THE BIG
FRONT YARD

THE BIG
FRONT YARD

AND OTHER STORIES

The Complete Short Fiction
of Clifford D. Simak,
Volume Two

Introduction by David W. Wixon

OPEN ROAD

INTEGRATED MEDIA
NEW YORK

All stories reprinted by permission of the Estate of Clifford D. Simak.

"The Big Front Yard" © 1958 by Street & Smith Publications, Inc. © 1986 by Clifford D. Simak. Originally published in *Astounding Science Fiction,* v. 62, no. 2, Oct., 1958.

"The Observer" © 1972 by The Conde Nast Publications, Inc. © 2000 by the Estate of Clifford D. Simak. Original appearance in *Analog,* v. 89, no. 4, May, 1972.

"Trail City's Hot-Lead Crusaders" © 1944 by Fictioneers, Inc. © 1972 by Clifford D. Simak. Originally published in *New Western Magazine,* v. 8, no. 2, Sept., 1944.

"Junkyard" © 1953 by Galaxy Publishing Corp. © 1981 by Clifford D. Simak. Originally published in *Galaxy Science Fiction,* v. 6, no. 2, May, 1953.

"Mr. Meek – Musketeer" © 1944 by Love Romances Publishing Co., Inc. © 1972 by Clifford D. Simak. Originally published in *Planet Stories,* v. 2, no. 7, Summer, 1944.

"Neighbor" © 1954 by Street & Smith Publications, Inc. © 1982 by Clifford D. Simak. Original appearance in *Astounding Science Fiction,* v. 53, no. 4, June, 1954.

"Shadow World" © 1957 by Galaxy Publishing Corp. © 1985 by Clifford D. Simak. Originally published in *Galaxy Science Fiction,* v. 14, no. 5, Sept., 1957.

"So Bright the Vision" © 1956 by King-Size Publications, Inc. © 1984 by Clifford D. Simak. Originally published in *Fantastic Universe,* v. 6, no. 1, Aug., 1956.

Copyright © 2016 by the Estate of Clifford D. Simak

Cover design by Jason Gabbert

978-1-5040-3945-1

Published in 2016 by Open Road Integrated Media, Inc.
180 Maiden Lane
New York, NY 10038
www.openroadmedia.com

CONTENTS

Clifford D. Simak: Learning All the Words   vii

The Big Front Yard   1
The Observer   63
Trail City's Hot-Lead Crusaders   77
Junkyard   115
Mr. Meek – Musketeer   159
Neighbor   191
Shadow World   219
So Bright the Vision   261

CLIFFORD D. SIMAK:
LEARNING ALL THE WORDS

"I'm looking for an alien, too. All of us, I think,
are looking for your alien."
—Clifford D. Simak in "So Bright the Vision"

Clifford Donald Simak was born on August 3, 1904, on a ridge-top farm a few miles from the village of Millville in Grant County, Wisconsin – a farm that belonged to his mother's parents. Cliff's grandfather, Edward "Ned" Wiseman, had been a member of the Second Wisconsin Volunteer Cavalry during the Civil War, taking part in the battles at Vicksburg and Gettysburg, and Cliff eventually became the proud possessor of Ned's cavalry saber. Cliff's grandmother, Ellen Wiseman (née Parker), seems to have had a special place in Cliff's heart, to judge by his clear use of her as his model for Ellen Forbes in "Over the River and Through the Woods" and his frequent uses of the names "Parker" and "Ellen." (Cliff also named his daughter after her.)

The Wiseman farm was located atop the broad, tall bluffs on the south side of the Wisconsin River; from just a little farther along the ridge, one can easily see, off to the west, the confluence of the Mississippi and Wisconsin Rivers.

Cliff's parents were John Lewis Simak and Margaret "Maggie" Olivia Wiseman Simak. The two met when John, who had emigrated at age twelve from a small town near Prague in the area that would become the Czech Republic, came to work for Ned Wiseman. John would eventually clear some land for himself and build a log cabin just to the east of the Wiseman farm to be a home for the small family, which would later come to include a younger son, Carson.

As was not uncommon in the early part of the twentieth century, Cliff, having been born on a farm, never had a birth certificate. And he never missed it, he told me, except on one occasion, in the fifties, when his newspaper wanted to send him out of the country on assignment. He could not get a passport until he got his mother to attest that she had indeed given birth to him in the United States.

Cliff started his education at what was known as a "country school," located a mile and a half from his home – a distance he walked every day. It was one of those stereotypical old-time schools in which students of all ages sat in a single room, to be taught by the same teacher. When finished in the little school, Cliff went to high school a few miles to the south, in the town of Patch Grove. To get there he rode a horse – an ornery gray mare, as he described her; he would say that although he loved her, and although he was sure she loved him, those feelings did not keep her from trying to kick him if she could.

The Wiseman and Simak farms were surrounded by woods where game abounded, cut by streams filled with fish, and the young Cliff Simak had the time of his life there. His boyhood, he would later say in an interview, was a sort of "Tom Sawyer existence" filled with hunting, fishing, and coon hunts, with horses and coon dogs – when the farm chores were done for the day. Later he would comment that although it was the twentieth century, life in that rural setting was much like living in pioneer days: He swam in exactly the kind of creeks he would later describe in stories, he rose before dawn to help with the morning chores, he went barefoot in the summers . . .

So how did he go on to become both a high-level newspaperman and a writer of award-winning fiction? It must have been built into him – he remembered that by the age of five, he knew he wanted to be a newspaperman, having been told by his mother that newspapers print all the news from all over the world, and that they print the truth. His family had a tradition of gathering around while one of the parents read aloud from a book or newspaper.

Cliff would later tell me that by the age of eight, he had developed a goal to learn all the words there were, and it may be no coincidence that the Simak family stone in the little cemetery between Bridgeport and Patch Grove depicts an open book – a Bible, no doubt, but still . . .

Finishing second in his high school class, Cliff took a two-year teacher-training program and then taught school, over the course of the next three years, at a number of small towns in the area. Already an avid reader of Verne, Wells, and Burroughs, when he chanced on a copy of *Amazing Stories* in 1927, he became a regular reader of the science fiction magazines.

It was while teaching in Cassville, a very small town, that Cliff, attending the local movie theater, met a young woman from the nearby town of Glen Haven. She was Agnes Kuchenberg, known always as Kay, and she would later become his wife.

In 1927 or 1928 the Simak family removed to Madison, the state capital, where Cliff attended the University of Wisconsin (studying journalism), Carson went to high school, and John went into carpentry and masonry. The new occupation did not work out well for John, and when Kay and Cliff got married in April of 1929 and decided that he would drop out of the university to take a job working for a newspaper in Michigan, the rest of the family returned to the ridge.

Cliff started as a reporter at the *Iron River Reporter*. He quickly got a column of his own, called "Driftwood," and within a few years had moved up to be editor. It was during this period that he began to try his hand at writing fiction.

He had already sold a number of stories when, in August 1932, the couple left Iron River for Spencer, Iowa, where Cliff became editor of the *Spencer Reporter*, and in July 1934 he moved on to North Dakota to become editor of the *Dickinson Press*.

At about that time, the Spencer newspaper was purchased by a Kansas City newspaper company, which persuaded Cliff to return to Spencer and convert the paper from a semiweekly to a daily. This went well, and the company made him a sort of trouble-shooter, transferring him first to Excelsior Springs, Missouri, then to Worthington, Minnesota, and finally to Brainerd, Minnesota.

In 1939 Cliff took a job at the copy desk of the *Minneapolis Star*, and within a few years he became chief of the copy desk. Years later, he could still remember that the day he started to work for the *Star* was June 16. In 1949 he would become the paper's news editor, and he stayed with the *Star* and its successors in various capacities until his retirement in 1976.

It's hard to know just when Cliff started writing stories himself. He kept a series of journals in which he recorded some of his submissions and sales – and occasionally other events – but he was sporadic, at best, in his data entry, and it appears that some of his journals did not survive. And although one of the surviving volumes contains a notation that a story entitled "Mutiny on Mercury" was submitted to a magazine at the end of 1930, there's no way to tell if that was his first attempt to write or submit fiction. The story was initially rejected, but Cliff's first sale came soon after, in 1931.

There was, however, one period during which Cliff left the *Star*. Early in World War II he accepted a job working for an intelligence agency of the US government. The nature of the job is not known, but it required Cliff and Kay to pack up their car and drive to Seattle . . . a trip that was probably torturous, since there were no freeways in those days – in fact, Kay recorded in her diary that it wasn't too long before they repacked the car, put it on a train to Seattle, and took another train themselves.

The stay in Seattle was short, though, and they returned to Minnesota before the end of 1942 – the newspaper was eager to have Cliff back.

That began a period during which Cliff churned out short stories in a number of genres, all the while working full time at the paper. In 1947 the Simak family had a son, Richard Scott, and in 1951 a daughter, Shelley Ellen.

In the fifties, Cliff began moving into the writing of novels – although he would always keep his hand in the short story field. And it was during this period too that he began to win awards for his fiction – awards that had not even existed in his first two decades in the field.

Clifford D. Simak retired from the *Minneapolis Tribune* (the *Star*'s successor) in 1976. He would continue writing, publishing his last novel, *Highway to Eternity*, in 1986. Predeceased by his beloved Kay, he died in Minneapolis in 1988.

David W. Wixon

THE BIG FRONT YARD

"The Big Front Yard," which started out identified in Cliff's notes as "Rats in the House," then "Errand Boy," and then "A Mouse in the House," before reaching its final name, may be the most lauded of the author's short fiction, even beyond the fact that it won the Hugo Award. I say this because it's a story that people often mention when speaking of Clifford D. Simak. And few stories have a submission history like this one: the story was sent to Galaxy Magazine *on April 2, 1958, only to be rejected and returned on the fourteenth; it was sent to Astounding on the following day and accepted there on the twenty-eighth – all this action, including two submissions, occurred in less than a month.*

The exotic and unusual is most effectively seen when positioned next to the commonplace.

—dww

I

Hiram Taine came awake and sat up in his bed.

Towser was barking and scratching at the floor.

"Shut up," Taine told the dog.

Towser cocked quizzical ears at him and then resumed the barking and scratching at the floor.

Taine rubbed his eyes. He ran a hand through his rat's-nest head of hair. He considered lying down again and pulling up the covers.

But not with Towser barking.

"What's the matter with you, anyhow?" he asked of Towser, with not a little wrath.

"*Whuff*," said Towser, industriously proceeding with his scratching at the floor.

"If you want out," said Taine, "all you got to do is open the screen door. You know how it is done. You do it all the time."

Towser quit his barking and sat down heavily, watching his master getting out of bed.

Taine put on his shirt and pulled on his trousers, but didn't bother with his shoes.

Towser ambled over to a corner, put his nose down to the baseboard and snuffled moistly.

"You got a mouse?" asked Taine.

"*Whuff*," said Towser, most emphatically.

"I can't ever remember you making such a row about a mouse," Taine said, slightly puzzled. "You must be off your rocker."

It was a beautiful summer morning. Sunlight was pouring through the open window.

Good day for fishing, Taine told himself, then remembered that there'd be no fishing, for he had to go out and look up that old four-poster maple bed that he had heard about up Woodman way. More than likely, he thought, they'd want twice as much as it was worth. It was getting so, he told himself, that a man couldn't make an honest dollar. Everyone was getting smart about antiques.

He got up off the bed and headed for the living room.

"Come on," he said to Towser.

Towser came along, pausing now and then to snuffle into corners and to whuffle at the floor.

"You got it bad," said Taine.

Maybe it's a rat, he thought. The house was getting old.

He opened the screen door and Towser went outside.

"Leave that woodchuck be today," Taine advised him. "It's a losing battle. You'll never dig him out."

Towser went around the corner of the house.

Taine noticed that something had happened to the sign that hung on the post beside the driveway. One of the chains had become unhooked and the sign was dangling.

He padded out across the driveway slab and the grass, still wet with dew, to fix the sign. There was nothing wrong with it – just the unhooked chain. Might have been the wind, he thought, or some passing urchin. Although probably not an urchin. He got along with kids. They never bothered him, like they did some others in the village. Banker Stevens, for example. They were always pestering Stevens.

He stood back a ways to be sure the sign was straight.

It read, in big letters:

HANDY MAN

And under that, in smaller lettering:

I fix anything

And under that:

ANTIQUES FOR SALE
What have you got to trade?

Maybe, he told himself, he'd ought to have two signs, one for his fix-it shop and one for antiques and trading. Some day, when he had the time, he thought, he'd paint a couple of new ones. One for each side of the driveway. It would look neat that way.

He turned around and looked across the road at Turner's

Woods. It was a pretty sight, he thought. A sizable piece of woods like that right at the edge of town. It was a place for birds and rabbits and woodchucks and squirrels and it was full of forts built through generations by the boys of Willow Bend.

Some day, of course, some smart operator would buy it up and start a housing development or something equally objectionable and when that happened a big slice of his own boyhood would be cut out of his life.

Towser came around the corner of the house. He was sidling along, sniffing at the lowest row of siding and his ears were cocked with interest.

"That dog is nuts," said Taine, and went inside.

He went into the kitchen, his bare feet slapping on the floor.

He filled the tea kettle, set it on the stove and turned the burner on underneath the kettle.

He turned on the radio, forgetting that it was out of kilter.

When it didn't make a sound, he remembered and, disgusted, snapped it off. That was the way it went, he thought. He fixed other people's stuff, but never got around to fixing any of his own.

He went into the bedroom and put on his shoes. He threw the bed together.

Back in the kitchen the stove had failed to work again. The burner beneath the kettle still was cold.

Taine hauled off and kicked the stove. He lifted the kettle and held his palm above the burner. In a few seconds he could detect some heat.

"Worked again," he told himself.

Some day, he knew, kicking the stove would fail to work. When that happened, he'd have to get to work on it. Probably wasn't more than a loose connection.

He put the kettle back onto the stove.

There was a clatter out in front and Taine went out to see what was going on.

Beasly, the Horton's yardboy-chauffeur-gardener-et cetera was backing a rickety old truck up the driveway. Beside him sat Abbie Horton, the wife of H. Henry Horton, the village's most important citizen. In the back of the truck, lashed on with ropes and half-protected by a garish red and purple quilt, stood a mammoth television set. Taine recognized it from of old. It was a good ten years out of date and still, by any standard, it was the most expensive set ever to grace any home in Willow Bend.

Abbie hopped out of the truck. She was an energetic, bustling, bossy woman.

"Good morning, Hiram," she said. "Can you fix this set again?"

"Never saw anything that I couldn't fix," said Taine, but nevertheless he eyed the set with something like dismay. It was not the first time he had tangled with it and he knew what was ahead.

"It might cost you more than it's worth," he warned her. "What you really need is a new one. This set is getting old and –"

"That's just what Henry said," Abbie told him, tartly. "Henry wants to get one of the color sets. But I won't part with this one. It's not just TV, you know. It's a combination with radio and a record player and the wood and style are just right for the other furniture, and, besides –"

"Yes, I know," said Taine, who'd heard it all before.

Poor old Henry, he thought. What a life the man must lead. Up at that computer plant all day long, shooting off his face and bossing everyone, then coming home to a life of petty tyranny.

"Beasly," said Abbie, in her best drill-sergeant voice, "you get right up there and get that thing untied."

"Yes'm," Beasly said. He was a gangling, loose-jointed man who didn't look too bright.

"And see you be careful with it. I don't want it all scratched up."

"Yes'm," said Beasly.

"I'll help," Taine offered.

The two climbed into the truck and began unlashing the old monstrosity.

"It's heavy," Abbie warned. "You two be careful of it."

"Yes'm," said Beasly.

It was heavy and it was an awkward thing to boot, but Beasly and Taine horsed it around to the back of the house and up the stoop and through the back door and down the basement stairs, with Abbie following eagle-eyed behind them, alert to the slightest scratch.

The basement was Taine's combination workshop and display room for antiques. One end of it was filled with benches and with tools and machinery and boxes full of odds and ends and piles of just plain junk were scattered everywhere. The other end housed a collection of rickety chairs, sagging bedposts, ancient highboys, equally ancient lowboys, old coal scuttles painted gold, heavy iron fireplace screens and a lot or other stuff that he had collected from far and wide for as little as he could possibly pay for it.

He and Beasly set the TV down carefully on the floor. Abbie watched them narrowly from the stairs.

"Why, Hiram," she said, excited, "you put a ceiling in the basement. It looks a whole lot better."

"Huh?" asked Taine.

"The ceiling. I said you put in a ceiling."

Taine jerked his head up and what she said was true. There was a ceiling there, but he'd never put it in.

He gulped a little and lowered his head, then jerked it quickly up and had another look. The ceiling still was there.

"It's not that block stuff," said Abbie with open admiration. "You can't see any joints at all. How did you manage it?"

Taine gulped again and got back his voice. "Something I thought up," he told her weakly.

"You'll have to come over and do it to our basement. Our basement is a sight. Beasly put the ceiling in the amusement room, but Beasly is all thumbs."

"Yes'm," Beasly said contritely.

"When I get the time," Taine promised, ready to promise anything to get them out of there.

"You'd have a lot more time," Abbie told him acidly, "if you weren't gadding around all over the country buying up that broken-down old furniture that you call antiques. Maybe you can fool the city folks when they come driving out here, but you can't fool me."

"I make a lot of money out of some of it," Taine told her calmly.

"And lose your shirt on the rest of it," she said.

"I got some old china that is just the kind of stuff you are looking for," said Taine. "Picked it up just a day or two ago. Made a good buy on it. I can let you have it cheap."

"I'm not interested," she said and clamped her mouth tight shut.

She turned around and went back up the stairs.

"She's on the prod today," Beasly said to Taine. "It will be a bad day. It always is when she starts early in the morning."

"Don't pay attention to her," Taine advised.

"I try not to, but it ain't possible. You sure you don't need a man? I'd work for you cheap."

"Sorry, Beasly. Tell you what – come over some night soon and we'll play some checkers."

"I'll do that, Hiram. You're the only one who ever asks me over. All the others ever do is laugh at me or shout."

Abbie's voice came bellowing down the stairs. "Beasly, are you coming? Don't go standing there all day. I have rugs to beat."

"Yes'm," said Beasly, starting up the stairs.

At the truck, Abbie turned on Taine with determination: "You'll get that set fixed right away? I'm lost without it."

"Immediately," said Taine.

He stood and watched them off, then looked around for Towser, but the dog had disappeared. More than likely he was at the woodchuck hole again, in the woods across the road. Gone off, thought Taine, without his breakfast, too.

The teakettle was boiling furiously when Taine got back to the kitchen. He put coffee in the maker and poured in the water. Then he went downstairs.

The ceiling was still there.

He turned on all the lights and walked around the basement, staring up at it.

It was a dazzling white material and it appeared to be translucent – up to a point, that is. One could see into it, but he could not see through it. And there were no signs of seams. It was fitted neatly and tightly around the water pipes and the ceiling lights.

Taine stood on a chair and rapped his knuckles against it sharply. It gave out a bell-like sound, almost exactly as if he'd rapped a fingernail against a thinly blown goblet.

He got down off the chair and stood there, shaking his head. The whole thing was beyond him. He had spent part of the evening repairing Banker Stevens' lawn mower and there'd been no ceiling then.

He rummaged in a box and found a drill. He dug out one of the smaller bits and fitted it in the drill. He plugged in the cord and climbed on the chair again and tried the bit against the ceiling. The whirling steel slid wildly back and forth. It didn't make a scratch. He switched off the drill and looked closely at the ceiling. There was not a mark upon it. He tried again, pressing against the drill with all his strength. The bit went *ping* and the broken end flew across the basement and hit the wall.

Taine stepped down off the chair. He found another bit and fitted it in the drill and went slowly up the stairs, trying to think. But he was too confused to think. That ceiling should not be up there, but there it was. And unless he went stark, staring crazy and forgetful as well, he had not put it there.

In the living room, he folded back one corner of the worn and faded carpeting and plugged in the drill. He knelt and started drilling in the floor. The bit went smoothly through the old oak flooring, then stopped. He put on more pressure and the drill spun without getting any bite.

And there wasn't supposed to be anything underneath that wood! Nothing to stop a drill. Once through the flooring, it should have dropped into the space between the joists.

Taine disengaged the drill and laid it to one side.

He went into the kitchen and the coffee now was ready. But before he poured it, he pawed through a cabinet drawer and found a pencil flashlight. Back in the living room he shined the light into the hole that the drill had made.

There was something shiny at the bottom of the hole.

He went back to the kitchen and found some day-old doughnuts and poured a cup of coffee. He sat at the kitchen table, eating doughnuts and wondering what to do.

There didn't appear, for the moment at least, much that he could do. He could putter around all day trying to figure out what had happened to his basement and probably not be any wiser than he was right now.

His money-making Yankee soul rebelled against such a horrid waste of time.

There was, he told himself, that maple four-poster that he should be getting to before some unprincipled city antique dealer should run afoul of it. A piece like that, he figured, if a man had any luck at all, should sell at a right good price. He might turn a handsome profit on it if he only worked it right.

Maybe, he thought, he could turn a trade on it. There was the table model TV set that he had traded a pair of ice skates for last winter. Those folks out Woodman way might conceivably be happy to trade the bed for a reconditioned TV set, almost like brand new. After all, they probably weren't using the bed and, he hoped fervently, had no idea of the value of it.

He ate the doughnuts hurriedly and gulped down an extra cup of coffee. He fixed a plate of scraps for Towser and set it outside the door. Then he went down into the basement and got the table TV set and put it in the pickup truck. As an afterthought, he added a reconditioned shotgun which would be perfectly all right if a man were careful not to use these far-reaching, powerful shells, and a few other odds and ends that might come in handy on a trade.

II

He got back late, for it had been a busy and quite satisfactory day. Not only did he have the four-poster loaded on the truck, but he had as well a rocking chair, a fire screen, a bundle of ancient magazines, an old-fashioned barrel churn, a walnut highboy and a Governor Winthrop on which some half-baked, slap-happy decorator had applied a coat of apple-green paint. The television set, the shotgun and five dollars had gone into the trade. And what was better yet – he'd managed it so well that the Woodman family probably was dying of laughter at this very moment about how they'd taken him.

He felt a little ashamed of it – they'd been such friendly people. They had treated him so kindly and had him stay for dinner and had sat and talked with him and shown him about the farm and even asked him to stop by if he went through that way again.

He'd wasted the entire day, he thought, and he rather hated that, but maybe it had been worth it to build up his reputation out that way as the sort of character who had softening of the head and didn't know the value of a dollar. That way, maybe some other day, he could do some more business in the neighborhood.

He heard the television set as he opened the back door, sounding loud and clear, and he went clattering down the basement stairs in something close to panic. For now that he'd traded off the table model, Abbie's set was the only one downstairs and Abbie's set was broken.

It was Abbie's set, all right. It stood just where he and Beasly had put it down that morning and there was nothing wrong with it – nothing wrong at all. It was even televising color.

Televising color!

He stopped at the bottom of the stairs and leaned against the railing for support.

The set kept right on televising color.

Taine stalked the set and walked around behind it.

The back of the cabinet was off, leaning against a bench that stood behind the set, and he could see the innards of it glowing cheerily.

He squatted on the basement floor and squinted at the lighted innards and they seemed a good deal different from the way that they should be. He'd repaired the set many times before and he thought he had a good idea of what the working parts would look like. And now they all seemed different, although just how he couldn't tell.

A heavy step sounded on the stairs and a hearty voice came booming down to him.

"Well, Hiram, I see you got it fixed."

Taine jackknifed upright and stood there slightly frozen and completely speechless.

Henry Horton stood foursquarely and happily on the stairs, looking very pleased.

"I told Abbie that you wouldn't have it done, but she said for me to come over anyway – Hey, Hiram, it's in color! How did you do it, man?"

Taine grinned sickly. "I just got fiddling around," he said.

Henry came down the rest of the stairs with a stately step and stood before the set, with his hands behind his back, staring at it fixedly in his best executive manner.

He slowly shook his head. "I never would have thought," he said, "that it was possible."

"Abbie mentioned that you wanted color."

"Well, sure. Of course I did. But not on this old set. I never would have expected to get color on this set. How did you do it, Hiram?"

Taine told the solemn truth. "I can't rightly say," he said.

Henry found a nail keg standing in front of one of the benches and rolled it out in front of the old-fashioned set. He sat down warily and relaxed into solid comfort.

"That's the way it goes," he said. "There are men like you, but not very many of them. Just Yankee tinkerers. You keep messing around with things, trying one thing here and another there and before you know it you come up with something."

He sat on the nail keg, staring at the set.

"It's sure a pretty thing," he said. "It's better than the color they have in Minneapolis. I dropped in at a couple of the places the last time I was there and looked at the color sets. And I tell you honest, Hiram, there wasn't one of them that was as good as this."

Taine wiped his brow with his shirtsleeve. Somehow or other, the basement seemed to be getting warm. He was fine sweat all over.

Henry found a big cigar in one of his pockets and held it out to Taine.

"No, thanks. I never smoke."

"Perhaps you're wise," said Henry. "It's a nasty habit."

He stuck the cigar into his mouth and rolled it east to west.

"Each man to his own," he proclaimed, expansively. "When it comes to a thing like this, you're the man to do it. You seem to think in mechanical contraptions and electronic circuits. Me, I don't know a thing about it. Even in the computer game, I still don't know a thing about it; I hire men who do. I can't even saw a board or drive a nail. But I can organize. You remember, Hiram, how everybody snickered when I started up the plant?"

"Well, I guess some of them did, at that."

"You're darn tooting they did. They went around for weeks with their hands up to their faces to hide smart-Aleck grins. They said, what does Henry think he's doing, starting up a computer factory out here in the sticks; he doesn't think he can compete with those big companies in the east, does he? And they didn't stop their grinning until I sold a couple of dozen units and had orders for a year or two ahead."

He fished a lighter from his pocket and lit the cigar carefully, never taking his eyes off the television set.

"You got something there," he said, judiciously, "that may be worth a mint of money. Some simple adaptation that will fit on any set. If you can get color on this old wreck, you can get color on any set that's made."

He chuckled moistly around the mouthful of cigar. "If RCA knew what was happening here this minute, they'd go out and cut their throats."

"But I don't know what I did," protested Taine.

"Well, that's all right," said Henry, happily. "I'll take this set up to the plant tomorrow and turn loose some of the boys on it. They'll find out what you have here before they're through with it."

He took the cigar out of his mouth and studied it intently, then popped it back in again.

"As I was saying, Hiram, that's the difference in us. You can do the stuff, but you miss the possibilities. I can't do a thing, but I can organize it once the thing is done. Before we get through with this, you'll be wading in twenty dollar bills clear up to your knees."

"But I don't have –"

"Don't worry. Just leave it all to me. I've got the plant and whatever money we may need. We'll figure out a split."

"That's fine of you," said Taine mechanically.

"Not at all," Henry insisted, grandly. "It's just my aggressive, grasping sense of profit. I should be ashamed of myself, cutting in on this."

He sat on the keg, smoking and watching the TV perform in exquisite color.

"You know, Hiram," he said, "I've often thought of this, but never got around to doing anything about it. I've got an old computer up at the plant that we will have to junk because it's taking up room that we really need. It's one of our early models, a sort of experimental job that went completely sour. It sure is a screwy thing. No one's ever been able to make much out of it. We tried some approaches that probably were wrong – or maybe they were right, but we didn't know enough to make them quite come off. It's been standing in a corner all these years and I should have junked it long ago. But I sort of hate to do it. I wonder if you might not like it – just to tinker with."

"Well, I don't know," said Taine.

Henry assumed an expansive air. "No obligation, mind you. You may not be able to do a thing with it – I'd frankly be surprised if you could, but there's no harm in trying. Maybe you'll decide to tear it down for the salvage you can get. There are several thousand dollars worth of equipment in it. Probably you could use most of it one way or another."

"It might be interesting," conceded Taine, but not too enthusiastically.

"Good," said Henry, with an enthusiasm that made up for Taine's lack of it. "I'll have the boys cart it over tomorrow. It's a heavy thing. I'll send along plenty of help to get it unloaded and down into the basement and set up."

Henry stood up carefully and brushed cigar ashes off his lap.

"I'll have the boys pick up the TV set at the same time," he said. "I'll have to tell Abbie you haven't got it fixed yet. If I ever let it get into the house, the way it's working now, she'd hold on to it."

Henry climbed the stairs heavily and Taine saw him out the door into the summer night.

Taine stood in the shadow, watching Henry's shadowed figure go across the Widow Taylor's yard to the next street behind his house. He took a deep breath of the fresh night air and shook his head to try to clear his buzzing brain, but the buzzing went right on.

Too much had happened, he told himself. Too much for any single day – first the ceiling and now the TV set. Once he had a good night's sleep he might be in some sort of shape to try to wrestle with it.

Towser came around the corner of the house and limped slowly up the steps to stand beside his master. He was mud up to his ears.

"You had a day of it, I see," said Taine. "And, just like I told you, you didn't get the woodchuck."

"*Woof*," said Towser, sadly.

"You're just like a lot of the rest of us," Taine told him, severely. "Like me and Henry Horton and all the rest of us. You're chasing something and you think you know what you are chasing, but you really don't. And what is even worse, you have no faint idea of why you're chasing it."

Towser thumped a tired tail upon the stoop.

Taine opened the door and stood to one side to let Towser in, then went in himself.

He went through the refrigerator and found part of a roast, a slice or two of luncheon meat, a dried out slab of cheese and half a bowl of cooked spaghetti. He made a pot of coffee and shared the food with Towser.

Then Taine went back downstairs and shut off the television set. He found a trouble lamp and plugged it in and poked the light into the innards of the set.

He squatted on the floor, holding the lamp, trying to puzzle out what had been done to the set. It was different, of course, but it was a little hard to figure out in just what ways it was different. Someone had tinkered with the tubes and had them twisted out of shape and there were little white cubes of metal tucked here and there in what seemed to be an entirely haphazard and illogical manner – although, Taine admitted to himself, there probably was no haphazardness. And the circuit, he saw, had been rewired and a good deal of wiring had been added.

But the most puzzling thing about it was that the whole thing seemed to be just jury-rigged – as if someone had done no more than a hurried, patch-up job to get the set back in working order on an emergency and temporary basis.

Someone, he thought!

And who had that someone been?

He hunched around and peered into the dark corners of the basement and he felt innumerable and many-legged imaginary insects running on his body.

Someone had taken the back off the cabinet and leaned it

against the bench and had left the screws which held the back laid neatly in a row upon the floor. Then they had jury-rigged the set and jury-rigged it far better than it had ever been before.

If this was a jury-job, he wondered, just what kind of job would it have been if they had had the time to do it up in style?

They hadn't had the time, of course. Maybe they had been scared off when he had come home – scared off even before they could get the back on the set again.

He stood up and moved stiffly away.

First the ceiling in the morning – and now, in the evening, Abbie's television set.

And the ceiling, come to think of it, was not a ceiling only. Another liner, if that was the proper term for it, of the same material as the ceiling, had been laid beneath the floor, forming a sort of boxed-in area between the joists. He had struck that liner when he had tried to drill into the floor.

And what, he asked himself, if all the house were like that, too?

There was just one answer to it all: *There was something in the house with him!*

Towser had heard that *something* or smelled it or in some other manner sensed it and had dug frantically at the floor in an attempt to dig it out, as if it were a woodchuck.

Except that this, whatever it might be, certainly was no woodchuck.

He put away the trouble light and went upstairs.

Towser was curled up on a rug in the living room beside the easy chair and beat his tail in polite decorum in greeting to his master.

Taine stood and stared down at the dog. Towser looked back at him with satisfied and sleepy eyes, then heaved a doggish sigh and settled down to sleep.

Whatever Towser might have heard or smelled or sensed this morning, it was quite evident that as of this moment he was aware of it no longer.

Then Taine remembered something else.

He had filled the kettle to make water for the coffee and had set it on the stove. He had turned on the burner and it had worked the first time.

He hadn't had to kick the stove to get the burner going.

III

He woke in the morning and someone was holding down his feet and he sat up quickly to see what was going on.

But there was nothing to be alarmed about; it was only Towser who had crawled into bed with him and now lay sprawled across his feet.

Towser whined softly and his back legs twitched as he chased dream-rabbits.

Taine eased his feet from beneath the dog and sat up, reaching for his clothes. It was early, but he remembered suddenly that he had left all of the furniture he had picked up the day before out there in the truck and should be getting it downstairs where he could start reconditioning it.

Towser went on sleeping.

Taine stumbled to the kitchen and looked out of the window and there, squatted on the back stoop, was Beasly, the Horton man-of-all-work.

Taine went to the back door to see what was going on.

"I quit them, Hiram," Beasly told him. "She kept on pecking at me every minute of the day and I couldn't do a thing to please her, so I up and quit."

"Well, come on in," said Taine. "I suppose you'd like a bite to eat and a cup of coffee."

"I was kind of wondering if I could stay here, Hiram. Just for my keep until I can find something else."

"Let's have breakfast first," said Taine, "then we can talk about it."

He didn't like it, he told himself. He didn't like it at all. In another hour or so Abbie would show up and start stirring up a ruckus about how he'd lured Beasly off. Because, no matter how dumb Beasly might be, he did a lot of work and took a lot of nagging and there wasn't anyone else in town who would work for Abbie Horton.

"Your ma used to give me cookies all the time," said Beasly. "Your ma was a real good woman, Hiram."

"Yes, she was," said Taine.

"My ma used to say that you folks were quality, not like the rest in town, no matter what kind of airs they were always putting on. She said your family was among the first settlers. Is that really true, Hiram?"

"Well, not exactly first settlers, I guess, but this house has stood here for almost a hundred years. My father used to say there never was a night during all those years that there wasn't at least one Taine beneath its roof. Things like that, it seems, meant a lot to father."

"It must be nice," said Beasly, wistfully, "to have a feeling like that. You must be proud of this house, Hiram."

"Not really proud; more like belonging. I can't imagine living in any other house."

Taine turned on the burner and filled the kettle. Carrying the kettle back, he kicked the stove. But there wasn't any need to kick it; the burner was already beginning to take on a rosy glow.

Twice in a row, Taine thought. This thing is getting better!

"Gee, Hiram," said Beasly, "this is a dandy radio."

"It's no good," said Taine. "It's broke. Haven't had the time to fix it."

"I don't think so, Hiram. I just turned it on. It's beginning to warm up."

"It's beginning to – Hey, let me see!" yelled Taine.

Beasly told the truth. A faint hum was coming from the tubes.

A voice came in, gaining in volume as the set warmed up.

It was speaking gibberish.

"What kind of talk is that?" asked Beasly.

"I don't know," said Taine, close to panic now.

First the television set, then the stove and now the radio!

He spun the tuning knob and the pointer crawled slowly across the dial face instead of spinning across as he remembered it, and station after station sputtered and went past.

He tuned in the next station that came up and it was strange lingo, too – and he knew by then exactly what he had.

Instead of a $39.50 job, he had here on the kitchen table an all-band receiver like they advertised in the fancy magazines.

He straightened up and said to Beasly: "See if you can get someone speaking English. I'll get on with the eggs."

He turned on the second burner and got out the frying pan. He put it on the stove and found eggs and bacon in the refrigerator.

Beasly got a station that had band music playing.

"How is that?" he asked.

"That is fine," said Taine.

Towser came out from the bedroom, stretching and yawning. He went to the door and showed he wanted out.

Taine let him out.

"If I were you," he told the dog, "I'd lay off that woodchuck. You'll have all the woods dug up."

"He ain't digging after any woodchuck, Hiram."

"Well, a rabbit, then."

"Not a rabbit, either. I snuck off yesterday when I was supposed to be beating rugs. That's what Abbie got so sore about."

Taine grunted, breaking eggs into the skillet.

"I snuck away and went over to where Towser was. I talked with him and he told me it wasn't a woodchuck or a rabbit. He said it was something else. I pitched in and helped him dig. Looks to me like he found an old tank of some sort buried out there in the woods."

"Towser wouldn't dig up any tank," protested Taine. "He wouldn't care about anything except a rabbit or a woodchuck."

"He was working hard," insisted Beasly. "He seemed to be excited."

"Maybe the woodchuck just dug his hole under this old tank or whatever it might be."

"Maybe so," Beasly agreed. He fiddled with the radio some more. He got a disk jockey who was pretty terrible.

Taine shoveled eggs and bacon onto plates and brought them to the table. He poured big cups of coffee and began buttering the toast.

"Dive in," he said to Beasly.

"This is good of you, Hiram, to take me in like this. I won't stay no longer than it takes to find a job."

"Well, I didn't exactly say –"

"There are times," said Beasly, "when I get to thinking I haven't got a friend and then I remember your ma, how nice she was to me and all –"

"Oh, all right," said Taine.

He knew when he was licked.

He brought the toast and a jar of jam to the table and sat down, beginning to eat.

"Maybe you got something I could help you with," suggested Beasly, using the back of his hand to wipe egg off his chin.

"I have a load of furniture out in the driveway. I could use a man to help me get it down into the basement."

"I'll be glad to do that," said Beasly. "I am good and strong. I don't mind work at all. I just don't like people jawing at me."

They finished breakfast and then carried the furniture down into the basement. They had some trouble with the Governor Winthrop, for it was an unwieldy thing to handle.

When they finally horsed it down, Taine stood off and looked at it. The man, he told himself, who slapped paint onto that beautiful cherry wood had a lot to answer for.

He said to Beasly: "We have to get the paint off that thing

there. And we must do it carefully. Use paint remover and a rag wrapped around a spatula and just sort of roll it off. Would you like to try it?"

"Sure, I would. Say, Hiram, what will we have for lunch?"

"I don't know," said Taine. "We'll throw something together. Don't tell me you are hungry."

"Well, it was sort of hard work, getting all that stuff down here."

"There are cookies in the jar on the kitchen shelf," said Taine. "Go and help yourself."

When Beasly went upstairs, Taine walked slowly around the basement. The ceiling, he saw, was still intact. Nothing else seemed to be disturbed.

Maybe that television set and the stove and radio, he thought, was just their way of paying rent to me. And if that were the case, he told himself, whoever they might be, he'd be more than willing to let them stay right on.

He looked around some more and could find nothing wrong.

He went upstairs and called to Beasly in the kitchen.

"Come on out to the garage, where I keep the paint. We'll hunt up some remover and show you how to use it."

Beasly, a supply of cookies clutched in his hand, trotted willingly behind him.

As they rounded the corner of the house they could hear Towser's muffled barking. Listening to him, it seemed to Taine that he was getting hoarse.

Three days, he thought – or was it four?

"If we don't do something about it," he said, "that fool dog is going to get himself wore out."

He went into the garage and came back with two shovels and a pick.

"Come on," he said to Beasly. "We have to put a stop to this before we have any peace."

IV

Towser had done himself a noble job of excavation. He was almost completely out of sight. Only the end of his considerably bedraggled tail showed out of the hole he had clawed in the forest floor.

Beasly had been right about the tanklike thing. One edge of it showed out of one side of the hole.

Towser backed out of the hole and sat down heavily, his whiskers dripping clay, his tongue hanging out of the side of his mouth.

"He says that it's about time that we showed up," said Beasly.

Taine walked around the hole and knelt down. He reached down a hand to brush the dirt off the projecting edge of Beasly's tank. The clay was stubborn and hard to wipe away, but from the feel of it the tank was heavy metal.

Taine picked up a shovel and rapped it against the tank. The tank gave out a clang.

They got to work, shoveling away a foot or so of topsoil that lay above the object. It was hard work and the thing was bigger than they had thought and it took some time to get it uncovered, even roughly.

"I'm hungry," Beasly complained.

Taine glanced at his watch. It was almost one o'clock.

"Run on back to the house," he said to Beasly. "You'll find something in the refrigerator and there is milk to drink."

"How about you, Hiram? Ain't you ever hungry?"

"You could bring me back a sandwich and see if you can find a trowel."

"What you want a trowel for?"

"I want to scrape the dirt off this thing and see what it is."

He squatted down beside the thing they had unearthed and watched Beasly disappear into the woods.

"Towser," he said, "this is the strangest animal you ever put to ground."

A man, he told himself, might better joke about it – if to do no more than keep his fear away.

Beasly wasn't scared, of course. Beasly didn't have the sense to be scared of a thing like this.

Twelve feet wide by twenty long and oval shaped. About the size, he thought, of a good-size living room. And there never had been a tank of that shape or size in all of Willow Bend.

He fished his jackknife out of his pocket and started to scratch away the dirt at one point on the surface of the thing. He got a square inch free of dirt and it was no metal such as he had ever seen. It looked for all the world like glass.

He kept on scraping at the dirt until he had a clean place as big as an outstretched hand.

It wasn't any metal. He'd almost swear to that. It looked like cloudy glass – like the milk-glass goblets and bowls he was always on the lookout for. There were a lot of people who were plain nuts about it and they'd pay fancy prices for it.

He closed the knife and put it back into his pocket and squatted, looking at the oval shape that Towser had discovered.

And the conviction grew: Whatever it was that had come to live with him undoubtedly had arrived in this same contraption. From space or time, he thought, and was astonished that he thought it, for he'd never thought such a thing before.

He picked up his shovel and began to dig again, digging down this time, following the curving side of this alien thing that lay within the earth.

And as he dug, he wondered. What should he say about this – or should he say anything? Maybe the smartest course would be to cover it again and never breathe a word about it to a living soul.

Beasly would talk about it, naturally. But no one in the village would pay attention to anything that Beasly said. Everyone in Willow Bend knew Beasly was cracked.

Beasly finally came back. He carried three inexpertly made sandwiches wrapped in an old newspaper and a quart bottle almost full of milk.

"You certainly took your time," said Taine, slightly irritated.

"I got interested," Beasly explained.

"Interested in what?"

"Well, there were three big trucks and they were lugging a lot of heavy stuff down into the basement. Two or three big cabinets and a lot of other junk. And you know Abbie's television set? Well, they took the set away. I told them that they shouldn't, but they took it anyway."

"I forgot," said Taine. "Henry said he'd send the computer over and I plumb forgot."

Taine ate the sandwiches, sharing them with Towser, who was very grateful in a muddy way.

Finished, Taine rose and picked up his shovel.

"Let's get to work," he said.

"But you got all that stuff down in the basement."

"That can wait," said Taine. "This job we have to finish."

It was getting dusk by the time they finished.

Taine leaned wearily on his shovel.

Twelve feet by twenty across the top and ten feet deep – and all of it, every bit of it, made of the milk-glass stuff that sounded like a bell when you whacked it with a shovel.

They'd have to be small, he thought, if there were many of them, to live in a space that size, especially if they had to stay there very long. And that fitted in, of course, for if they weren't small they couldn't now be living in the space between the basement joists.

If they were really living there, thought Taine. If it wasn't all just a lot of supposition.

Maybe, he thought, even if they had been living in the house, they might be there no longer – for Towser had smelled or heard or somehow sensed them in the morning, but by that very night he'd paid them no attention.

Taine slung his shovel across his shoulder and hoisted the pick. "Come on," he said, "let's go. We've put in a long, hard day."

They tramped out through the brush and reached the road.

Fireflies were flickering off and on in the woody darkness and the street lamps were swaying in the summer breeze. The stars were hard and bright.

Maybe they still were in the house, thought Taine. Maybe when they found out that Towser had objected to them, they had fixed it so he'd be aware of them no longer.

They probably were highly adaptive. It stood to good reason they would have to be. It hadn't taken them too long, he told himself grimly, to adapt to a human house.

He and Beasly went up the gravel driveway in the dark to put the tools away in the garage and there was something funny going on, for there was no garage.

There was no garage and there was no front on the house and the driveway was cut off abruptly and there was nothing but the curving wall of what apparently had been the end of the garage.

They came up to the curving wall and stopped, squinting unbelieving in the summer dark.

There was no garage, no porch, no front of the house at all. It was as if someone had taken the opposite corners of the front of the house and bent them together until they touched, folding the entire front of the building inside the curvature of the bent-together corners.

He now had a curved-front house. Although it was, actually, not as simple as all that, for the curvature was not in proportion to what actually would have happened in case of such a feat. The curve was long and graceful and somehow not quite apparent. It was as if the front of the house had been eliminated and an illusion of the rest of the house had been summoned to mask the disappearance.

Taine dropped the shovel and the pick and they clattered on the driveway gravel. He put his hand up to his face and wiped it across his eyes, as if to clear his eyes of something that could not possibly be there.

And when he took the hand away it had not changed a bit.

There was no front to the house.

Then he was running around the house, hardly knowing he was running, and there was a fear inside of him at what had happened to the house.

But the back of the house was all right. It was exactly as it had always been.

He clattered up the stoop with Beasly and Towser running close behind him. He pushed open the door and burst into the entry and scrambled up the stairs into the kitchen and went across the kitchen in three strides to see what had happened to the front of the house.

At the door between the kitchen and the living room he stopped and his hands went out to grasp the door jamb as he stared in disbelief at the windows of the living room.

It was night outside. There could be no doubt of that. He had seen the fireflies flickering in the brush and weeds and the street lamps had been lit and the stars were out.

But a flood of sunlight was pouring through the windows of the living room and out beyond the windows lay a land that was not Willow Bend.

"Beasly," he gasped, "look out there in front!"

Beasly looked.

"What place is that?" he asked.

"That's what I'd like to know."

Towser had found his dish and was pushing it around the kitchen floor with his nose, by way of telling Taine that it was time to eat.

Taine went across the living room and opened the front door. The garage, he saw, was there. The pickup stood with its nose against the open garage door and the car was safe inside.

There was nothing wrong with the front of the house at all.

But if the front of the house was all right, that was all that was.

For the driveway was chopped off just a few feet beyond the tail end of the pickup and there was no yard or woods or road. There was just a desert – a flat, far-reaching desert, level as a floor, with occasional boulder piles and haphazard clumps of vegetation and all of the ground covered with sand and pebbles. A big blinding sun hung just above a horizon that seemed much too far away and a funny thing about it was that the sun was in the north, where no proper sun should be. It had a peculiar whiteness, too.

Beasly stepped out on the porch and Taine saw that he was shivering like a frightened dog.

"Maybe," Taine told him, kindly, "you'd better go back in and start making us some supper."

"But, Hiram –"

"It's all right," said Taine. "It's bound to be all right."

"If you say so, Hiram."

He went in and the screen door banged behind him and in a minute Taine heard him in the kitchen.

He didn't blame Beasly for shivering, he admitted to himself. It was a sort of shock to step out of your front door into an unknown land. A man might eventually get used to it, of course, but it would take some doing.

He stepped down off the porch and walked around the truck and around the garage corner and when he rounded the corner he was half prepared to walk back into familiar Willow Bend – for when he had gone in the back door the village had been there.

There was no Willow Bend. There was more of the desert, a great deal more of it.

He walked around the house and there was no back to the house. The back of the house now was just the same as the front had been before – the same smooth curve pulling the sides of the house together.

He walked on around the house to the front again and there was desert all the way. And the front was still all right. It hadn't changed at all. The truck was there on the chopped-off driveway and the garage was open and the car inside.

Taine walked out a ways into the desert and hunkered down and scooped up a handful of the pebbles and the pebbles were just pebbles.

He squatted there and let the pebbles trickle through his fingers.

In Willow Bend there was a back door and there wasn't any front. Here, wherever here might be, there was a front door, but there wasn't any back.

He stood up and tossed the rest of the pebbles away and wiped his dusty hands upon his britches.

Out of the corner of his eye he caught a sense of movement on the porch and there they were.

A line of tiny animals, if animals they were, came marching down the steps, one behind the other. They were four inches high or so and they went on all four feet, although it was plain to see that their front feet were really hands, not feet. They had rat-like faces that were vaguely human, with noses long and pointed. They looked like they might have scales instead of hide, for their bodies glistened with a rippling motion as they walked. And all of them had tails that looked very much like the coiled-wire tails one finds on certain toys and the tails stuck straight up above them, quivering as they walked.

They came down the steps in single file, in perfect military order, with half a foot or so of spacing between each one of them.

They came down the steps and walked out into the desert in a straight, undeviating line as if they knew exactly where they might be bound. There was something deadly purposeful about them and yet they didn't hurry.

Taine counted sixteen of them and he watched them go out into the desert until they were almost lost to sight.

There go the ones, he thought, who came to live with me. They are the ones who fixed up the ceiling and who repaired Abbie's television set and jiggered up the stove and radio. And more than likely, too, they were the ones who had come to Earth in the strange milk-glass contraption out there in the woods.

And if they had come to Earth in that deal out in the woods, then what sort of place was this?

He climbed the porch and opened the screen door and saw the neat, six-inch circle his departing guests had achieved in the screen to get out of the house. He made a mental note that some day, when he had the time, he would have to fix it.

He went in and slammed the door behind him.

"Beasly," he shouted.

There was no answer.

Towser crawled from beneath the love seat and apologized.

"It's all right, pal," said Taine. "That outfit scared me, too."

He went into the kitchen. The dim ceiling light shone on the overturned coffee pot, the broken cup in the center of the floor, the upset bowl of eggs. One broken egg was a white and yellow gob on the linoleum.

He stepped down on the landing and saw that the screen door in the back was wrecked beyond repair. Its rusty mesh was broken – exploded might have been a better word – and a part of the frame was smashed.

Taine looked at it in wondering admiration.

"The poor fool," he said. "He went straight through it without opening it at all."

He snapped on the light and went down the basement stairs. Halfway down he stopped in utter wonderment.

To his left was a wall – a wall of the same sort of material as had been used to put in the ceiling.

He stooped and saw that the wall ran clear across the basement, floor to ceiling, shutting off the workshop area.

And inside the workshop, what?

For one thing, he remembered, the computer that Henry had sent over just this morning. Three trucks, Beasly had said – three truckloads of equipment delivered straight into their paws!

Taine sat down weakly on the steps.

They must have thought, he told himself, that he was co-operating! Maybe they had figured that he knew what they were about and so went along with them. Or perhaps they thought he was paying them for fixing up the TV set and the stove and radio.

But to tackle first things first, why had they repaired the TV set and the stove and radio? As a sort of rental payment? As a friendly gesture? Or as a sort of practice run to find out what they could about this world's technology? To find, perhaps, how their technology could be adapted to the materials and conditions on this planet they had found?

Taine raised a hand and rapped with his knuckles on the wall beside the stairs and the smooth white surface gave out a pinging sound.

He laid his ear against the wall and listened closely and it seemed to him he could hear a low-key humming, but if so it was so faint he could not be absolutely sure.

Banker Stevens' lawn mower was in there, behind the wall, and a lot of other stuff waiting for repair. They'd take the hide right off him, he thought, especially Banker Stevens. Stevens was a tight man.

Beasly must have been half-crazed with fear, he thought. When he had seen those things coming up out of the basement, he'd gone clean off his rocker. He'd gone straight through the door without even bothering to try to open it and now he was down in the village yapping to anyone who'd stop to listen to him.

No one ordinarily would pay Beasly much attention, but if he yapped long enough and wild enough, they'd probably do some checking. They'd come storming up here and they'd give the place a going over and they'd stand goggle-eyed at what they found in front and pretty soon some of them would have worked their way around to sort of running things.

And it was none of their business, Taine stubbornly told himself, his ever-present business sense rising to the fore. There was a lot of real estate lying around out there in his front yard and the only way anyone could get to it was by going through his house. That being the case, it stood to reason that all that land out there was his. Maybe it wasn't any good at all. There might be nothing there. But before he had other people overrunning it, he'd better check and see.

He went up the stairs and out into the garage.

The sun was still just above the northern horizon and there was nothing moving.

He found a hammer and some nails and a few short lengths of plank in the garage and took them in the house.

Towser, he saw, had taken advantage of the situation and was sleeping in the gold-upholstered chair. Taine didn't bother him.

Taine locked the back door and nailed some planks across it. He locked the kitchen and the bedroom windows and nailed planks across them, too.

That would hold the villagers for a while, he told himself, when they came tearing up here to see what was going on.

He got his deer rifle, a box of cartridges, a pair of binoculars and an old canteen out of a closet. He filled the canteen at the kitchen tap and stuffed a sack with food for him and Towser to eat along the way, for there was no time to wait and eat.

Then he went into the living room and dumped Towser out of the gold-upholstered chair.

"Come on, Tows," he said. "We'll go and look things over."

He checked the gasoline in the pickup and the tank was almost full.

He and the dog got in and he put the rifle within easy reach. Then he backed the truck and swung it around and headed out, north, across the desert.

It was easy traveling. The desert was as level as a floor. At times it got a little rough, but no worse than a lot of the back roads he traveled hunting down antiques.

The scenery didn't change. Here and there were low hills, but the desert itself kept on mostly level, unraveling itself into that far-off horizon. Taine kept on driving north, straight into the sun.

He hit some sandy stretches, but the sand was firm and hard and he had no trouble.

Half an hour out he caught up with the band of things – all sixteen of them – that had left the house. They were still traveling in line at their steady pace.

Slowing down the truck, Taine traveled parallel with them for a time, but there was no profit in it; they kept on traveling their course, looking neither right or left.

Speeding up, Taine left them behind.

The sun stayed in the north, unmoving, and that certainly was queer. Perhaps, Taine told himself, this world spun on its axis far more slowly than the Earth and the day was longer. From the way the sun appeared to be standing still, perhaps a good deal longer.

Hunched above the wheel, staring out into the endless stretch of desert, the strangeness of it struck him for the first time with its full impact.

This was another world – there could be no doubt of that – another planet circling another star, and where it was in actual space no one on Earth could have the least idea. And yet, through some machination of those sixteen things walking straight in line, it also was lying just outside the front door of his house.

Ahead of him a somewhat larger hill loomed out of the flatness of the desert. As he drew nearer to it, he made out a row of shining objects lined upon its crest. After a time he stopped the truck and got out with the binoculars.

Through the glasses, he saw that the shining things were the same sort of milk-glass contraptions as had been in the woods. He counted eight of them, shining in the sun, perched upon some sort of rock-gray cradles. And there were other cradles empty.

He took the binoculars from his eyes and stood there for a moment, considering the advisability of climbing the hill and investigating closely. But he shook his head. There'd be time for that later on. He'd better keep on moving. This was not a real exploring foray, but a quick reconnaissance.

He climbed into the truck and drove on, keeping watch upon the gas gauge. When it came close to half full he'd have to turn around and go back home again.

Ahead of him he saw a faint whiteness above the dim horizon line and he watched it narrowly. At times it faded away and then came in again, but whatever it might be was so far off he could make nothing of it.

He glanced down at the gas gauge and it was close to the halfway mark. He stopped the pickup and got out with the binoculars.

As he moved around to the front of the machine he was puzzled at how slow and tired his legs were and then remembered – he should have been in bed many hours ago. He looked at his watch and it was two o'clock and that meant, back on Earth, two o'clock in the morning. He had been awake for more than twenty hours and much of that time he had been engaged in the back-breaking work of digging out the strange thing in the woods.

He put up the binoculars and the elusive white line that he had been seeing turned out to be a range of mountains. The great, blue, craggy mass towered up above the desert with the gleam of snow on its peaks and ridges. They were a long way off, for even the powerful glasses brought them in as little more than a misty blueness.

He swept the glasses slowly back and forth and the mountains extended for a long distance above the horizon line.

He brought the glasses down off the mountains and examined the desert that stretched ahead of him. There was more of the same that he had been seeing – the same floorlike levelness, the same occasional mounds, the self-same scraggy vegetation.

And a house!

His hands trembled and he lowered the glasses, then put them up to his face again and had another look. It was a house, all right. A funny-looking house standing at the foot of one of the hillocks, still shadowed by the hillock so that one could not pick it out with the naked eye.

It seemed to be a small house. Its roof was like a blunted cone and it lay tight against the ground, as if it hugged or crouched against the ground. There was an oval opening that probably was a door, but there was no sign of windows.

He took the binoculars down again and stared at the hillock. Four or five miles away, he thought. The gas would stretch that far and even if it didn't he could walk the last few miles into Willow Bend.

It was queer, he thought, that a house should be all alone out here. In all the miles he'd traveled in the desert he'd seen no sign of life beyond the sixteen little ratlike things that marched in single file, no sign of artificial structure other than the eight milk-glass contraptions resting in their cradles.

He climbed into the pickup and put it into gear. Ten minutes later he drew up in front of the house, which still lay within the shadow of the hillock.

He got out of the pickup and hauled his rifle after him. Towser leaped to the ground and stood with his hackles up, a deep growl in his throat.

"What's the matter, boy?" asked Taine.

Towser growled again.

The house stood silent. It seemed to be deserted.

The walls were built, Taine saw, of rude, rough masonry crudely set together, with a crumbling, mudlike substance used in lieu of mortar. The roof originally had been of sod and that was queer, indeed, for there was nothing that came close to sod upon this expanse of desert. But now, although one could see the lines where the sod strips had been fit together, it was nothing more than earth baked hard by the desert sun.

The house itself was featureless, entirely devoid of any ornament, with no attempt at all to soften the harsh utility of it as a simple shelter. It was the sort of thing that a shepherd people might have put together. It had the look of age about it; the stone had flaked and crumbled in the weather.

Rifle slung beneath his arm, Taine paced toward it. He

reached the door and glanced inside and there was darkness and
no movement.

He glanced back for Towser and saw that the dog had crawled
beneath the truck and was peering out and growling.

"You stick around," said Taine. "Don't go running off."

With the rifle thrust before him, Taine stepped through the
door into the darkness. He stood for a long moment to allow his
eyes to become accustomed to the gloom.

Finally he could make out the room in which he stood. It
was plain and rough, with a rude stone bench along one wall and
queer unfunctional niches hollowed in another. One rickety piece
of wooden furniture stood in a corner, but Taine could not make
out what its use might be.

An old and deserted place, he thought, abandoned long ago.
Perhaps a shepherd people might have lived here in some long-
gone age, when the desert had been a rich and grassy plain.

There was a door into another room and as he stepped through
it he heard the faint, far-off booming sound and something else as
well – the sound of pouring rain! From the open door that led out
through the back he caught a whiff of salty breeze and he stood
there frozen in the center of that second room.

Another one!

Another house that led to another world!

He walked slowly forward, drawn toward the outer door, and he
stepped out into a cloudy, darkling day with the rain streaming down
from wildly racing clouds. Half a mile away, across a field of jumbled,
broken, iron-gray boulders, lay a pounding sea that raged upon the
coast, throwing great spumes of angry spray high into the air.

He walked out from the door and looked up at the sky and
the rain drops pounded at his face with a stinging fury. There was
a chill and a dampness in the air and the place was eldritch – a
world jerked straight from some ancient Gothic tale of goblin and
of sprite.

He glanced around and there was nothing he could see,

for the rain blotted out the world beyond this stretch of coast, but behind the rain he could sense or seemed to sense a presence that sent shivers down his spine. Gulping in fright, Taine turned around and stumbled back again through the door into the house.

One world away, he thought, was far enough; two worlds away was more than one could take. He trembled at the sense of utter loneliness that tumbled in his skull and suddenly this long-forsaken house became unbearable and he dashed out of it.

Outside the sun was bright and there was welcome warmth. His clothes were damp from rain and little beads of moisture lay on the rifle barrel.

He looked around for Towser and there was no sign of the dog. He was not underneath the pickup; he was nowhere in sight.

Taine called and there was no answer. His voice sounded lone and hollow in the emptiness and silence.

He walked around the house, looking for the dog, and there was no back door to the house. The rough rock walls of the sides of the house pulled in with that funny curvature and there was no back to the house at all.

But Taine was not interested; he had known how it would be. Right now he was looking for his dog and he felt the panic rising in him. Somehow it felt a long way from home.

He spent three hours at it. He went back into the house and Towser was not there. He went into the other world again and searched among the tumbled rocks and Towser was not there. He went back to the desert and walked around the hillock and then he climbed to the crest of it and used the binoculars and saw nothing but the lifeless desert, stretching far in all directions.

Dead-beat with weariness, stumbling, half asleep even as he walked, he went back to the pickup.

He leaned against it and tried to pull his wits together.

Continuing as he was would be a useless effort. He had to get some sleep. He had to go back to Willow Bend and fill the tank and get some extra gasoline so that he could range farther afield in his search for Towser.

He couldn't leave the dog out here – that was unthinkable. But he had to plan, he had to act intelligently. He would be doing Towser no good by stumbling around in his present shape.

He pulled himself into the truck and headed back for Willow Bend, following the occasional faint impressions that his tires had made in the sandy places, fighting a half-dead drowsiness that tried to seal his eyes shut.

Passing the higher hill on which the milk-glass things had stood, he stopped to walk around a bit so he wouldn't fall asleep behind the wheel. And now, he saw, there were only seven of the things resting in their cradles.

But that meant nothing to him now. All that meant anything was to hold off the fatigue that was closing down upon him, to cling to the wheel and wear off the miles, to get back to Willow Bend and get some sleep and then come back again to look for Towser.

Slightly more than halfway home he saw the other car and watched it in numb befuddlement, for this truck that he was driving and the car at home in his garage were the only two vehicles this side of his house.

He pulled the pickup to a halt and stumbled out of it.

The car drew up and Henry Horton and Beasly and a man who wore a star leaped quickly out of it.

"Thank God we found you, man!" cried Henry, striding over to him.

"I wasn't lost," protested Taine. "I was coming back."

"He's all beat out," said the man who wore the star.

"This is Sheriff Hanson," Henry said. "We were following your tracks."

"I lost Towser," Taine mumbled. "I had to go and leave him. Just leave me be and go and hunt for Towser. I can make it home."

He reached out and grabbed the edge of the pickup's door to hold himself erect.

"You broke down the door," he said to Henry. "You broke into my house and you took my car –"

"We had to do it, Hiram. We were afraid that something might have happened to you. The way that Beasly told it, it stood your hair on end."

"You better get him in the car," the sheriff said. "I'll drive the pickup back."

"But I have to hunt for Towser!"

"You can't do anything until you've had some rest."

Henry grabbed him by the arm and led him to the car and Beasly held the rear door open.

"You got any idea what this place is?" Henry whispered conspiratorially.

"I don't positively know," Taine mumbled. "Might be some other –"

Henry chuckled. "Well, I guess it doesn't really matter. Whatever it may be, it's put us on the map. We're in all the newscasts and the papers are plastering us in headlines and the town is swarming with reporters and cameramen and there are big officials coming. Yes, sir, I tell you, Hiram, this will be the making of us –"

Taine heard no more. He was fast asleep before he hit the seat.

V

He came awake and lay quietly in the bed and he saw the shades were drawn and the room was cool and peaceful.

It was good, he thought, to wake in a room you knew – in a room that one had known for his entire life, in a house that had been the Taine house for almost a hundred years.

Then memory clouted him and he sat bolt upright.

And now he heard it – the insistent murmur from outside the window.

He vaulted from the bed and pulled one shade aside. Peering out, he saw the cordon of troops that held back the crowd that overflowed his back yard and the backyards back of that.

He let the shade drop back and started hunting for his shoes, for he was fully dressed. Probably Henry and Beasly, he told himself, had dumped him into bed and pulled off his shoes and let it go at that. But he couldn't remember a single thing of it. He must have gone dead to the world the minute Henry had bundled him into the back seat of the car.

He found the shoes on the floor at the end of the bed and sat down upon the bed to pull them on.

And his mind was racing on what he had to do.

He'd have to get some gasoline somehow and fill up the truck and stash an extra can or two into the back and he'd have to take some food and water and perhaps his sleeping bag. For he wasn't coming back until he found his dog.

He got on his shoes and tied them, then went out into the living room. There was no one there, but there were voices in the kitchen.

He looked out the window and the desert lay outside, unchanged. The sun, he noticed, had climbed higher in the sky, but out in his front yard it still was forenoon.

He looked at his watch and it was six o'clock and from the way the shadows had been falling when he'd peered out of the bedroom window, he knew that it was 6:00 p.m. He realized with a guilty start that he must have slept almost around the clock. He had not meant to sleep that long. He hadn't meant to leave Towser out there that long.

He headed for the kitchen and there were three persons there – Abbie and Henry Horton and a man in military garb.

"There you are," cried Abbie merrily. "We were wondering when you would wake up."

"You have some coffee cooking, Abbie?"

"Yes, a whole pot full of it. And I'll cook up something else for you."

"Just some toast," said Taine. "I haven't got much time. I have to hunt for Towser."

"Hiram," said Henry, "this is Colonel Ryan. National Guard. He has his boys outside."

"Yes, I saw them through the window."

"Necessary," said Henry. "Absolutely necessary. The sheriff couldn't handle it. The people came rushing in and they'd have torn the place apart. So I called the governor."

"Taine," the colonel said, "sit down. I want to talk with you."

"Certainly," said Taine, taking a chair. "Sorry to be in such a rush, but I lost my dog out there."

"This business," said the colonel, smugly, "is vastly more important than any dog could be."

"Well, colonel, that just goes to show that you don't know Towser. He's the best dog I ever had and I've had a lot of them. Raised him from a pup and he's been a good friend all these years –"

"All right," the colonel said, "so he is a friend. But still I have to talk with you."

"You just sit and talk," Abbie said to Taine. "I'll fix up some cakes and Henry brought over some of that sausage that we get out on the farm."

The back door opened and Beasly staggered in to the accompaniment of a terrific metallic banging. He was carrying three empty five-gallon gas cans in one hand and two in the other hand and they were bumping and banging together as he moved.

"Say," yelled Taine, "what is going on here?"

"Now, just take it easy," Henry said. "You have no idea the problems that we have. We wanted to get a big gas tank moved through here, but we couldn't do it. We tried to rip out the back of the kitchen to get it through, but we couldn't –"

"You did what!"

"We tried to rip out the back of the kitchen," Henry told him calmly. "You can't get one of those big storage tanks through an ordinary door. But when we tried, we found that the entire house is boarded up inside with the same kind of material that you used down in the basement. You hit it with an axe and it blunts the steel –"

"But, Henry, this is my house and there isn't anyone who has the right to start tearing it apart."

"Fat chance," the colonel said. "What I would like to know, Taine, what is that stuff that we couldn't break through?"

"Now you take it easy, Hiram," cautioned Henry. "We have a big new world waiting for us out there –"

"It isn't waiting for you or anyone," yelled Taine.

"And we have to explore it and to explore it we need a stock-pile of gasoline. So since we can't have a storage tank, we're getting together as many gas cans as possible and then we'll run a hose through here –"

"But, Henry –"

"I wish," said Henry sternly, "that you'd quit interrupting me and let me have my say. You can't even imagine the logistics that we face. We're bottlenecked by the size of a regulation door. We have to get supplies out there and we have to get transport. Cars and trucks won't be so bad. We can disassemble them and lug them through piecemeal, but a plane will be a problem."

"You listen to me, Henry. There isn't anyone going to haul a plane through here. This house has been in my family for almost a hundred years and I own it and I have a right to it and you can't come in highhanded and start hauling stuff through it."

"But," said Henry plaintively, "we need a plane real bad. You can cover so much more ground when you have a plane."

Beasly went banging through the kitchen with his cans and out into the living room.

The colonel sighed. "I had hoped, Mr. Taine, that you would understand how the matter stood. To me it seems very plain that it's your patriotic duty to co-operate with us in this. The government, of course, could exercise the right of eminent domain and start condemnation action, but it would rather not do that. I'm speaking unofficially, of course, but I think it's safe to say the government would much prefer to arrive at an amicable agreement."

"I doubt," Taine said, bluffing, not knowing anything about it, "that the right of eminent domain would be applicable. As I understand it, it applies to buildings and to roads –"

"This is a road," the colonel told him flatly. "A road right through your house to another world."

"First," Taine declared, "the government would have to show it was in the public interest and that refusal of the owner to relinquish title amounted to an interference in government procedure and –"

"I think," the colonel said, "that the government can prove it is in the public interest."

"I think," Taine said angrily, "I better get a lawyer."

"If you really mean that," Henry offered, ever helpful, "and you want to get a good one – and I presume you do – I would be pleased to recommend a firm that I am sure would represent your interests most ably and be, at the same time, fairly reasonable in cost."

The colonel stood up, seething. "You'll have a lot to answer, Taine. There'll be a lot of things the government will want to know. First of all, they'll want to know just how you engineered this. Are you ready to tell that?"

"No," said Taine, "I don't believe I am."

And he thought with some alarm: They think that I'm the one who did it and they'll be down on me like a pack of wolves to find out just how I did it. He had visions of the FBI and the state department and the Pentagon and, even sitting down, he felt shaky in the knees.

The colonel turned around and marched stiffly from the kitchen. He went out the back and slammed the door behind him.

Henry looked at Taine speculatively.

"Do you really mean it?" he demanded. "Do you intend to stand up to them?"

"I'm getting sore," said Taine. "They can't come in here and take over without even asking me. I don't care what anyone may think, this is my house. I was born here and I've lived here all my life and I like the place and –"

"Sure," said Henry. "I know just how you feel."

"I suppose it's childish of me, but I wouldn't mind so much if they showed a willingness to sit down and talk about what they meant to do once they'd taken over. But there seems no disposition to even ask me what I think about it. And I tell you, Henry, this is different than it seems. This is not a place where we can walk in and take over, no matter what Washington may think. There is something out there and we better watch our step –"

"I was thinking," Henry interrupted, "as I was sitting here, that your attitude is most commendable and deserving of support. It has occurred to me that it would be most unneighborly of me to go on sitting here and leave you in the fight alone. We could hire ourselves a fine array of legal talent and we could fight the case and in the meantime we could form a land and development company and that way we could make sure that this new world of yours is used the way it should be used.

"It stands to reason, Hiram, that I am the one to stand beside you, shoulder to shoulder, in this business since we're already partners in this TV deal."

"What's this about TV?" shrilled Abbie, slapping a plate of cakes down in front of Taine.

"Now, Abbie," Henry said patiently, "I have explained to you already that your TV set is back of that partition down in the basement and there isn't any telling when we can get it out."

"Yes, I know," said Abbie, bringing a platter of sausages and pouring a cup of coffee.

Beasly came in from the living room and went bumbling out the back.

"After all," said Henry, pressing his advantage, "I would suppose I had some hand in it. I doubt you could have done much without the computer I sent over."

And there it was again, thought Taine. Even Henry thought he'd been the one who did it.

"But didn't Beasly tell you?"

"Beasly said a lot, but you know how Beasly is."

And that was it, of course. To the villagers it would be no more than another Beasly story – another whopper that Beasly had dreamed up. There was no one who believed a word that Beasly said.

Taine picked up the cup and drank his coffee, gaining time to shape an answer and there wasn't any answer. If he told the truth, it would sound far less believable than any lie he'd tell.

"You can tell me, Hiram. After all, we're partners."

He's playing me for a fool, thought Taine. Henry thinks he can play anyone he wants for a fool and sucker.

"You wouldn't believe me if I told you, Henry."

"Well," Henry said, resignedly, getting to his feet, "I guess that part of it can wait."

Beasly came tramping and banging through the kitchen with another load of cans.

"I'll have to have some gasoline," said Taine, "if I'm going out for Towser."

"I'll take care of that right away," Henry promised smoothly. "I'll send Ernie over with his tank wagon and we can run a hose through here and fill up those cans. And I'll see if I can find some-one who'll go along with you."

"That's not necessary. I can go alone."

"If we had a radio transmitter. Then you could keep in touch."

"But we haven't any. And, Henry, I can't wait. Towser's out there somewhere –"

"Sure, I know how much you thought of him. You go out and look for him if you think you have to and I'll get started on this other business. I'll get some lawyers lined up and we'll draw up some sort of corporate papers for our land development –"

"And, Hiram," Abbie said, "will you do something for me, please?"

"Why, certainly," said Taine.

"Would you speak to Beasly. It's senseless the way he's acting. There wasn't any call for him to up and leave us. I might have been a little sharp with him, but he's so simple-minded he's infuriating. He ran off and spent half a day helping Towser at digging out that woodchuck and –"

"I'll speak to him," said Taine.

"Thanks, Hiram. He'll listen to you. You're the only one he'll listen to. And I wish you could have fixed my TV set before all this came about. I'm just lost without it. It leaves a hole in the living room. It matched my other furniture, you know."

"Yes, I know," said Taine.

"Coming, Abbie?" Henry asked, standing at the door.

He lifted a hand in a confidential farewell to Taine. "I'll see you later, Hiram. I'll get it all fixed up."

I just bet you will, thought Taine.

He went back to the table, after they were gone, and sat down heavily in a chair.

The front door slammed and Beasly came panting in, excited.

"Towser's back!" he yelled. "He's coming back and he's driving in the biggest woodchuck you ever clapped your eyes on."

Taine leaped to his feet.

"Woodchuck! That's an alien planet. It hasn't any woodchucks."

"You come and see," yelled Beasly.

He turned and raced back out again, with Taine following close behind.

It certainly looked considerably like a woodchuck – a sort of man-size woodchuck. More like a woodchuck out of a children's book, perhaps, for it was walking on its hind legs and trying to look dignified even while it kept a weather eye on Towser.

Towser was back a hundred feet or so, keeping a wary distance from the massive chuck. He had the pose of a good sheep-herding dog, walking in a crouch, alert to head off any break that the chuck might make.

The chuck came up close to the house and stopped. Then it did an about-face so that it looked back across the desert and it hunkered down.

It swung its massive head to gaze at Beasly and Taine and in the limpid brown eyes Taine saw more than the eyes of an animal.

Taine walked swiftly out and picked up the dog in his arms and hugged him tight against him. Towser twisted his head around and slapped a sloppy tongue across his master's face.

Taine stood with the dog in his arms and looked at the man-size chuck and felt a great relief and an utter thankfulness.

Everything was all right now, he thought. Towser had come back.

He headed for the house and out into the kitchen.

He put Towser down and got a dish and filled it at the tap. He placed it on the floor and Towser lapped at it thirstily, slopping water all over the linoleum.

"Take it easy, there," warned Taine. "You don't want to overdo it."

He hunted in the refrigerator and found some scraps and put them in Towser's dish. Towser wagged his tail with doggish happiness.

"By rights," said Taine, "I ought to take a rope to you, running off like that."

Beasly came ambling in.

"That chuck is a friendly cuss," he announced. "He is waiting for someone."

"That's nice," said Taine, paying no attention.

He glanced at the clock.

"It's seven thirty," he said. "We can catch the news. You want to get it, Beasly?"

"Sure. I know right where to get it. That fellow from New York."

"That's the one," said Taine.

He walked into the living room and looked out the window. The man-size chuck had not moved. He was sitting with his back to the house, looking back the way he'd come.

Waiting for someone, Beasly had said, and it looked as if he might be, but probably it was all just in Beasly's head.

And if he were waiting for someone, Taine wondered, who might that someone be? *What* might that someone be? Certainly by now the word had spread out there that there was a door into another world. And how many doors, he wondered, had been opened through the ages?

Henry had said that there was a big new world out there waiting for Earthmen to move in. And that wasn't it at all. It was the other way around.

The voice of the news commentator came blasting from the radio in the middle of a sentence:

". . . Finally got into the act. Radio Moscow said this evening that the Soviet delegate will make representations in the U.N. tomorrow for the internationalization of this other world and the gateway to it.

"From that gateway itself, the home of a man named Hiram Taine, there is no news. Complete security had been clamped down and a cordon of troops form a solid wall around the house, holding back the crowds. Attempts to telephone the residence are blocked by a curt voice which says that no calls are being accepted for that number. And Taine himself has not stepped from the house."

Taine walked back into the kitchen and sat down.

"He's talking about you," Beasly said importantly.

"Rumor circulated this morning that Taine, a quiet village repair man and dealer in antiques, and until yesterday a relative unknown, had finally returned from a trip which he made out into this new and unknown land. But what he found, if anything, no one yet can say. Nor is there any further information about this other place beyond the fact that it is a desert and, to the moment, lifeless.

"A small flurry of excitement was occasioned late yesterday by the finding of some strange object in the woods across the road from the residence, but this area likewise was swiftly cordoned off and to the moment Colonel Ryan, who commands the troops, will say nothing of what actually was found.

"Mystery man of the entire situation is one Henry Horton, who seems to be the only unofficial person to have entry to the Taine house. Horton, questioned earlier today, had little to say, but managed to suggest an air of great conspiracy. He hinted he and Taine were partners in some mysterious venture and left hanging in midair the half impression that he and Taine had collaborated in opening the new world.

"Horton, it is interesting to note, operates a small computer plant and it is understood on good authority that only recently he delivered a computer to Taine, or at least some sort of machine to which considerable mystery is attached. One story is that this particular machine had been in the process of development for six or seven years.

"Some of the answers to the matter of how all this did happen and what actually did happen must wait upon the findings of a team of scientists who left Washington this evening after an all-day conference at the White House, which was attended by representatives from the military, the state department, the security division and the special weapons section.

"Throughout the world the impact of what happened yesterday at Willow Bend can only be compared to the sensation of the news, almost twenty years ago, of the dropping of the first atomic bomb. There is some tendency among many observers to believe that the implications of Willow Bend, in fact, may be even more Earth-shaking than were those of Hiroshima.

"Washington insists, as is only natural, that this matter is of internal concern only and that it intends to handle the situation as it best affects the national welfare.

"But abroad there is a rising storm of insistence that this is not a matter of national policy concerning one nation, but that it necessarily must be a matter of worldwide concern.

"There is an unconfirmed report that a U.N. observer will arrive in Willow Bend almost momentarily. France, Britain, Bolivia, Mexico and India have already requested permission of Washington to send observers to the scene and other nations undoubtedly plan to file similar requests.

"The world sits on edge tonight, waiting for the word from Willow Bend and –"

Taine reached out and clicked the radio to silence.

"From the sound of it," said Beasly, "we are going to be over-run by a batch of foreigners."

Yes, thought Taine, there might be a batch of foreigners, but not exactly in the sense that Beasly meant. The use of the word, he told himself, so far as any human was concerned, must be outdated now. No man of Earth ever again could be called a foreigner with alien life next door – literally next door. What were the people of the stone house?

And perhaps not the alien life of one planet only, but the alien life of many. For he himself had found another door into yet another planet and there might be many more such doors and what would these other worlds be like, and what was the purpose of the doors?

Someone, *something,* had found a way of going to another planet short of spanning light-years of lonely space – a simpler and a shorter way than flying through the gulfs of space. And once the way was open, then the way stayed open and it was as easy as walking from one room to another.

But one thing – one ridiculous thing – kept puzzling him and that was the spinning and the movement of the connected planets, of all the planets that must be linked together. You could not, he argued, establish solid, factual links between two objects that move independently of one another.

And yet, a couple of days ago, he would have contended just as stolidly that the whole idea on the face of it was fantastic and impossible. Still it had been done. And once one impossibility was accomplished, what logical man could say with sincerity that the second could not be?

The doorbell rang and he got up to answer it.

It was Ernie, the oil man.

"Henry said you wanted some gas and I came to tell you I can't get it until morning."

"That's all right," said Taine. "I don't need it now."

And swiftly slammed the door.

He leaned against it, thinking: I'll have to face them sometime. I can't keep the door locked against the world. Sometime, soon or late, the Earth and I will have to have this out.

And it was foolish, he thought, for him to think like this, but that was the way it was.

He had something here that the Earth demanded; something that Earth wanted or thought it wanted. And yet, in the last analysis, it was his responsibility. It had happened on his land, it had happened in his house; unwittingly, perhaps, he'd even aided and abetted it.

And the land and house are mine, he fiercely told himself, and that world out there was an extension of his yard. No matter how far or where it went, an extension of his yard.

Beasly had left the kitchen and Taine walked into the living room. Towser was curled up and snoring gently in the gold-upholstered chair.

Taine decided he would let him stay there. After all, he thought, Towser had won the right to sleep anywhere he wished.

He walked past the chair to the window and the desert stretched to its far horizon and there before the window sat the man-size woodchuck and Beasly side by side, with their backs turned to the window and staring out across the desert.

Somehow it seemed natural that the chuck and Beasly should be sitting there together – the two of them, it appeared to Taine, might have a lot in common.

And it was a good beginning – that a man and an alien creature from this other world should sit down companionably together.

He tried to envision the setup of these linked worlds, of which Earth was now a part, and the possibilities that lay inherent in the fact of linkage rolled thunder through his brain.

There would be contact between the Earth and these other worlds and what would come of it?

And come to think of it, the contact had been made already, but so naturally, so undramatically, that it failed to register as a great, important meeting. For Beasly and the chuck out there were contact and if it all should go like that, there was absolutely nothing for one to worry over.

This was no haphazard business, he reminded himself. It had been planned and executed with the smoothness of long practice. This was not the first world to be opened and it would not be the last.

The little ratlike things had spanned space – how many light-years of space one could not even guess – in the vehicle which he had unearthed out in the woods. They then had buried it, perhaps as a child might hide a dish by shoving it into a pile of sand. Then they had come to this very house and had set up the apparatus that had made this house a tunnel between one world and another. And once that had been done, the need of crossing space had been canceled out forever. There need be but one crossing and that one crossing would serve to link the planets.

And once the job was done the little ratlike things had left, but not before they had made certain that this gateway to their planet would stand against no matter what assault. They had sheathed the house inside the studdings with a wonder-material that would resist an ax and that, undoubtedly, would resist much more than a simple ax.

And they had marched in drill-order single file out to the hill where eight more of the space machines had rested in their cradles. And now there were only seven there, in their cradles on the hill, and the rat-like things were gone and, perhaps, in time to come, they'd land on another planet and another doorway would be opened, a link to yet another world.

But more, Taine thought, than the linking of mere worlds. It would be, as well, the linking of the peoples of those worlds.

The little ratlike creatures were the explorers and the pioneers who sought out other Earth-like planets and the creature waiting with Beasly just outside the window must also serve its purpose and perhaps in time to come there would be a purpose which Man would also serve.

He turned away from the window and looked around the room and the room was exactly as it had been ever since he could remember it. With all the change outside, with all that was happening outside, the room remained unchanged.

This is the reality, thought Taine, this is all the reality there is. Whatever else may happen, this is where I stand – this room with its fireplace blackened by many winter fires, the bookshelves with the old thumbed volumes, the easy-chair, the ancient worn carpet – worn by beloved and unforgotten feet through the many years.

And this also, he knew, was the lull before the storm.

In just a little while the brass would start arriving – the team of scientists, the governmental functionaries, the military, the observers from the other countries, the officials from the U.N.

And against all these, he realized, he stood weaponless and shorn of his strength. No matter what a man might say or think, he could not stand off the world.

This was the last day that this would be the Taine house. After almost a hundred years, it would have another destiny.

And for the first time in all those years there'd be no Taine asleep beneath its roof.

He stood looking at the fireplace and the shelves of books and he sensed the old, pale ghosts walking in the room and he lifted a hesitant hand as if to wave farewell, not only to the ghosts but to the room as well. But before he got it up, he dropped it to his side.

What was the use, he thought.

He went out to the porch and sat down on the steps.

Beasly heard him and turned around.

"He's nice," he said to Taine, patting the chuck upon the back. "He's exactly like a great big teddy bear."

"Yes, I see," said Taine.

"And best of all, I can talk with him."

"Yes, I know," said Taine, remembering that Beasly could talk with Towser, too.

He wondered what it would be like to live in the simple world of Beasly. At times, he decided, it would be comfortable.

The ratlike things had come in the spaceship, but why had they come to Willow Bend, why had they picked this house, the only house in all the village where they would have found the equipment that they needed to build their apparatus so easily and so quickly? For there was no doubt that they had cannibalized the computer to get the equipment they needed. In that, at least, Henry had been right. Thinking back on it, Henry, after all, had played quite a part in it.

Could they have foreseen that on this particular week in this particular house the probability of quickly and easily doing what they had come to do had stood very high?

Did they, with all their other talents and technology, have clairvoyance as well?

"There's someone coming," Beasly said.

"I don't see a thing."

"Neither do I," said Beasly, "but Chuck told me that he saw them."

"Told you!"

"I told you we been talking. There, I can see them too."

And so could Taine.

They were far off, but they were coming fast – three dots that rode rapidly up out of the desert.

He sat and watched them come and he thought of going in to get the rifle, but he didn't stir from his seat upon the steps. The rifle would do no good, he told himself. It would be a senseless thing to get it; more than that, a senseless attitude. The least that Man could do, he thought, was to meet these creatures of another world with clean and empty hands.

They were closer now and it seemed to him that they were sitting in invisible easy-chairs that traveled very fast.

He saw that they were humanoid, to a degree at least, and there were only three of them.

They came in with a rush and stopped very suddenly a hundred feet or so from where he sat upon the steps.

He didn't move or say a word – there was nothing he could say. It was too ridiculous.

They were, perhaps, a little smaller than himself, and black as the ace of spades, and they wore skintight shorts and vests that were somewhat oversize and both the shorts and vests were the blue of April skies.

But that was not the worst of it.

They sat on saddles, with horns in front and stirrups and a sort of bedroll tied on the back, but they had no horses.

The saddles floated in the air, with the stirrups about three feet above the ground and the aliens sat easily in the saddles and stared at him and he stared back at them.

Finally he got up and moved forward a step or two and when he did that the three swung from the saddles and moved forward, too, while the saddles hung there in the air, exactly as they'd left them.

Taine walked forward and the three walked forward until they were no more than six feet apart.

"They say hello to you," said Beasly. "They say welcome to you."

"Well, all right, then, tell them – Say, how do you know all this!"

"Chuck tells me what they say and I tell you. You tell me and I tell him and he tells them. That's the way it works. That is what he's here for."

"Well, I'll be –" said Taine. "So you can really talk to him."

"I told you that I could," stormed Beasly. "I told you that I could talk to Towser, too, but you thought that I was crazy."

"Telepathy!" said Taine. And it was worse than ever now. Not only had the ratlike things known all the rest of it, but they'd known of Beasly, too.

"What was that you said, Hiram?"

"Never mind," said Taine. "Tell that friend of yours to tell them I am glad to meet them and what can I do for them?"

He stood uncomfortably and stared at the three and he saw that their vests had many pockets and that the pockets were all crammed, probably with their equivalent of tobacco and hand-kerchiefs and pocket knives and such.

"They say," said Beasly, "that they want to dicker."

"Dicker?"

"Sure, Hiram. You know, trade."

Beasly chuckled thinly. "Imagine them laying themselves open to a Yankee trader. That's what Henry says you are. He says you can skin a man on the slickest —"

"Leave Henry out of this," snapped Taine. "Let's leave Henry out of something."

He sat down on the ground and the three sat down to face him.

"Ask them what they have in mind to trade."

"Ideas," Beasly said.

"Ideas! That's a crazy thing —"

And then he saw it wasn't.

Of all the commodities that might be exchanged by an alien people, ideas would be the most valuable and the easiest to handle. They'd take no cargo room and they'd upset no economies — not immediately, that is — and they'd make a bigger contribution to the welfare of the cultures than trade in actual goods.

"Ask them," said Taine, "what they'll take for the idea back of those saddles they are riding."

"They say, what have you to offer?"

And that was the stumper. That was the one that would be hard to answer.

Automobiles and trucks, the internal gas engine — well, probably not. Because they already had the saddles. Earth was out-of-date in transportation from the viewpoint of these people.

Housing architecture – no, that was hardly an idea and, anyhow, there was that other house, so they knew of houses.

Cloth? No, they had cloth.

Paint, he thought. Maybe paint was it.

"See if they are interested in paint," Taine told Beasly.

"They say, what is it? Please explain yourself."

"O.K., then. Let's see. It's a protective device to be spread over almost any surface. Easily packaged and easily applied. Protects against weather and corrosion. It's decorative, too. Comes in all sorts of colors. And it's cheap to make."

"They shrug in their mind," said Beasly. "They're just slightly interested. But they will listen more. Go ahead and tell them."

And that was more like it, thought Taine.

That was the kind of language that he could understand.

He settled himself more firmly on the ground and bent forward slightly, flicking his eyes across the three dead-pan, ebony faces, trying to make out what they might be thinking.

There was no making out. Those were three of the deadest pans he had ever seen.

It was all familiar. It made him feel at home. He was in his element.

And in the three across from him, he felt somehow subconsciously, he had the best dickering opposition he had ever met. And that made him feel good too.

"Tell them," he said, "that I'm not quite sure. I may have spoken up too hastily. Paint, after all, is a mighty valuable idea."

"They say, just as a favor to them, not that they're really interested, would you tell them a little more."

Got them hooked, Taine told himself. If he could only play it right –

He settled down to dickering in earnest.

VI

Hours later Henry Horton showed up. He was accompanied by a very urbane gentleman, who was faultlessly turned out and who carried beneath his arm an impressive attaché case.

Henry and the man stopped on the steps in sheer astonishment.

Taine was squatted on the ground with a length of board and he was daubing paint on it while the aliens watched. From the daubs here and there upon their anatomies, it was plain to see the aliens had been doing some daubing of their own. Spread all over the ground were other lengths of half-painted boards and a couple of dozen old cans of paint.

Taine looked up and saw Henry and the man.

"I was hoping," he said, "that someone would show up."

"Hiram," said Henry, with more importance than usual, "may I present Mr. Lancaster. He is a special representative of the United Nations."

"I'm glad to meet you, sir," said Taine. "I wonder if you would –"

"Mr. Lancaster," Henry explained grandly, "was having some slight difficulty getting through the lines outside, so I volunteered my services. I've already explained to him our joint interest in this matter."

"It was very kind of Mr. Horton," Lancaster said. "There was this stupid sergeant –"

"It's all in knowing," Henry said, "how to handle people."

The remark, Taine noticed, was not appreciated by the man from the U.N.

"May I inquire, Mr. Taine," asked Lancaster, "exactly what you're doing?"

"I'm dickering," said Taine.

"Dickering. What a quaint way of expressing –"

"An old Yankee word," said Henry quickly, "with certain connotations of its own. When you trade with someone you are exchanging goods, but if you're dickering with him you're out to get his hide."

"Interesting," said Lancaster. "And I suppose you're out to skin these gentlemen in the sky-blue vests –"

"Hiram," said Henry, proudly, "is the sharpest dickerer in these parts. He runs an antique business and he has to dicker hard –"

"And may I ask," said Lancaster, ignoring Henry finally, "what you might be doing with these cans of paint? Are these gentlemen potential customers for paint or –"

Taine threw down the board and rose angrily to his feet.

"If you'd both shut up!" he shouted. "I've been trying to say something ever since you got here and I can't get in a word. And I tell you, it's important –"

"Hiram!" Henry exclaimed in horror.

"It's quite all right," said the U.N. man. "We *have* been jabbering. And now, Mr. Taine?"

"I'm backed into a corner," Taine told him, "and I need some help. I've sold these fellows on the idea of paint, but I don't know a thing about it – the principle back of it or how it's made or what goes into it or –"

"But, Mr. Taine, if you're selling them the paint, what difference does it make –"

"I'm not selling them the paint," yelled Taine. "Can't you understand that? They don't want the paint. They want the *idea* of paint, the principle of paint. It's something that they never thought of and they're interested. I offered them the paint idea for the idea of their saddles and I've almost got it –"

"Saddles? You mean those things over there, hanging in the air?"

"That is right. Beasly, would you ask one of our friends to demonstrate a saddle?"

"You bet I will," said Beasly.

"What," demanded Henry, "has Beasly got to do with this?"

"Beasly is an interpreter. I guess you'd call him a telepath. You remember how he always claimed he could talk with Towser?"

"Beasly was always claiming things."

"But this time he was right. He tells Chuck, that funny-looking monster, what I want to say and Chuck tells these aliens. And these aliens tell Chuck and Chuck tells Beasly and Beasly tells me."

"Ridiculous!" snorted Henry. "Beasly hasn't got the sense to be . . . what did you say he was?"

"A telepath," said Taine.

One of the aliens had gotten up and climbed into a saddle. He rode it forth and back. Then he swung out of it and sat down again.

"Remarkable," said the U.N. man. "Some sort of antigravity unit, with complete control. We could make use of that, indeed."

He scraped his hand across his chin.

"And you're going to exchange the idea of paint for the idea of that saddle?"

"That's exactly it," said Taine, "but I need some help. I need a chemist or a paint manufacturer or someone to explain how paint is made. And I need some professor or other who'll understand what they're talking about when they tell me the idea of the saddle."

"I see," said Lancaster. "Yes, indeed, you have a problem. Mr. Taine, you seem to me a man of some discernment –"

"Oh, he's all of that," interrupted Henry. "Hiram's quite astute."

"So I suppose you'll understand," said the U.N. man, "that this whole procedure is quite irregular –"

"But it's not," exploded Taine. "That's the way they operate. They open up a planet and then they exchange ideas. They've been doing that with other planets for a long, long time. And ideas are all they want, just the new ideas, because that is the way to keep on building a technology and culture. And they have a lot of ideas, sir, that the human race can use."

"That is just the point," said Lancaster. "This is perhaps the most important thing that has ever happened to we humans. In just a short year's time we can obtain data and ideas that will put us ahead – theoretically, at least – by a thousand years. And in a thing that is so important, we should have experts on the job –"

"But," protested Henry, "you can't find a man who'll do a better dickering job than Hiram. When you dicker with him your back teeth aren't safe. Why don't you leave him be? He'll do a job for you. You can get your experts and your planning groups together and let Hiram front for you. These folks have accepted him and have proved they'll do business with him and what more do you want? All he needs is just a little help."

Beasly came over and faced the U.N. man.

"I won't work with no one else," he said. "If you kick Hiram out of here, then I go along with him. Hiram's the only person who ever treated me like a human –"

"There, you see!" Henry said, triumphantly.

"Now, wait a second, Beasly," said the U.N. man. "We could make it worth your while. I should imagine that an interpreter in a situation such as this could command a handsome salary."

"Money don't mean a thing to me," said Beasly. "It won't buy me friends. People still will laugh at me."

"He means it, mister," Henry warned. "There isn't anyone who can be as stubborn as Beasly. I know; he used to work for us."

The U.N. man looked flabbergasted and not a little desperate.

"It will take you quite some time," Henry pointed out, "to find another telepath – leastwise one who can talk to these people here."

The U.N. man looked as if he were strangling. "I doubt," he said, "there's another one on Earth."

"Well, all right," said Beasly, brutally, "let's make up our minds. I ain't standing here all day."

"All right," cried the U.N. man. "You two go ahead. Please, will you go ahead? This is a chance we can't let slip through our fingers. Is there anything you want? Anything I can do for you?"

"Yes, there is," said Taine. "There'll be the boys from Washington and bigwigs from other countries. Just keep them off my back."

"I'll explain most carefully to everyone. There'll be no interference."

"And I need that chemist and someone who'll know about the saddles. And I need them quick. I can stall these boys a little longer, but not for too much longer."

"Anyone you need," said the U.N. man. "Anyone at all. I'll have them here in hours. And in a day or two there'll be a pool of experts waiting for you whenever you may need them – on a moment's notice."

"Sir," said Henry, unctuously, "that's most co-operative. Both Hiram and I appreciate it greatly. And now, since this is settled, I understand that there are reporters waiting. They'll be interested in your statement."

The U.N. man, it seemed, didn't have it in him to protest. He and Henry went tramping up the stairs. Taine turned around and looked out across the desert.

"It's a big front yard," he said.

THE OBSERVER

Presaging, perhaps, the until-now-unpublished "I Had No Head and My Eyes Were Floating Way Up in the Air," "The Observer" probably represents an experiment on the author's part, one in which he sought to portray a being discovering itself after an event that reminds me, irresistibly, of a computer recovering from a forced shutdown.

—dww

It existed. Whether it had slept and wakened, or been turned on, or if this might be the first instant of its creation, it had no way of knowing. There was no memory of other time, or place.

Words came to fit where it found itself. Words emerging out of nowhere, symbols quite unbidden – awakened or turned on or first appearing, as it had itself.

It was in a place of red and yellow. The land was red. The sky was yellow. A brightness stood straight above the red land in the yellow sky. Liquid ran gurgling down a channel in the land.

In a little time it knew more, had a better understanding. It knew the brightness was a sun. It knew the running liquid was a brook. It thought of the liquid as a compound, but it wasn't water. Life forms sprang from the redness of the soil. Their stems were green. They had purple fruits at the top of them.

It had the names now, identifying symbols it could use – life, liquid, land, sky, red, yellow, purple, green, sun, bright, water. Each instant it had more words, more names, more terms. And it could see, although seeing might not be the proper term, for it had no eyes. Nor legs. Nor arms. Nor body.

It had no eyes and seemed to have no body, either. It had no idea of position – standing up or lying down or sitting. It could look anywhere it wished without turning its head, since it hadn't any head. Although, strangely, it did seem to occupy a specific position in relation to the landscape.

It looked straight up into the sky at the brightness of the sun and could look directly at the brightness since it was seeing without eyes, without frail organic structures that might be harmed by brilliance.

The sun was a B8 star, five times more massive than the Sun, and it lay 3.76 A.U. distant from this planet.

Sun, capitalized? A.U.? Five? 3.76? Planet?

Sometime in the past – when past, where past, what past – it had known the terms, a sun that was capitalized, water that ran in brooks, the idea of a body and eyes. Or had it known them? Had it ever had a past in which it could have known them? Or were they simply terms that were being fed into it from another source, to be utilized as the need arose, tools – and there was yet another term – to be used in interpreting this place where it found itself? Interpreting this place for what? For itself? That was ridiculous, for it did not need to know, did not even care to know.

Knowing, how did it know? how did it know the sun was a B8 star, and what was a B8 star? How know its distance, its diameter, its mass just by looking at it? How know a star, for it had never seen a star before?

Then, even thinking this, it knew it had. It had known many suns, a long string of suns across the galaxy and it had looked at each of them and known its spectral type, its distance and diameter, its mass, its very composition, its age and probable length of remaining life, stable or variable, its spectral lines, any small peculiarities that might set it apart from other stars. Red giants, supergiants, white dwarfs, even one black dwarf. But mostly main sequence stars and the planets that went with them, for it made few stops at stars that had no planets.

Perhaps nothing had ever known more suns than it. Or knew more of suns than it.

And the purpose of all this? It tried to think of purpose, but there seemed no purpose. The purpose utterly escaped it. If there were, in fact, a purpose.

It stopped looking at the sun and looked at the rest of it, at all of it at once, at all the planetary surface in its sight – as if, it thought, it had eyes all around its nonexistent head. Why did it, it wondered, keep dwelling on this idea of a head and eyes? Had it, at one time perhaps, had a head and eyes? Was the ideal of head and eyes an old residual, perhaps a primitive, memory that persistently refused to go away, but that for some reason must linger and thrust itself forward at the slightest opportunity?

It tried to think it out, to reach back and grasp the idea or the memory and drag it squalling from its hole. And failed.

It concentrated on the surface. It was located – if located was the word – on a steep hillside with massive rock outcroppings. The hill shut off the view of one portion of the surface, but the rest lay bare before it to the horizon line.

The rest of the surface was level, except for one place, far distant, where what appeared to be a circular prominence arose. The top of the prominence was jagged and the sides were furrowed and it looked very like an ancient crater.

But the rest was level and through it ran several little streams of something that was liquid but was not water. The sparse vegetation stood up on its dark green stems, surmounted by its purple fruit and now it was apparent that there were several kinds of vegetation. The purple fruit vegetation at first had seemed to be the only vegetation because it was more abundant, and certainly more spectacular.

The soil seemed to be little more than sand. It put out a hand – no, not a hand, for it had no hand – but it thought of its action as putting out a hand. It put out a hand and thrust the fingers deep into the soil and the data on the soil came flowing into it. Sand. Almost pure sand. Silicon, some iron, some aluminum, traces of oxygen, hydrogen, potassium, magnesium. Almost no acidity. There were figures, percentages, but it hardly noticed. They simply passed along.

The atmosphere was deadly. Deadly to what? The radiation lancing in from the B-type star was deadly and again, deadly to what?

What do I have to know, it wondered. And there was another word it had not used before. I. Me. Myself. An entity. A self. A single thing, standing all alone, no part of another. A personality.

What am I? it asked. Where am I? And why? Why must I go on collecting all this data? What care I for soil, or radiation, or the atmosphere? Why should I have to know what kind of star is standing overhead? I have no body that can be affected by any of it. I seem to have no form. I only have a being. A disembodied entity. A nebulous I.

It desisted for a time, unmoving, doing nothing, collecting no more data, only looking at the red and yellow of the planet, the purple of the flowers.

Then, after a time, it took up its work again. It touched the rocky outcrops on the hillside, found the planes that lay between the layers, seeped into the rock, following the cleavages.

Limestone. Massive, hard limestone. Put down millennia ago at the bottom of the sea.

It paused for a moment, vaguely disturbed, then recognized the cause of its disturbance. Fossils!

Why should fossils disturb it, it asked itself and then suddenly it knew with something that amounted to excitement, or as close as it could come to what might be excitement. These were not the fossils of plants, primordial ancestors to those purple plants growing on the present surface. These were animals – well-organized forms of life, sophisticated in their structure, well up the evolutionary ladder.

So few of the other planets had any life at all, the few that did more often than not had only the simplest of vegetable life or, perhaps, tiny organisms on the borderline, things that might be slightly more than vegetable, but not yet animal. I should have known, it thought. The purple plants should have alerted me. For they are highly organized; they are not simple plants. On this planet, despite its deadly atmosphere and it deadly radiation and its liquid that is not water, evolutionary forces still had been at work.

It traced one particular fossil. Not large. A chitin covering, apparently, but still it had a skeleton of sorts. It had a head, a body, legs. It had a flattened tail for swimming in whatever evil chemical brew the ocean might have been. It had jaws for seizing and for holding. It had eyes, a great many more eyes, perhaps, than it had any need of. There were faint tracings of an alimentary canal, fragments of nerves here and there that were still preserved, or at least the canals in which they ran had been preserved.

And it thought of that faint, misty time when he –

He? First an I. And then a he.

Two identities – or rather two terms of identity.

No longer an it, but an I and he.

He lay thin and spread out along the tight seams of the limestone and knew the fossils and pondered on them. Especially that one particular fossil and that other misty time in which the first fossil had been found, the first time he had ever known there was such a thing as fossil. He recalled the finding of it and recalled its name as well. It had been called a trilobite. Someone had told him the name, but he could not remember who it might have been. A place so faint in time, so far in space, that all he had left of it was a fossil called a trilobite.

But there had been another time and another place and he was not new – he had not in that first instant of awareness been turned on, or newly hatched, or born. He had a history. There had been times of other awarenesses and he had held identity in those other times. Not new, he thought, but old. A creature with a past.

The thought of eyes, of body, or arms and legs – could all of them be memories from that other time or times? Could there have been a time when he did have a head and eyes, a body?

Or could he be mistaken? Could all of this be a phantom memory fashioned out of some happening, or event, or some combination of happenings and events that had occurred to some other being? Was it, perhaps, a misplaced memory, not of himself, but of something else? If the memory should prove to be his own, what had happened to him – what changes had been made?

He forgot the limestone and the fossils. He lay spread out in the fissures of the rock and stayed quiet and limp, hoping that out of the limpness and the quietness he might devise an answer. A partial answer came, an infuriating answer, unspecific and tantalizing. Not one place, but many; not one time, but many times. Not on one planet, but on many planets spaced over many light-years.

If all of this were true, he thought, there must be purpose in it. Otherwise, why the many planets and the data on those planets? And this was a new, unbidden thought – the data on the planets. Why the data? For what purpose was it gathered? Certainly not for himself, for he did not need the data, had no use for it. Could it be that he was only the gatherer, the harvester, the storer and communicator of the data that he gathered?

If not for himself, for whom? He waited for the answer to come welling up, for the memory to reassert itself, and in time he realized that he had gone groping back as far as he could go.

Slowly he withdrew from the rock, once more was upon the hillside above the red land beneath the yellow sky.

A portion of the nearby surface moved and as it moved, he saw that it was not a portion of the surface, but a creature that had a coloration which made it seem to be a part of the planet's surface. It moved quickly, as if a shadow had brushed along and blurred the surface. It moved in short and flowing motions, and when it stopped its motion it became a part of the surface, blending into it.

It was watching him, he knew, looking him over, although what there was to see of him he could not imagine. Sensitive, perhaps, to another personality, to another thing that shared with it that strange and undefinable quality which made up life. A force field, he wondered – was that what he was, a disembodied intelligence carried in a force field?

He stayed still so the thing could look him over. It moved in its short, flowing dashes, all around him. It left a furrowed track behind it, it kicked up little spurts of sand as it made its dashes. It moved in closer.

And he had it. He held it motionless, wrapped up as if he held it in many hands. He examined it, not closely, not analytically, but only enough so he could tell what kind of thing it was. Protoplasmic and heavily shielded against the radiations, even designed, perhaps – although he could not be sure – to take advantage of the energy contained in the radiation. An organism, more than likely, that could not exist without the radiations, that needed them as other creatures might need warmth, or food, or oxygen. Intelligent and laced with a multitude of emotions – not, perhaps, the kind of intelligence that could build a complex culture, but a high level of animal intelligence. Perhaps still evolving in its intelligence. Give it a few more million years and it might contrive a culture.

He turned it loose. It flowed away, moving rapidly, straight away from him. He lost sight of it, but still could follow its movement for a time by its unreeling track and the spurts of sand it kicked into the air.

There was much work to do. an atmospheric profile, an analysis of the soil and of the micro-organisms that it might contain, a determination of the liquid in the brook, an examination of the plant life, a geological survey, measurement of the magnetic field, the intensity of the radiation. But first there should be a general survey of the planet to determine what sort of place it was, a pinpointing of those areas that might be of economic interest.

And there it was again, another word he had not had before. Economic.

He searched inside himself, inside the theoretical intelligence enclosed within the hypothetical force field, for the purpose that was hinted in that single word. When he found it, it stood out sharp and clear – the one thing he had found that was sharp and clear. What was here that could be used and what would be the cost of obtaining it? A treasure hunt, he thought. That was the purpose of him. It was clear immediately that he, himself, had no use for treasure of any kind at all. There must be someone else who would have a use for it. Although when he thought of treasure a pleasurable thrill went through him.

What might there be in it for him, he wondered, this location of a treasure? What had been the profit to him in the finding of all those other treasures on all those other planets – although, come to think of it, there had not been treasure on every one of them. And on some of the others where there'd been, it had been meaningless, for planetary conditions had been such that it could not be got at. Many of the planets, he recalled, far too many of them, were such that only a thing such as himself would dare even to approach them.

There had been attempts, he remembered now, to recall him from some of the planets when it had become apparent they had no economic worth and that to further explore them would be a waste of time. He had resisted those attempts; he had ignored the summons to return to wherever it was he went when he did return. Because, in his simplistic ethic, when there was a job to do he did it and he did not quit until the job was done. Having started something, he was incapable of leaving off until it had been finished. It was a part of him, this single-minded stubbornness; it was a characteristic that was necessary to do the work he did.

If they had it one way, they could not have it two. He either was, or wasn't. He did the job, or didn't. He was so made that he had an interest in each problem that was presented him and would not leave off until he'd wrung the problem dry. They had to go along with that and they knew it now; they no longer bothered trying to recall him from a non-productive planet.

They? he asked himself, and remembered faintly other creatures such as he had been. They had indoctrinated him, they had made him what he was and they used him as they used the priceless planets he had found, but he did not mind the using, for it was a life and the only life he had. It either had been this life, or no life at all. He tried to recall circumstances, but something moved to block the recall. Exactly as he never could recall in all entirety, but only in fragments, the other planets he had visited. That, he thought at the time, might be a great mistake, for experience he had gathered on the other planets might have been valuable as guide lines on the one to which he currently had been sent. But for some reason, they did not allow it, but did their imperfect best to wipe from his memory all past experiences before he was sent out again. To keep him clear, they said; to guard him from confusion; to send a bright new mind, freed of all encumbrances, out to each new planet. That was why, he knew, he always arrived upon each planet groping for a meaning and purpose, with the feeling of being newly born to this particular planet and to nowhere else.

He did not mind. It still was a life and he saw a lot of places – very different places – and saw them, no matter what conditions might obtain, in perfect safety. For there was nothing that could touch him – tooth, or claw, or poison, no matter what the atmosphere, no matter what the radiation, there was nothing that could touch him. There was nothing of him to be touched. He walked – no, not walked, but moved – in utter nonchalance through all the hells the galaxy could muster.

A second sun was rising, a great swollen, brick-red star pushing its way above the horizon, with the first one just beginning to slide towards the west – as a matter of convenience, he thought of the big red one as rising in the east.

K2, he read it, thirty times, or so, the diameter of the Sun with a surface temperature that was possibly no more than 4,000 degrees. A binary system and maybe more than that; there might be other suns that he still had yet to see. He tried to calculate the distance, but that would not be possible with any accuracy until the giant had moved higher in the sky, until it had moved above the horizon that now bisected it.

But the second sun could wait, all the rest of it could wait. There was one thing he must see. He had not realized it before, but now he knew there was one thing about the landscape that had been nagging him. The crater did not fit. It had all the appearances of a crater, but it had no right to be there. It could not be volcanic, for it sat in the middle of a sandy terrain and the limestone thrusting from the hillside was sedimentary rock. There was no trace of igneous rock, no ancient lava flows. And the same objections still would hold if the crater had been formed by meteoric impact, for any meteorite that threw up a crater of that size would have turned tons of material into a molten mass and would have thrown out a sheet of magma, of which there was no sign.

He began drifting slowly in the direction of the crater. Beneath him the terrain remained unchanged – the red soil, the purple fruit and little else.

He came to rest – if that is what his action could be called – on the crater's rim and for a moment failed to understand what he was seeing.

Some sort of shining substance extended all around the rim

and sloped inward to the center to form what appeared to be a concave mirror. But it was not a mirror, for it was nonreflective.

Then, quite suddenly, an image formed upon it and if he could have caught his breath, he would have.

Two creatures, one large, the other smaller, stood on a ledge above a deep cut in the earth, with a striated sandstone bluff rising up above them. The smaller one was digging in the bluff with a hand tool of some sort – a hand tool that was grasped in what must be a hand, which was attached to an arm and the arm hooked up to a body, which had a head and eyes.

Myself, he thought – the smaller one, myself.

He felt a weakness and a haziness and the image in the mirror seemed to be trying to pull him down to join and coalesce with this image of himself. The gates of memory opened and the old, restricted data came pouring in upon him – the terms and relationships – and he cried out against it and tried to push it back, but it would not push back. It was as if someone were holding him so he could not get away and, with a mouth close against his ear, was telling him things he did not wish to know.

Humans, father, son, a railroad cut, the Earth, the finding of that first trilobite. Relentlessly the information came pouring into him, into the intellectual force field that he had become, that he had evolved into, or been engineered into, and that had been a comfort and a refuge until this very moment.

His father wore an old sweater, with holes in the elbows of the sleeves, and an old pair of black trousers that were baggy at the knees. He smoked an ancient pipe with a fire-charred bowl and a stem half-bitten through, and he watched with deep paternal interest as the boy, working carefully, dug out the tiny slab of stone that bore the imprint of an ancient form of life.

Then the image flickered and went out and he sat (?) upon the crater's rim, with the dead mirror sweeping downward to its center, showing nothing but the red and blue reflections of the suns.

Now he knew, he thought. He knew, not what he was, but

what he once had been – a creature that had walked upon two legs, that had a body and two arms, a head and eyes and a mouth that cried out in excited triumph at the finding of a trilobite. A creature that walked proudly and with misplaced confidence, for it had none of the immunity against its environment such as he now possessed.

From that feeble, vulnerable creature, how had he evolved?

Could it be death, he wondered, and was aghast at death, which was a new concept. Death, an ending, and there was no end, never would be one; a thing that was an intellect trapped within a force field could exist forever. But somewhere along the way, somewhere in the course of evolution, or of engineering, could death have played a part? Must a man come to death before he came to this?

He sat upon the crater's rim and knew the surface of the planet all about him – the red of land, the yellow of the sky, the green and purple of the flowers, the gurgle of the liquid running in its courses, the red and blue of suns and the shadows that they cast, the running thing that threw up spurts of sand, the limestone and the fossils.

And something else as well and with the sensing of that something else a fear and panic he had never known before. Had never had the need to know, for he had been protected and immune, untouchable, secure, perhaps even in the center of a sun. There had been nothing that could get at him, no way he could be reached.

But that was true no longer, for now he could be reached. Something had torn from him an ancient memory and had shown it to him. Here, on this planet, there was a factor that could get at him, that could reach into him and tear from him something even he had not suspected.

He screamed a question and phantom echoes ran across the land, bouncing back to mock him. Who are you? Who are you? Who are you? Fainter and fainter and the only answers were the echoes.

It could afford not to answer him, he knew. It need not answer him. It could sit smug and silent while he screamed the question, waiting until it wished to strip other memories from him, memories for its own strange use, or to further mock him.

He was safe no longer. He was vulnerable. Naked to this thing that used a mirror to convince him of his own vulnerability.

He screamed again and this time the scream was directed to those others of his kind who had sent him out.

Take me back! I am naked! Save me!

Silence.

I have worked for you – I have dug out the data for you – I have done my job – You owe me something now!

Silence.

Please!

Silence.

Silence – and something more than silence. Not only silence, but an absence, a not being there, a vacuum.

The realization came thudding hard into his understanding. He had been abandoned, all ties with him had been cut – in the depth of unguessed space, he had been set adrift. They had washed their hands of him and he was not only naked, but alone.

They knew what had happened. They knew everything that ever happened to him, they monitored him continuously and would know everything he knew. And they had sensed the danger, perhaps even before he, himself, had sensed it. Had recognized the danger, not only to himself, but to themselves as well. If something could get to him, it could trace back the linkage and get to them as well. So the linkage had been cut and would not be restored. They weren't taking any chances. It had been something that had been emphasized time and time again. You must remain not only unrecognized, but entirely unsuspected. You must do nothing that will make you known. You must never point a finger at us.

Cold, callous, indifferent. And frightened. More frightened, perhaps, than he was. For now they knew there was something in the galaxy that could become aware of the disembodied observer they had been sending out. They could never send another, if indeed they had another, for the old fear would be there. And perhaps an even greater fear – based upon the overriding suspicion that the linkage had been cut not quite soon enough, that this factor which had spotted their observer had already traced it back to them.

Fear for their bodies and their profits . . .

Not for their bodies, a voice said inside him. Not their biologic bodies. There are no longer any of your kind who have biologic bodies . . .

Then what? he asked.

An extension of their bodies, carrying on the purpose those with bodies gave them in a time when the bodies still existed. Carried on mindlessly ever since, but without a purpose, only with a memory of a purpose . . .

Who are you? he asked. How do you know all this? What will you do with me?

In a very different way, it said, I am one like you. You can be like me. You have your freedom now.

I have nothing, he said.

You have yourself, it said. Is that not enough?

But is self enough? he asked.

And did not need an answer.

For self was the basis of all life, all sentience. The institutions, the cultures, the economics were no more than structures for the enhancement of the self. Self now was all he had and self belonged to him. It was all he needed.

Thank you, sir, said he, the last human in the universe.

TRAIL CITY'S
HOT-LEAD CRUSADERS

*Cliff Simak wrote this story under the name "Gunsmoke Goes to Press,"
but it was published, in the September 1944 issue of* New Western
Magazine, *under a new title . . . and these days it's likely that many
readers will miss the play on words in the new title. If you've read a
few Westerns, you probably know that "hot lead" is a euphemism for a
gunfight – but the protagonist of this story is a frontier newspaper editor
in the days when newspaper publishing often required melting down
and recasting the lead alloy used to set type on the printing press. (As it
turned out, "Gunsmoke Goes to Press" was retained as a chapter heading in the newly titled story.)*

*Clifford D. Simak seems to have had some following in West-
ern literature of the era – in this case, his story was the topmost of
the two listed on the front cover of the magazine, and it appeared
as the first story in the magazine. Cliff's journal shows that he
was paid $120 for it during a period when the cover price of the
magazine was fifteen cents. Several characters in the story bear the
names of towns in the area of Wisconsin where Cliff grew up, and
the protagonist bears as a last name the name of Cliff's younger
brother, Carson.*

—dww

CHAPTER ONE

Hit the Trail, Or Die!

Morgan Carson, editor of the *Trail City Tribune,* knew trouble when he saw it – and it was walking across the street straight toward his door.

Dropping in alone, either Jackson Quinn, the town's lone lawyer, or Roger Delavan, the banker, would have been just visitors stopping by to pass the time of day. But when they came together, there was something in the wind.

Jake the printer clumped in from the back room, stick of type clutched in his fist, bottle joggling in hip pocket with every step he took, wrath upon his ink-smeared face.

"Ain't you got that damned editorial writ yet?" he demanded. "Holy hoppin' horntoads, does a feller have to wait all day?"

Carson tucked the pencil behind his ear. "We're getting visitors," he said.

Jake shifted the cud of tobacco to the left side of his face and squinted beneath bushy eyebrows at the street outside.

"Slickest pair of customers I ever clapped an eye on," he declared. "I'd sure keep my peepers peeled, with them jaspers coming at me."

"Delavan's not so bad," said Carson.

"Just pick pennies off a dead man's eyes, that's all," said Jake.

He spat with uncanny accuracy at the mouse-hole in the corner.

"Trouble with you," he declared, "is you're sweet on that dotter of hisn. Because she's all right, you think her old man is too. Nobody that goes around with Quinn is all right. They're just a couple of cutthroats, in with that snake Fennimore clear up to their hips."

Quinn and Delavan were stepping to the boardwalk outside the *Tribune* office. Jake turned and shuffled toward the back.

The door swung open and the two came in, Quinn huge, square-shouldered, flashy even in a plain black suit; Delavan quiet and dignified with his silvery hair and bowler hat.

"This is a pleasure," Carson said. "Two of the town's most distinguished citizens, both at once. Could I offer you a drink?"

He bent and rummaged in a deep desk drawer, came up empty-handed.

"Nope," he said, "I can't. Jake found it again."

"Forget the drink," said Quinn. He seated himself on Carson's desk and swung one leg back and forth. Delavan sat down in a chair, prim and straight, like a man who dreads the job he has to do.

"We came in with a little business proposition," said Quinn. "We have a man who's interested in the paper."

Carson shook his head. "The *Tribune*'s not for sale."

Quinn grinned, pleasantly enough. "Don't say that too quickly, Carson. You haven't heard the price."

"Tempt me," invited Carson.

"Ten thousand," said Quinn, bending over just a little as if to keep it confidential.

"Not enough," said Carson.

"Not enough!" gasped Quinn. "Not enough for this?" He swept his hand at the dusty, littered room. "You didn't pay a thousand for everything you have in the whole damned place."

"Byron Fennimore," Carson told him levelly, "hasn't got enough to buy me out."

"Who said anything about Fennimore?"

"I did," snapped Carson. "Who else would be interested? Who else would be willing to pay ten thousand to get me out of town?"

Delavan cleared his throat. "I would say, Morgan, that should have nothing to do with it. After all, a business deal is a business deal. What does it matter who makes the offer?"

He cleared his throat again. "I offer the observation," he pointed out, "merely as a friend. I have no interests in this deal myself. I just came along to take care of the financial end should you care to sell."

Carson eyed Delavan. "Ten thousand," he asked, "spot cash? Ten thousand on the barrel-head?"

"Say the word," said Quinn, "and we'll hand it to you."

Carson laughed harshly. "I'd never get out of town with it."

Quinn spoke softly. "That could be part of the deal," he said.

"Nope," Carson told him, "ten thousand is too much for the paper. I'd sell the paper – just the paper, mark you – for ten thousand. But I won't sell my friends. I won't sell myself."

"You'd be making a stake out of it, wouldn't you?" asked Quinn. "Isn't that what you came here for?"

Carson leaned back in his chair, hooked his thumbs in his vest and stared at Quinn. "I don't suppose," he said, "that you or Fennimore could understand why I came here. You aren't built that way. You wouldn't know what I was talking about if I told you I saw Trail City as a little cowtown that might grow up into a city.

"Gentlemen, that's exactly what I saw. And I'm here, in on the ground floor. I'll grow up with the town."

"Have you stopped to think," Quinn pointed out, "that you might not grow up at all? Might just drop over dead, suddenlike, some day?"

"All your gunslicks are poor shots," said Carson. "They've missed me every time so far."

"Maybe up to now the boys haven't been trying too hard?"

"I take it," said Carson, "they'll try real hard from now on."

He flicked a look at Delavan. The man was uneasy, embarrassed, twirling the bowler hat in his hands.

"Let's stop beating around the bush," suggested Carson. "I don't know why you tried it in the first place. As I understand it, Fennimore will give me ten thousand if I quit bucking him, forget about electing Purvis for sheriff and get out of town. If not, the Bar Y boys turn me into buzzard bait."

"That's about it," said Quinn.

"You don't happen to be hankering after my blood, person-ally?" asked Carson.

Quinn shook his head. "Not me. I'm no gunslinger."

"Neither am I," Carson told him. "Leastwise not profession-ally. But from now on I'm not wearing this gun of mine for an ornament. I'm going to start shooting back. You can noise that around, sort of gentle-like."

"The boys," said Quinn, sarcastically, "will appreciate the warning."

"And you can tell Fennimore," said Carson, "that his days are over. The days of free range and squeezing out the little fellow are at an end. Maybe Fennimore can stop me with some slugs. Maybe he can stop a lot of men. But he can't stop them forever.

"The day is almost here when Fennimore can't fix elections and hand-pick his sheriffs, when he can't levy tribute on all the busi-nessmen in town, when he can't hog all the water on the range."

"Better put that in an editorial," said Quinn.

"I have," declared Carson. "Don't you read my paper?"

Quinn turned toward the door and Delavan arose. He fum-bled just a little with his hat before he put it on. "You're coming to the house tonight for supper, aren't you?" he asked.

"I thought so, up to now," said Carson.

"Kathryn is expecting you," the banker said.

Quinn swung around. "Sure, go ahead, Carson. Nothing per-sonal in this, you understand."

Carson rose slowly. "I didn't think there was. You wouldn't have a man planted along the way, would you?"

"What a thought," said Quinn. "No, my friend, when we get you, it'll be in broad daylight."

Carson followed them to the door, stood on the stoop outside to watch them leave. They crossed the street toward the bank, the dust puffing up from their boots to shimmer momentarily in the slanting rays of the westering sun.

A horse cantered down the street, coming from the east, its

rider slouching in the saddle. A hen scratched industriously in the dust and clucked to an imaginary brood. The sun caught the windows of the North Star Saloon, directly opposite the newspaper office, and turned the glass to glittering silver.

Trail City, thought Editor Morgan Carson, looking at it. Just a collection of shacks today. The North Star and the bank and sheriff's office with the jail behind it. The livery stable and the new store with the barber shop in one corner.

A frontier town, with chickens clucking in the dust and slinking dogs that stopped to scratch for fleas. But someday a great town, a town with trains and water tower instead of a creaking windmill, a town of shining glass and brick.

A man was coming down the steps of the North Star, a big man stepping lightly. Carson watched him abstractedly, recognized him as one of Fennimore's hired hands, probably in town on some errand.

The man started across the street and stopped. His voice came quietly across the narrow stretch of dust.

"Carson!"

"Yes," said Carson. And something in the way the man stood there, something in the single word, something in the way the man's face looked beneath the droopy hat, made him stiffen, tensed every nerve within him.

"I'm calling you," said the man, and it was as if he had asked for a match to light his smoke. No anger, no excitement, just a simple statement.

For a single instant time stood still and stared. Even as the man's hands drove for the gun-butts at his thighs, the street seemed frozen in a motionlessness that went on forever.

And in that timeless instant, Carson knew his own hand was swooping for his gun, that the weapon's butt was in his fist and coming out.

Then time exploded and took up again and Carson's gun was swinging up, easily, effortless, simple as pointing one's finger. The other man's guns were coming up, too, a glitter of steel in the sunlight.

Carson felt his gun buck against his hand, saw the look of surprise that came upon the other's face, heard the blast of the single shot ringing in his ears.

The man out in the street was sagging, sagging like a slowly collapsing sack, as if the strength were draining from him in the dying day. His knees buckled and the guns, still unfired, dropped from his loosened fingers. As if something had pushed him gently, he pitched forward on his face.

For an instant more, the stillness held, a stillness even deeper than before. The man on the horse had reined up and was motionless, the scratching hen was a feathery statue of bewilderment.

Then doors slammed and voices shouted; feet pounded on the sidewalks. The saloon porch boiled with men. Bill Robinson, white apron around his middle, ducked out of the store. The barber came out and yelled. His customer, white towel around his neck, lather on his face, was pawing for his gun, swearing at the towel.

Two men came from the sheriff's office and walked down the street, walked toward Carson, standing there, still with gun in hand. They walked past the dead man in the street and came on, while the town stood still and watched.

Carson waited for them, fighting down the fear that welled within him, the fear and anger. Anger at the trap, at how neatly it had worked.

The door slammed behind him and Jake was beside him, a rifle in his hand.

"What's the matter, kid?" he asked.

Carson motioned toward the man lying in the dust.

"Called me," he said.

Jake shifted his cud of tobacco to the north cheek.

"Dang neat job," he said.

Sheriff Bert Bean and Stu Leonard, the deputy, stopped short of the sidewalk.

"You do that?" asked Bean, jerking a thumb toward the dust.

"I did," admitted Carson.

"That bein' the case," announced Bean, "I'm placin' you under arrest."

"I'm not submitting to arrest," said Carson.

The sheriff's jaw dropped. "You ain't submittin' – you what!"

"You heard him," roared Jake. "He ain't a-going with you. Want to do anything about it?"

Bean lifted his hands towards his guns, thought better of it, dropped them to his side again.

"You better come," Bean said with something that was almost pleading in his voice. "If you don't, I got ways to make you."

"If you got ways," yelped Jake, "get going on 'em. He's calling your bluff."

The four men stood motionless for a long, dragging moment.

Jake broke the tension by jerking his rifle down. "Get going," he yelled. "Start high-tailing it back to your den, or I'll bullet-dance you back there. Get out of here and tell Fennimore you dassn't touch Carson 'cause you're afraid he'll gun-whip you out of town."

The crowd, silent, motionless until now, stirred restlessly.

"Jake," snapped Carson, "keep an eye on that crowd out there."

Jake spat with gusto, snapped back the hammer of the gun. The click was loud and ominous in the quiet.

Carson walked slowly down the steps toward the sidewalk, and Bean and Leonard backed away. Carson's gun was in his hand, hanging at his side, and he made no move to raise it, but as he advanced the two backed across the street.

Quinn pushed his way through the crowd in front of the bank and strode across the dust.

"Carson," he yelled, "you're crazy. You can't do this. You can't buck law and order."

"The hell he can't," yelped Jake. "He's doing it."

"I'm not bucking law and order," declared Carson. "Bean isn't law and order. He's Fennimore's hired hand. He tried to do a job for Fennimore and he didn't get away with it. That man I killed was planted on me. You had Bean sitting over there, all ready to gallop out and slap me into jail."

Quinn snarled. "You got it all doped out, haven't you?"

"I'm way ahead of you," said Carson. "You used a man that was just second-rate with his guns. Probably had him all primed up with liquor so he thought he was greased hell itself. You knew that I'd outshoot him and then you could throw a murder charge at me. Smart idea, Quinn. Better than killing me outright. Never give the other side a martyr."

"So what about it?" asked Quinn.

"So it didn't work."

"But it'll work," Quinn declared. "You will be arrested."

"Come ahead, then," snapped Carson. He half-lifted the six-gun. "I'll get you first, Quinn. The sheriff next –"

"Hey," yelled Jake, "what order do you want me to take 'em in? Plumb senseless for the two of us to be shooting the same people."

Quinn moved closer to Carson, lowered his voice. "Listen, Carson," he said, "you've got until tomorrow to disappear."

"What?" asked Carson in mock surprise. "No ten thousand?"

CHAPTER TWO

Gunsmoke Goes to Press

Jake scrubbed the back of his neck with a grimy hand, his brow wrinkled like a worried hound's.

"You sure didn't make yourself popular with the sheriff," he declared. "Now he ain't going to rest content until you're plumb perforated."

"The sheriff," announced Carson, "won't make a move toward me until he's heard from Fennimore."

"I'm half-hoping," said Jake, "that Fennimore decides on shootin'. This circlin' around, sort of growlin' at one another like two dogs on the prod has got me downright nervous. Ain't nothin' I'd welcome more than a lively bullet party."

Carson tapped a pencil on the desk. "You know, Jake, I figure maybe we won that election right out there on the street. Before tomorrow morning there won't be a man in Rosebud County that hasn't heard how Bean backed down. A story like that is apt to lose him a pile of votes. Fennimore can scare a lot of people from voting for Purvis, but this sort of takes the edge off the scare. People are going to figure that since that happened to Bean, maybe Fennimore ain't so tough himself."

"They'll sure be makin' a mistake," said Jake. "Fennimore is just about the orneriest hombre that ever forked a horse."

Carson nodded gravely. "I can't figure Fennimore will take it lying down. Maybe you better sneak out the back door, Jake, and tell Lee Weaver, over at the livery barn, to do a bit of riding. Tell the boys all hell is ready to pop."

"Good idea," agreed Jake. He shuffled toward the back, and a moment later Carson heard the back door slam behind hm.

There was no question, Carson told himself, tapping a pencil on the desk, that the showdown would be coming soon. Maybe tonight, maybe tomorrow morning . . . but it couldn't be long in coming.

Fennimore wasn't the sort of man who would wait when a challenge was thrown at him, and what had happened that afternoon was nothing short of a challenge. First the refusal of the offer to buy the paper off, then the refusal to submit to arrest, and finally the bluffing that had sent Bean skulking back to the sheriff's office.

In his right mind, Carson told himself, he never would have done it, never would have had the nerve to do it. But he was sore clear through, and he'd done it without thinking.

The front door opened and Carson looked up. A girl stood

there, looking at him: a girl with foamy lace at her throat, silk gloves, dainty parasol.

"I heard what happened," she said. "I came right down."

Carson stood up. "You shouldn't have," he said. "I'm a fugitive from justice."

"You should skulk," she said. "Don't all fugitives skulk?"

"Only when they are in hiding," he said. "I'm not exactly in hiding."

"That's fine," said the girl. "Then you'll be able to eat with us tonight."

"A murderer?" he asked. "Kathryn, your father might not like that. Think of it, a murderer eating with the banker and his charming daughter."

Kathryn Delavan looked squarely at him. "I'll have Daddy come over when he's through work and walk home with you. Probably he'll have something to talk with you about."

"If you do that," Carson said, "I'll come."

They stood for a minute, silent in the room. A fly buzzed against a windowpane and the noise was loud.

"You understand, don't you, Kathryn?" asked Carson. "You understand why I have to fight Fennimore – fight for decent government? Fennimore came in here ten years ago. He had money, cattle and men. He settled down and took over the country – free range, he calls it now, but that's just a term that he and men like him invented to keep for themselves things that were never theirs in the first place. It's not democracy, Kathryn, it's not American. It isn't building the sort of country or the sort of town that common, everyday, ordinary folks want to live in."

He hesitated, almost stammering. "It's sometimes a dirty business, I know, but if gunsmoke's the only answer, then it has to be gunsmoke."

She reached out a hand and touched his arm. "I think I do understand," she said.

She turned away then, walked toward the door.

"Daddy," she told him, "will be over around six o'clock to bring you home."

Carson moved to the window, watched her cross the street and enter Robinson's store. He stood there for a long time, listening to the buzzing of the fly. Then he went back to the desk and settled down to work.

It was almost seven o'clock when Roger Delavan came, profuse with apology.

"Kathryn will be angry with me," he said, fidgeting with his hat, "but I had some work to do, forgot all about the time."

Outside, dusk had fallen on the street and the windows of the business places glowed with yellow light. There was a sharp nip in the rising wind, and Delavan turned up the collar of his coat. A few horses stood huddled, heads drooping at the hitching post in front of the North Star. Up the street a dog-fight suddenly erupted, as suddenly ceased.

Carson and Delavan turned west, their boots ringing on the sidewalk. The wind whispered and talked in the weeds and grass that grew in the vacant space surrounding the creaking, groaning windmill tower.

"I want to talk with you," said Delavan, head bent into the wind, hat socked firmly on his head. "About what happened today. I am afraid you may think –"

"It was a business deal," Carson told him. "You said so, yourself."

"No, it wasn't," protested Delavan. "It was the rankest sort of bribery and attempt at intimidation I have ever seen. I've played along with Fennimore because of business reasons. Fennimore, after all, was the only business in Trail City for a long time. I blinked at a lot of his methods, thinking they were no more than the growing pains of any normal city. But after what happened today, I had to draw the line. I told Quinn this afternoon –"

Red flame flickered in the weeds beside the tower, and a gun bellowed in the dusk. Delavan staggered, coughed, fell to his knees. His bowler hat fell off, rolled into the street. The wind caught it and it rolled on its rim, like a spinning wagon-wheel.

A man, bent low, was running through the weeds, half-seen in the thickening dark.

Carson's hand dipped for his gun, snatched it free, but the man was gone, hidden in the thicker shadows where no lamplight reached from the windows on the street.

Carson slid back the gun, knelt beside Delavan and turned him over. The man was a dead weight in his arms; his head hung limply. Carson tore open his coat, bent one ear to his chest, heard no thudding heart.

Slowly, he laid the banker back on the ground, pulled the coat about him, then straightened up. The bowler hat no longer was in sight, but a half-dozen men were running down the street. Among them, he recognized Bill Robinson, the new store owner, by the white apron tied around his middle.

"That you, Robinson?" asked Carson.

"Yeah, it's me," said Robinson. "We heard a shot."

"Someone shot Delavan," said Carson. "He's dead."

They came up and stood silently for a moment, looking at the black shape on the ground. One of them, Carson saw, was Caleb Storm, the barber. Another was Lee Weaver, the liveryman. The others he knew only from having seen them about town. Men from some of the ranches.

Robinson glanced over his shoulder at the North Star. "Guess they didn't hear the shot in there," he said. "Probably helling it up a bit."

"I'm thinking about Kathryn," said Carson. "Delavan's daughter. Someone will have to tell her."

"That's right," declared Robinson. He considered it a moment, a square, blocky man, almost squatty in the semi-darkness of the street.

"My old woman will go and stay with her," he said, "but she can't break the news to her, not all alone. Someone else will have to help her do it."

He looked at Carson. "You were going there just now. Kathryn told me when she came in to buy some spuds."

Carson nodded. "I suppose you're right, Bill. Let's get Delavan in someplace."

Storm and two of the other men lifted the body, started down the street.

"Come down to the store for a minute," said Robinson. "The old lady will be ready to go in a minute or so."

Carson followed Robinson. Weaver lagged until he fell in step with the editor. He stepped close to Carson and pitched his voice low.

"I got word to Purvis," he said. "He sent out riders. Some of the boys will be coming into town."

"I'll be back at the office," Carson told him, "as soon as I can get away."

Feet pattered on the sidewalk behind them and a woman's voice cried out: "Daddy! Daddy!"

Weaver and Carson spun around.

It was Kathryn Delavan, running across the street, sobs catching in her throat. She would have rushed by, but Carson reached out and stopped her. "No, Kathryn," he said. "Stay back here with us."

She clung to him. "You were so late," she said, "that I came to see –"

He held her close, awkward in his comforting.

"You don't know who –"

Carson shook his head. "It was too dark."

Robinson lumbered through the dusk toward them. "Perhaps," he said, "she might want to come to the store. My wife is there."

The girl stepped away from Carson. "No," she said, "I want to go back home. Martha is there. I'll be all right there with her."

She dabbed at her eyes with a handkerchief. "You will bring him home, too?"

Robinson's voice was understanding, almost soft. "Yes, miss, just as soon – In an hour or two."

She moved closer, took Carson's arm, and they moved west up the street, toward the house where supper waited for a man who would not eat it.

The clock on the bar said ten when Carson pushed open the door of the North Star.

The place was half-full, and in the crowd Carson singled out a handful of Fennimore's riders – Clay Duffy, John Nobles, Madden and Farady at the bar; Saunders and Downey at a table in a listless poker game. The rest of the men were in from other ranches or were from the town.

Carson walked to the bar and signaled to the bartender.

The man came over. "What'll it be?"

"Fennimore around?" asked Carson.

"You don't give a damn for your life, do you?" snarled the man.

Carson's voice turned to ice. "Is Fennimore here?"

The man motioned with his head. "In the back."

For a moment the room had grown silent, but once again it took up its ordinary clatter of tongue and glass and poker chip. One or two men smiled at Carson as he walked by, but others either turned their heads or did not change expression.

Without knocking, Carson pushed open the back door, stepped into the smoke-filled room.

Three men stared at him from a single round table decorated by two whisky bottles, staring with that suddenly vacant, vicious stare that marks an interrupted conversation.

One was Fennimore, a huge man, wisps of black hair hanging out from under his broad-brimmed hat. Quinn and Bean were on either side of him.

For a moment the stare was unbroken and the silence held. Fennimore was the one who broke it. "What do you want?" he asked, and his voice was like a lash, hard and cold and with a sting in every word.

"I came," said Carson, "to see what was being done about Delavan's murder."

"So," said Fennimore slowly. "So, what do you want to be done about it?"

"I want the man who killed him found."

"And if we don't?"

"I'll say that you don't want him found. On the front page of the *Tribune*."

"Look here, Morgan," said Quinn, "you're in no position to say that. When you yourself are wanted for murder."

"I'm here," said Carson. "Go ahead and take me."

The three sat unmoving. Fennimore's tongue licked his upper lip, briefly. Bean's whisky-flushed face drained to pasty white.

"No," said Carson. "All right, then –"

"Quinn," interrupted Fennimore, "gave you until tomorrow morning to get out of town. That still holds."

"I'm not getting out," said Carson. "The day when you can tell a man to get out and make it stick is over, Fennimore. Because in another week we're electing a new sheriff, one who will uphold the law of the country and not the law of one cow-boss."

"It's your damned paper," snarled Fennimore. "You and your lousy stories that give me all the trouble. Stirring up the people –"

"What Fennimore means," said Quinn, smiling, "is that you'll never go to press again . . ."

"But I will," said Carson. "Tonight. I'm not waiting until tomorrow. We go to press tonight instead of tomorrow afternoon. And I'm going to tell how Delavan was shot down from ambush and nothing's being done about it. And I'm going to point out that when I killed a man on fair call this afternoon you wanted to run me in for murder."

"You can't blame any of my boys for killing Delavan," said Fennimore. "Delavan was my friend."

"He was your friend, you mean," said Carson, "until he told Quinn this afternoon that he was all through. After that, Fennimore, you couldn't afford to let him live."

Fennimore hunched forward in his chair. "If you think you

can get me to raise the ten thousand ante," he declared, "you're wrong. It was worth that much to get you out of the way, but it's not worth any more."

Carson laughed at him, a laugh that came between his teeth.

"You're still willing to pay that ten thousand?"

Fennimore nodded. "If you leave within the hour. If you get a horse and ride. If you never go back to the office again."

"I knew I had you scared," said Carson, "but I didn't know I could scare you quite so thoroughly."

Slowly he backed out of the door, closed it and strode across the barroom.

CHAPTER THREE

One Against the Town

Light glowed in the windows of the *Tribune* and Carson, hurrying across the street, saw the tiny office was filled with men.

Cries of greeting rose as he stepped through the door, and he stopped for a moment to recognize the faces. There was Gordon Purvis, the candidate for sheriff, Jim Owens, Dan Kelton, Humphrey Ross and others. Lee Weaver was there and so was Bill Robinson.

Jake shambled out of the back room, stick of type clutched in one hand, gunbelt joggling on his hip.

"Ain't you got that damned editorial writ yet?" he demanded. "Holy hoppin' horntoads –"

"Jake," snapped Carson, "how soon can you get out a paper? An extra?"

Jake gasped. "A whole paper? A whole danged paper?"

"No, just one page. Sort of a circular."

"Couple, three hours," said Jake, "if I can use big type."

"All right," said Carson, "get ready for it. I'll start writing."

Jake shifted the cud of tobacco to the left side of his jaw, spat at the mouse-hole.

Owens had risen, was making his way toward Carson. "What you planning to do?" he asked, and his question quieted the room so that Jake's feet, shuffling to the back, sounded almost like a roll of thunder.

"I'm going to blow Fennimore sky-high," said Carson. "I'm going to force him to produce Delavan's murderer or face the assumption that it was he, himself, that ordered the killing."

"You can't do that," said Owens, softly.

"I can't!"

"No, you can't. This thing is getting out of hand. Range-war is apt to break wide open any minute. You know what that means. Our homes will be burned. Our families run out or murdered. Ourselves shot down from ambush."

Purvis leaped to his feet. "You don't know what you're saying, Owens," he shouted. "If they want to shoot it out, we have to shoot it out. If we back down this time, we're done. We'll never –"

"You're safe enough," snarled Owens, "you're all alone. You haven't any family to be worried about. The rest of us –"

"Wait a minute," yelled Carson. "Wait a minute."

They quieted.

"Do you remember when you came in here six months ago to talk this thing over with me?" asked Carson. "You told me then that if I went with you, you'd string along with me. You swore you wouldn't let me down. You agreed this was the show-down. You said you wanted Purvis for sheriff and you'd back him –"

"We know that," yelled Owens, "but it's different now –"

"Let me talk, Owens," snapped Carson, his voice like a knife. "I want to tell you something. Something that happened this afternoon. Fennimore offered me ten thousand if I would sell you out – ten thousand, cash on the barrel-head and a promise that I'd get safely out of town. I turned him down. I told him I wouldn't sell you fellows out. And because I told him that, I have a murder charge hanging over me and Delavan is dead . . ."

He looked from one to another of them in the deadly quiet, each of them staring in turn at him.

"I refused to sell you men out," said Carson, "and now you're selling me out. You won't back my play. I should have taken that ten thousand."

Their eyes were shifty, refusing to meet his. A strange fear was upon them.

Kelton said, "But you don't understand, Morgan. Our wives and kids. We never thought it would come to this –"

From the street outside came wild shouts and the sound of running feet.

"Fire!" the single word ran through the startled night, crashed into the lamp-lighted *Tribune* office. "Fire! Fire!"

Carson spun toward the window, saw the leaping flames across the street.

"It's my place!" yelled Bill Robinson. "My store! Every dime I have – every dime –"

He was rushing for the door, clawing at the jamb, sobbing in his haste.

The room exploded in a surge of men leaping for the door. Across the street dark figures of men, silhouetted against the windows, hurdled the porch railing of the North Star, hit the street running. At the hitching posts the horses reared and screamed and pawed at the air in terror.

Flames were leaping and racing through the store, staining the whole street red. Smoke mushroomed like an angry cloud, blotting out the stars. Glass tinkled as a window was shattered by the heat.

Carson pounded through the dust. Running figures bumped into him. Voices bellowed – yelling for pails, for someone to start the windmill.

The flames shot through the roof with a gusty sigh, curled skyward, painting the pall of smoke with a bloody hue. One peak of the roof crumbled in as the fire raced through the seasoned timber. In the back something exploded with a whoosh, and for a moment the street was lighted by a garish flare that seemed to illuminate even the racing flames, then thick black clouds of smoke blotted it out.

The kerosene drum had gone up.

The building was dissolving, tongues of fire licking through the solid wall. Someone screamed a warning and the building went, the upper structure plunging in upon the flame-eaten nothingness that lay beneath it. Burning embers sailed into the street and the men ducked as they thudded in the dust.

For a moment the crowd stood stricken into silence, and all that could be heard was the hungry soughing of the fire as it ate its way into oblivion.

Men who had been rushing from the windmill with water to douse the side and roof of the sheriff's office to keep it from catching fire, lowered their buckets and as the fire died down a new sound came: the clanking of the windmill.

Through the crowd came Bill Robinson, face white, shirt smoldering where a brand had fallen. He stopped in front of Carson.

"Everything is gone," he said, almost as if he were talking to himself. His eyes were looking beyond Carson, scarcely seeing him. "Everything. I'm ruined. Everything. . . ."

Carson reached out a hand and gripped the man by the shoulder, but he wrenched away and shook his head, and plodded down the street. Men stood aside to let him pass, not knowing what to say.

Gordon Purvis was at Carson's elbow. He said quietly: "We'll have to figure out something. Pass the hat –"

Carson nodded. "We may as well go back to the office. Nothing we can do here."

A man came leaping through the open door of the *Tribune*, saw them and headed toward them at a run. Carson saw that it was Jake. And as the man drew near he knew there was something wrong.

"The type!" gasped Jake. "All over the floor and throwed out the door. And someone's used a sledge on the press –"

Carson broke into a run, heart down in his stomach, his stomach squeezing to put it back in place, the cold feet of apprehension jigging on his spine.

What Jake said was true.

The back shop was a shambles. Every type case had been jerked out of the cabinets and emptied, some of it heaved out of the door into the grass along the path that ran to the livery stable. The press was smashed as if by a heavy sledge. The same sledge had smashed the cans of ink and left them lying in sticky gobs upon the floor.

The work of a moment – of just the few minutes while the fire was racing through Robinson's store.

Carson stood slump-shouldered and stared at the wreckage.

He finally turned wearily to Purvis. "I guess," he said, "we don't print that extra after all."

Purvis shook his head. "Now we know that fire was no accident," he declared. "They wanted us out of here, and they picked a way that was sure to get us out."

They went back to the office and sat down to wait, but no one came in. Outside, hoofs pounded now and again as men mounted their horses and headed out of town. The hum of voices finally subsided until the street was quiet. Sound of occasional revelry still came from the North Star. The windmill, which no one had remembered to shut off, clanked on in the rising wind. The embers of the fire across the street still glowed redly.

Purvis, tilted back in his chair, fashioned a smoke with steady fingers. Jake hauled a bottle from his pocket, took a drink and passed it around.

"I guess they aren't coming back," said Purvis, finally. "I guess all of them feel the way that Owens felt. All of them plumb scared."

"What the hell," asked Jake, "can you do for a gang like that? They come in here wantin' help, and now –"

"You can't blame them," said Carson, shortly. "After all, they have families to think of. They have too much at stake."

He picked up a pencil from his desk, deliberately broke it in one hand, hurled the pieces on the floor.

"They burned out Robinson," he said. "Cold-bloodedly. They burned him out so they could wreck the shop. So they could stop that extra, scare us out of town. A gang like that would do anything. No wonder the other fellows didn't come back. No wonder they high-tailed for home."

He glanced at Purvis. "How do you feel?" he asked.

Purvis' face didn't change. "Got a place where I can stretch out for the night?"

"Sure you want to?"

"Might as well," said Purvis. "All they can do is burn down my shanty and run off my stock." He puffed smoke through his nostrils. "And maybe, come morning, you'll need an extra gun."

Carson awoke once in the night, saw Jake sitting with his back against the door, his head drooping across one shoulder, his mouth wide open, snoring lustily. The rifle lay across his knees.

Moonlight painted a white oblong on the floor and the night was quiet except for the racing windmill, still clattering in the wind.

Carson pulled the blanket closer around his throat and settled his head back on his coat-covered boots which were serving as a pillow. In the cot, Purvis was a black huddle.

So this is it, thought Carson, staring at the moonlight coming through the window.

The press broken, the type scattered, the men he had been working for deserting, scared out once again by the guns that backed Fennimore. Nothing left at all.

He shrugged off the despair that reached out for him and screwed his eyes tight shut. After a while he went to sleep.

It was morning when he awoke again, with the smell of brewing coffee in his nostrils. Jake, he knew, had started a small fire in the old air-tight heater in the back. He heard the hiss of bacon hit the pan, sat up and hauled on his boots, shucked into his coat.

The cot was empty.

"Where's Purvis?" he called to Jake.

"Went out to get a pail of water," said Jake. "Ought to be good and cold after running all night long."

Somewhere a rifle coughed, a sullen sound in the morning air. Like a man trying to clear a stubborn throat.

For a moment Carson stood stock still, as if his boot-soles were riveted to the floor.

Then he ran to the side window, the window looking out on the windmill lot, half knowing what he would see there, half afraid of what he'd see.

Purvis was a crumpled pile of clothes not five feet from the windmill. The pail lay on its side, shining in the sun. A vagrant breeze fluttered the handkerchief around Purvis' neck.

The town was quiet. The rifle had coughed and broken the silence and then the silence had come again. Nothing stirred, not even the wind after that one solitary puff that had moved the handkerchief.

Carson swung slowly from the window, saw Jake standing in the door to the back room, fork in one hand, pan of bacon in the other.

"What was it?" Jake demanded. "Too tarnation early in the morning to start shootin'."

"Purvis," said Carson. "He's out there, dead."

Jake carefully set the pan of bacon on a chair, laid the fork across it, walked to the corner and picked up his rifle. When he turned around his eyes were squinted as if they already looked along the gun-barrel.

"Them fellers," he announced, "have gone a mite too far. All right, maybe, to shoot a hombre when he's half-expectin' it and has a chance at least to make a motion toward his own artillery. But 'taint right bushwhackin' a man out to get a pail of water."

Jake spat at the mouse-hole, missed it. "Especially," he declared, "before he's had his breakfast."

"Look, Jake," said Carson, "this fight isn't yours. Why don't you crawl out the back window and make a break for it? You could make it now. Maybe later you can't."

"The hell it ain't my fight," yelped Jake. "Don't you go hoggin' all the credit for this brawl. Me, I've had somethin' to do with it, too. Maybe you writ all them pieces takin' the hide off Fennimore, but I set 'em up in type and run 'em off the press."

A voice was bawling outside.

"Carson!" it shouted. "Carson!"

Stalking across the room, but keeping well away from the window, Carson looked out.

Sheriff Bean stood in front of the North Star, badge of office prominently pinned on his vest, two guns at his sides.

"Carson!"

"Watch out," said Jake. "If they see a move in here, they'll fill us full of lead."

Carson nodded, stepped out of line of the window and walked to the wall. Drawing his gun, he reached out and smashed a window-pane with the barrel, then slumped into a crouch.

"What is it?" he yelled.

"Come out and give yourself up," bawled Bean. "That's all we want."

"Haven't got someone posted to pick me off?" asked Carson.

"There won't be a shot fired," said Bean. "Just come out that door, hands up, and no one will get hurt."

Jake's whisper cut fiercely through the room. "Don't believe a word that coyote says. He's got a dozen men in the North Star. Open up that door and you'll be first cousin to a sieve."

Carson nodded grimly.

"Say the word," urged Jake, "and I'll pick 'im off. Easy as blastin' a buzzard off a fence."

"Hold your fire," snapped Carson. "If you start shooting now we haven't got a chance. Probably haven't anyway. As it is they've got us dead to rights. Bean, over there, technically is the law and he can kill us off legal-like. Can say later we were outlaws or had resisted arrest or anything he wants to. . . ."

"They killed Delavan and Purvis," yelped Jake. "They –"

"We can't prove it," said Carson bitterly. "We can't prove a thing. And now they've got us backed into a hole. There's nothing we can gain by fighting. I'm going to go out and give myself up."

"You can't do that," gasped Jake. "You'd never get three feet from the door before they opened up on you."

"Listen to me," snapped Carson. "I'm going to give myself up. I'll take a chance on getting shot. You get out of here, through the back. Weaver will let you have a horse. Ride out and tell the boys that Purvis is dead and I'm in jail. Tell them the next move is up to them. They can do what they want."

"But – but –" protested Jake.

"There's been enough killing," declared Carson. "A bit of gunning was all right, maybe, when there still was something to fight for, but what's the use of fighting if the men you're fighting for won't help? That's what I'm doing. Giving them a chance to show whether they want to fight or knuckle down to Fennimore."

He raised his voice. "Bean. Bean."

"What is it?" Bean called back.

"I'm coming out," yelled Carson.

There was silence, a heavy silence.

"Get going," Carson said to Jake. "Out the back. Crawl through the weeds."

Jake shifted the rifle across his arm.

"After you're safe," he insisted. "Until I see you cross that street, I'll stay right here."

"Why?" asked Carson.

"If they get you," Jake told him, "I'm plumb bent on drillin' Bean."

Carson reached out and yanked the door open. He stood for a moment in the doorway, looking across at Bean, who waited in front of the North Star.

The dawn was clean and peaceful, and the street smelled of cool dust and the wind of the day had not yet arisen, but only stirred here and there, in tiny, warning puffs.

Carson took a step forward, and even as he stepped a rifle barked; a throaty, rasping bark that echoed among the wooden buildings.

Across the street something lifted Bean off his feet, as if a mighty fist had smote him – struck so hard that it slammed him off his feet and sprawled him in the dust.

At the sound of the shot, Carson had ducked and spun on his heel, was back in the room again, slamming shut the door.

The windows of the North Star sprouted licking spurts of gunflame and the smashing of the *Tribune's* windows for an instant drowned the crashing of the guns. Bullets snarled through the thin sheathing and plowed furrows in the floor, hurling bright showers of splinters as they gouged along the wood.

Carson hurled himself toward his heavy desk, hit the floor and skidded hard into the partition behind it. A slug thudded into the wall above his head and another screamed, ricocheting, from the desk top.

Thunder pounded Carson's ears, a crashing, churning thunder that seemed to shake the room. Out of the corner of his eye he saw Jake crouched, half-shielded by the doorway into the back shop, pouring lead through the broken windows. Shell cases rolled and clattered on the floor as the old printer, eye squinted under bushy brow, tobacco tucked carefully in the northeast corner of his cheek, worked the lever action.

From the corner of the desk, Carson flipped two quick shots at one North Star window where he thought he saw for an instant the hint of shadowy motion.

And suddenly he realized there were no sounds of guns, no more bullets thudding into the floor, throwing showers of splinters.

Jake was clawing at the pockets of his printer's apron, spilling cartridges on the floor in his eagerness to fill the magazine.

He spat at the mouse-hole with uncanny accuracy. "Wonder who in tarnation knocked off Bean," he said.

"Somebody out in the windmill lot," said Carson.

Jake picked up the cartridges he had dropped, put them back in the apron pocket again. "Kind of nice," he declared, "to know you got some backin'. Probably somebody that hates Fennimore's guts just as much as we do."

"Whoever he was," declared Carson, "he sure messed up my plans. No sense of trying to surrender now."

"Never was in the fust place," Jake told him. "Damndest fool thing I ever heard of. Steppin' out to get yourself shot up."

He squatted in the doorway, rifle across his knee.

"They didn't catch us unawares," he said. "Now they'll be up to something else. Thought maybe they'd wipe us out by shooting the place plumb full of holes." He patted the rifle stock. "Sort of discouraged them," he said.

"It'll be sniping now," declared Carson. "Waiting for one of us to show ourselves."

"And us," said Jake, "waiting for them to show themselves."

"They'll be spreading out," said Carson, "trying to come at us from different directions. We got to keep our eyes peeled. One of us watch from the front and the other from the back."

"Okay by me," said Jake. "Want to flip for it?"

"No time to flip," said Carson. "You take the back. I'll watch up here."

He glanced at the clock on the wall. "If we only can hold out until dark," he declared, "maybe –"

A furtive tapping came against the back of the building.

"Who's there?" called out Jake, guardedly.

A husky whisper came through the boards. "Open up. It's me. Robinson."

The man slipped in, dragging his rifle behind him, when Jake eased the door open. The merchant slapped the dust from his clothes.

"So you're the jasper what hauled down on Bean," said Jake.

Robinson nodded. "They burned my store," he said. "So they could bust up your shop. They burned everything I had – for no reason at all except to let them get in here and stop that extra you were planning."

"That's what we figured, too," said Jake.

"I ain't no fighting man," Robinson declared. "I like things peaceable . . . like them peaceable so well I'll fight to make them that way. That's why I shot Bean. That's why I came here. My way of figurin', there ain't no peace around these parts until we run out Fennimore."

"Instead of coming here," Carson told him, "you should have ridden out and told the ranchers what was happening. Told them we needed help."

"Lee Weaver is already out," said Robinson. "I was just over there. The stable boy told me he left half an hour ago."

A flurry of shots blazed from the North Star, and bullets chunked into the room. One of them, aimed higher than the rest, smashed the clock and it hung drunkenly from its nail, a wrecked thing that drooled wheels and broken spring.

"Just tryin' us out," said Jake.

To the north, far away, came the sound of shooting. They strained their ears, waiting. "Wonder what's going on up there?" asked Jake.

Robinson shook his head. "Sure hope it isn't Lee," he said.

After that one burst there were no further shots.

The sun climbed up the sky and the town dozed, its streets deserted.

"Everyone's staying under cover," Jake opined. "Ain't nobody wants to get mixed up in this."

Just after noon Lee Weaver came, flat on his belly through the weeds and tall grass back of the building, dragging himself along with one hand, the right arm dragging limply at his side, its elbow a bloody ruin bound with a red-stained handkerchief.

"Came danged near lettin' you have it," Jake told him. "Sneakin' through them weeds like a thievin' redskin."

Weaver slumped into a chair, gulped the dipper of water that Carson brought him.

"I couldn't get through," he told them. "Fennimore's got men posted all around the town, watching. Shot my horse, but I got away. Had to shoot it out with three of them. Laid for two hours in a clump of sage while they hunted me."

Carson frowned, worried. "That leaves us on the limb," he said. "There isn't any help coming. They got us cornered. Come night –"

"Come night," suggested Jake, "and we fade out of here. No use in tryin' it now. They'd get us sure as shootin'. In the dark we'd have some chance to get away."

Carson shook his head. "Come night," he declared, "I'm going into that saloon the back way. While you fellows keep them busy up here."

"If they don't get us first," Weaver reminded him. "They'll rush us as soon as it's dark."

"In that case," snapped Carson, "I'm starting now. That weed-patch out there is tall enough to shield a man if he goes slow, inches at a time, and doesn't cause too much disturbance. I'll circle wide before I try crossing the street. I'll be waiting to get into the North Star long before it's dark."

CHAPTER FOUR
The Plans of Mice and Men . . .

The doorknob turned easily, and Carson let out his breath. For long hours he had lain back of the North Star, his mind conjuring up all the things that might go wrong. The door might be locked, he might be seen before he could reach it, he might run into someone just inside. . . .

But he reached the door without detection and now the

knob turned beneath his fingers. He shoved it slowly, fearful of a squeaking hinge.

The smell of liquor and of stale cooking hit him in the face as the door swung open. From inside came the dull rumble of occasional words, the scrape of boot-heels.

Holding his breath, he moved inside, slid along the wall, shoved the door shut. Standing still, shoulders pressed against the wall, he waited for his eyes to become accustomed to the dark.

He was, he saw, in a sort of warehouse. Liquor cases and barrels were piled against the walls, half-blocking the lone window in the room. Straight ahead was another door and he guessed that it opened into a hallway that ran up to the barroom, with another room, the one in which he had faced Fennimore the night before, off to the side.

A gun crashed ahead of him. A single shot. And then another one. Then a flurry of shots.

He felt the hair crawl at the base of his scalp, and his grip tightened on the gun in his hand. There had been occasional firing all afternoon, a few shots now and then. This might be just another fusillade, or it might mean that the kill had started, that the office would be rushed.

On tiptoe he moved across the room, reached the second door. And even as he reached for the knob, he felt it turn beneath his hand before his fingers gripped it.

Someone else had hold of the knob on the other side – was coming through the door!

Twisting on his boot-heel, he swung away, staggered back against the piled-up cases. The door swung open and a figure stepped into the room.

With all his strength, Carson swung at the head of the shadowy man, felt the barrel of his sixgun crash through the resistance of the hat, slam against the skull. The man gasped, pitched forward on buckling knees.

Moving swiftly, Carson scooped the guns from the holsters of the fallen man. He bent close to try to make out who it was, but in the dark the face was a white splotch, unrecognizable.

He straightened and stood tense, listening. There was no sound. No more shots from up in front.

He reached up to place the two guns he had taken from the holsters on top of the whisky cases, and as he stretched on tiptoe to shove them back away from the edge, something drilled into his back, something hard and round.

Rigid, he did not move, and a voice that he knew spoke just behind him.

"Well, well, Morgan, imagine finding you here."

Mocking, hard – the voice of Jackson Quinn. Quinn, hearing the thud of the falling body, coming on quiet feet down the hallway to investigate, catching him when he was off guard.

"Mind if I turn around?" asked Carson, trying to keep his voice easy.

Quinn gurgled with delight. "Not at all. Turn around by all means. I never did like shooting in the back." He chuckled again. "Not even you."

Carson twisted slowly around. The gun muzzle never left his body, following it around from back to belly.

"Drop your gun," said Quinn.

Carson loosened his fingers and the gun thudded on the floor.

"You've given me so much trouble," Quinn told him, "that I should bust you up a bit. But I don't think I will. I don't think I'll even bother." He chuckled. "I think I'll just shoot you here and have it over with."

Iron squealed against iron, an eerie sound that leaped at them from the dark.

Quinn jerked around, and for the first time his gun-muzzle lifted from Carson's body.

Carson moved like lightning, clenched fist coming up and striking down, smashing against the wrist that held the gun; striking entirely by instinct, for it was too dark to see.

Quinn cried out and the gun clanged to the floor.

The back door was open. A figure stood outlined against the lesser dark outside, a crouching figure that carried a rifle at the ready.

Shoulders hunched, head down, one foot braced hard for leverage against the whisky cases, Carson hurled himself at Quinn. He felt the man go over at the impact of the flow, knew he was falling on top of him, hauled back his arm for a blow.

But a foot came up, lashing at his stomach. He sensed its coming, twisted, caught it in the ribs instead and went reeling back against the whisky cases, limp with pain.

Quinn was crouching, springing toward him. A fist exploded in his face, thumped his head against the cases. He ducked his head, ears ringing, and bored in, fists playing a tattoo on Quinn's midriff, driving the man out into the center of the room.

A vicious punch straightened Carson, rocked him. The white blur of Quinn's face was coming toward him and he aimed at it, smashed with all his might – and the face retreated as Quinn staggered backward on his heels.

Carson stepped in, and out of the dark came piledriver blows that shook him with their viciousness.

The face was there again. Carson measured it, brought his fist up almost from the floor in a whistling, singing loop. Pain lanced down his arm as the blow connected with the whiteness of the face and then the face was gone and Quinn was on the floor.

Feet were pounding in the hallway and shouts came from the barroom. Behind him a rifle crashed, thunderous in the closeness of the room, the red breath of its muzzle lighting the place for a single instant.

The rifle crashed again and yet again and the room was full of powder-fumes that stung the nostrils.

"Jake!" yelled Carson.

"You bet your boots," said the man with the rifle. "You didn't think I'd let you do it all alone!"

"Quick!" gasped Carson. "Get in here, back by the door. They can't reach us here!"

A sixgun blasted and bullets chunked into the cases. Glass crashed and the reek of whisky mingled with the smell of gun-smoke.

Jake came leaping across the room, crouched in the angle back of the door.

Scraping his feet along the floor, Carson located his sixgun, picked it up.

Jake's whisper was rueful. "They got us bottled like a jug of rum."

Carson nodded in the dark. "Been all right," he said, "If Quinn hadn't found me."

"That Quinn you had the shindy with?"

"That's right."

"Had a mind to step in and do some work with the gunstock," Jake told him, "but decided it was too risky. Couldn't tell which of you was which."

Guns thundered in the passageway, the explosions deafening. Bullets thudded into the cases, chewing up the boards, smashing the bottles.

Carson reached up and grasped a case from those stacked behind him. Jake's rifle bellowed. Carson flung the case over his head. It smashed into the doorway. He heaved another one.

Jake blasted away again. The guns in the hallway cut off.

"Keep watch," Carson told Jake. He heaved more cases in the doorway, blocking it to shoulder-height.

From across the street came the sound of firing – the ugly snarling of a high-powered rifle.

"That's Robinson," said Jake. "Some of them buzzards tried to sneak out the front door and come at us from behind, but Robinson was Johnny at the rat-hole."

"Robinson can't stop them for long," snapped Carson. "They'll get at us in a minute or two –"

A gun hammered almost in their ears and something stabbed

Carson in the face. He brushed at it with his hand, pulled away a splinter. The gun roared again, as if it were just beside their heads.

"They're in the back room," gasped Jake, "shooting at us through the partition!"

"Quick!" yelled Carson. "We got to get out of here! Here, you grab Quinn and haul him out. I'll take the other fellow."

He grasped the man he had stuck down with the gun-barrel, started to tug him toward the door.

"Why don't we leave 'em here?" yelped Jake. "What in tarnation is the sense of luggin' 'em?"

"Don't argue with me," yelled Carson. "Just get Quinn out of here."

The gun in the back room was hammering, was joined by another. Through the holes already punched by the bullets, Carson could see the red flare of the blasting runs. One of the bullets brushed past Carson's face, buried itself with a thud in the stacked cases. Another flicked burning across his ribs.

Savagely he yanked the door open, hauled his man through and dumped him on the ground. Reaching in, he gave the panting, puffing Jake a hand with Quinn.

"Pull them a bit farther away," said Carson. "We don't want them to get scorched."

"Scorched?" yipped Jake. "Now you're plumb out of your head!"

"I said scorched," declared Carson, "and I mean scorched. Things are going to get hot in the next five minutes."

He plunged his hand into a pocket, brought out a match, scratched it across the seat of his breeches. For a moment he held it in his cupped hand, nursing the flame, then with a flip of his fingers sent it sailing into the whisky-reeking room.

The flame sputtered for a moment on the floor, almost went out, then blazed brilliantly, eating its way along a track of liquor flowing from one of the broken cases.

Carson lit another match, hurled it into the room. The blaze puffed rapidly, leaping along the floor, climbing the cases, snapping and snarling.

Carson turned and ran, Jake pelting at his heels. In the long grass back of the North Star they flung themselves prone, and watched.

The single window in the building was an angry maw of fire, and tiny tongues of flame were pushing their way through the shingled roof.

A man leaped from one of the side windows in a shower of broken glass. Beside Carson, almost in his ear, Jake's rifle bellowed. The man's hat, still on his head despite the leap, was whipped off as if by an unseen hand.

From the *Tribune* office across the street came the flickering of blasting guns, covering the front windows and the door of the burning saloon.

"Listen!" hissed Jake. His hand reached out and grasped Carson by the shoulder. "Horses!"

It was horses – there could be no mistaking that. The thrum of hoofs along the dusty street – the whoop of a riding man, then a crash of thunder as sixguns cut loose.

Men were spilling out of the North Star now, running men with guns blazing in their hands. And down upon them swept the riders, yelling, sixguns tonguing flame.

The riders swept past the North Star, whirled and came back, and in their wake they left quiet figures lying in the dust.

Jake was on his knee, rifle at his shoulder, firing steadily at the running, dodging figures scurrying for cover.

A running man dashed around the corner of the flaming saloon, ducked into the broken, weedy ground back of the jail. For a moment the light of the fire swept across his face and in that moment, Carson recognized him.

It was Fennimore! Fennimore, making a getaway.

Carson leaped to his feet, crouched low and ran swiftly in the direction Fennimore had taken. Ahead of him a gun barked and a bullet sang like an angry bee above his head.

For an instant he saw a darting darker shape in the shadows and brought up his own gun, triggered it swiftly. Out of the darkness, Fennimore's gun answered and the bullet, traveling low, whispered wickedly in the knee-high grass.

Carson fired at the gun-flash, and at the same instant something jerked at his arm and whirled him half-around. Staggering, his boot caught in a hummock and he went down, plowing ground with his shoulder.

He tried to put out his arm to help himself up again and he found he couldn't. His right arm wouldn't move. It was a dead thing hanging on him, a dead thing that was numb, almost as if it were not a part of him.

Pawing in the grass with his left hand, he found the gun and picked it up, while dull realization beat into his brain.

Running after Fennimore, he'd been outlined against the burning North Star, had been a perfect target. Fennimore had shot him through the arm, perhaps figured he had killed him when he saw him stumble.

Crouching in the grass, he raised his head cautiously. But there was nothing but darkness.

Behind him the saloon's roof fell in with a gush of flames and for a moment the fire leaped high, twisting in the air. And in that moment he saw Fennimore on a rise of ground above him. The man was standing there, looking at the flames.

Carson surged to his feet.

"Fennimore!" he shouted.

The man spun toward him, and for an instant the two stood facing one another in the flare of the gutted building.

Then Fennimore's gun was coming up and to Carson it was almost as if he stood off to one side and watched with cold, deliberate, almost scientific interest.

But he knew his own hand was coming up, too, the left hand with the feel of the gun a bit unfamiliar in it.

Fennimore's gun drooled fire and something brushed with a

blast of air past Carson's cheek. Then Carson's gun bucked against his wrist, and bucked again.

On the rise of ground, in the dying light of the sinking fire, Fennimore doubled over slowly. And across the space of the few feet that separated them, Carson heard him coughing, coughs wrenched out of his chest. The man pitched slowly forward, crashed face-first into the grass.

Slowly, Carson turned and walked down to the street, his wounded arm hanging at his side, blood dripping from his dangling fingers.

The guns were quiet. The fire was dying down. Black, grotesque figures still lay huddled in the dust. In front of the *Tribune* office the horses milled, and inside the office someone had lighted a lamp.

Voices yelled at him as he stepped up on the board sidewalk and headed for the office. He recognized some of the voices. Owens, Kelton, Ross – the men who had ridden away the night before, afraid of what might happen to their homes.

Owens was striding down the walk to meet him. He stared at Carson's bloody arm.

"Fennimore plugged me," Carson said.

"Fennimore got away. He isn't here."

"He's out back of the jail," Carson told him.

"We're glad we got here in time," said Owens, gravely. "Glad we came to our senses. The boys feel pretty bad about last night. It took Miss Delavan to show us –"

"Miss Delavan?" asked Carson, dazed. "What did Kathryn have to do with it?"

Owens looked surprised. "I thought you knew. She rode out and told us."

"But Fennimore had guards posted!"

"She outrode them," Owens declared. "They didn't shoot at her. Guess even a Fennimore gunman doesn't like to gun a woman. They took out after her, but she was on that little Star horse of hers –"

"Yes, I know," said Carson. "Star can outrun anything on four legs."

"She told us how it was our chance to make a decent land out here, a decent place to live – a decent place for our kids."

"Where is she now?" asked Carson. "You made her stay behind. You –"

Owens shook his head. "She wouldn't listen to us. Nothing doing but she'd ride along with us. She said her father –"

"You left her at the house?"

Owens nodded. "She said –"

But Cason wasn't listening. He wasn't even staying. He stepped down into the street and walked away, his stride changing in a moment to a run.

"Kathryn!" he cried.

She was running down the street toward him, arms outstretched.

Jake, prodding Quinn and Clay Duffy toward the *Tribune* at rifle-point, saw them when they met. He watched interestedly, and spat judiciously in the dust.

"Beats all hell," he told Quinn, "how that feller gets along with women."

JUNKYARD

Originally published in Galaxy Science Fiction *in May 1953, "Junk-yard" fits neatly inside a particular subspecies of Simak stories – those starring what we might call "freebooters." By this I mean stories in which human exploitation of the galaxy is being carried out not by human governmental agencies, but by the agents of commercial organizations, who are generally out to make a buck. In interstellar space, there are a lot of places a story with such a background can take you . . .*

—dww

I

They had solved the mystery – with a guess, a very erudite and educated guess – but they didn't know a thing, not a single thing, for certain. That wasn't the way a planetary survey team usually did a job. Usually they nailed it down and wrung a lot of information out of it and could parade an impressive roll of facts. But here there was no actual, concrete fact beyond the one that would have been obvious to a twelve-year-old child.

Commander Ira Warren was worried about it. He said as much to Bat Ears Brady, ship's cook and slightly disreputable pal of his younger days. The two of them had been planet-checking together for more than thirty years. While they stood at opposite poles on the table of organization, they were able to say to one another things they could not have said to any other man aboard the survey ship or have allowed another man to say to them.

"Bat Ears," said Warren, "I'm just a little worried."

"You're always worried," Bat Ears retorted. "That's part of the job you have."

"This junkyard business . . ."

"You wanted to get ahead," said Bat Ears, "and I told you what would happen. I warned you you'd get yourself weighed down with worry and authority and pomp – pomp –"

"Pomposity?"

"That's the word," said Bat Ears. "That's the word, exactly."

"I'm not pompous," Warren contradicted.

"No, you're worried about his junkyard business. I got a bottle stowed away. How about a little drink?"

Warren waved away the thought. "Someday I'll bust you wide open. Where you hide the stuff, I don't know, but every trip we make . . ."

"Now, Ira! Don't go losing your lousy temper."

"Every trip we make, you carry enough dead weight of liquor to keep you annoyingly aglow for the entire cruise."

"It's baggage," Bat Ears insisted. "A man is allowed some baggage weight. I don't have hardly nothing else. I just bring along my drinking."

"Someday," said Warren savagely, "it's going to get you booted off the ship about five light-years from nowhere."

The threat was an old one. It failed to dismay Bat Ears.

"This worrying you're doing," Bat Ears said, "ain't doing you no good."

"But the survey team didn't do the job," objected Warren. "Don't you see what this means? For the first time in more than a hundred years of survey, we've found what appears to be evidence that some other race than Man has achieved space flight. And we don't know a thing about it. We should know. With all that junk out there, we'd ought to be able by this time to write a book about it."

Bat Ears spat in contempt. "You mean them scientists of ours."

The way he said "scientist" made it a dirty word.

"They're good," said Warren. "The very best there is."

"Remember the old days, Ira?" asked Bat Ears. "When you was second looey and you used to come down and we'd have a drink together and . . ."

"That has nothing to do with it."

"We had real men in them days. We'd get ourselves a club and go hunt us up some natives and beat a little sense into them and we'd get more facts in half a day than these scientists, with all their piddling around, will get in a month of Sundays."

"This is slightly different," Warren said. "There are no natives here."

There wasn't, as a matter of fact, much of anything on this particular planet. It was strictly a low-grade affair and it wouldn't amount to much for another billion years. The survey, understandably, wasn't too interested in planets that wouldn't amount to much for another billion years.

Its surface was mostly rock outcroppings and tumbled boulder fields. In the last half million years or so, primal plants had gotten started and were doing well. Mosses and lichens crept into the crevices and crawled across the rocks, but aside from that there seemed to be no life. Although, strictly speaking, you couldn't be positive, for no one had been interested in the planet. They hadn't looked it over and they hadn't searched for life; everyone had been too interested in the junkyard.

They had never intended to land, but had circled the planet, making routine checks and entering routine data in the survey record.

Then someone at a telescope had seen the junkyard and they'd gone down to investigate and had been forthrightly pitchforked into a maddening puzzle.

They had called it the junkyard and that was what it was. Strewn about were what probably were engine parts, although no one was quite sure. Pollard, the mech engineer, had driven himself to the verge of frenzy trying to figure out how to put some of the parts together. He finally got three of them assembled, somehow, and they didn't mean a thing, so he tried to take them apart again to figure out how he'd done it. He couldn't get them apart. It was about that time that Pollard practically blew his top.

The engine parts, if that was what they were, were scattered all over the place, as if someone or something had tossed them away, not caring where they fell. But off to one side was a pile of other stuff, all neatly stacked, and it was apparent even to the casual glance that this stuff must be a pile of supplies.

There was what more than likely was food, though it was a rather strange kind of food (if that was what it was), and strangely fabricated bottles of plastic that held a poison liquid, and other stuff that was fabric and might have been clothing, although it gave one the shudders trying to figure out what sort of creatures would have worn that kind of clothing, and bundles of metallic bars, held together in the bundles by some kind of gravitational attraction instead of the wires that a human would have used to tie them in bundles. And a number of other objects for which there were no names.

"They should have found the answer," Warren said. "They've cracked tougher nuts than this. In the month we've been here, they should have had that engine running."

"If it is an engine," Bat Ears pointed out.

"What else could it be?"

"You're getting so that you sound like them. Run into something that you can't explain and think up the best guess possible and when someone questions you, you ask what else it could be. And that ain't proof, Ira."

"You're right, Bat Ears," Warren admitted. "It certainly isn't proof and that's what worries me. We have no doubt the junk out there is a spaceship engine, but we have no proof of it."

"Nobody's going to land a ship," said Bat Ears testily, "and rip out the engine and just throw it away. If they'd done that, the ship would still be here."

"But if that's not the answer," demanded Warren, "what is all that stuff out there?"

"I wouldn't know. I'm not even curious. I ain't the one that's worrying."

He got up from the chair and moved toward the door.

"I still got that bottle, Ira."

"No, thanks," Warren said.

He sat and listened to Bar Ears' feet going down the stairs.

II

Kenneth Spencer, the alien psychologist, came into the cabin and sat down in the chair across the desk from Warren.

"We're finally through," he said.

"You aren't through," challenged Warren. "You haven't even started."

"We've done all we can."

Warren grunted at him.

"We've run all sorts of tests," said Spencer. "We've got a book full of analyses. We have a complete photographic record and everything is down on paper in diagrams and notes and –"

"Then tell me: What is that junk out there?"

"It's a spaceship engine."

"If it's an engine," Warren said, "let's put it together. Let's find out how it runs. Let's figure out the kind of intelligence most likely to have built it."

"We tried," replied Spencer. "All of us tried. Some of us didn't have applicable knowledge or training, but even so we worked; we helped the ones who had training."

"I know how hard you worked."

And they had worked hard, only snatching stolen hours to sleep, eating on the run.

"We are dealing with alien mechanics," Spencer said.

"We've dealt with other alien concepts," Warren reminded him. "Alien economics and alien religions and alien psychology . . ."

"But this is different."

"Not so different. Take Pollard, now. He is the key man in this situation. Wouldn't you have said that Pollard should have cracked it?"

"If it can be cracked, Pollard is your man. He has everything – the theory, the experience, the imagination."

"You think we should leave?" asked Warren. "That's what you came in here to tell me? You think there is no further use of staying here?"

"That's about it," Spencer admitted.

"All right," Warren told him. "If you say so, I'll take your word for it. We'll blast off right after supper. I'll tell Bat Ears to fix us up a spread. A sort of achievement dinner."

"Don't rub it in so hard," protested Spencer. "We're not proud of what we've done."

Warren heaved himself out of the chair.

"I'll go down and tell Mac to get the engines ready. On the way down, I'll stop in on Bar Ears and tell him."

Spencer said, "I'm worried, Warren."

"So am I. What is worrying you?"

"Who are these things, these other people, who had the other spaceship? They're the first, you know, the first evidence we've ever run across of another race that had discovered space flight. And what happened to them here?"

"Scared?"

"Yes. Aren't you?"

"Not yet," said Warren. "I probably will be when I have the time to think it over."

He went down the stairs to talk to Mac about the engines.

III

He found Mac sitting in his cubby hole, smoking his blackened pipe and reading his thumb-marked Bible.

"Good news," Warren said to him.

Mac laid down the book and took off his glasses.

"There's but one thing you could tell me that would be good news," he said.

"This is it. Get the engines ready. We'll be blasting off."

"When, sir? Not that it can be too soon."

"In a couple of hours or so," said Warren. "We'll eat and get settled in. I'll give you the word."

The engineer folded the spectacles and slid them in his pocket. He tapped the pipe out in his hand and tossed away the ashes and put the dead pipe back between his teeth.

"I've never liked this place," he said.

"You never like any place."

"I don't like them towers."

"You're crazy, Mac. There aren't any towers."

"The boys and me went walking," said the engineer. "We found a bunch of towers."

"Rock formations, probably."

"Towers," insisted the engineer doggedly.

"If you found some towers," Warren demanded, "why didn't you report them?"

"And have them science beagles go baying after them and have to stay another month?"

"It doesn't matter," Warren said. "They probably aren't towers. Who would mess around building towers on this backwash of a planet?"

"They were scary," Mac told him. "They had that black look about them. And the smell of death."

"It's the Celt in you. The big, superstitious Celt you are, rocketing through space from world to world – and still believing in banshees and spooks. The medieval mind in the age of science."

Mac said, "They fair give a man the shivers."

They stood facing one another for a long moment. Then Warren put out a hand and tapped the other gently on the shoulder.

"I won't say a word about them," he said. "Now get those engines rolling."

IV

Warren sat in silence at the table's head, listening to the others talk.

"It was a jury-rigged job," said Clyne, the physicist. "They tore out a lot of stuff and rebuilt the engine for some reason or other and there was a lot of the stuff they tore out that they didn't use again. For some reason, they had to rebuild the engine and they rebuilt it simpler than it was before. Went back to basic principles and cut out the fancy stuff – automatics and other gadgets like that – but the one they rebuilt must have been larger and more unwieldy, less compact, than the one that they ripped down. That would explain why they left some of their supplies behind."

"But," said Dyer, the chemist, "what did they jury-rig it with? Where did they get the material?"

Briggs, the metallurgist, said, "This place crawls with ore. If it wasn't so far out, it would be a gold mine."

"We saw no signs of mining," Dyer objected. "No signs of mining or smelting and refining or of fabrication."

"We didn't go exploring," Clyne pointed out. "They might have done some mining a few miles away from here and we'd have never known it."

Spencer said, "That's the trouble with us on this whole project. We've adopted suppositions and let them stand as fact. If they had to do some fabrication, it might be important to know a little more about it."

"What difference does it make?" asked Clyne. "We know the basic facts – a spaceship landed here in trouble, they finally repaired their engines, and they took off once again."

Old Doc Spears, down at the table's end, slammed his fork on his plate.

"You don't even know," he said, "that it was a spaceship. I've listened to you caterwauling about this thing for weeks. I've never seen so damn much motion and so few results in all my born days."

All of them looked a little surprised. Old Doc was normally a mild man and he usually paid little attention to what was going on, bumbling around on his regular rounds to treat a smashed thumb or sore throat or some other minor ailment. All of them had wondered, with a slight sickish feeling, how Old Doc might perform if he faced a real emergency, like major surgery, say. They didn't have much faith in him, but they liked him well enough. Probably they liked him mostly because he didn't mix into their affairs.

And here he was, mixing right into them truculently.

Lang, the communications man, said, "We found the scratches, Doc. You remember that. Scratches on the rock. The kind of scratches that a spaceship could have made in landing."

"*Could* have made," said Doc derisively.

"*Must* have made!"

Old Doc snorted and went on with his eating, holding his head down over the plate, napkin tucked beneath his chin, shoveling in the food with fork and knife impartially. Doc was noted as a messy eater.

"I have a feeling," Spencer said, "that we may be off the beaten track in thinking of this as a simple repair job. From the amount of parts that are down there in the junkyard, I'd say that they found it necessary to do a redesigning job, to start from the beginning and build an entirely new engine to get them out of here. I have a feeling that those engine parts out there represent the whole engine, that if we knew how, we could put those parts together and we'd have an engine."

"I tried it," Pollard answered.

"I can't quite buy the idea that it was a complete redesigning job," Clyne stated. "That would mean a new approach and some new ideas that would rule out the earlier design and all the parts that had been built into the original engine as it stood. The theory would explain why there are so many parts strewn around, but it's just not possible. You don't redesign an engine when you're stranded on a barren planet. You stick to what you know."

Dyer said, "Accepting an idea like redesigning sends you back again to the problem of materials."

"And tools," added Lang. "Where would they get the tools?"

"They'd probably have a machine shop right on board the ship," said Spencer.

"For minor repairs," Lang corrected. "Not the kind of equipment you would need to build a complete new engine."

"What worries me," said Pollard, "is our absolute inability to understand any of it. I tried to fit those parts together, tried to figure out the relationship of the various parts – and there must be some sort of relationship, because unrelated parts would make no sense at all. Finally I was able to fit three of them together and that's as far as I could get. When I got them together, they didn't spell a thing. They simply weren't going anywhere. Even with three of them together, you were no better off, no further along in understanding, than before you'd put them together. And when I tried to get them apart, I couldn't do that, either. You'd think, once a man had got a thing together, he could take it apart again, wouldn't you?"

"It was an alien ship," Spencer offered, "built by alien people, run by alien engines."

"Even so," said Pollard, "there should have been some basic idea that we could recognize. In some way or other, their engine should have operated along at least one principle that would be basic with human mechanics. An engine is a piece of mechanism that takes raw power and controls it and directs it into useful energy. That would be its purpose, no matter what race built it."

"The metal," said Briggs, "is an alien alloy, totally unlike anything we have ever run across. You can identify the components, all right, but the formula, when you get it down, reads like a metallic nightmare. It shouldn't work. By Earth standards, it *wouldn't* work. There's some secret in the combination that I can't even guess at."

Old Doc said, from the table's end, "You're to be congratulated, Mr. Briggs, upon your fine sense of restraint."

"Cut it out, Doc," Warren ordered sharply, speaking for the first time.

"All right," said Doc. "If that's the way you want it, Ira, I will cut it out."

V

Standing outside the ship, Warren looked across the planet. Evening was fading into night and the junkyard was no more than a grotesque blotch of deeper shadow on the hillside.

Once, not long ago, another ship had rested here, just a little way from where they rested now. Another ship – another race.

And something had happened to that ship, something that his survey party had tried to ferret out and had failed to discover.

It had not been a simple repair job; he was sure of that. No matter what any of them might say, it had been considerably more than routine repair.

There had been some sort of emergency, a situation with a strange urgency about it. They had left in such a hurry that they had abandoned some of their supplies. No commander of any spaceship, be he human or alien, would leave supplies behind except when life or death was involved in his escape.

There was what appeared to be food in the stack of supplies – at least, Dyer had said that it was food, although it didn't look edible. And there were the plastic-like bottles filled with a poison that might be, as like as not, the equivalent of an alien whisky. And no man, Warren said, leaves food and whisky behind except in the direst emergency.

He walked slowly down the trail they'd beaten between the ship's lock and the junkyard and it struck him that he walked in a silence that was as deep as the awful stillness of far space. There was nothing here to make any sound at all. There was no life except the mosses and the lichens and the other primal plants that crept among the rocks. In time there would be other life, for the planet had the air and water and the basic ingredients for soil and here, in another billion years or so, there might arise a life economy as complex as that of Earth.

But a billion years, he thought, is a long, long time.

He reached the junkyard and walked its familiar ground, dodging the larger pieces of machinery that lay all about, stumbling on one or two of the smaller pieces that lay unseen in the darkness.

The second time he stumbled, he stooped and picked up the thing he had stumbled on and it was, he knew, one of the tools that the alien race had left behind them when they fled. He could picture them, dropping their tools and fleeing, but the picture was not clear. He could not decide what these aliens might have looked like or what they might have fled from.

He tossed the tool up and down, catching it in his hand. It was light and handy and undoubtedly there was some use for it, but he did not know the use nor did any of the others up there in the ship. Hand or tentacle, claw or paw – what appendage had it been that had grasped the tool? What mind lay behind the hand or tentacle, claw or paw that had grasped and used it?

He stood and threw back his head and looked at the stars that shone above the planet and they were not the familiar stars he had known when he was a child.

Far out, he thought, far out. The farthest out that Man had ever been.

A sound jerked him around, the sound of running feet coming down the trail.

"Warren!" cried a voice. "Warren! Where are you?"

There was fright in that voice, the frantic note of panic that one hears in the screaming of a terrified child.

"Warren!"

"Here!" shouted Warren. "Over here. I'm coming."

He swung around and hurried to meet the man who was running in the dark.

The runner would have charged on past him if he had not put out a hand and gripped him by the shoulder and pulled him to a halt.

"Warren! Is that you?"

"What's the matter, Mac?" asked Warren.

"I can't . . . I can't . . . I . . ."

"What's wrong? Speak up? You can't what, Mac?"

He felt the engineer's fumbling hands reaching out for him, grasping at his coat lapels, hanging onto him as if the engineer were a drowning man.

"Come on, come on," Warren urged with the impatience of alarm.

"I can't start the engines, sir," said Mac.

"Can't start the . . ."

"I can't start them, sir. And neither can the others. None of us can start them, sir."

"The engines!" said Warren, terror rising swiftly. "What's the matter with the engines?"

"There's nothing the matter with the engines. It's us, sir. We can't start them."

"Talk sense, man. Why can't you?"

"We can't remember how. We've forgotten how to start the engines!"

VI

Warren switched on the light above the desk and straightened, seeking out the book among the others on the shelf.

"It's right here, Mac," he said. "I knew I had it here."

He found it and took it down and opened it beneath the light. He leafed the pages rapidly. Behind him he could hear the tense, almost terrified breathing of the engineer.

"It's all right, Mac. It's all here in the book."

He leafed too far ahead and had to back up a page or two and reached the place and spread the book wide beneath the lamp.

"Now," he said, "we'll get those engines started. It tells right here . . ."

He tried to read and couldn't.

He could understand the words all right and the symbols, but the sum of the words he read made little sense and the symbols none at all.

He felt the sweat breaking out on him, running down his forehead and gathering in his eyebrows, breaking out of his armpits and trickling down his ribs.

"What's the matter, Chief?" asked Mac. "What's the matter now?"

Warren felt his body wanting to shake, straining every nerve to tremble, but it wouldn't move. He was frozen stiff.

"This is the engine manual," he said, his voice cold and low. "It tells all about the engines – how they operate, how to locate trouble, how to fix them."

"Then we're all right," breathed Mac, enormously relieved.

Warren closed the book.

"No, we aren't, Mac. I've forgotten all the symbols and most of the terminology."

"You what?"

"I can't read the book," said Warren.

VII

"It just isn't possible," argued Spencer.

"It's not only possible," Warren told him. "It happened. Is there any one of you who can read that book?"

They didn't answer him.

"If there's anyone who can," invited Warren. "Step up and show us how."

Clyne said quietly, "There's none of us can read it."

"And yet," declared Warren, "an hour ago any one of you – any single one of you – probably would have bet his life that he not only could start the engines if he had to, but could take the manual if he couldn't and figure how to do it."

"You're right," Clyne agreed. "We would have bet our lives. An hour ago we would have. It would have been a safe, sure bet."

"That's what you think," said Warren. "How do you know how long it's been since you couldn't read the manual?"

"We don't, of course," Clyne was forced to admit.

"There's something more. You didn't find the answer to the junkyard. You *guessed* an answer, but you didn't *find* one. And you should have. You know damn well you should have."

Clyne rose to his feet. "Now see here, Warren . . ."

"Sit down, John," said Spencer. "Warren's got us dead to rights. We didn't find an answer and we know we didn't. We took a guess and substituted it for the answer that we didn't find. And

Warren's right about something else – we should have found the answer."

Under any other circumstances, Warren thought, they might have hated him for those blunt truths, but now they didn't. They just sat there and he could see the realization seeping into them.

Dyer finally said, "You think we failed out there because we forgot – just like Mac forgot."

"You lost some of your skills," replied Warren, "some of your skills and knowledge. You worked as hard as ever. You went through the motions. You didn't have the skill or knowledge any more, that's all."

"And now?" asked Lang.

"I don't know."

"This is what happened to that other ship," said Briggs emphatically.

"Maybe," Warren said with less conviction.

"But they got away," Clyne pointed out.

"So will we," promised Warren. "Somehow."

VIII

The crew of that other, alien ship had evidently forgotten, too. But somehow or other they had blasted off – somehow or other they had remembered, or forced themselves to remember. But if it had been the simple matter of remembering, why had they rebuilt the engines? They could have used their own.

Warren lay in his bunk, staring into the blackness, knowing that a scant two feet above his head there was a plate of steel, but he couldn't see the steel. And he knew there was a way to start the engines, a simple way once you knew it or remembered it, but he couldn't see that, either.

Man experienced incidents, gathered knowledge, knew emotion – and then, in the course of time, forgot the incident and knowledge and emotion. Life was a long series of forgettings. Memories were wiped out and old knowledge dulled and skill was lost, but it took time to wipe it out or dull it or lose it. You couldn't know a thing one day and forget it on the next.

But here on this barren world, in some impossible way, the forgetting had been speeded up. On Earth it took years to forget an incident or to lose a skill. Here it happened overnight.

He tried to sleep and couldn't. He finally got up and dressed and went down the stairs, out the lock into the alien night.

A low voice asked, "That you, Ira?"

"It's me, Bat Ears. I couldn't sleep. I'm worried."

"You're always worried," said Bat Ears. "It's an occu . . . occu . . ."

"Occupational?"

"That's it," said Bat Ears, hiccoughing just a little. "That's the word I wanted. Worry is an occupational disease with you."

"We're in a jam, Bat Ears."

"There's been planets," Bat Ears said, "I wouldn't of minded so much being marooned on, but this ain't one of them. This here place is the tail end of creation."

They stood together in the darkness with the sweep of alien stars above them and the silent planet stretching off to a vague horizon.

"There's something here," Bat Ears went on. "You can smell it in the air. Them fancy-pants in there said there wasn't nothing here because they couldn't see nothing and the books they'd read said nothing much could live on a planet that was just rocks and moss. But, me, I've seen planets. Me, I was planet-checking when most of them was in diapers and my nose can tell me more about a planet than their brains all lumped together, which, incidentally, ain't a bad idea."

"I think you're right," confessed Warren. "I can feel it myself. I couldn't before. Maybe it's just because we're scared that we can feel it now."

"I felt it before I was scared."

"We should have looked around. That's where we made our mistake. But there was so much work to do in the junkyard that we never thought of it."

"Mac took a little jaunt," said Bat Ears. "Says he found some towers."

"He told me about them, too."

"Mac was just a little green around the gills when he was telling me."

"He told me he didn't like them."

"If there was any place to run to, Mac would be running right now."

"In the morning," Warren said, "we'll go and see those towers."

IX

They were towers, all right, and there were eight of them in line, like watchtowers that at one time had stretched across the planet, but something had happened and all the others had been leveled except the eight that were standing there.

They were built of undressed native rock, crudely piled, without mortar and with little wedges and slabs of stone used in the interstices to make the stones set solid. They were the kind of towers that might have been built by a savage race and they had an ancient look about them. They were about six feet at the base and tapered slightly toward the top and each of them was capped by a huge flat stone with an enormous boulder placed upon the slab to hold it in its place.

Warren said to Ellis, "This is your department. Take over."

The little archaeologist didn't answer. He walked around the nearest tower and went up close to it and examined it. He put out his hands and acted as if he meant to shake the tower, but it didn't shake.

"Solid," he said. "Well built and old."

"Type F culture, I would say," guessed Spencer.

"Maybe less than that. No attempt at an aesthetic effect – pure utility. But good craftsmanship."

Clyne said, "Its purpose is the thing. What were the towers built for?"

"Storage space," said Spencer.

"A marker," Lang contradicted. "A claim marker, a cache marker . . ."

"We can find the purpose," Warren said. "That is something we needn't argue nor speculate about. All we have to do is knock off the boulder and lift the cap and have a look inside."

He strode up to the tower and started climbing it.

It was an easy thing to climb, for there were niches in the stones and hand and toe holds were not too hard to find.

He reached the top.

"Look out below," he yelled, and heaved at the boulder.

It rolled and then slowly settled back. He braced himself and heaved again and this time it toppled. It went plunging off the tower, smashed to the ground, went rumbling down the slope, gathering speed, hitting other boulders in its path, zigzagging with the deflection of its course, thrown high into the air by the boulders that it hit.

Warren said, "Throw a rope up to me. I'll fasten it to the capstone and then we can haul it off."

"We haven't got a rope," said Clyne.

"Someone run back to the ship and get one. I'll wait here till he returns."

Briggs started back toward the ship.

Warren straightened up. From the tower he had a fine view of the country and he swiveled slowly, examining it.

Somewhere nearby, he thought, the men – well, not men, but the things that built these towers – must have had their dwelling. Within a mile or so there had been at one time a habitation. For the towers would have taken time in building and that meant that the ones who built them must have had at least a semi-permanent location.

But there was nothing to see – nothing but tumbled boulder fields and great outcroppings and the blankets of primal plants that ran across their surfaces.

What did they live on? Why were they here? What would have attracted them? What would have held them here?

He halted in his pivoting, scarcely believing what he saw. Carefully he traced the form of it, making sure that the light on some boulder field was not befuddling his vision.

It couldn't be, he told himself. It couldn't happen three times. He must be wrong.

He sucked in his breath and held it and waited for the illusion to go away.

It didn't go away. The thing was there.

"Spencer," he called. "Spencer, please come up here."

He continued watching it. Below him, he heard Spencer scrabbling up the tower. He reached down a hand and helped him.

"Look," Warren said, pointing. "What is that out there?"

"A ship!" cried Spencer. "There's another ship out there!"

X

The spaceship was old, incredibly old. It was red with rust; you could put your hand against its metal hide and sweep your hand across it and the flakes of rust would rain down upon the rock and your hand would come away painted with rust.

The airlock once had been closed, but someone or something had battered a hole straight through it without opening it, for the rim was still in place against the hull and the jagged hole ran to the ship's interior. For yards around the lock, the ground was red with violently scattered rust.

They clambered through the hole. Inside, the ship was bright and shining, without a trace of rust, although there was a coating of dust over everything. Through the dust upon the floor was a beaten track and many isolated footprints where the owners of the prints had stepped out of the path. They were alien tracks, with a heavy heel and three great toes, for all the world like the tracks of a mighty bird or some long-dead dinosaur.

The trail led through the ship back to the engine room and there the empty platform stood, with the engines gone.

"That's how they got away," said Warren, "the ones who junked their engines. They took the engines off this ship and put them in their ship and then they took off."

"But they wouldn't know –" argued Clyne.

"They evidently did," Warren interrupted bluntly.

Spencer said, "They must have been the ones. This ship has been here for a long time – the rust will tell you that. And it was closed, hermetically sealed, because there's no rust inside. That hole was punched through the lock fairly recently and the engines taken."

"That means, then," said Lang, "that they did junk their engines. They ripped them out entire and heaved them in the junkpile. They tore them out and replaced them with the engines from this ship."

"But why?" asked Clyne. "Why did they have to do it?"

"Because," said Spencer, "they didn't know how to operate their own engines."

"But if they didn't know how to operate their engines, how could they run this one?"

"He's got you there," said Dyer. "That's one that you can't answer."

"No, I can't," shrugged Warren. "But I wish I could, because then we'd have the answer ourselves."

"How long ago," asked Spencer, "would you say this ship landed here? How long would it take for a spaceship hull to rust?"

"It's hard to tell," Clyne answered. "It would depend on the kind of metal they used. But you can bet on this – any spaceship hull, no matter who might have built it, would be the toughest metal the race could fabricate."

"A thousand years?" Warren suggested.

"I don't know," said Clyne. "Maybe a thousand years. Maybe more than that. You see this dust. That's what's left of whatever organic material there was in the ship. If the beings that landed here remained within the ship, they still are here in the form of dust."

Warren tried to think, tried to sort out the chronology of the whole thing.

A thousand years ago, or thousands of years ago, a spaceship had landed here and had not got away.

They another spaceship landed, a thousand or thousands of years later, and it, too, was unable to get away. But it finally escaped when the crew robbed the first ship of its engines and substituted them for the ones that had brought it here.

Then years, or months, or days later, the Earth survey ship had landed here, and it, too, couldn't get away – because the men who ran it couldn't remember how to operate its engines.

He swung around and strode from the engine room, leaving the others there, following the path in the dust back to the shattered lock.

And just inside the port, sitting on the floor, making squiggles in the dust with an awkward finger, sat Briggs, who had gone back to the ship to get a length of rope.

"Briggs," said Warren sharply. "Briggs, what are you doing here?"

Briggs looked up with vacant, laughing eyes.

"Go away," he said.

Then he went back to making squiggles in the dust.

XI

Doc Spears said, "Briggs reverted to childhood. His mind is wiped as clean as a one-year-old's. He can talk, which is about the only difference between a child and him. But his vocabulary is limited and what he says makes very little sense."

"He can be taught again?" asked Warren.

"I don't know."

"Spencer had a look at him. What does Spencer say?"

"Spencer said a lot," Doc told him. "It adds up, substantially, to practically total loss of memory."

"What can we do?"

"Watch him. See he doesn't get hurt. After a while we might try re-education. He may even pick up some things by himself. Something happened to him. Whether whatever it was that took his memory away also injured his brain is something I can't say for sure. It doesn't appear injured, but without a lot of diagnostic equipment we don't have, you can't be positive."

"There's no sign of injury?"

"There's not a single mark anywhere," said Doc. "He isn't hurt. That is, not physically. It's only his mind that's been injured. Maybe not his mind, either – just his memory gone."

"Amnesia?"

"Not amnesia. When you have that, you're confused. You are haunted by the thought that you have forgotten something. You're all tangled up. Briggs isn't confused or tangled. He seems to be happy enough."

"You'll take care of him, Doc? Kind of keep an eye on him?"

Doc snorted and got up and left.

Warren called after him. "If you see Bat Ears down there, tell him to come up."

Doc clumped down the stairs.

Warren sat and stared at the blank wall opposite him.

First Mac and his crew had forgotten how to run the engines. That was the first sign of what was happening – the first recognizable sign – for it had been going on long before Mac found he'd forgotten all his engine lore.

The crew of investigators had lost some of their skills and their knowledge almost from the first. How else could one account for the terrible mess they'd made of the junkyard business? Under ordinary circumstances, they would have wrung some substantial information from the engine parts and the neatly stacked supplies. They had gotten information of a sort, of course, but it added up to nothing. Under ordinary circumstances, it should have added up to an extraordinary something.

He heard feet coming up the stairs, but the tread was too crisp for Bat Ears.

It was Spencer.

Spencer flopped into one of the chairs. He sat there opening and closing his hands, looking down at them with helpless anger.

"Well?" asked Warren. "Anything to report?"

"Briggs got into that first tower," said Spencer. "Apparently he came back with the rope and found us gone, so he climbed up and threw a hitch around the capstone, then climbed down again and pulled it off. The capstone is lying on the ground, at the foot of the tower, with the rope still hitched around it."

Warren nodded. "He could have done that. The capstone wasn't too heavy. One man could have pulled it off."

"There's something in that tower."

"You took a look?"

"After what happened to Briggs? Of course not. I posted a guard to keep everyone away. We can't go monkeying around with the tower until we've thought a few things through."

"What do you think is in there?"

"I don't know," said Spencer. "All I have is an idea. We know what it can do. It can strip your memory."

"Maybe it's fright that did it," Warren said. "Something down in the tower so horrible . . ."

Spencer shook his head. "There is no evidence of fright in Briggs. He's calm. Sits there happy as a clam, playing with his fingers and talking silly sentences – happy sentences. The way a kid would talk."

"Maybe what he's saying will give us a hint. Keep someone listening all the time. Even if the words don't mean much . . ."

"It wouldn't do any good. Not only is his memory gone, but even the memory of what took it away."

"What do you plan to do?"

"Try to get into the tower," said Spencer. "Try to find out what's in there. There must be a way of getting at whatever is there and coming out okay."

"Look," Warren stated, "we have enough as it is."

"I have a hunch."

"This is the first time I've ever heard you use that word. You gents don't operate on hunches. You operate on fact."

Spencer put up an outspread hand and wiped it across his face.

"I don't know what's the matter with me, Warren. I know I've never thought in hunches before. Perhaps because now I can't help myself, the hunch comes in and fills the place of knowledge that I've lost."

"You admit there's been knowledge lost?"

"Of course I do," said Spencer. "You were right about the junkyard. We should have done a better job."

"And now you have a hunch."

"It's crazy," said Spencer. "At least, it sounds crazy. That memory, that lost knowledge and lost skill went somewhere. Maybe there's something in the tower that took it away. I have the silly feeling we might get it back again, take it back from the thing that has it."

He looked challengingly at Warren. "You think I'm cracked."

Warren shook his head. "No, not that. Just grasping at straws."

Spencer got up heavily. "I'll do what I can. I'll talk with the others. We'll try to think it out before we try anything."

When he had gone, Warren buzzed the engine room communicator.

Mac's voice came reedily out of the box.

"Having any luck, Mac?"

"None at all," Mac told him. "We sit and look at the engines. We are going out of our heads trying to remember."

"I guess that's all you can do, Mac."

"We could mess around with them, but I'm afraid if we do, we'll get something out of kilter."

"Keep your hands off everything," commanded Warren in sudden alarm. "Don't touch a single thing. God knows what you might do."

"We're just sitting," Mac said, "and looking at the engines and trying to remember."

Crazy, thought Warren.

Of course it was crazy.

Down there were men trained to operate spaceship engines, men who had lived and slept with engines for year on lonesome year. And now they sat and looked at engines and wondered how to run them.

Warren got up from his desk and went slowly down the stairs.

In the cook's quarters, he found Bat Ears.

Bat Ears had fallen off a chair and was fast asleep upon the floor, breathing heavily. The room reeked with liquor fumes. An almost empty bottle sat upon the table.

Warren reached out a foot and prodded Bat Ears gently. Bat Ears moaned a little in his sleep.

Warren picked up the bottle and held it to the light. There was one good, long drink.

He tilted the bottle and took the drink, then hurled the empty bottle against the wall. The broken plastiglass sprayed in a shower down on Bat Ears' head.

Bat Ears raised a hand and brushed it off, as if brushing away a fly. Then he slept on, smiling, with his mind comfortably drugged against memories he no longer had.

XII

They covered the tower with the capstone once again and rigged a tripod and pulley above it. then they took the capstone off and used the pulley to lower an automatic camera into the pit and they got their pictures.

There was something in the tower, all right.

They spread the pictures out on the table in the mess room and tried to make out what they had.

It was shaped like a watermelon or an egg stood on one end with the lower end slightly mashed so that it would stand upright. It sprouted tiny hairs all over and some of the hairs were blurred in the pictures, as if they might have been vibrating. There was tubing and what seemed to be wiring, even if it didn't look exactly the way you thought of wiring, massed around the lower end of the egg.

They made other tests, lowering the instruments with the pulley, and they determined that the egg was alive and that it was the equivalent of a warm-blooded animal, although they were fairly sure that its fluids would not be identical with blood.

It was soft and unprotected by any covering shell and it pulsed and gave out some sort of vibrations. They couldn't determine what sort of vibrations. The little hairs that covered it were continually in motion.

They put the capstone back in place again, but left the tripod and the pulley standing.

Howard, the biologist, said, "It's alive and it's an organism of some kind, but I'm not at all convinced that it's pure animal. Those wires and that piping lead straight into it, as if, you'd almost swear, the piping and the wires were a part of it. And look at these – what would you call them? – these studs, almost like connections for other wires."

"It's not conceivable," said Spencer, "that an animal and a mechanism should be joined together. Take Man and his machines. Man and the machines work together, but Man maintains his individual identity and the machines maintain their own. In a lot of cases it would make more sense, economically, if not socially, that Man and machine should be one, that the two of them be joined together, become, in fact, one organism."

Dyer said, "I think that may be what we have here."

"Those other towers?" asked Ellis.

"They could be connected," Spencer suggested, "associated in some way. All eight of them could be, as a matter of principle, one complex organism."

"We don't know what's in those other towers," said Ellis.

"We could find out," Howard answered.

"No, we can't," objected Spencer. "We don't dare. We've fooled around with them more than was safe. Mac and his crew went for a walk and found the towers and examined them, just casually, you understand, and they came back not knowing how to operate the engines. We can't take the chance of fooling around with them a minute longer than is necessary. Already we may have lost more than we suspect."

"You mean," said Clyne, "that the loss of memory we may have experienced will show up later? That we may not know now we've lost it, but will find later that we did?"

Spencer nodded. "That's what happened to Mac. He or any member of his crew would have sworn, up to the minute that they tried to start the engines, that they could start them. They took it for granted, just as we take our knowledge for granted.

Until we come to use the specific knowledge we have lost, we won't realize we've lost it."

"It scares you just to think about it," Howard said.

Lang said, "It's some sort of communications system."

"Naturally you'd think so. You're a communications man."

"Those wires."

"And what about the pipes?" asked Howard.

"I have a theory on that one," Spencer told them. "The pipes supply the food."

"Attached to some food supply," said Clyne. "A tank of food buried in the ground."

"More likely roots," Howard put in. "To talk of tanks of food would mean these are transplanted things. They could just as easily be native to this planet."

"They couldn't have built those towers," said Ellis. "If they were native, they'd have had to build those towers themselves. Something or someone else built the towers, like a farmer builds a barn to protect his cattle. I'd vote for tanks of food."

Warren spoke for the first time. "What makes you think it's a communications set up?"

Lang shrugged. "Nothing specific. Those wires, I guess, and the studs. It *looks* like a communications rig."

"Communications might fill the bill," Spencer nodded. "But a communications machine built to take in information rather than to pass information along or disseminate it."

"What are you getting at?" demanded Lang. "How would that be communication?"

"I mean," said Spencer, "that something has been robbing us of our memory. It stole our ability to run the engines and it took enough knowledge away from us so we bungled the junkyard job."

"It couldn't be that," said Dyer.

"Why couldn't it?" asked Clyne.

"It's just too damn fantastic."

"No more fantastic," Spencer told him, "than a lot of other things we've found. Say that egg is a device for gathering knowledge . . ."

"But there's no knowledge to gather here," protested Dyer. "Thousands of years ago, there was knowledge to gather from the rusted ship out there. And then, just a while ago, there was knowledge to gather from the junkyard ship. And now there's us. But the next shipload of knowledge won't come along for maybe uncounted thousands of years. It's too long to wait, too big a gamble. Three ships we know of have come here; it would be just as reasonable to suppose that no ship would ever come here. It doesn't make any sense."

"Who said that the knowledge had to be collected here? Even back on Earth we forget, don't we?"

"Good Lord!" gasped Clyne, but Spencer rushed ahead.

"If you were some race setting out fish traps for knowledge and had plenty of time to gather it, where would you put your traps? On a planet that swarmed with sentient beings, where the traps might be found and destroyed or their secrets snatched away? Or would you put them on some uninhabited, out-of-the-way planet, some second-rate world that won't be worth a tinker's damn to anyone for another billion years?"

Warren said, "I'd put them on a planet just like this."

"Let me give you the picture," Spencer continued. "Some race is bent on trapping knowledge throughout the Galaxy. So they hunt up the little, insignificant, good-for-nothing planets where they can hide their traps. That way, with traps planted on strategically spaced planets, they sweep all space and there's little chance that their knowledge traps ever will be found."

"You think that's what we've found here?" asked Clyne.

"I'm tossing you the idea," said Spencer, "to see what you think of it. Now let's hear your comments."

"Well, the distance, for one thing –"

"What we have here," said Spencer, "is mechanical telepathy

hooked up with a recording device. We know that distance has little to do with the speed of thought waves."

"There's no other basis for this belief beyond speculation?" asked Warren.

"What else can there be? You certainly can't expect proof. We don't dare to get close enough to find out what this egg is. And maybe, even if we could, we haven't got enough knowledge left in us to make an intelligent decision or a correct deduction."

"So we guess again," said Warren.

"Have you some better method?"

Warren shook his head. "No, I don't think I have."

XIII

Dyer put on a spacesuit, with a rope running from it to the pulley in the tripod set above the tower. He carried wires to connect to the studs. The other ends of the wires were connected to a dozen different instruments to see what might come over them – if anything.

Dyer climbed the tower and they lowered him down into the inside of the tower. Almost immediately, he quit talking to them, so they pulled him out.

When they loosened the spacesuit helmet and hinged it back, he gurgled and blew bubbles at them.

Old Doc gently led him back to sick bay.

Clyne and Pollard worked for hours designing a lead helmet with television installed instead of vision plates. Howard, the biologist, climbed inside the spacesuit and was lowered into the tower.

When they hauled him out a minute later, he was crying – like a child. Ellis hurried him after Old Doc and Dyer, with Howard clutching his hands and babbling between sobs.

After ripping the television unit out of the helmet, Pollard was all set to go in the helmet made of solid lead when Warren put a stop to it.

"You keep this up much longer," he told them, "and we'll have no one left."

"This one has a chance of working," Clyne declared. "It might have been the television lead-ins that let them get at Howard."

"It has a chance of not working, too."

"But we have to try."

"Not until I say so."

Pollard started to put the solid helmet on his head.

"Don't put that thing on," said Warren. "You're not going anywhere you'll be needing it."

"I'm going in the tower," Pollard said flatly.

Warren took a step toward him and without warning lashed out with his fist. It caught Pollard on the jaw and crumpled him.

Warren turned to face the rest of them. "If there's anyone else who thinks he wants to argue, I'm ready to begin the discussion – in the same way."

None of them wanted to argue. He could see the tired disgust for him written on their faces.

Spencer said, "You're upset, Warren. You don't know what you're doing."

"I know damned well what I'm doing," Warren retorted. "I know there must be a way to get into that tower and get out again with some of your memory left. But the way you're going about it isn't the right way."

"You know another?" asked Ellis bitterly.

"No, I don't," said Warren. "Not yet."

"What do you want us to do?" demanded Ellis. "Sit around and twiddle our thumbs?"

"I want you to behave like grown men," said Warren, "not like a bunch of crazy kids out to rob an orchard."

He stood and looked at them and none of them had a word to say.

"I have three mewling babies on my hands right now," he added. "I don't want any more."

He walked away, up the hill, heading for the ship.

XIV

Their memory had been stolen, probably by the egg that squatted in the tower. And although none of them had dared to say the thought aloud, the thing that all of them were thinking was that maybe there was a way to steal the knowledge back, to tap and drain all the rest of the knowledge that was stored within the egg.

Warren sat at his desk and held his head in his hands, trying to think.

Maybe he should have let them go ahead with what they had been doing. But if he had, they'd have kept right on, using variations of the same approach – and when the approach had failed twice, they should have figured out that approach was wrong and tried another.

Spencer had said that they'd lost knowledge and not known they had lost it, and that was the insidious part of the whole situation. They still thought of themselves as men of science, and they were, of course, but not as skilled, not as knowledgeable as they once had been.

That was the hell of it – they still thought they were.

They despised him now and that was all right with him. Anything was all right with him if it would help them discover a way to escape.

Forgetfulness, he thought. All through the Galaxy, there was forgetfulness. There were explanations for that forgetfulness, very learned and astute theories on why a being should forget something it had learned. But might not all these explanations be wrong? Might it not be that forgetfulness could be traced, not to some kink within the brain, not to some psychic cause, but to thousands upon thousands of memory traps planted through the Galaxy, traps that tapped and drained and nibbled away at the mass memory of all the sentient beings which lived among the stars?

On Earth a man would forget slowly over the span of many years and that might be because the memory traps that held Earth in their orbit were very far away. But here a man forgot completely and suddenly. Might that not be because he was within the very shadow of the memory traps?

He tried to imagine Operation Mind Trap and it was a shocking concept too big for the brain to grasp. Someone came to the backwoods planets, the good-for-nothing planets, the sure-to-be-passed-by planets and set out the memory traps.

They hooked them up in series and built towers to protect them from weather or from accident, and set them operating and connected them to tanks of nutrients buried deep within the soil. Then they went away.

And years later – how many years later, a thousand, ten thousand? – they came back again and emptied the traps of the knowledge they had gathered. As a trapper sets out traps to catch animals for fur, or a fisherman should set the pots for lobsters or drag the seine for fish.

A harvest, Warren thought – a continual, never-ending harvest of the knowledge of the Galaxy.

If this were true, what kind of race would it be that set the traps? What kind of trapper would be plodding the starways, gathering his catch?

Warren's reason shrank away from the kind of race that it would be.

The creatures undoubtedly came back again, after many years, and emptied the traps of the knowledge they had snared. That must be what they'd do, for why otherwise would they bother to set out the traps? And if they could empty the traps of the knowledge they had caught, that meant there was some way to empty them. And if the trappers themselves could drain off the knowledge, so could another race.

If you could only get inside the tower and have a chance to figure out the way, you could do the job, for probably it was a simple thing, once you had a chance to see it. But you couldn't get inside. If you did, you were robbed of all memory and came out a squalling child. The moment you got inside, the egg grabbed onto your mind and wiped it clean and you didn't even know why you were there or how you'd got there or where you were.

The trick was to get inside and still keep your memory, to get inside and still know what there was to do.

Spencer and the others had tried shielding the brain and shielding didn't work. Maybe there was a way to make it work, but you'd have had to use trial and error methods and that meant too many men coming out with their memories gone before you had the answer. It meant that maybe in just a little while you'd have no men at all.

There must be another way.

When you couldn't shield a thing, what did you do?

A communications problem, Lang had said. Perhaps Lang was right – the egg was a communications set up. And what did you do to protect communications? When you couldn't shield a communication, what did you do with it?

There was an answer to that one, of course – you scrambled it.

But there was no solution there, nor any hint of a solution. He sat and listened and there was no sound. No one had stopped by to see him; no one had dropped in to pass the time of day.

They're sore, he thought. They're off sulking in a corner. They're giving me the silent treatment.

To hell with them, he said.

He sat alone and tried to think and there were no thoughts, just a mad merry-go-round of questions revolving in his skull.

Finally there were footsteps on the stair and from their unsteadiness, he knew whose they were.

It was Bat Ears coming up to comfort him and Bat Ears had a skin full.

He waited, listening to the stumbling feet tramping up the stairs, and Bat Ears finally appeared. He stood manfully in the doorway, putting out both hands and bracing them against the jambs on either side of him to keep the place from swaying.

Bat Ears nerved himself and plunged across the space from doorway to chair and grabbed the chair and hung onto it and wrestled himself into it and looked up at Warren with a smirk of triumph.

"Made it," Bat Ears said.

"You're drunk," snapped Warren disgustedly.

"Sure, I'm drunk. It's lonesome being drunk all by yourself. Here . . ."

He found his pocket and hauled the bottle out and set it gingerly on the desk.

"There you are," he said. "Let's you and me go and hang one on."

Warren stared at the bottle and listened to the little imp of thought that jigged within his brain.

"No, it wouldn't work."

"Cut out the talking and start working on that jug. When you get through with that one, I got another hid out."

"Bat Ears," said Warren.

"What do you want?" asked Bat Ears. "I never saw a man that wanted —"

"How much more have you got?"

"How much more what, Ira?"

"Liquor. How much more do you have stashed away?"

"Lots of it. I always bring along a marg . . . a marg . . ."

"A margin?"

"That's right," said Bat Ears. "That is what I meant. I always figure what I need and then bring along a margin just in case we get marooned or something."

Warren reached out and took the bottle. He uncorked it and threw the cork away.

"Bat Ears," he said, "go and get another bottle."

Bat Ears blinked at him. "Right away, Ira? You mean right away?"

"Immediately," said Warren. "And on your way, would you stop and tell Spencer that I want to see him soon as possible?"

Bat Ears wobbled to his feet.

He regarded Warren with forthright admiration.

"What you planning on doing, Ira?" he demanded.

"I'm going to get drunk," said Warren. "I'm going to hang one on that will make history in the survey fleet."

XV

"You can't do it, man," protested Spencer. "You haven't got a chance."

Warren put out a hand against the tower and tried to hold himself a little steadier, for the whole planet was gyrating at a fearful pace.

"Bat Ears," Warren called out.

"Yes, Ira."

"Shoot the – *hic* – man who tries to shtop me."

"I'll do that, Ira," Bat Ears assured him.

"But you're going in there unprotected," Spencer said anxiously. "Without even a spacesuit."

"I'm trying out a new appro . . . appro . . ."

"Approach?" supplied Bat Ears.

"Thash it," said Warren. "I thank you, Bat Ears. Thash exactly what I'm doing."

Lang said, "It's got a chance. We tried to shield ourselves and it didn't work. He's trying a new approach. He's scrambled up his mind with liquor. I think he might have a chance."

"The shape he's in," said Spencer, "he'll never get the wires connected."

Warren wobbled a little. "The hell you shay."

He stood and blurredly watched them. Where there had been three of each of them before, there now, in certain cases, were only two of them.

"Bat Ears."

"Yes, Ira."

"I need another drink. It's wearing off a little."

Bat Ears took the bottle from his pocket and handed it across. It was not quite half full. Warren tipped it up and drank, his Adam's apple bobbing. He did not quit drinking until the last of it was gone. He let the bottle drop and looked at them again. This time there were three of each of them and it was all right.

He turned to face the tower.

"Now," he said, "if you gen'men will jush –"

Ellis and Clyne hauled on the rope and Warren sailed into the air.

"Hey, there!" he shouted. "Wha' you trying to do?"

He had forgotten about the pulley rigged on the tripod above the tower.

He dangled in the air, kicking and trying to get his balance, with the blackness of the tower's mouth looming under him and a funny, shining glow at the bottom of it.

Above him the pulley creaked and he shot down and was inside the tower.

He could see the thing at the bottom now. He hiccoughed politely and told it to move over, he was coming down. It didn't move an inch. Something tried to take his head off and it didn't come off.

The earphones said, "Warren, you all right? You all right? Talk to us."

"Sure," he said. "Sure, all right. Wha' matter wish you?"

They let him down and he stood beside the funny thing that

pulsated in the pit. He felt something digging at his brain and laughed aloud, a gurgling, drunken laugh.

"Get your handsh out my hair," he said. "You tickle."

"Warren," said the earphones. "The wires. The wires. You remember, we talked about the wires."

"Sure," he said. "The wires."

There were little studs on the pulsating thing and they'd be fine things to attach a wire to.

Wires? What the hell were wires?

"Hooked on your belt," said the earphones. "The wires are hooked on your belt."

His hand moved to his belt and he found the wires. He fumbled with them and they slipped out of his fingers and he got down and scrabbled around and grabbed hold of them again. They were all tangled up and he couldn't make head or tail of them and what was he messing around with wires for, anyhow?

What he wanted was another drink – another little drink.

He sang: *"I'm a ramblin' wreck from Georgia Tech and a hell of an engineer!"*

He said to the egg: "Friend, I'd be mosh pleased if you'd join me in a drink."

The earphones said, "Your friend can't drink until you get those wires hooked up. He can't hear without the wires hooked up. He can't tell what you're saying until you get those wires hooked up.

"You understand, Warren? Hook up the wires. He can't hear till you do."

"Now, thash too bad," said Warren. "Thash an awful thing."

He did the best he could to get the wires hooked up and he told his new friend just to be patient and hold still, he was doing the best he could. He yelled for Bat Ears to hurry with the bottle and he sang a ditty which was quite obscene. And finally he got the wires hooked up, but the man in the earphones said that wasn't right, to try it once again. He changed the wires around some more and they still weren't right, and so he changed them around again, until the man in the earphones said, "That's fine! We're getting something now!"

And then someone hauled him out of there before he even had a drink with his pal.

XVI

He stumbled up the stairs and negotiated his way around the desk and plopped into the chair. Someone had fastened a steel bowl securely over the top half of his head and two men, or possibly three, were banging it with a hammer, and his mouth had a wool blanket wadded up in it, and he could have sworn that at any moment he'd drop dead of thirst.

He heard footsteps on the stairs and hoped that it was Bat Ears, for Bat Ears would know what to do.

But it was Spencer.

"How're you feeling?" Spencer asked.

"Awful," Warren groaned.

"You turned the trick!"

"That tower business?"

"You hooked up the wires," said Spencer, "and the stuff is rolling out. Lang has a recorder hooked up and we're taking turns listening in and the stuff we're getting is enough to set your teeth on edge."

"Stuff?"

"Certainly. The knowledge that mind trap has been collecting. It'll take us years to sort out all the knowledge and try to correlate it. Some of it is just in snatches and some of it is fragmentary, but we're getting lots of it in hunks."

"Some of our own stuff being fed back to us?"

"A little. But mostly alien."

"Anything on the engines?"

Spencer hesitated. "No, not on *our* engines. That is –"

"Well?"

"We got the dope on the junkyard engine. Pollard's already at work. Mac and the boys are helping him get it assembled."

"It'll work?"

"Better than what we have. We'll have to modify our tubes and make some other changes."

"And you're going to –"

Spencer nodded. "We're ripping out our engines."

Warren couldn't help it. He couldn't have helped it if he'd been paid a million dollars. He put his arms down on the desk and hid his face in them and shouted raucously with incoherent laughter.

After a time he looked up again and mopped at laughter-watered eyes.

"I fail to see –" Spencer began stiffly.

"Another junkyard," Warren said. "Oh, God, another junk-yard!"

"It's not so funny, Warren. It's brain-shaking – a mass of knowledge such as no one ever dreamed of. Knowledge that had been accumulating for years, maybe a thousand years. Ever since that other race came and emptied the trap and then went away again."

"Look," said Warren, "couldn't we wait until we came across the knowledge of our engines? Surely it will come out soon. It went in, was fed in, whatever you want to call it, later than any of the rest of this stuff you are getting. If we'd just wait, we'd have the knowledge that we lost. We wouldn't have to go to all the work of ripping out the engines and replacing them."

Spencer shook his head. "Lang figured it out. There seems to be no order or sequence in the way we get the information. The chances are that we might have to wait for a long, long time. We have no way of knowing how long the information will keep pouring out. Lang thinks for maybe years. But there's something else. We've got to get away as soon as possible."

"What's the matter with you, Spencer?"

"I don't know."

"You're afraid of something. Something's got you scared."

Spencer bent over and grasped the desk edge with his hands, hanging on.

"Warren, it's not only knowledge in that thing. We're monitoring it and we know. There's also –"

"I'll take a guess," said Warren. "There's personality."

He saw the stricken look on Spencer's face.

"Quit monitoring it," ordered Warren sharply. "Turn the whole thing off. Let's get out of here."

"We can't. Don't you understand? We can't! There are certain points. We are –"

"Yes, I know," said Warren. "You are men of science. Also downright fools."

"But there are things coming out of that tower that –"

"Shut it off!"

"No," said Spencer obstinately. "I can't. I won't."

"I warn you," Warrant said grimly, "if any of you turn alien, I'll shoot you without hesitation."

"Don't be a fool," Spencer turned sharply about and went out the door.

Warren sat, sober now, listening to Spencer's feet go down the steps.

It was all very clear to Warren now.

Now he knew why there had been evidence of haste in that other ship's departure, why supplies had been left behind and tools still lying where they had been dropped as the crew had fled.

After a while Bat Ears came up the stairs, lugging a huge pot of coffee and a couple of cups.

He set the cups down on the desk and filled them, then banged down the pot.

"Ira," he said, "it was a black day when you gave up your drinking."

"How is that?" asked Warren.

"Because there ain't no one, nowhere, who can hang one on like you."

They sat silently, gulping the hot, black coffee.

Then Bat Ears said, "I still don't like it."

"Neither do I," admitted Warren.

"The cruise is only half over," said Bat Ears.

"The cruise is completely over," Warren told him bluntly. "When we lift out of here, we're heading straight for Earth."

They drank more coffee.

Warren asked: "How many on our side, Bat Ears?"

"There's you and me," said Bat Ears, "and Mac and the four engineers. That's seven."

"Eight," corrected Warren. "Don't forget Doc. He hasn't been doing any monitoring."

"Doc don't count for nothing one way or the other."

"In a pinch, he still can handle a gun."

After Bat Ears had gone, Warren sat and listened to the sound of Mac's crew ripping out the engines and he thought of the long way home. Then he got up and strapped on a gun and went out to see how things were shaping up.

MR. MEEK – MUSKETEER

Cliff referred to this story, before he ever sent it to a publisher, by the name of "Space Calls Mr. Meek," and he was paid one hundred dollars for it by Planet Stories. *It will remind you irresistibly of the stereotypical pulp Westerns of the sort he'd been writing during the preceding couple of years, the sort that had been a staple of American literature for several decades – complete with a saloon on an asteroid and gunfights – but it has so much humor that one has to call it satire. And something about it must have tickled Cliff, because he wrote a sequel before this one was even published and, perhaps, a third one – and with the exception of the* City *stories, he wasn't a writer who did sequels.*

And another familiar feature of many Simak stories from the thirties reappears: good old Martian bocca.

—dww

I

Now that he'd done it, Oliver Meek found the thing he'd done hard to explain.

Under the calm, inquiring eyes of Mr. Richard Belmont,

president of Lunar Exports, Inc., he stammered a little before he could get started.

"For years," he finally said, "I've been planning a trip . . ."

"But, Oliver," said Belmont, "we would give you a leave of absence. You'll be back. There's no reason to resign."

Oliver Meek shuffled his feet and looked uncomfortable, a little guilty.

"Maybe I won't be back," he declared. "You see, it isn't just an ordinary trip. It may take a long, long time. Something might happen. I'm going out to see the Solar System."

Belmont laughed lightly, reared back in his chair, matching fingertips. "Oh, yes. One of the tours. Nothing dangerous about them. Nothing at all. You needn't worry about that. I went on one a couple of years ago. Mighty interesting. . . ."

"Not one of the tours," interrupted Meek. "Not for me. I have a ship of my own."

Belmont thumped forward in his chair, looking almost startled.

"A ship of your own!"

"Yes, sir," Oliver admitted, squirming uncomfortably. "Over thirty years I've saved for it . . . for it and the other things I'll need. It sort of got to be . . . well, an obsession, you might say."

"I see," said Belmont. "You planned it."

"Yes, sir, I planned it."

Which was a masterpiece of understatement.

For Belmont could not know and Oliver Meek, stoop-shouldered, white-haired bookkeeper, could not tell of those thirty years of thrift and dreams. Thirty years of watching ships of the void taking off from the space port, just outside the window where he sat hunched over ledgers and calculators. Thirty years of catching scraps of talk from the men who ran those ships. Men and ships with the alien dust of far off planets still clinging to their skins. Ships with strange marks and scars upon them, and men with strange words upon their tongues.

Thirty years of reducing high adventure to cold figures. Thirty years of recording strange cargoes and stranger tales into accounts. Thirty years of watching through a window while rockets, outbound, dug molten pits into the field. Thirty years of being on the edge, the very fringe of life . . . but *never* in it.

Nor could Belmont have guessed or Meek formed in words the romanticism that glowed within the middle-aged bookkeeper's heart . . . a thing that sometimes hurt . . . something earthbound that forever cried for space.

Nor the night classes Oliver Meek had attended to learn the theory of space navigation and after that more classes to gain an understanding of the motors and controls that drove the ships between the planets.

Nor how he had stood before the mirror in his room hour after hour, practicing, perfecting the art of pistol handling. Nor of the afternoons he had spent at the shooting gallery.

Nor of the nights he had read avidly, soaking up the lore and information and color of those other worlds that seemed to beckon him.

"How old are you, Oliver?" asked Belmont.

"Fifty next month, sir," Meek answered.

"I wish you were taking one of the passenger ships," said Belmont. "Now, those tours aren't so bad. They're comfortable and . . ."

Meek shook his head and there was a stubborn glint in the weak blue eyes behind the thick lensed glasses.

"No tour for me, sir. I'm going to some of those places the tours never take you. I've missed a lot in these thirty years. I've waited a long time and now I'm going out and see the things I've dreamed about."

Oliver Meek pushed open the swinging doors of the Silver Moon and stepped timidly inside. Just through the door he stopped and stared, for the place hit him squarely in the face . . . the acrid smoke of Venusian leaf, the high-pitched laughter of the Martian dancing girls, the soft whirr of wheels, the click of balls as they bounced around the spinning wheels, the clatter of poker chips, the odor of strange liquors, the chirping and growling of a dozen tongues, the strange, exotic music of Ganymede.

Meek blinked through his heavy lenses, moved forward cautiously.

In the far corner of the place stood a table occupied by one man . . . an old, grizzled veteran of the Asteroids with his muzzle in a flagon of cheap beer.

Meek sidled toward the table, drew out a chair.

"Do you mind if I sit here?" he asked, and Old Stiffy Grant choked on a mouthful of beer in his amazement.

"Go ahead, stranger," he finally croaked. "I don't give a dang. I don't own the joint."

Meek sat down on the edge of the chair. His eyes swept the room. He smelled the smoke, the raw liquor, the sweat-stained clothing of the men, the cheap perfumery of the dancing girls.

He shifted his gun belt so the two energy pistols hung more easily, and cautiously slid farther back upon the chair.

So this was Asteroid City on Juno. The place he'd read about. The place the pulp paper writers used as background for their more lurid tales. This was the place where guns flamed and men were found dead in the streets and a girl or a game of chance or just one spoken word could start a fight.

The tours didn't include places such as this. They took one to the nice, civilized places . . . towns like Gusta Pahn on Mars and Radium City on Venus and out to Satellite City on Ganymede. Civilized, polished places . . . places hardly different than New York or Chicago or Denver back home. But this was different . . . here one could sense something that made the blood run faster, made a thrill scamper up one's spine.

"You're new here, ain't you?" asked Stiffy.

Meek jumped, then recovered his composure.

"Yes," he said. "Yes, I am. I always wanted to see this place. I read about it."

"Ever read about an Asteroid Prowler?" asked Stiffy.

"I believe I have somewhere. In a magazine section. A crazy story. . . ."

"It ain't crazy," protested Stiffy. "I saw one of them . . . this afternoon. Right here on Juno. None of these dad-blamed fools will believe me."

Furtively, Meek studied the man opposite him. He didn't seem to be such a bad fellow. Almost like any other human being. A little rough, maybe, but a good fellow just the same.

"Say," he suggested impulsively, "maybe you'd have a drink with me."

"You're dang tootin'," agreed Stiffy. "I never turn down no drinks."

"You order it," said Meek.

Stiffy bawled across the room. "Hey, Joe, bring us a couple snorts."

"What kind of an animal was this you were speaking of?" asked Meek.

"Asteroid Prowler," said Stiffy. "Most of these hoodlums don't think there is one, but I know different. I saw him this afternoon and he was the dad-blamest thing I ever laid my eyes on. He boiled right out from behind a big rock and started coming after me. I let him have one in the face but that didn't even nick him. Full-power, too. When that happened I didn't waste no more time. I took it on the lam. Got to my ship and got out of there."

"What did he look like?"

Stiffy leaned across the table and wagged a forefinger solemnly. "Mister, you won't believe me when I tell you. But it's the truth, so help me. He had a beak. And eyes. Danged if them eyes weren't something. Like they were reaching out and trying to grab you. Not really reaching out, you know. But there was something in them that tried to talk to you. Big as plates and they shimmered like there was fire inside of them.

"These dod-rotted rock-blasters here laughed at me when I told them about it. Insinuated I held the truth lightly, they did. Laughed their fool heads off.

"It's pretty near as big as a house . . . that animal, and it's got a body like a barrel. It's got a long neck and a little head with big teeth. It's got a tail, too, and it's kind of set close to the ground. You see, I was out looking for the Lost Mine."

"Lost Mine?"

"Sure, ain't you ever heard of the Lost Mine?"

Stiffy blew beer in amazement.

Oliver Meek shook his head, feeling that probably he was the victim of tales reserved for the greenest of the tenderfeet, not knowing what he could do about it if he were.

Stiffy settled more solidly in his chair.

"The Lost Mine story," he declared, "has been going around for years. Seems a couple of fellows found it a few years after the first dome was built. They came in and told about it, stocked up with grub and went out. They never did come back."

He leaned across the table.

"You know what I think?" he demanded gustily.

"No," said Meek. "What do you think?"

"The Prowler got 'em," Stiffy said, triumphantly.

"But how could there be a lost mine?" asked Meek. "Asteroid City was one of the first mining domes built out here. There was no prospecting done until about that time."

Stiffy shook his head, waggling his beard.

"How should I know," he defended himself. "Maybe some early space traveler set down here, dug a mine, never got back to Earth to tell about it."

"But Juno is only one hundred and eighteen miles in diameter," Meek argued. "If there had been a mine someone would have found it."

Stiffy snorted. "That's all you know about it, stranger. Only one hundred and eighteen miles, sure . . . but one hundred and eighteen miles of the worst danged country man ever set a boot on. Mostly up and down."

The drinks came, the bartender slapping them down on the table before them. Meek gasped first at their price, then choked on the drink itself. But he smothered the choke manfully and asked:

"What kind of stuff is this?"

"*Bocca*," replied Stiffy. Good old Martian *bocca*. Puts hair on your chest."

He gulped his drink with gusto, blew noisily through his whiskers, eyed Meek disapprovingly.

"Don't you like it?" he demanded.

"Sure," liked Meek. "Sure I like it."

He shut his eyes and poured the liquor into his mouth, gulped fiercely, desperately, almost strangling.

Said Stiffy: "Tell you what let's do. Let's get into a game."

Meek opened his mouth to accept the invitation, then closed it, caution stealing over him. After all, he didn't know much about this place. Maybe he'd better go a little easy, at least at first.

He shook his head. "No, I'm not very good at cards. Just a few games of penny-ante now and then."

Stiffy looked his disbelief. "Penny-ante," he said, then guffawed as if he sensed humor in what Meek had said. "Say, you're good," he roared. "Don't s'pose you can use them lightnin' throwers of yours either."

"Some," admitted Meek. "Practiced in front of a looking glass a little."

He wondered why Stiffy rolled in his chair with mirth until tears ran down into his whiskers.

Stiffy held a full house . . . aces with kings . . . and his eyes had the look of a cat talking a saucer full of cream.

There were only two in the game, Stiffy and an oily gentleman called Luke. As the stakes mounted and the game grew hotter the others at the table dropped out.

Standing behind Stiffy, Oliver Meek watched in awe, scarcely breathing.

Here was life . . . the kind of life one would never dream of back in the little cubby hole with its calculators and dusty books at Lunar Exports, Inc.

In the space of an hour, he had seen more money pass across the table than he had ever owned in all his life. Pots that climbed and pyramided, fortunes gambled on the flip of a single card.

But there was something else too . . . something wrong about the dealing. He couldn't figure quite what it was, but he had read an article about how gamblers dealt the cards when they didn't aim to give the other fellow quite an even break. And there had been something about Luke's dealing . . . something that he had read about in that article.

Across the table Luke grimaced.

"I'll have to call you," he announced. "I'm afraid you're too strong for me."

Stiffy slapped down his hand triumphantly.

"Match that, dang you!" he exulted. "The kind of cards I been waiting for all night."

He reached out a gnarled hand to rake in the coin but Luke stopped him with a gesture.

"Sorry," he said.

He flipped the cards down slowly, one at a time. First a trey, then a four and then three more fours.

Stiffy gulped, reached for the bottle.

But even as he did, Oliver Meek reached out and placed his hand upon the money on the table, fingers wide spread. He'd remembered what he had read in that article. . . .

"Just a minute, gentlemen," he said. "I've remembered something. . . ."

Silence thudded in the room.

Meek looked across the table straight into the eyes of Luke.

Luke said: "You better explain yourself, mister."

Meek suddenly was flustered. "Why, maybe I acted too hastily. It really was nothing. I just noticed something about the deal. . . ."

Luke jerked erect, kicking his chair away with the single

motion of rising. The crowd suddenly surged away, out of the line of fire. The bartender ducked behind the bar. Stiffy flung himself with a howl out of his chair, skidded along the floor. Meek, suddenly straightening from the table, saw Luke's hand streaking for the gun at his belt and in a split second he realized that here he faced a situation that demanded action.

He didn't think about those days of practice in front of the mirror. He didn't call upon a single iota of the gun-lore he had read in hundreds of books. His mind, for a bare instant, was almost a blank, but he acted as if by instinct.

His hands moved like driving pistons, snapped the twin guns from their holsters, heaved them clear of leather, grabbed them in mid-air.

He saw Luke's gun muzzle swinging up, tilted down the muzzle of his own left gun, pressed the activator. There was a screeching hiss, a streak of blue that crackled in the air and the gun that Luke held in his hand was suddenly red hot.

But Meek wasn't watching Luke. His eyes were for the crowd and even as he pressed the firing button he saw a hand pick a bottle off the bar, lift it to throw. The gun in his right hand shrieked and the bottle smashed into a million pieces, the liquor turned to steam.

Slowly Meek backed away, his tread almost cat-like, his weak blue eyes like cold ice behind the thick lensed spectacles, his hunched shoulders still hunched, his lean jaw like a steel trap.

He felt the wall at his back and stopped.

Out in the room before him no one stirred. Luke stood like a statue, gripping his right hand, badly burned by the smoking gun that lay at his feet. Luke's face was a mask of hatred.

The rest of them simply stared. Stared at this outlander. A man who wore clothing such as the Asteroid Belt had never seen before. A man who looked as if he might be a clerk or even a retired farmer out on a holiday. A man with glasses and hunched shoulders and a skin that had never known the touch of sun in space.

And yet a man who had given Luke Blaine a head start for his gun, had beaten him to the draw, had burned the gun out of his hand.

Oliver Meek heard himself speaking, but he couldn't believe it was himself. It was as if some other person had taken command of his tongue, was forcing it to speak. He hardly recognized his voice, for it was hard and brittle and sounded far away.

It was saying: "Does anyone else want to argue with me?"

It was immediately apparent no one did.

II

Oliver Meek tried to explain it carefully, but it was hard when people were so insistent. Hard, too, to collect his thoughts so early in the day.

He sat on the edge of the bed, white hair tousled, his night shirt wrinkled, his bony legs sticking out beneath it.

"But I'm not a gun fighter," he declared. "I'm just on a holiday. I never shot at a man before in all my life. I can't imagine what came over me."

The Rev. Harold Brown brushed his argument aside.

"Don't you see, sir," he insisted, "what you can do for us? These hoodlums will respect you. You can clean up the town for us. Blacky Hoffman and his mob run the place. They make decent government and decent living impossible. They levy protection tribute on every businessman, they rob and cheat the miners and prospectors who come here, they maintain vice conditions. . . ."

"All you have to do," said Andrew Smith brightly, "is run Blacky and his gang out of town."

"But," protested Meek, "you don't understand."

"Five years ago," the Rev. Brown went on, disregarding him, "I would have hesitated to pit force against force. It is not my way nor the way of the church . . . but for five years I've tried to bring the gospel to this place, have worked for better conditions and each year I see them steadily getting worse."

"This could be a swell place," enthused Smith, "if we could get rid of the undesirables. Fine opportunities. Capital would come in. Decent people could settle. We could have some civic improvements. Maybe a Rotary club."

Meek wiggled his toes despairingly.

"You would earn the eternal gratitude of Asteroid City," urged the Rev. Brown. "We've tried it before but it never worked."

"They always killed our man," Smith explained, "or he got scared, or they bought him off."

"We never had a man like you before," the Rev. Brown declared. "Luke Blaine is a notorious gunman. No one, ever before, has been able to beat him to . . ."

"There must be some mistake," insisted Meek. "I'm just a bookkeeper. I don't know a thing. . . ."

"We'd swear you in as marshal," said Smith. "The office is vacant now. Has been for three months or more. We can't find anyone to take it."

"But I'm not staying long," protested Meek. "I'm leaving pretty soon. I just want to try to get a look at the Asteroid Prowler and scout around to see if I can't find some old rocks I read about once."

The two visitors stared open mouthed at hm. Meek brightened. "You've heard about those old rocks, maybe. Some funny inscriptions on them. Fellow who found them thought they had been made recently, probably just before Earthmen first came here. But no one can read them. Maybe some other race . . . from somewhere far away."

"But it won't take you long," pleaded Smith. "We got warrants for all of them. All you got to do is serve them."

"Look," said Meek in desperation, "you have got me wrong. It must have been an accident, shooting that gun out of Mr. Blaine's hand."

Meek felt dull anger stirring within him. What right did these people have of insisting that he help them with their troubles? What did they think he was? A desperado or space runner? Another gangster? Just because he'd been lucky at the Silver Moon.

"By gosh," he declared flatly, "I just won't do it!"

They looked pained, rose reluctantly.

"I suppose we shouldn't have expected that you would," said the Reverend Brown bitingly.

The Silver Moon was quiet. The bartender was languidly wiping the top of the bar. A Venusian boy was as languidly sweeping out. The dancing girls were gone, the music was silent.

Stiffy and Oliver Meek were among the few customers.

Stiffy gulped a drink and blew fiercely through his whiskers.

"Oliver," he said, "you sure are a ring-tailed bearcat with them guns of yours. I wonder, would you tell me how you do it?"

"Look here, Mr. Grant," said Meek. "I wish you'd quit talking about what I did. It was just an accident, anyhow. What I'm mainly interested in is this Asteroid Prowler you were telling me about. Is there any chance I might find him if I went out and looked?"

Stiffy choked, almost purple with astonishment.

"Good gravy," he said, "now you want to go out and tangle with the Prowler!"

"Not tangle with him," Meek declared. "Just look at him."

"Mister," Stiffy warned, "the best way to look at that thing is with a telescope. A good, powerful telescope."

The swinging doors swung open and a man walked in.

The newcomer walked directly toward the table occupied by Stiffy and Meek. He halted beside it, black beard jutting fearsomely, eyes bleakly cold.

"I'm Blacky Hoffman," he said. "I suppose you're Meek." He disregarded Stiffy.

Meek stood up and held out his hand.

"Glad to know you, Mr. Hoffman," he said.

Blacky took the proffered hand in some surprise.

"Seems I should know you, Meek, but I don't. Should have

heard of you at some time or other. A man like you would get talked about."

Meek shook his head. "I don't think you ever have. I never did anything to get talked about."

"Sit down," said Hoffman and it sounded like a command.

"I got to be going," Stiffy piped, already halfway to the door.

Hoffman poured out a drink and shoved the bottle at Meek. Meek gritted his teeth and poured a short one.

"No use beating around the bush," said Blacky. "We may as well get down to cases. I guess we understand one another."

Oliver Meek didn't know what the other meant, but he had to say something.

"I guess we do," he agreed.

"All right, then," said Hoffman. "I've built up a sweet little racket here and I don't like fellows butting in."

Meek essayed to down his liquor, succeeded, gasped for breath.

"But I could use a man like you," said Hoffman. "Luke tells me you are handy with the blasters."

"I practice sometimes," Meek admitted.

A smile twitched Hoffman's bearded lips. "We have the town just where we want it. The officials can't do a thing. Scared to. Marshals always eat rock or skip town. Maybe you would like to throw in with us. Not much to do, easy pickings."

"I'm sorry," said Meek, "but I can't do that."

"Listen, Meek," warned Hoffman, "you're either with us or you aren't. We don't like chiselers here. We know what to do with guys who try to muscle in. I don't know who you are or where you come from, but I'm telling you this . . . straight. If you don't come in, all right . . . but if you stick around after tonight I can't promise you protection."

Meek was silent, mulling the threat.

"You mean," he finally asked, "that you're ordering me out if I don't join your gang?"

Hoffman nodded. "That, big boy, is just exactly what I mean."

Slow anger and resentment ate at Meek. Who was this Hoffman to order him out of Asteroid City? This was a free Solar System, wasn't it? No wonder the Rev. Brown was jittery. No wonder the decent people wanted a clean-up.

Meek's anger mounted, a cold deadly anger that shook him like a frigid hand. An anger that almost frightened him, for very seldom in his life had he been really angry.

He rose slowly from the table, hitched his gun belt to a comfortable position.

"The town's been without a marshal for a long time, hasn't it?" he asked.

Hoffman's laugh boomed out. "You bet it has. And it's going to stay that way. The last one took it on the lam. The one before that got killed. The one before that sort of disappeared. . . ."

Meek spoke slowly, weak eyes burning.

"Horrible condition," he said. "Something's got to be done about it."

The streets were deserted, quiet, a deadly quiet that lurked and hovered, waiting for something to happen.

Oliver Meek polished his marshal's star with his coat sleeve, glanced up at the dome. Stars glittered, their light distorted by the heavy quartz. Stars in a dead black sky.

Bathed in the weak starlight, the mighty walls of the canyon reared above the dome. A canyon, the only sort of place where a city could rise on one of the planetoids. For the walls protected the dome against the deadly barrage of whizzing debris that continually shrieked down from space. Those mighty cragged mountains and dizzy cliffs were pocked with the blows dealt, through long eons, by that hail of armor-piercing projectiles.

Meek returned his gaze to the street, saw the lights of the Silver Moon. Nervously he felt of the papers in his inside pocket. Warrants for the arrest of John Hoffman for murder, Luke Blaine for murder, Jim Smithers for reckless shooting, Jake Loomis for assault and battery, Robert Blake for robbery.

And suddenly, Oliver Meek was afraid. For death waited him, he knew, inside the swinging doors of the Silver Moon. A death preluded by this quiet street.

Almost as if he were awaking from a dream, he found questions filling his brain. What was he doing here? Why had he gotten himself into a jam like this? What difference did it make to him what happened to Asteroid City?

It had been anger that had made him do it . . . that unaccountable anger which had flared when Hoffman told him to get out.

After all, what difference would a few days make? He was going to leave anyhow. He'd seen about all there was to see in Asteroid City. He wanted to see the Prowler and the stones with the strange inscriptions on them, but they were sights he could get along without.

If he turned around and walked the other way he could reach his space ship in just a few minutes. There was fuel enough to take him to Ganymede. No one would know until he was already gone. And after he was gone, what would he care what anybody thought?

He stood irresolutely, arguing with himself. Then he shook his head, resumed his march toward the Silver Moon.

A figure stepped from a dark doorway. Meek saw the threatening gleam of steel. His hands streaked toward his gun-butts, but something prodded him in the back and he froze, fingers touching metal.

"All right, marshal," said a mocking voice. "You just turn around and walk the other way."

He felt his guns lifted from their holsters and he turned around and walked. Footsteps crunched beside him and behind him, but otherwise he walked in silence.

"Where are you taking me?" he asked, his voice just a trifle shaky.

One of the men laughed.

"Just on a little trip, marshal. Out to take a look at Juno. It's a right pretty sight at night."

Juno wasn't pretty. For the most part, there was little of it one could see. The stars shed little light and the depressions were in shadow, while the cragged mountain tops seemed like shimmering mirages in the ghostly starlight.

The ship lay on a plateau between a needle-like range and a deep, shadowed valley.

"Now, marshal," said one of the men, "you stay right here. You'll see the Sun come up over that mountain back there. Interesting. Dawn on Juno is something to remember."

Meek started forward, but the other waved him back with his pistol.

"You're leaving me here?" shrieked Meek.

"Why sure," the man said. "You wanted to see the Solar System, didn't you?"

They backed away from him, guns in hand. Frozen in terror, he watched them enter the ship, saw the port close. An instant later the ship roared away, the backwash of its tubes buffeting Meek to the ground.

He struggled to his feet, watching the blasting tubes until they were out of sight. Clumsily he stepped forward and then stopped. There was no place to go . . . nothing to do.

Loneliness and fear swept over him in terrible waves of anguish. Fear that dwarfed any emotion he had ever felt. Fear of the ghostly shimmer of the peaks, fear of the shadow-blackened valley, fear of space and the mad, cold intensity of unwinking stars.

He fought for a grip on himself. It was fear such as this that drove men mad in space. He'd read about that, heard about it. Fear of the loneliness and the terrible depths of space . . . fear of the indifference of endless miles of void, fear of the unknown that always lurked just at elbow distance.

"Meek," he told himself, "you should have stayed at home."

Dawn came shortly, but no such dawn as one would see on Earth. Just a gradual dimming of the stars, a gradual lifting of the blacker darkness as a larger star, the Sun, swung above the peaks.

The stars still shone, but a gray light filtered over the landscape, made the mountains solid things instead of ghostly shapes.

Jagged peaks loomed on one side of the plateau, fearsome depths on the other. A meteor thudded somewhere to his right and Meek shuddered. There was no sound of the impact but he could feel the vibrations of the blow as the whizzing mass struck the cliffs.

But it was foolish to be afraid of meteors, he told himself. He had greater and more immediate worries.

There were less than eight hours of air left in the tanks of his space suit. He had no idea where he was, although he knew that many miles of rugged, fearsome country stretched between him and Asteroid City.

The space suit carried no food and no water, but that was of minor moment, he realized, for his air would give out long before he felt the pangs of thirst or hunger.

He sat down on a massive boulder and tried to think. There wasn't much to think about. Everywhere his thoughts met black walls. The situation, he told himself, was hopeless.

If only he hadn't come to Asteroid City in the first place! Or having come, if he had only minded his business, this never would have happened. If he hadn't been so anxious to show off what he knew about card dealing tricks. If only he hadn't agreed to be sworn in as marshal. If he'd swallowed his pride and left when Hoffman told him to.

He brushed away such thoughts as futile, took stock of his surroundings.

The cliff on the right hand side was undercut, overhanging several hundred feet of level ground.

Ponderously, he heaved himself off the boulder, wandered aimlessly up the wider tongue of plateau. The undercut, he saw, grew deeper, forming a deep cleft, as if someone had furrowed out the mountain side. Heavy shadows clung within it.

Suddenly he stopped, riveted to the ground, scarcely daring to breathe.

Something was moving in the deep shadow of the undercut. Something that seemed to glint faintly with reflected light.

The thing lurched forward and, in the fleeting instant before he turned and ran, Oliver Meek had an impression of a barrel-like body, a long neck, a cruel mouth, monstrous eyes that glowed with hidden fires.

There was no speculation in Oliver Meek's mind. From the description given him by Stiffy, from the very terror of the thing, he knew the being shambling toward him was the Asteroid Prowler.

With a shriek of pure fear, Meek turned and fled and behind him came the Prowler, its head swaying on the end of its whip-like neck.

Meek's legs worked like pistons, his breath gasping in his throat, his body soaring through space as he covered long distances at each leap under the influence of lesser gravity.

Thunderous blasts hammered at the earphones in his helmet and as he ran he craned his head skyward.

Shooting down toward the plateau, forward rockets braking, was a small spaceship!

Hope rose within him and he glanced back over his shoulder. Hope died instantly. The Prowler was gaining on him, gaining fast.

Suddenly his legs gave out. Simply folded up, worn out with the punishment they had taken. He threw up his arms to shield his helmet plate and sobbed in panic.

The Asteroid Prowler would get him now. Sure as shooting. Just at the minute rescue came, the Prowler would get him.

But the Prowler didn't get him. Nothing happened at all. Surprised, he sat up and spun around, crouching.

The ship had landed, almost at the edge of the plateau and a man was tumbling out of the port. The Prowler had changed his course, was galloping toward the ship.

The man from the ship ran in leaping bounds, a pistol in one gloved hand, and his yelp of terror rang in Meek's earphones.

"Run, dang you. Run! That dad-blamed Prowler will be after us any minute now."

"Stiffy," yelled Meek. "Stiffy, you came out to get me."

Stiffy landed beside him, hauled him to his feet.

"Dang right I came to get you," he panted. "I thought them hoodlums would be up to some dirty tricks, so I stuck around and watched."

He jerked at Meek's arm.

"Come on, Oliver, we got to get along."

But Meek jerked his arm away.

"Look what he's doing!" he shouted. "Just look at him!"

The Prowler seemed to be bent on systematic destruction of the space ship. His jaws were ripping at the steel plating . . . Ripping at it and tearing it away, peeling it off the frame as one might peel an orange.

"Hey," howled Stiffy. "You can't do that. Get out of there, you danged . . ."

The Prowler turned to look at them, a heavy power cable in its mouth.

"You'll be electrocuted," yelped Stiffy. "Danged if it won't serve you right."

But, far from being electrocuted, the Prowler seemed to be enjoying himself. He sucked at the power cable and his eyes glowed blissfully.

Stiffy flourished his pistol.

"Get away," he yelled. "Get away or I'll blister your danged hide."

Almost playfully the Prowler minced away from the ship, feet dancing.

"He did it!" said Meek.

"Did what?" Stiffy scowled bewilderedly.

"Got away from that ship, just like you told him to."

Stiffy snorted. "Don't even kid yourself he did it because I told him to. He couldn't even hear me, probably. Living out here like this, he wouldn't have anything to hear with. Probably he's just trying to decide which one of us he'll catch first. Better be ready to kick you up some dust."

The Prowler trotted toward them, head bobbing up and down.

"Get going," Stiffy yelled at Meek and brought up his pistol. A blue shaft of light whipped out, smacked the Prowler in the head, but the Prowler didn't even falter in his stride. The energy charge seemed to have no power at all. It didn't even spatter . . . it looked as if the blue pencil of raging death was boring straight into the spread of forehead between the monstrous eyes.

"Run, you danged fool," Stiffy screeched at Meek. "I can't hold him off."

But Meek didn't run . . . instead he sprang straight into the Prowler's path, arm upraised.

"Stop!" he yelled.

III

The Prowler skidded to a stop, his metal hooves leaving scratches on the solid rock.

For a moment the three of them stood stock still, Stiffy's jaw hanging in astonishment.

Meek reached out a hand and patted the Prowler's massive shoulder.

"Good boy," he said. "Good boy."

"Come away from there!" Stiffy yelled in sudden terror. "Just one good gulp and that guy would have you."

"Ah, shucks," said Meek, "he won't hurt anybody. He's only hungry, that's all."

"That," declared Stiffy, "is just what I'm afraid of."

"You don't understand," insisted Meek. "He isn't hungry for us. He's starved for energy. Give him another shot from the gun."

Stiffy stared at the gun hanging in his hand.

"You're sure it wouldn't make him sore?" he asked.

"Gosh, no," said Meek. "That's what he wants. He soaks it up. Didn't you notice how the beam went right into him without spattering or anything. And the way he sucked that power cable. He drained your ship of every drop of energy it had."

"He did what?" yelped Stiffy.

"He drained the ship of energy. That's what he lives on. That's why he chased you. He wanted you to keep on shooting."

Stiffy clapped a hand to his forehead.

"We're sunk for certain, now," he declared. "There might have been a chance to get back with just a few plates ripped off the ship. But with all the energy gone . . ."

"Hey, Stiffy," yelled Meek, "take a look at this."

Stiffy moved nearer, cautiously.

"What you got now?" he demanded irritably.

"These marks on his shoulder," said Meek. His gloved finger shook excitedly as he pointed. "They're the same kind of marks as were on those stones I read about in the book. Marks no one could read. Fellow who wrote the book figured they were made by some other race that had visited Juno. Maybe a race from outside the Solar System, even."

"Good gravy," said Stiffy, in awe, "you don't think . . ."

"Sure, I do," Meek declared with the air of a man who is sure of his knowledge. "A race came here one time and they had the Prowler along. For some reason they left him. Maybe he was just a robot and they didn't have room for him, or maybe something happened to them . . ."

"Say," said Stiffy, "I bet you that's just what he is. A robot. Attuned to thought waves. That's why he minds you."

"That's what I figured," Meek agreed. "Thought waves would be the same, no matter who thought them . . . human being or a . . . well . . . or something else."

A sudden thought struck Stiffy. "Maybe them guys found

the Lost Mine! By cracky, that would be something, wouldn't it? Maybe this critter could lead us to it."

"Maybe?" Meek said doubtfully.

Meek patted the Prowler's rocky shoulder gently, filled with wonder. In some unguessed time, in some unknown sector of space, the Prowler had been fashioned by an alien people. For some reason they had made him, for some reason they had left him here. Abandonment or purpose?

Meek shook his head. That would be something to puzzle over later, something to roll around in his brain on some monotonous flight into the maw of space.

Space! Startled at the thought clanging on his brain he jerked a quick glance upward, saw the bleak stars staring at him. Eyes that seemed to be laughing at him, cruel, ironic laughter.

"Stiffy," he whispered. "Stiffy, I just thought of something."

"Yeah, what is it?"

Stark terror walked in Meek's words. "My oxygen tank is better than half gone. And the ship is wrecked. . . ."

"Cripes," said Stiffy, "I guess we just forgot. We sure are behind the eight ball. Somehow we got to get back to Asteroid City. And we got to get there quick."

Meek's eyes brightened. "Stiffy, maybe . . . Maybe we could ride the Prowler."

Stiffy backed away. But Meek reached out and grasped his arm. "Come on. It's the only way, Stiffy. We have to get there and the Prowler can take us."

"But . . . but . . . but . . ." Stiffy stammered.

"Give me a leg up," Meek ordered.

Stiffy complied and Meek leaped astride the broad metal back, reached down and hauled Stiffy aboard.

"Get going, you flea-bitten nag!" Meek yipped, in sudden elation.

There was reason for elation. Not until that moment had he stopped to consider the Prowler might object to being ridden. Might consider it an insult.

The Prowler apparently was astonished, but that was all. He shook his head in bewilderment and weaved his neck around as if he wasn't quite sure just what to do. But at least he hadn't started to take the place apart.

"Giddap!" yelled Stiffy, bringing the butt of his pistol down.

The Prowler jigged a little, then gathered himself together and started. The landscape blurred with speed as he leaped a mighty boulder, skipped along a narrow ledge around a slick-faced mountain, skidded a hairpin turn.

Meek and Stiffy fought desperately to hang on. The metal back was slick and broad and there weren't any handholds. They bounced and thumped, almost fell off a dozen times.

"Stiffy," yelled Meek, "how do we know he's taking us to Asteroid City?"

"Don't fret about that," said Stiffy. "He knows where we want to go. He read our minds."

"I hope so," Meek said, prayerfully.

The Prowler whished around a right angle turn on a narrow ledge and the distant peaks wheeled sickeningly against the sky.

Meek lay flat on his belly and hugged the Prowler's sides. The mountains whistled past. He stole a look at the jagged peaks on the near horizon and they looked like a tight board fence.

Oliver Meek fought manfully to get back his composure as the Prowled pranced down the main street of Asteroid City.

The sidewalks were lined with hundreds of staring faces, faces that dropped in astonishment and disbelief.

Stiffy was yelling at someone. "Now, doggone you, will you believe there is a Prowler?"

And the man he yelled at didn't have a word to say, just stood and stared.

In the swarm of faces, Meek saw those of the Reverend Harold Brown and Andrew Smith and, almost as if in a dream, he waved jauntily to them. At least, he hoped the wave was jaunty. Wouldn't do to let them know his knees were too weak to hold him up.

Smith waved back and shouted something, but the Reverend Brown's jaw hung open and he seemed too wonder-struck to move.

This, thought Meek, is the kind of thing you read about. The conquering hero coming home astride his mighty charger. Only the conquering hero, he remembered with a sudden twinge, usually was a young lad who sat straight in the saddle instead of an old man with shoulders hunched from thirty years of poring over dusty ledgers.

A man was stepping out into the street, a man who carried a gun in hand and suddenly Meek realized they were abreast of the Silver Moon.

The armed man was Blacky Hoffman.

Here, thought Meek, is where I get it. This is what I get for playing the big shot . . . for being a smart alec, for remembering how cards shouldn't be dealt and for shooting a man's gun out of his hand and letting myself be talked into being a marshal.

But he sat stiff and as straight as he could on the Prowler and kept his eyes on Hoffman. That was the only way to do. That was the way all the heroes did in the stories he had read. And doggone, he was a hero. Whether he liked it or not, he was one.

The street was hushed with sudden tension and the very air seemed to be crackling with the threat of direful happenings.

Hoffman's voice rang crisply through the stillness.

"Go for your blasters, Meek!"

"I have no blasters," Meek told him calmly. "Your hoodlums took them from me."

"Borrow Stiffy's," snapped Hoffman, and added, with a nasty laugh: "You won't need them long."

Meek nodded, watching Hoffman narrowly. Slowly he reached back for Stiffy's gun. He felt it in his hand, wrapped his fingers tightly around it.

Funny, he thought, how calm he was. Like he had been in the Silver Moon that night. There was something about a gun. It changed him, turned him into another man.

He didn't have a chance, he knew. Hoffman would shoot

before he could ever get the gun around. But despite that, he felt foolishly sure. . . .

Hoffman's gun flashed in the weak sunlight, blooming with blue brilliance.

For an instant, a single fraction of a second, Meek saw the flash of the beam straight in his eyes, but even before he could involuntarily flinch, the beam had bent. True to its mark, it would have drilled Meek straight between the eyes . . . but it didn't go straight to its mark. Instead, it bent and slapped itself straight between the Prowler's eyes.

And the Prowler danced a little jig of happiness as the blue spear of energy knifed into its metal body.

"Cripes," gasped Stiffy, "he draws it! He ain't satisfied with just taking it when you give it to him. He reaches out and gets it. Just like a lightning rod reaching up and grabbing lightning."

Puzzlement flashed across Hoffman's face, then incredulity and finally something that came close to fear. The gun's beam snapped off and his hands sagged. The gun dropped in the dust. The Prowler stood stock still.

"Well, Hoffman?" Meek asked quietly, and his voice seemed to run all along the street.

Hoffman's face twitched.

"Get down and fight like a man," he rasped.

"No," said Meek, "I don't do that. Because it wouldn't be man to man. It would be me against your entire gang."

Hoffman started to back away, slowly, step by furtive step. Step by step the Prowler stalked him there in the silent street.

Then Hoffman, with a scream of terror, broke and ran.

"Get him!" Meek roared at the Prowler.

The Prowler, with one lightning lunge, one flip of its whip-like neck, got him. Got him, gently, as Meek had meant he should.

Howling in mingled rage and terror, Hoffman dangled by the seat of his pants from the Prowler's beak. Neatly as any circus horse, the Prowler wheeled and trotted back to the Silver Moon, carrying Hoffman with a certain gentle grace that was not lost upon the crowd.

Hoffman quieted and the crowd's jeers rang against the dome. The Prowler pranced a bit, jiggled Hoffman up and down.

Meek raised a hand for silence, spoke to Hoffman. "O.K., Mr. Hoffman, call out your men. All of them. Out into the middle of the street. Where we can see them."

Hoffman swore at him.

"Jiggle him some," Meek told the Prowler. The Prowler jiggled him and Hoffman bawled and clawed at empty air.

"Damn you," shrieked Hoffman, "get out into the street. All of you. Just like he said."

No one stirred.

"Blaine," yelled Hoffman. "Get out there! You, too, Smithers. Loomis. Blake!"

They came slowly, shame-faced. At a command from Meek they unholstered their blasters and heaved them in a pile.

The Prowler deposited Hoffman with them.

Meek saw Andrew Smith standing at the edge of the sidewalk and nodded to him.

"There you are, Mr. Smith. Rounded up, just like you wanted them."

"Neat," said Stiffy, "but not gaudy."

Slowly, carefully, bones aching, Meek slid from the Prowler's back, was surprised his legs would hold him up.

"Come in and have a drink," yelled a dozen voices all at once.

"Bet your life," agreed Stiffy, licking his chops.

Men were slapping Meek on the back, yelling at him. Yelling friendly things, calling him an old he-wolf.

He tried to thrust out his chest but didn't succeed too well. He hoped they wouldn't insist on his drinking a lot of *bocca*.

A hand tugged at Meek's elbow. It was the Reverend Brown.

"You aren't going to leave that beast out here all alone?" he asked. "No telling what he might do."

"Ah, shucks," protested Stiffy, "he's gentle as a kitten. Stands without hitching."

But even as he spoke, the Prowler lifted his head, almost as if he were sniffing, started down the street at a swinging trot.

"Hey," yelled Stiffy, "come back here, you cross-eyed crow-bait!"

The Prowler didn't falter in his stride. He went even faster.

Cold fear gripped Meek by the throat. He tried to speak and gulped instead. He'd just thought of something. The power plant that supplied Asteroid City with its power and light, the very oxygen it breathed, was down that way.

A power plant and an alien robot that was starved for energy!

"My stars!" gasped Meek.

He shook off the minister's hand and galloped down the street, shrieking at the Prowler. But the Prowler had no thought of stopping.

Panting, Meek slowed from a gallop to a trot, then to a labored walk. Behind him, he heard Stiffy puffing along. Behind Stiffy trailed practically the entire population of Asteroid City.

Far ahead came the sound of rending steel and crashing structure as the Prowler ripped the plant apart to get at the juice.

Stiffy gained Meek's side and panted at him. "Cripes, they'll crucify us for this. We got to get him out of there."

"How?" asked Meek.

"Danged if I know," said Stiffy.

One side of the plant was a mass of tangled wreckage, surrounding a hole out of which protruded the Prowler's hind quarters. Terrified workers and maintenance men were running for their lives. Live wires spat and crackled with flaming energy.

IV

Meek and Stiffy halted a half block away, breath whistling in their throats. The Prowler's tail, protruding from the hole in the side of the plant, twitched happily. Meek regarded the scene with doleful thoughts.

"I wish," Stiffy declared, "we'd stayed out there and died. It would have been easier than what's liable to happen to us now."

Feet thumped behind them and a hand grabbed Meek's shoulder, grabbed it hard. It was Andrew Smith, a winded, apoplectic Andrew Smith.

"What are you going to do?" he shouted at Meek.

Meek swallowed hard, tried to make his voice even. "Just studying over the situation, Mr. Smith. I'll figure out something in a minute."

"Sure he will," insisted Stiffy. "Leave him alone. Give him time. He always does what he says he'll do. He said he'd round up Blacky for you, and he did. He went out single-handed and captured the Prowler. He . . ."

"Yeah," yelled Smith, "and he said the Prowler would stand without hitching, too. And did he stand? I ask you . . ."

"He didn't say that," Stiffy interrupted, testily. "I said that."

"It don't make a bit of difference who said it," shrieked Smith. "I got stock in that plant there. And the Prowler's ruining it. He's jeopardizing the life of this whole city. And it's all your fault. You brought him here. I'll sue you, the both of you, so help me . . ."

"Ah, shut up," snapped Stiffy. "Who can think with you blabbering around?"

Smith danced in rage. "Who's blabbering? I got a good mind to . . ."

He doubled up his fist and started toward Stiffy.

And once again Oliver Meek did something he never would have thought of doing back on Earth. He put out his gloved hand, deliberately, and pushed Smith in the face. Pushed hard, so hard that Smith thumped down in the dust of the street and sat there, silenced by surprise.

Without even looking back, Meek strode purposefully down the street toward the Prowler. What he meant to do he did not know. What he possibly could do he had no idea. But anything was better than standing there while the crowd screamed at him and men shook their fists at him.

Why, they might even lynch him! He shivered at the thought. But men still did things like that. Especially when someone monkeyed around with the very things they depended on for life out here in naked space. Maybe they'd turn him out on Juno with only an hour or two of oxygen. Maybe they'd . . .

Stiffy was yelling at him. "Come back, you danged old fool . . ."

Suddenly the ground leaped and bucked beneath Meek's feet. The power reeled before his startled eyes and then, somehow, he was on his back, watching the dome wheel and weave above him.

Fighting for breath that had been knocked out of him, he clawed his way to his knees, tried to stand erect, but the ground still was crawling with motion.

It was like an earthquake, he told himself, startled that he could even think. But it couldn't be an earthquake. Juno didn't have earthquakes, there was no reason for Juno to have earthquakes. The little planetoid eons ago had cooled through and through, each rock, each strata had found its place. Juno was dead, dead as the reaches of space itself, and earthquakes don't happen on dead planets.

Out of the corner of his eyes he saw the Prowler had backed out of the hole in the power plant, was standing with four legs spread wide, bracing himself. His long neck was stretched high in the air and the ugly, toothy head had the look of quick alertness.

Meek gained his feet, stood tottering, keeping upright by some fancy footwork. The Prowler started toward him, legs gathering speed, heading down the street.

With a hoarse whoop, Meek steadied himself, half crouched and held his breath. Sprawling, he leaped, leaped so hard he almost vaulted over the beast's broad back. He scrambled into position astride the running robot, saw Stiffy leaping at him. Quickly he shot out a hand, grasped Stiffy and hauled him aboard.

Ahead of them the crowd rushed for safety, leaving a broad avenue for the storming Prowler and his two riders.

"Get the locks open," yelled Stiffy. "Here we come!"

The crowd took up the shriek. "Get the locks open!"

The Prowler swept down the street, hoofs clattering like hammer blows. Ahead of them the inner lock swung open. As the Prowler bulleted into the entrance tunnel, the outer lock swung out and for a few wild seconds air screamed and howled, rushing from the city into the vacuum of space.

In frantic haste, Meek and Stiffy worked with their helmets, getting them clamped down. Then they were out in the open, the gleaming city behind them.

Less than half a mile away loomed a massive boulder towering a hundred feet or more above the level of the canyon floor. The Prowler made a beeline for it.

"Oliver," yelled Stiffy, "that thing wasn't there before. Look, it almost blocks the canyon!"

The bounder was black but it crawled with a greenish glow, a faint network of somber fire.

The breath caught in Meek's throat.

"Stiffy," he whispered.

Behind him, Stiffy almost sobbed in excitement. "Yeah, I know. it's a meteor. And it's lousy with radium."

"If just fell," said Meek, voice unsteady. "That's what shook up the place. Wonder is it didn't crack the dome wide open."

"We better jump for it," urged Stiffy. "If we don't want to get plumb burned. Can't go near that thing without lead sheathing."

Meek flung himself sidewise, throwing up his arms to shield his helmet, struck on his shoulders and rolled. Slowly, benumbed from the fall, he crept out of the shadow of a high rock wall into the starlight.

Stiffy was sitting on the ground, rubbing his shins.

"Barked them up some," he admitted.

Up the valley the Prowler was arching its back and rubbing against the green-glowing boulder.

"Just like a dad-blamed cat that has found some catnip," said Stiffy. "Must sort of like that radium."

He rose slowly, dusted off his suit.

"Well," he suggested, "let's you and me go into action."

"Action?"

"Sure. Let's go back and file us a claim on that meteor. Don't need to worry about anybody else jumping it, cause every dad-blamed one of them is scared speechless of the Prowler. They won't go near the meteor long as he's around."

Meek stared at the meteor speculatively. "That's worth a lot of money, isn't it, Stiffy? Filled with radium like that."

"Bet your boots," said Stiffy cheerfully. "We go fifty-fifty on her. Split equal ways. We're pardners."

"Tell you what you do," Meek said slowly. "You take it all. Just take out enough to fix up the damage back there and call that my share."

Stiffy's jaw drooped. "Say, what you getting at?"

"I'm leaving," said Meek.

"Good gravy! Leaving! And just when we made us a strike."

"You don't understand," said Meek. "I didn't come out here to find radium. Or to arrest gangs. Or even to capture an Asteroid Prowler. I just came out to look around. Nice and quiet. Didn't want to bother anybody. Didn't want anybody to bother me."

"Doggone it," said Stiffy, "and I was just figuring maybe, soon as we cleaned up the radium, we might get that Prowler to lead us to the Lost Mine."

Meek brightened. "I have a hunch I know where that Lost Mine is, Stiffy. Remember there was a cut-back in the cliff near where we found the Prowler. Well, when I first saw him, he was in that place. Got a hunch maybe that's the mine."

Stiffy grinned. "So you're sticking with me."

Meek shook his head. "No, I'm still leaving."

"Just like that?" said Stiffy.

Stiffy held out his hand, "O.K., if that's what you want to do.

I'll bank your half in the First Martian back on Earth. Leave my address there. Might want to get in touch with me some time."

Meek gripped his hand. "You don't need to do that. Take all of it. Just see the plant's fixed up."

Stiffy's eyes shone queerly, moistly in the starlight. "Shucks, there's enough for both of us. More than enough." His voice was rough. "Now get along with you."

Meek started to walk away.

"Goodbye, Stiffy," he called.

"So long," Stiffy shouted.

Meek hesitated. It seemed there should have been more he could have said. Some way to let Stiffy know he liked him. Some way to tell him he was a friend in a life which had known few friends.

He tried to think of ways to put what he felt in words, but there wasn't any way, none that didn't sound awkward and sentimental.

He wheeled about, headed for the space port. His feet went faster and faster, until finally he was running.

He had to get out of here, he told himself, before he got into another jam. His luck was stretched too thin already. A fellow just couldn't go on having luck like that.

And besides, there was all of space to roam in, other places to see. That was what he had set out to do. To see the Solar System in his own ship, to do all the things he'd dreamed about back in the cubby hole at Lunar Exports, Inc.

And he was going to do just that, he promised himself. Although he hoped the next stop would be more peaceable.

Oliver Meek sighed happily – *this was the life*.

NEIGHBOR

If one were forced to choose a single particular story that would most represent Clifford D. Simak's best-known literary image, this would be that story: a story of the alien coming to backcountry middle America, told from the point of view of one of those country people. No one else – not even Cliff himself – ever did this better, nor ever will.

—dww

Coon Valley is a pleasant place, but there's no denying it's sort of off the beaten track and it's not a place where you can count on getting rich because the farms are small and a lot of the ground is rough. You can farm the bottomlands, but the hillsides are only good for pasture and the roads are just dirt roads, impassable at certain times of year.

The old-timers, like Bert Smith and Jingo Harris and myself, are well satisfied to stay here, for we grew up with the country and we haven't any illusions about getting rich and we'd feel strange and out-of-place anywhere but in the valley. But there are others, newcomers, who move in and get discouraged after a while and up and move away, so there usually is a farm or two standing idle, waiting to be sold.

We are just plain dirt farmers, with emphasis on the dirt, for we can't afford a lot of fancy machinery and we don't go in for blooded stock – but there's nothing wrong with us; we're just everyday, the kind of people you meet all over these United States. Because we're out of the way and some of the families have lived here for so long, I suppose you could say that we have gotten clannish. But that doesn't mean we don't like outside folks; it just means we've lived so long together that we've got to know and like one another and are satisfied with things just as they are.

We have radios, of course, and we listen to the programs and the news, and some of us take daily papers, but I'm afraid that we may be a bit provincial, for it's fairly hard to get us stirred up much about world happenings. There's so much of interest right here in the valley we haven't got the time to worry about all those outside things. I imagine you'd call us conservative, for most of us vote Republican without even wondering why and there's none of us who has much time for all this government interference in the farming business.

The valley has always been a pleasant place – not only the land, but the people in it, and we've always been fortunate in the new neighbors that we get. Despite new ones coming in every year or so, we've never had a really bad one and that means a lot to us.

But we always worry a little when one of the new ones up and moves away and we speculate among ourselves, wondering what kind of people will buy or rent the vacant farm.

The old Lewis farm had been abandoned for a long time, the buildings all run down and gone to ruin and the fields gone back to grass. A dentist over at Hopkins Corners had rented it for several years and run some cattle in it, driving out on weekends to see how they were doing. We used to wonder every now and then if anyone would ever farm the place again, but finally we quit wondering, for the buildings had fallen into such disrepair that we figured no one ever would. I went in one day and talked to the banker at Hopkins Corners, who had the renting of the place, and told him I'd like to take it over if the dentist ever gave it up. But he told me the owners, who lived in Chicago then, were anxious to sell rather than to rent it, although he didn't seem too optimistic that anyone would buy it.

Then one spring a new family moved onto the farm and in time we learned it had been sold and that the new family's name was Heath – Reginald Heath. And Bert Smith said to me, "Reginald! That's a hell of a name for a farmer!" But that was all he said.

Jingo Harris stopped by one day, coming home from town, when he saw Heath out in the yard, to pass the time of day. It was a neighborly thing to do, of course, and Heath seemed glad to have him stop, although Jingo said he seemed to be a funny kind of man to be a farmer.

"He's a foreigner," Jingo told me. "Sort of dark. Like he might be a Spaniard or from one of those other countries. I don't know how he got that Reginald. Reginald is English and Heath's no Englishman."

Later on we heard that the Heaths weren't really Spanish, but were Rumanians or Bulgarians and that they were refugees from the Iron Curtain.

But Spanish, or Rumanian, or Bulgarian, the Heaths were workers. There was Heath and his wife and a half-grown girl and all three of them worked all the blessed time. They paid attention to their business and didn't bother anyone and because of this we liked them, although we didn't have much to do with them. Not that we didn't want to or that they didn't want us to; it's just that in a community like ours new folks sort of have to grow in instead of being taken in.

Heath had an old beaten-up, wired-together tractor that made a lot of noise, and as soon as the soil was dry enough to plow he started out to turn over the fields that through the years had grown up to grass. I used to wonder if he worked all night long, for many times when I went to bed I heard the tractor running. Although that may not be as late as it sounds to city dwellers, for here in the valley we go to bed early – and get up early, too.

One night after dark I set out to hunt some cows, a couple of fence-jumping heifers that gave me lots of trouble. Just let a man come in late from work and tired and maybe it's raining a little and dark as the inside of a cat and those two heifers would turn up missing and I'd have to go and hunt them. I tried all the different kinds of pokes and none of them did any good. When a heifer gets to fence-jumping there isn't much that can be done with her.

So I lit a lantern and set out to hunt for them, but I hunted for two hours and didn't find a trace of them. I had just about decided to give up and go back home when I heard the sound of a tractor running and realized that I was just above the west field of the old Lewis place. To get home I'd have to go right past the field and I figured it might be as well to wait when I reached the field until the tractor came around and ask Heath if he had seen the heifers.

It was a dark night, with thin clouds hiding the stars and a wind blowing high in the treetops and there was a smell of rain in the air. Heath, I figured, probably was staying out extra late to finish up the field ahead of the coming rain, although I remember that I thought he was pushing things just a little hard. Already he was far ahead of all the others in the valley with his plowing.

So I made my way down the steep hillside and waded the creek at a shallow place I knew and while I was doing this I heard the tractor make a complete round of the field. I look for the headlight, but I didn't see it and I thought probably the trees had hidden it from me.

I reached the edge of the field and climbed through the fence, walking out across the furrows to intercept the tractor. I heard it make the turn to the east of me and start down the field toward me and although I could hear the noise of it, there wasn't any light.

I found the last furrow and stood there waiting, sort of wondering, not too alarmed as yet, how Heath managed to drive the rig without any light. I thought that maybe he had cat's eyes and could see in the dark and although it seemed funny later when I remembered it, the idea that a man might have cat's eyes did not seem funny then.

The noise kept getting louder and it seemed to be coming pretty close, when all at once the tractor rushed out of the dark and seemed to leap at me. I guess I must have been afraid that it would run over me, for I jumped back a yard or two, with my heart up in my neck. But I needn't have bothered, for I was out of the way to start with.

The tractor went on past me and I waved the lantern and yelled for Heath to stop and as I waved the lantern the light was thrown onto the rear of the tractor and I saw there was no one on it.

A hundred things went through my mind, but the one idea that stuck was that Heath had fallen off the tractor and might be lying injured, somewhere in the field.

I ran after the tractor, thinking to shut it down before it got loose and ran into a tree or something, but by the time I reached it, it had reached a turn and it was making that turn as neatly as if it had been broad daylight and someone had been driving it.

I jumped up on the drawbar and grabbed the seat, hauling myself up. I reached out a hand, grabbing for the throttle, but with my hand upon the metal I didn't pull it back. The tractor had completed the turn now and was going down the furrow – and there was something else.

Take an old tractor, now – one that wheezed and coughed and hammered and kept threatening to fall apart, like this one did – and you are bound to get a lot of engine vibration. But in this tractor there was no vibration. It ran along as smooth as a high-priced car and the only jolts you got were when the wheels hit a bump or slight gully in the field.

I stood there, hanging onto the lantern with one hand and clutching the throttle with the other, and I didn't do a thing. I just rode down to the point where the tractor started to make another turn. Then I stepped off and went on home. I didn't hunt for Heath lying in the field, for I knew he wasn't there.

I suppose I wondered how it was possible, but I didn't really fret myself too much trying to figure it all out. I imagine, in the first place, I was just too numb. You may worry a lot about little things that don't seem quite right, but when you run into a big thing, like that self-operating tractor, you sort of give up automatically, knowing that it's too big for your brain to handle, that it's something you haven't got a chance of solving. And after a while you forget it because it's something you can't live with. So your mind rejects it.

I got home and stood out in the barnyard for a moment, listening. The wind was blowing fairly hard by then and the first drops of rain were falling, but every now and then, when the wind would quiet down, I could hear the tractor.

I went inside the house and Helen and the kids were all in bed and sound asleep, so I didn't say anything about it that night. And the next morning, when I had a chance to think about it, I didn't say anything at all. Mostly, I suppose, because I knew no one would believe me and that I'd have to take a lot of kidding about automatic tractors.

Heath got his plowing done and his crops in, well ahead of everyone in the valley. The crops came up in good shape and we had good growing weather; then along in June we got a spell of wet, and everyone got behind with corn plowing because you can't go out in the field when the ground is soggy. All of us chored around our places, fixing fences and doing other odd jobs, cussing out the rain and watching the weeds grow like mad in the unplowed field.

All of us, that is, except Heath. His corn was clean as a whistle and you had to hunt to find a weed. Jingo stopped by one day and asked him how he managed, but Heath just laughed a little, in that quiet way of his, and talked of something else.

The first apples finally were big enough for green-apple pies and there is no one in the county makes better green-apple pies than Helen. She wins prizes with her pies every year at the county fair and she is proud of them.

One day she wrapped up a couple of pies and took them over to the Heaths. It's a neighborly way we have of doing in the valley, with the women running back and forth from one neighbor to another with their cooking. Each of them has some dish she likes to show off to the neighbors and it's a sort of harmless way of bragging.

Helen and the Heaths got along just swell. She was late in getting home and I was starting supper, with the kids yelling they were hungry when-do-we-eat-around-here, when she finally showed up.

She was full of talk about the Heaths – how they had fixed up the house, you never would have thought anyone could do so much to such a terribly run-down place as they had, and about the garden they had – especially about the garden. It was a big one, she said, and beautifully taken care of and it was full of vegetables she had never seen before. The funniest things you ever saw, she said. Not the ordinary kind of vegetables.

We talked some about those vegetables, speculating that maybe the Heaths had brought the seeds out with them from behind the Iron Curtain, although so far as I could remember, vegetables were vegetables, no matter where you were. They grew the same things in Russia or Rumania or Timbuktu as we did. And, anyhow, by this time I was getting a little skeptical about that story of their escaping from Rumania.

But we didn't have the time for much serious speculation on the Heaths, although there was plenty of casual gossip going around the neighborhood. Haying came along and then the small-grain harvest and everyone was busy. The hay was good and the small-grain crop was fair, but it didn't look like we'd get much corn. For we hit a drought. That's the way it goes – too much rain in June, not enough in August.

We watched the corn and watched the sky and felt hopeful when a cloud showed up, but the clouds never meant a thing. It just seems at times that God isn't on your side.

Then one morning Jingo Harris showed up and stood around, first on one foot, then the other, talking to me while I worked on an old corn binder that was about worn out and which it didn't look nohow I'd need to use that year.

"Jingo," I said, after I'd watched him fidget for an hour or more, "you got something on your mind?"

He blurted it out then. "Heath got rain last night," he said.

"No one else did," I told him.

"I guess you're right," said Jingo. "Heath's the only one."

He told me how he'd gone to cut through Heath's north corn-field, carrying back a couple of balls of binder twine he'd bor-rowed from Bert Smith. It wasn't until he'd crawled through the fence that he noticed the field was wet, soaked by a heavy rain.

"It must have happened in the night," he said.

He thought it was funny, but figured maybe there had been a shower across the lower end of the valley, although as a rule rains travel up and down the valley, not across it. But when he had crossed the corner of the field and crawled through the fence, he noticed it hadn't rained at all. So he went back and walked around the field and the rain had fallen on the field, but nowhere else. It began at the fence and ended at the fence.

When he'd made a circuit of the field he sat down on one of the balls of twine and tried to get it all thought out, but it made no sense – furthermore, it was plain unbelievable.

Jingo is a thorough man. He likes to have all the evidence and know all there is to know before he makes up his mind. So he went over to Heath's second corn patch, on the west side of the valley. And once again, he found that it had rained on that field – on the field, but not around the field.

"What do you make of it?" Jingo asked me and I said I didn't know. I came mighty close to telling him about the unmanned tractor, but I thought better of it. After all, there was no point in getting the neighborhood stirred up.

After Jingo left I got in the car and drove over to the Heath farm, intending to ask him if he could loan me his posthole digger for a day or two. Not that I was going to dig any postholes, but you have to have some excuse for showing up at a neighbor's place.

I never got a chance to ask him for that posthole digger, though. Once I got there I never even thought of it.

Heath was sitting on the front steps of the porch and he seemed glad to see me. He came down to the car and shook my hand and said, "It's good to see you, Calvin." The way he said it made me feel friendly and sort of important, too – especially that Calvin business, for everyone else just calls me Cal. I'm not down-right sure, in fact, that anyone in the neighborhood remembers that my name is Calvin.

"I'd like to show you around the place," he said. "We've done some fixing up."

Fixing up wasn't exactly the word for it. The place was spick-and-span. It looked like some of those Pennsylvania and Connecticut farms you see in the magazines. The house and all the other buildings had been ramshackle with all the paint peeled off them and looking as if they might fall down at any minute. But now they had a sprightly, solid look and they gleamed with paint. They didn't look new, of course, but they looked as if they'd always been well taken care of and painted every year. The fences were all fixed up and painted, too, and the weeds were cut and a couple of old unsightly scrap-lumber piles had been cleaned up and burned. Heath had even tackled an old iron and machinery junk pile and had it sorted out.

"There was a lot to do," said Heath, "but I feel it's worth it. I have an orderly soul. I like to have things neat."

Which might be true, of course, but he'd done it all in less than six months' time. He'd come to the farm in early March and it was only August and he'd not only put in some hundred acres of crops and done all the other farm work, but he'd got the place fixed up. And that wasn't possible, I told myself. One man couldn't do it, not even with his wife and daughter helping – not even if he worked twenty-four hours a day and didn't stop to eat. Or unless he could take time and stretch it out to make one hour equal three or four.

I trailed along behind Heath and thought about that time-stretching business and was pleased at myself for thinking of it, for it isn't often that I get foolish thoughts that are likewise pleasing. Why, I thought, with a deal like that you could stretch out any day so you could get all the work done you wanted to. And if you could stretch out time, maybe you could compress it, too, so that a trip to a dentist, for example, would only seem to take a minute.

Heath took me out to the garden and Helen had been right. There were the familiar vegetables, of course – cabbages and tomatoes and squashes and all the other kinds that are found in every garden – but in addition to this there were as many others I had never seen before. He told me the names of them and they seemed to be queer names then, although now it seems a little strange to think they once had sounded queer, for now everyone in the valley grows these vegetables and it seems like we have always had them.

As we talked he pulled up and picked some of the strange vegetables and put them in a basket he had brought along.

"You'll want to try them all," he said. "Some of them you may not like at first, but there are others that you will. This one you eat raw, sliced like a tomato, and this one is best boiled, although you can bake it, too –"

I wanted to ask him how he'd come on the vegetables and where they had come from, but he didn't give me a chance; he kept on telling me about them and how to cook them and that this one was a winter keeper and that one you could can and he gave me one to eat raw and it was rather good.

We'd got to the far end of the garden and were starting to come back when Heath's wife ran around the corner of the house.

Apparently she didn't see me at first or had forgotten I was there, for she called to him and the name she called him wasn't Reginald or Reggie, but a foreign-sounding name. I won't even try to approximate it, for even at the time I wasn't able to recall it a second after hearing it. It was like no word I'd ever heard before.

Then she saw me and stopped running and caught her breath, and a moment later said she'd been listening in on the party line and that Bert Smith's little daughter, Ann, was terribly sick.

"They called the doctor," she said, "but he is out on calls and he won't get there in time."

"Reginald," she said, "the symptoms sound like –"

And she said another name that was like none I'd ever heard or expect to hear again.

Watching Heath's face, I could swear I saw it pale despite his olive tinge of skin.

"Quick!" he shouted and grabbed me by the arm.

We ran around in front to his old clunk of a car. He threw the basket of vegetables in the back seat and jumped behind the wheel. I scrambled in after him and tried to close the door, but it wouldn't close. The lock kept slipping loose and I had to hang onto the door so it wouldn't bang.

We lit out of there like a turpentined dog and the noise that old car made was enough to deafen one. Despite my holding onto it, the door kept banging and all the fenders rattled and there was every other kind of noise you'd expect a junk-heap car to make, with an extra two or three thrown in.

I wanted to ask him what he planned to do, but I was having trouble framing the question in my mind and even if I had known how to phrase it I doubt he could have heard me with all the racket that the car was making.

So I hung on as best I could and tried to keep the door from banging and all at once it seemed to me the car was making more noise than it had any call to. Just like the old haywire tractor made more noise than any tractor should. Too much noise, by far, for the way that it was running. Just like on the tractor, there was no engine vibration and despite all the banging and the clanking we were making time. As I've said, our valley roads are none too good, but even so I swear there were places we hit seventy and we went around sharp corners where, by rights, we should have gone into the ditch at the speed that we were going, but the car just seemed to settle down and hug the road and we never even skidded.

We pulled up in front of Bert's place and Heath jumped out and ran up the walk, with me following him.

Amy Smith came to the door and I could see that she'd been crying, and she looked a little surprised to see the two of us.

We stood there for a moment without saying anything, until Heath spoke to her and here is a funny thing: Heath was wearing a pair of ragged overalls and a sweat-stained shirt and he didn't have a hat and his hair was all rumpled up, but there was a single instant when it seemed to me that he was well-dressed in an expensive business suit and that he took off a hat and bowed to Amy.

"I understand," he said, "that the little girl is sick. Maybe I can help."

I don't know if Amy had seen the same thing that I had seemed to see, but she opened the door and stood to one side so that we could enter.

"In there," she said.

"Thank you, ma'am," said Heath, and went into the room.

Amy and I stood there for a moment, then she turned to me and I could see the tears in her eyes again.

"Cal, she's awful sick," she said.

I nodded miserably, for now the spell was gone and common sense was coming back again and I wondered at the madness of this farmer who thought that he could help a little girl who was terribly sick. And at my madness for standing there, without even going in the room with him.

But just then Heath came out of the room and closed the door softly behind him.

"She's sleeping now," he said to Amy. "She'll be all right."

Then, without another word, he walked out of the door. I hesitated a moment, looking at Amy, wondering what to do. And it was pretty plain there was nothing I could do. So I followed him.

We drove back to his farm at a sober rate of speed, but the car banged and thumped just as bad as ever.

"Runs real good," I yelled at him.

He smiled a bit.

"I keep it tinkered up," he yelled back at me.

When we got to his place, I got out of his car and walked over to my own.

"You forgot the vegetables," he called after me.

So I went back to get them.

"Thanks a lot," I said.

"Any time," he told me.

I looked straight at him, then, and said: "It sure would be fine if we could get some rain. It would mean a lot to us. A soaking rain right now would save the corn."

"Come again," he told me. "It was good to talk with you."

And that night it rained, all over the valley, a steady, soaking rain, and the corn was saved.

And Ann got well.

The doctor, when he finally got to Bert's, said that she had passed the crisis and was already on the mend. One of those virus things, he said. A lot of it around. Not like the old days, he said, before they got to fooling around with all their miracle drugs, mutating viruses right and left. Used to be, he said, a doctor knew what he was treating, but he don't know any more.

I don't know if Bert or Amy told Doc about Heath, although I imagine that they didn't. After all, you don't tell a doctor that a neighbor cured your child. And there might have been someone who would have been ornery enough to try to bring a charge against Heath for practicing medicine without a license, although that would have been pretty hard to prove. But the story got around the valley and there was a lot of talk. Heath, I heard, had been a famous doctor in Vienna before he'd made his getaway. But I didn't believe it. I don't even believe those who started the story believed it, but that's the way it goes in a neighborhood like ours.

That story, and others, made quite a flurry for a month or so, but then it quieted down and you could see that the Heaths had become one of us and belonged to the valley. Bert went over and had quite a talk with Heath and the womenfolks took to calling Mrs. Heath on the telephone, with some of those who were listening in breaking in to say a word or two, thereby initiating Mrs. Heath into the round-robin telephone conversations that are going on all the time on our valley party line, with it getting so that you have to bust in on them and tell them to get off the line when you want to make an important call. We had Heath out with us on our coon hunts that fall and some of the young bloods started paying attention to Heath's daughter. It was almost as if the Heaths were old-time residents.

As I've said before, we've always been real fortunate in getting in good neighbors.

When things are going well, time has a way of flowing along so smoothly that you aren't conscious of its passing, and that was the way it was in the valley.

We had good years, but none of us paid much attention to that. You don't pay much attention to the good times, you get so you take them for granted. It's only when bad times come along that you look back and realize the good times you have had.

A year or so ago I was just finishing up the morning chores when a car with a New York license pulled up at the barnyard gate. It isn't very often we see an out-of-state license plate in the valley, so I figured that it probably was someone who had gotten lost and had stopped to ask directions. There was a man and woman in the front seat and three kids and a dog in the back seat and the car was new and shiny.

I was carrying the milk up from the barn and when the man got out I put the pails down on the ground and waited for him.

He was a youngish sort of fellow and he looked intelligent and he had good manners.

He told me his name was Rickard and that he was a New York newspaperman on vacation and had dropped into the valley on his way out west to check some information.

It was the first time, so far as I knew, that the valley had ever been of any interest news-wise and I said so. I said we never did much here to get into the news.

"It's no scandal," Rickard told me, "if that is what you're thinking. It's just a matter of statistics."

There are a lot of times when I don't catch a situation as quickly as I should, being a sort of deliberate type, but it seems to me now that as soon as he said statistics I could see it coming.

"I did a series of farm articles a few months back," said Rickard, "and to get my information I had to go through a lot of government statistics. I never got so sick of anything in my entire life."

"And?" I asked, not feeling too well myself.

"I found some interesting things about this valley," he went on. "I remember that I didn't catch it for a while. Went on past the figures for a ways. Almost missed the significance, in fact. Then I did a doubletake and backed up and looked at them again. The full story wasn't in that report, of course. Just a hint of something. So I did some more digging and came up with other facts."

I tried to laugh it off, but he wouldn't let me.

"Your weather, for one thing," he said. "Do you realize you've had perfect weather for the past ten years?"

"The weather's been pretty good," I admitted.

"It wasn't always good. I went back to see."

"That's right," I said. "It's been better lately."

"Your crops have been the best they've ever been in the last ten years."

"Better seed," I said. "Better ways of farming."

He grinned at me. "You guys haven't changed your way of farming in the last quarter-century."

And he had me there, of course.

"There was an army worm invasion two years ago," he said. "It hit all around you, but you got by scot-free."

"We were lucky. I remember we said so at the time."

"I checked the health records," he said. "Same thing once again. For ten solid years. No measles, no chickenpox, no pneumonia. No nothing. One death in ten full years – complications attendant on old age."

"Old Man Parks," I said. "He was going on to ninety. Fine old gentleman."

"You see," said Rickard.

I did see.

The fellow had the figures. He had tracked it down, this thing we hadn't even realized, and he had us cold.

"What do you want me to do about it?" I asked.

"I want to talk to you about a neighbor."

"I won't talk about any of my neighbors. Why don't you talk to him yourself?"

"I tried to, but he wasn't at home. Fellow down the road said he'd gone into town. Whole family had gone into town."

"Reginald Heath," I said. There wasn't much sense in playing dumb with Rickard, for he knew all the angles.

"That's the man. I talked to folks in town. Found out he'd never had to have any repair work done on any of his machinery or his car. Has the same machinery he had when he started farming. And it was worn out then."

"He takes good care of it," I told him. "He keeps it tinkered up."

"Another thing," said Rickard. "Since he's been here he hasn't bought a drop of gasoline."

I'd known the rest of it, of course, although I'd never stopped to think about it. But I didn't know about the gasoline. I must have shown my surprise, for Rickard grinned at me.

"What do you want?" I asked.

"A story."

"Heath's the man to talk to. I don't know a thing to help you."

And even when I said it I felt easy in my mind. I seemed to have an instinctive faith that Heath could handle the situation, that he'd know just what to do.

But after breakfast I couldn't settle down to work. I was pruning the orchard, a job I'd been putting off for a year or two and that badly needed doing. I kept thinking of that business of Heath not buying gasoline and that night I'd found the tractor plowing by itself and how smooth both the car and tractor ran despite all the noise they made.

So I laid down my pruning hook and shears and struck out across the fields. I knew the Heath family was in town, but I don't think it would have made any difference to me if they'd been at home. I think I would have gone just the same. For more than ten years now, I realized, I'd been wondering about that tractor and it was time that I found out.

I found the tractor in the machine shed and I thought maybe I'd have some trouble getting into it. But I didn't have a bit. I slipped the catches and the hood lifted up and I found exactly what I had thought I'd find, except that I hadn't actually worked out in my mind the picture of what I'd find underneath that hood.

It was just a block of some sort of shining metal that looked almost like a cube of heavy glass. It wasn't very big, but it had a massive look about it, as if it might have been a heavy thing to lift.

You could see the old bolt holes where the original internal combustion engine had been mounted and a heavy piece of some sort of metal had been fused across the frame to seat that little power plant. And up above the shiny cube was an apparatus of some sort. I didn't take the time to find out how it worked, but I could see that it was connected to the exhaust and knew it was a dingus that disguised the power plant. You know how in electric trains they have it fixed up so that the locomotive goes *chuff-chuff* and throws out a stream of smoke. Well, that was what that contraption was. It threw out little puffs of smoke and made a tractor noise.

I stood there looking at it and I wondered why it was, if Heath had an engine that worked better than an internal combustion engine, he should have gone to so much trouble to hide the fact he had it. If I'd had a thing like that, I knew I'd make the most of it. I'd get someone to back me and go into production and in no time at all I'd be stinking rich. And there'd be nothing in the world to prevent Heath from doing that. But instead he'd fixed the tractor so it looked and sounded like an ordinary tractor and he'd fixed his car to make so much noise that it hid the fact it had a new type motor. Only he had overdone it. He'd made both the car and tractor make more noise than they should. And he'd missed an important bet in not buying gasoline. In his place I'd have bought the stuff, just the way you should, and thrown it away or burned it to get rid of it.

It almost seemed to me that Heath might have had something he was hiding all these years, that he'd tried deliberately to keep himself unnoticed. As if he might really have been a refugee from the Iron Curtain – or from somewhere else.

I put the hood back in place again and snapped the catches shut and when I went out I was very careful to shut the machine shed door securely.

I went back to my pruning and I did quite a bit of thinking and while I was doing it I realized that I'd been doing this same thinking, piecemeal, ever since that night I'd found the tractor running by itself. Thinking of it in snatches and not trying to correlate all my thinking and that way it hadn't added up to much, but now it did and I suppose I should have been a little scared.

But I wasn't scared. Reginald Heath was a neighbor, and a good one, and we'd gone hunting and fishing together and we'd helped one another with haying and threshing and one thing and another and I liked the man as well as anyone I had ever known. Sure, he was a little different and he had a funny kind of tractor and a funny kind of car and he might even have a way of stretching time and since he'd come into the valley we'd been fortunate in weather and in health. All true, of course, but nothing to be scared of. Nothing to be scared of, once you knew the man.

For some reason or other I remembered the time several years before when I'd dropped by of a summer evening. It was hot and the Heath family had brought chairs out on the lawn because it was cooler there. Heath got me a chair and we sat and talked, not about anything in particular, but whatever came into our heads.

There was no moon, but there were a lot of stars and they were the prettiest I have ever seen them.

I called Heath's attention to them and, just shooting off my mouth, I told him what little I'd picked up about astronomy.

"They're a long ways off," I said. "So far off that their light takes years to reach us. And all of them are suns. A lot of them bigger than our sun."

Which was about all I knew about the stars.

Heath nodded gravely.

"There's one up there," he said, "that I watch a lot. That blue one, over there. Well, sort of blue, anyhow. See it? See how it twinkles. Like it might be winking at us. A friendly sort of star."

I pretended that I saw the one he was pointing at, although I wasn't sure I did, there were so many of them and a lot of them were twinkling.

Then we got to talking about something else and forgot about the stars. Or at least I did.

Right after supper, Bert Smith came over and said that Rickard had been around asking him some questions and that he'd been down to Jingo's place and that he'd said he'd see Heath just as soon as Heath got back from town.

Bert was a bit upset about it, so I tried to calm him down.

"These city folks get excited easy," I told him. "There's nothing to it."

I didn't worry much about it because I felt sure that Heath could handle things and even if Rickard did write a story for the New York papers it wouldn't bother us. Coon Valley is a long piece from New York.

I figured we'd probably seen and heard the last from Rickard.

But in all my life, I've never been more wrong.

About midnight or so I woke up with Helen shaking me.

"There's someone at the door," she said. "Go see who it is."

So I shucked into my overalls and shoes and lit the lamp and went downstairs to see.

While I'd been getting dressed there'd been some knocking at the door, but as soon as I lit the lamp it quit.

I went to the door and opened it and there stood Rickard and he wasn't near as chipper as he'd been in the morning.

"Sorry to get you up," he said, "but it seems that I'm lost."

"You can't be lost," I told him. "There isn't but one road through the valley. One end of it ties up to Sixty and the other to Eighty-five. You follow the valley road and you're bound to hit one or the other of them."

"I've been driving," he told me, "for the last four hours and I can't find either of them."

"Look," I said, "all you do is drive one way or the other. You can't get off the road. Fifteen minutes either way and you're on a state highway."

I was exasperated with him, for it seemed a silly thing to do. And I don't take kindly to being routed out at midnight.

"But I tell you I'm lost," he said in a sort of desperation and I could see that he was close to panic. "The wife is getting scared and the kids are dead on their feet —"

"All right," I told him. "Let me get on my shirt and tie my shoes. I'll get you out of here."

He told me he wanted to get to Sixty, so I got out my car and told him to follow me. I was pretty sore about it, but I figured the only thing to do was to help him out. He'd upset the valley and the sooner out the better.

I drove for thirty minutes before I began to get confused myself. That was twice as long as it should have taken to get out to the highway. But the road looked all right and there seemed to be nothing wrong, except for the time it took. So I kept on going. At the end of forty-five minutes we were back in front of my place again.

I couldn't figure it out for the life of me. I got out of my car and went back to Rickard's car.

"You see what I mean," he said.

"We must have got turned around," I said.

His wife was almost hysterical.

"What's going on?" she asked me in a high, shrill voice. "What is going on around here?"

"We'll try again," I said. "We'll drive slower this time so we don't make the same mistake."

I drove slower and this time it took an hour to get back to the farm. So we tried for Eighty-five and forty minutes later were right back where we started.

"I give up," I told them. "Get out and come in. We'll fix up some beds. You can spend the night and we'll get you out come light."

I cooked up some coffee and found stuff to make sandwiches while Helen fixed up beds to take care of the five of them. "The dog can sleep out here in the kitchen," she said.

I got an apple box and quilt and fixed the dog a bed.

The dog was a nice little fellow, a wirehair who was full of fun, and the Rickard kids were about as fine a bunch of kids as you'd find anywhere.

Mrs. Rickard was all set to have hysterics, but Helen got her to drink some coffee and I wouldn't let them talk about not being able to get out.

"Come daylight," I told them, "and there'll be nothing to it."

After breakfast they were considerably calmed down and seemed to have no doubt they could find Number Sixty. So they started out alone, but in an hour were back again. I took my car and started out ahead of them and I don't mind admitting I could feel bare feet walking up and down my spine.

I watched closely and all at once I realized that somehow we were headed back into the valley instead of heading out of it. So I stopped the car and we turned our cars around and headed back in the right direction. But in ten minutes we were turned around again. We tried again and this time we fairly crawled, trying to spot the place where we got turned around. But we could never spot it.

We went back to my place and I called up Bert and Jingo and asked them to come over.

Both of them tried to lead the Rickards out, one at a time then the two of them together, but they were no better at it than I was. Then I tried it alone, without the Rickards following me and I had no trouble at all. I was out to highway Sixty and back in half an hour. So we thought maybe the jinx was broken and I tried to lead out the Rickard car, but it was no soap.

By mid-afternoon we knew the answer. Any of the natives could get out of the valley, but the Rickards couldn't.

Helen put Mrs. Rickard to bed and fed her some sedative and I went over to see Heath.

He was glad to see me and he listened to me, but all the time I was talking to him I kept remembering how one time I had wondered if maybe he could stretch out time. When I had finished he was silent for a while, as if he might have been going over some decision just to be certain that it was right.

"It's a strange business, Calvin," he said finally, "and it doesn't seem right the Rickards should be trapped in this valley if they don't want to stay here.

"Yet, it's a fortunate thing for us, actually. Rickard was planning on writing a story about us and if he'd written as he planned to, there'd been a lot of attention paid us. There would have been a crowd of people coming in – other newspapermen and government men and people from the universities and the idly curious. They'd have upset our lives and some of them would have offered us big sums of money for our farms, much more than they're worth, and all of it would spoil the valley for us. I don't know about you, but I like the valley as it is. It reminds me of . . . well, of another place."

"Rickard still can telephone that story," I told him, "or he can mail it out. Just keeping Rickard here won't prevent that story being printed."

"Somehow I think it will," he said. "I am fairly certain he won't telephone it or send it in the mails."

I had come half prepared to go to bat for Rickard, but I thought over what Heath had pointed out to me and I didn't do it.

I saw that if there were some principle or power which kept the valley healthy and insured good weather and made living pleasant, why, then, the rest of the world would be hell-bent to use the same principle or power. It might have been selfish of me, but I felt fairly certain the principle or power couldn't be spread thin enough to cover all the world. And if anyone were to have it, I wanted it kept right here, where it rightfully belonged.

And there was another thing: If the world should learn there was such a power or principle and if we couldn't share it or refused to share it, then all the world would be sore at us and we'd live in the center of a puddle of hatred.

I went back home and had a talk with Rickard and I didn't try to hide anything from him. He was all set to go and have it out with Heath, but I advised against it. I pointed out that he didn't have a shred of proof and he'd only make himself look silly, for

Heath would more than likely act as if he didn't know what he was getting at. After quite a tussle, he took my advice.

The Rickards stayed on at our place for several days and occasionally Rickard and I would make a trial run just to test the situation out, but there was no change.

Finally Bert and Jingo came over and we had a council of war with the Rickard family. By this time Mrs. Rickard was taking it somewhat better and the Rickard kids were happy with the outdoor life and the Rickard dog was busily engaged in running all the valley rabbits down to skin and bones.

"There's the old Chandler place up at the head of the valley," said Jingo. "No one's been living there for quite a while, but it's in good shape. It could be fixed up so it was comfortable."

"But I can't stay here," protested Rickard. "I can't settle down here."

"Who said anything about settling down?" asked Bert. "You just got to wait it out. Some day whatever is wrong will get straightened out and then you can get away."

"But my job," said Rickard.

Mrs. Rickard spoke up then. You could see she didn't like the situation any better than he did, but she had that queer, practical, everyday logic that a woman at times surprises a man by showing. She knew that they were stuck here in the valley and she was out to make the best of it.

"Remember that book you're always threatening to write?" she asked. "Maybe this is it."

That did it.

Rickard mooned around for a while, making up his mind, although it already was made up. Then he began talking about the peace in the valley – the peace and quietness and the lack of hurry – just the place to write a book.

The neighbors got together and fixed up the house on the old Chandler place and Rickard called his office and made some excuse and got a leave of absence and wrote a letter to his bank, transferring whatever funds he had. Then he settled down to write.

Apparently in his phone calls and his letter-writing he never even hinted at the real reason for his staying – perhaps because it would have sounded downright silly – for there was no ruckus over his failure to go back.

The valley settled down to its normal life again and it felt good after all the uproar. The neighbors shopped for the Rickards and carried out from town all the groceries and other things they needed and once in a while Rickard took the car and had a try at finding the state highways.

But mostly he wrote and in about a year he sold this book of his. Probably you have read it: *You Could Hear the Silence.* Made him a hunk of money. But his New York publishers still are going slowly mad trying to understand why he steadfastly refuses to stir out of the valley. He has refused lecture tours, has declined dinners in his honor and turned down all the other glitter that goes with writing a bestseller.

The book didn't change Rickard at all. By the time he sold it he was well liked in the valley and seemed to like everyone – except possibly Heath. He stayed rather cold to Heath. He used to do a lot of walking, to get exercise, he said, although I think that he thought up most of his book out on those walks. And he'd stop by and chew the fat when he was out on those walks and that way everyone got to know him. He used to talk a lot about when he could get out of the valley and all of us were beginning to feel sorry that a time would come when he would leave, for the Rickards had turned out to be good neighbors. There must be something about the valley that brings out the best there is in everyone. As I have said before, we have yet to get a bad neighbor and that is something most neighborhoods can't say.

One day I had stopped on my way from town to talk a while with Heath and as we stood talking, up the road came Rickard. You could see he wasn't going anywhere, but was just out for a walk.

He stopped and talked with us for a few minutes, then suddenly he said, "You know, we've made up our minds that we would like to stay here."

"Now, that is fine," said Heath.

"Grace and I were talking about it the other night," said Rickard. "About the time when we could get out of here. Then suddenly we stopped our talking and looked at one another and we knew right then and there we didn't want to leave. It's been so peaceful and the kids like the school here so much better than in the city and the people are so fine we couldn't bear to leave."

"I'm glad to hear you say that," Heath told him. "But it seems to me you've been sticking pretty close. You ought to take the wife and kids in town to see a show."

And that was it. It was as simple as all that.

Life goes on in the valley as it always has, except it's even better now. All of us are healthy. We don't even seem to get colds any more. When we need rain we get it and when there's need of sun the sun is sure to shine. We aren't getting rich, for you can't get rich with all this Washington interference, but we're making a right good living. Rickard is working on his second book and once in a while I go out at night and try to locate the star Heath showed me that evening long ago.

But we still get some publicity now and then. The other night I was listening to my favorite newscaster and he had an item he had a lot of fun with.

"Is there really such a place as Coon Valley?" he asked and you could hear the chuckle just behind the words. "If there is, the government would like to know about it. The maps insist there is and there are statistics on the books that say it's a place where there is no sickness, where the climate is ideal, where there's never a crop failure – a land of milk and honey. Investigators have gone out to seek the truth of this and they can't find the place, although people in nearby communities insist there's such a valley. Telephone calls have been made to people listed as residents of the valley, but the calls can't be completed. Letters have been written to them, but the letters are returned to the sender for one or another of the many reasons the post office has for non-delivery. Investigators have waited in nearby trading centers, but Coon Valley people never came to town while the investigators were there. If there is such a place and if the things the statistics say of it are true, the government would be very interested, for there must be data in the valley that could be studied and applied to other sectors. We have no way of knowing whether this broadcast can reach the valley – if it is any more efficient than investigators or telephone or the postal service. But if it does – and if there is such a place as Coon Valley – and if one of its residents should be listening, won't he please speak up!"

He chuckled then, chuckled very briefly, and went on to tell the latest rumor about Khrushchev.

I shut off the radio and sat in my chair and thought about the times when for several days no one could find his way out of the valley and of the other times when the telephones went dead for no apparent reason. And I remembered how we'd talked about it among ourselves and wondered if we should speak to Heath about it, but had in each case decided not to, since we felt that Heath knew what he was doing and that we could trust his judgment.

It's inconvenient at times, of course, but there are a lot of compensations. There hasn't been a magazine solicitor in the valley for more than a dozen years – nor an insurance salesman, either.

SHADOW WORLD

Originally published in the September 1957 issue of Galaxy Science
Fiction, *"Shadow World" was the relatively rare result of a decision
by Cliff Simak to replot a story. He had originally submitted the story
(then named "Who Cares for Shadows?") to Horace Gold in Febru-
ary 1957, but Gold had rejected it. Cliff received the rejected manuscript on March 4, and by March 11 he had done enough work that
when he sent it back to Gold on that date, it was accepted. It would
be good to know what the alleged replotting consisted of . . .*

*This would be the third of three Simak stories using the word
shadow prominently in their titles, but there is no discernible pattern
or relationship among them.*

—dww

I rolled out early to put in an hour or so of work on my sector
model before Greasy got breakfast slopped together. When I came
out of my tent, Benny, my Shadow, was waiting for me. Some of
the other Shadows also were standing around, waiting for their
humans, and the whole thing, if one stopped to think of it, was
absolutely crazy. Except that no one ever stopped to think of it;
we were used to it by now.

Greasy had the cookshack stove fired up and smoke was curl-
ing from the chimney. I could hear him singing lustily amid the

clatter of his pans. This was his noisy time. During the entire morning, he was noisy and obnoxious, but toward the middle of the afternoon, he turned mousy quiet. That was when he began to take a really dangerous chance and hit the peeper.

There were laws which made it very rough on anyone who had a peeper. Mack Baldwin, the project superintendent, would have raised merry hell if he had known that Greasy had one. But I was the only one who knew it. I had found out by accident and not even Greasy knew I knew and I had kept my mouth shut.

I said hello to Benny, but he didn't answer me. He never answered me; he had no mouth to answer with. I don't suppose he even heard me, for he had no ears. Those Shadows were a screwy lot. They had no mouths and they had no ears and they hadn't any noses.

But they did have an eye, placed in the middle of the face, about where the nose would have been if they'd had noses. And that eye made up for the lack of ears and mouth and nose.

It was about three inches in diameter and, strictly speaking, it wasn't built exactly like an eye; it had no iris or no pupil, but was a pool of light and shadow that kept shifting all around so it never looked the same. Sometimes it looked like a bowl of goop that was slightly on the spoiled side, and at other times it was hard and shining like a camera lens, and there were other times when it looked sad and lonely, like a mournful hound dog's eyes.

They were a weird lot for sure, those Shadows. They looked mostly like a rag doll before any one had gotten around to painting in the features. They were humanoid and they were strong and active and I had suspected from the very first that they weren't stupid. There was some division of opinion on that latter point and a lot of the boys still thought of them as howling savages. Except they didn't howl – they had no mouths to howl with. No mouths to howl or eat with, no nose to smell or breathe with, and no ears to hear with.

Just on bare statistics, one would have put them down as plain impossible, but they got along all right. They got along just fine.

They wore no clothes. On the point of modesty, there was

no need of any. They were as bare of sexual characteristics as they were of facial features. They were just a gang of rag dolls with massive eyes in the middle of their faces.

But they did wear what might have been a decoration or a simple piece of jewelry or a badge of Shadowhood. They wore a narrow belt, from which was hung a bag or sack in which they carried a collection of trinkets that jingled when they walked. No one had ever seen what was in those sacks. Cross straps from the belt ran over the shoulders, making the whole business into a simple harness, and at the juncture of the straps upon their chest was mounted a huge jewel. Intricately carved, the jewel sparkled like a diamond, and it might have been a diamond, but no one knew if it was or not. No one ever got close enough to see. Make a motion toward that jewel and the Shadow disappeared.

That's right. Disappeared.

I said hello to Benny and he naturally didn't answer and I walked around the table and began working on the model. Benny stood close behind me and watched me as I worked. He seemed to have a lot of interest in that model. He had a lot of interest in everything I did. He went everywhere I went. He was, after all, my Shadow.

There was a poem that started out: *I have a little shadow* . . . I had thought about it often, but couldn't recall who the poet was or how the rest of it went. It was an old, old poem and I remembered I had read it when I was a kid. I could close my eyes and see the picture that went with the words, the brightly colored picture of a kid in his pajamas, going up a stairs with a candle in his hand and the shadow of him on the wall beyond the stairs.

I took some satisfaction in Benny's interest in the sector model, although I was aware his interest probably didn't mean a thing. He might have been just as interested if I'd been counting beans.

I was proud of that model and I spent more time on it than I had any right to. I had my name, Robert Emmett Drake, spelled out in full on the plaster base and the whole thing was a bit more ambitious than I originally had intended.

I had let my enthusiasm run away with me and that was not too hard to understand. It wasn't every day that a conservationist got a chance to engineer from scratch an absolutely virgin Earth-type planet. The layout was only one small sector of the initial project, but it included almost all the factors involved in the entire tract and I had put in the works – the dams and roads, the power sites and the mill sites, the timber management and the water-conservation features and all the rest of it.

I had just settled down to work when a commotion broke out down at the cookshack. I could hear Greasy cussing and the sound of thudding whacks. The door of the shack burst open and a Shadow came bounding out with Greasy just a leap behind him. Greasy had a frying pan and he was using it effectively, with a nifty backhand technique that was beautiful to see. He was laying it on the Shadow with every leap he took and he was yelling maledictions that were enough to curl one's hair.

The Shadow legged it across the camp with Greasy close behind. Watching them, I thought how it was a funny thing that a Shadow would up and disappear if you made a motion toward its jewel, but would stay and take the kind of treatment Greasy was handing out with that frying pan.

When they came abreast of my model table, Greasy gave up the chase. He was not in the best of condition.

He stood beside the table and put both fists belligerently on his hips, so that the frying pan, which he still clutched, stood out at a right angle from his body.

"I won't allow that stinker in the shack," he told me, wheezing and gasping. "It's bad enough to have him hanging around outside and looking in the windows. It's bad enough falling over him every time I turn around. I will not have him snooping in the kitchen; he's got his fingers into everything he sees. If I was Mack, I'd put the lug on all of them. I'd run them so fast, so far, that it would take them –"

"Mack's got other things to worry about," I told him rather

sharply. "The project is way behind schedule, with all the break-downs we've been having."

"Sabotage," Greasy corrected me. "That's what it is. You can bet your bottom dollar on that. It's them Shadows, I tell you, sabotaging the machines. If it was left to me, I'd run them clear out of the country."

"It's their country," I protested. "They were here before we came."

"It's a big planet," Greasy said. "There are other parts of it they could live in."

"But they have got a right here. This planet is their home."

"They ain't got no homes," said Greasy.

He turned around abruptly and walked back toward the shack. His Shadow, which had been standing off to one side all the time, hurried to catch up with him. It didn't look as if it had minded the pounding he had given it. But you could never tell what a Shadow was thinking. Their thoughts don't show on them.

What Greasy had said about their not having any homes was a bit unfair. What he meant, of course, was that they had no village, that they were just a sort of carefree bunch of gypsies, but to me the planet was their home and they had a right to go any place they wanted on it and use any part of it they wished. It should make no difference that they settled down on no particular spot, that they had no villages and possibly no shelters or that they raised no crops.

Come to think of it, there was no reason why they should raise crops, for they had no mouths to eat with, and if they didn't eat, how could they keep on living and if . . .

You see how it went. That was the reason it didn't pay to think too much about the Shadows. Once you started trying to get them figured out, you got all tangled up.

I sneaked a quick look sidewise to see how Benny might be taking this business of Greasy beating up his pal, but Benny was just the same as ever. He was all rag doll.

Men began to drift out of the tents and the Shadows galloped over to rejoin their humans, and everywhere a man might go, his Shadow tagged behind him.

The project center lay there on its hilltop, and from where I stood beside my sector table, I could see it laid out like a blueprint come to life.

Over there, the beginning of the excavation for the administration building, and there the gleaming stakes for the shopping center, and beyond the shopping center, the ragged, first-turned furrows that in time would become a street flanked by neat rows of houses.

It didn't look much like a brave beginning on a brand-new world, but in a little while it would. It would even now, if we'd not run into so much hard luck. And whether that hard luck could be traced to the Shadows or to something else, it was a thing that must be faced and somehow straightened out.

For this was important. Here was a world on which Man would not repeat the ancient, sad mistakes that he had made on Earth. On this, one of the few Earth-like planets found so far, Man would not waste the valuable resources which he had let go down the drain on the old home planet. He'd make planned use of the water and the soil, of the timber and the minerals, and he'd be careful to put back as much as he took out. This planet would not be robbed and gutted as Earth had been. It would be used intelligently and operated like a well-run business.

I felt good, just standing there, looking out across the valley and the plains toward the distant mountains, thinking what a fine home this would be for mankind.

The camp was becoming lively now. Out in front of the tents, the men were washing up for breakfast and there was a lot of friendly shouting and a fair amount of horseplay. I heard considerable cussing down in the equipment pool and I knew exactly what was going on. The machines, or at least a part of them, had gone daffy again and half the morning would be wasted getting them repaired. It certainly was a funny deal, I thought, how those machines got out of kilter every blessed night.

After a while, Greasy rang the breakfast bell and everyone dropped everything and made a dash for it and their Shadows hustled along behind them.

I was closer to the cookshack than most of them and I am no slouch at sprinting, so I got one of the better seats at the big outdoor table. My place was just outside the cookshack door, where I'd get first whack at seconds when Greasy lugged them out. I went past Greasy on the run and he was grumbling and muttering the way he always was at chow, although sometimes I thought that was just a pose to hide his satisfaction at knowing his cooking still was fit to eat.

I got a seat next to Mack, and a second later Rick Thorne, one of the equipment operators, grabbed the place on the other side of me. Across from me was Stan Carr, a biologist, and just down the table, on the other side, was Judson Knight, our ecologist.

We wasted no time in small talk; we dived into the wheat cakes and the side pork and the fried potatoes. There is nothing in all the Universe like the morning air of Stella IV to hone an edge on the appetite.

Finally we had enough of the edge off so we would waste time being civil.

"It's the same old story again this morning," Thorne said bitterly to Mack. "More than half the equipment is all gummed up. It'll take hours to get it moving."

He morosely shoveled food into his mouth and chewed with unnecessary savagery. He shot an angry glance at Carr across the table. "Why don't you get it figured out?" he asked.

"Me?" said Carr, in some astonishment. "Why should I be the one to get it figured out? I don't know anything about machines and I don't want to know. They're stupid contraptions at best."

"You know what I mean," said Thorne. "The machines are not to blame. They don't gum up themselves. It's the Shadows and you're a biologist and them Shadows are your business and –"

"I have other things to do," said Carr. "I have this earthworm problem to work out, and as soon as that is done, Bob here wants me to run some habit-patterns on a dozen different rodents."

"I wish you would," I said. "I have a hunch some of those little rascals may cause us a lot of trouble once we try our hand at crops. I'd like to know ahead of time what makes the critters tick."

That was the way it went, I thought. No matter how many factors you might consider, there were always more of them popping up from under rocks and bushes. It seemed somehow that a man never quite got through the list.

"It wouldn't be so bad," Thorne complained, "if the Shadows would leave us alone and let us fix the damage after they've done their dirty work. But not them. They breathe down our necks while we're making the repairs, and they've got their faces buried in those engines clear up to their shoulders, and every time you move, you bump into one of them. Someday," he said fiercely, "I'm going to take a monkey wrench and clear some space around me."

"They're worried about what you're doing to their machines," said Carr. "The Shadows have taken over those machines just like they've adopted us."

"That's what you think," Thorne said.

"Maybe they're trying to find out about the machines," Carr declared. "Maybe they gum them up so that, when you go to fix them, they can look things over. They haven't missed a single part of any machine so far. You were telling me the other day it's a different thing wrong every time."

Knight said, solemn as an owl: "I've been doing a lot of thinking about this situation."

"Oh, you have," said Thorne, and the way he said it, you could see he figured that what Knight might think would cut no ice.

"I've been seeking out some motive," Knight told him. "Because if the Shadows are the ones who are doing it, they'd have to have a motive. Don't you think so, Mack?"

"Yeah, I guess so," said Mack.

"For some reason," Knight went on, "those Shadows seem to

like us. They showed up as soon as we set down and they've stayed with us ever since. The way they act, they'd like us to stay on and maybe they're wrecking the machines so we'll have to stay."

"Or drive us away," Thorne answered.

"That's all right," said Carr, "but why should they want us to stay? What exactly is it they like about us? If we could only get that one on the line, we might be able to do some bargaining with them."

"Well, I wouldn't know," Knight admitted. "There might be a lot of different reasons."

"Name just three of them," Thorne challenged him nastily.

"Gladly," said Knight, and he said it as if he were slipping a knife into the left side of Thorne's gizzard. "They may be getting something from us, only don't ask me what it is. Or they may be building us up to put the bite on us for something that's important. Or they may be figuring on reforming us, although just what's in us they object to, I can't faintly imagine. Or they may worship us. Or maybe it's just love."

"Is that all?" asked Thorne.

"Just a start," said Knight. "They may be studying us and they may need more time to get us puzzled out. They may be prodding us to get some reactions from us —"

"Studying us!" yelled Thorne, outraged. "They're just lousy savages!"

"I don't think they are," Knight replied.

"They don't wear any clothes," Thorne thundered, slamming the table with his fist. "They don't have any tools. They don't have a village. They don't know how to build a hut. They don't have any government. They can't even talk or hear."

I was disgusted with Thorne.

"Well, we got that settled," I said. "Let's go back to work."

I got up off the bench, but I hadn't gone more than a step or two before a man came pounding down from the radio hut, waving a piece of paper in his hand. It was Jack Pollard, our communications man, who also doubled in brass as an electronics expert.

"Mack!" he was hollering. "Hey, Mack!"

Mack lumbered to his feet.

Pollard handed him the paper. "It was coming in when Greasy blew the horn," he gasped. "I was having trouble getting it. Relayed a long way out."

Mack read the paper and his face turned hard and red.

"What's the matter, Mack?" I wanted to know.

"There's an inspector coming out," he said, and he choked on each and every word. He was all burned up. And maybe scared as well.

"Is it likely to be bad?"

"He'll probably can the lot of us," said Mack.

"But he can't do that!"

"That's what you think. We're six weeks behind schedule and this project is hotter than a pile. Earth's politicians have made a lot of promises, and if those promises don't pay off, there'll be hell to pay. Unless we can do something and do it fast, they'll bounce us out of here and send a new gang in."

"But considering everything, we haven't done so badly," Carr said mildly.

"Don't get me wrong," Mack told him. "The new gang will do no better, but there has to be some action for the record and we're the ones who'll get it in the neck. If we could lick this breakdown business, we might have a chance. If we could say to that inspector: 'Sure, we've had a spot of trouble, but we have it licked and now we're doing fine –' if we could say that to him, then we might save our hides."

"You think it's the Shadows, Mack?" asked Knight.

Mack reached up and scratched his head. "Must be them. Can't think of anything else."

Somebody shouted from another table: "Of course it's them damn Shadows!"

The men were getting up from their seats and crowding around.

Mack held up his hands. "You guys get back to work. If any

of you got some good ideas, come up to the tent and we'll talk them over."

They started jabbering at him.

"Ideas!" Mack roared. "I said *ideas!* Anyone that comes up without a good idea, I'll dock him for being off the job."

They quieted down a little.

"And another thing," said Mack. "No rough stuff on the Shadows. Just go along the way we always have. I'll fire the man who strongarms them."

He said to me: "Let's go."

I followed him, and Knight and Carr fell in beside me. Thorne didn't come. I had expected that he would.

Inside Mack's tent, we sat down at a table littered with blueprints and spec sheets and papers scribbled with figures and off-hand diagrams.

"I suppose," said Carr, "that it has to be the Shadows."

"Some gravitational peculiarity?" suggested Knight. "Some strange atmospheric condition? Some space-warping quality?"

"Maybe," said Mack. "It all sounds a bit far-fetched, but I'm ready to grab any straw you shove at me."

"One thing that puzzles me," I put in, "is that the survey crew didn't mention Shadows. Survey believed the planet was uninhabited by any sort of intelligence. It found no signs of culture. And that was good, because it meant the project wouldn't get all tangled up with legalities over primal rights. And yet the minute we landed, the Shadows came galloping to meet us, almost as if they'd spotted us a long way off and were waiting for us to touch down."

"Another funny thing," said Carr, "is how they paired off with us – one Shadow to every man. Like they had it all planned out. Like they'd married us or something."

"What are you getting at?" growled Mack.

I said: "Where were the Shadows, Mack, when the survey gang was here? Can we be absolutely sure they're native to this planet?"

"If they aren't native," demanded Mack, "how did they get here? They have no machines. They haven't even got tools."

"There's another thing about that survey report," said Knight, "that I've been wondering about. The rest of you have read it –"

We nodded. We had not only read it, we had studied and digested it. We'd lived with it day and night on the long trip out to Stella IV.

"The survey report told about some cone-shaped things," said Knight. "All sitting in a row, as if they might be boundary markers. But they never saw them except from a long way off. They had no idea what they were. They just wrote them off as something that had no real significance."

"They wrote off a lot of things as having no significance," said Carr.

"We aren't getting anywhere," Mack complained. "All we do is talk."

"If we could talk to the Shadows," said Knight, "we might be getting somewhere."

"But we can't!" argued Mack. "We tried to talk to them and we couldn't raise a ripple. We tried sign language and we tried pantomime and we filled reams of paper with diagrams and drawings and we got exactly nowhere. Jack rigged up that electronic communicator and he tried it on them and they just sat and looked at us, all bright and sympathetic, with that one big eye of theirs, and that was all there was. We even tried telepathy –"

"You're wrong there, Mack," said Carr. "We didn't try telepathy, because we don't know a thing about it. All we did was sit in a circle, holding hands with them and thinking hard at them. And of course it was no good. They probably thought it was just a game."

"Look," pleaded Mack, "that inspector will be here in ten days or so. We have to think of something. Let's get down to cases."

"If we could run the Shadows off somehow," said Knight. "If we could scare them away –"

"You know how to scare a Shadow?" Mack asked, "You got any idea what they might be afraid of?"

Knight shook his head.

"Our first job," said Carr, "is to find out what a Shadow is like. We have to learn what kind of animal he is. He's a funny kind, we know. He doesn't have a mouth or nose or ears . . ."

"He's impossible," Mack said. "There ain't no such animal."

"He's alive," said Carr, "and doing very well. We have to find out how he gets his food, how he communicates, what tolerances he may have, what his responses are to various kinds of stimuli. We can't do a thing about the Shadows until we have some idea of what we're dealing with."

Knight agreed with him. "We should have started weeks ago. We made a stab at it, of course, but our hearts were never in it. We were too anxious to get started on the project."

Mack said bitterly: "Fat lot of good it did us."

"Before you can examine one, you have to have a subject," I answered Knight. "Seems to me we should try to figure out how to catch a Shadow. Make a sudden move toward one and he disappears."

But even as I said it, I knew that was not entirely right. I remembered how Greasy had chased his Shadow from the cook-shack, lamming him with the frying pan.

And I remembered something else and I had a hunch and got a big idea, but I was scared to say anything about it. I didn't even, for the moment, dare to let on to myself I had it.

"We'd have to take one by surprise somehow and knock him out before he had a chance to disappear," Carr said. "And it has to be a sure way, for if we try it once and fail we've put the Shadows on their guard and we'll never have another chance."

Mack warned, "No rough stuff. You can't go using violence until you know your critter. You don't do any killing until you have some idea how efficiently the thing that you are killing can up and kill you back."

"No rough stuff," Carr agreed. "If a Shadow can bollix up the innards of some of those big earthmovers, I wouldn't like to see what he could do to a human body."

"It's got to be fast and sure," said Knight, "and we can't even start until we know it is. If you hit one on the head with a baseball bat, would the bat bounce or would you crush the Shadow's skull? That's about the way it would be with everything we could think of at the moment."

Carr nodded. "That's right. We can't use gas, because a Shadow doesn't breathe."

"He might breathe through his pores," said Knight.

"Sure, but we'd have to know before we tried using gas. We might jab a hypo into one, but what would you use in the hypo? First you'd have to find something that would knock a Shadow out. You might try hypnotism –"

"I'd doubt hypnotism," said Knight.

"How about Doc?" I asked. "If we could knock out a Shadow, would Doc give him a going over? If I know Doc, he'd raise a lot of hell. Claim the Shadow was an intelligent being and that it would be in violation of medical ethics to examine one without first getting its consent."

"You get one," Mack promised grimly, "and I'll handle Doc."

"He'll do a lot of screaming."

"I'll handle Doc," repeated Mack. "This inspector is going to be here in a week or so –"

"We wouldn't have to have it *all* cleared up," said Knight. "If we could show the inspector that we had a good lead, that we were progressing, he might play ball with us."

I was seated with my back to the entrance of the tent and I heard someone fumbling with the canvas.

Mack said: "Come in, Greasy. Got something on your mind?"

Greasy walked in and came up to the table. He had the bottom of his apron tucked into his trouser band, the way he always did when he wasn't working, and he held something in his hand. He tossed it on the table.

It was one of the bags that the Shadows carried at their belts! We all sucked in our breath and Mack's hair fairly stood on end.

"Where did you get this?" he demanded.

"Off my Shadow, when he wasn't looking."

"When he wasn't looking!"

"Well, you see, it was this way, Mack. That Shadow is always into things. I stumble over him everywhere I go. And this morning he had his head halfway into the dishwasher and that bag was hanging on his belt, so I grabbed up a butcher knife and just whacked it off."

As Mack got up and pulled himself to his full height, you could see it was hard for him to keep his hands off Greasy.

"So that was all you did," he said in a low, dangerous voice.

"Sure," said Greasy. "There was nothing hard about it."

"All you've done is spill the beans to them! All you've done is made it almost impossible —"

"Maybe not," Knight interrupted in a hurry.

"Now that the damage has been done," said Carr, "we might as well have a look. Maybe there's a clue inside that bag."

"I can't open it," grumbled Greasy. "I tried every way I know. There's no way to open it."

"And while you were trying to open it," asked Mack, "what was the Shadow doing?"

"He didn't even notice. He had his head inside that washer. He's as stupid as —"

"Don't say that! I don't want anyone thinking a Shadow's stupid. Maybe they are, but there's no sense believing it until we're sure."

Knight had picked up the bag and was turning it around and around in his hand. Whatever was inside was jingling as he turned and twisted it.

"Greasy's right," he said. "I don't see any way to get it open."

"You get out of here!" Mack roared at Greasy. "Get back to your work. Don't you ever make another move toward any of the Shadows."

Greasy turned around and left, but he was no more than out of the tent when he gave a yelp that was enough to raise your scalp.

I almost knocked the table over getting out of there to see what was going on.

What was happening was no more than plain solemn justice.

Greasy was running for all he was worth, and behind him was the Shadow with a frying pan, and every jump that Greasy took, the Shadow let him have it, and was every bit as good with that frying pan as Greasy was.

Greasy was weaving and circling, trying to head back for the cookshack, but each time the Shadow got him headed off and went on chasing him.

Everyone had stopped work to watch. Some of them were yelling advice to Greasy and some of the others were cheering on the Shadow. I'd have liked to stay and watch, but I knew that if I was going to put my hunch into execution, I'd never have a better chance to do it.

So I turned and walked swiftly down the street to my own tent and ducked inside and got a specimen bag and came out again.

I saw that Greasy was heading for the equipment pool and that the Shadow still was one long stride behind. Its arm was holding up well, for the frying pan never missed a lick.

I ran down to the cookshack and, at the door, I stopped and looked back. Greasy was shinnying up the derrick of a shovel and the Shadow was standing at the bottom, waving the frying pan as though daring him to come down and take it like a man. Everyone else was running toward the scene of action and there was no one, I was sure, who had noticed me.

So I opened the cookshack door and stepped inside.

The dishwasher was chugging away and everything was peaceable and quiet.

I was afraid I might have trouble finding what I was looking for, but I found it in the third place I looked – underneath the mattress on Greasy's bunk.

I pulled the peeper out and slipped it in the bag and got out of there as fast as I could go.

Stopping at my tent, I tossed the bag into a corner and threw some old clothes over it and then went out again.

The commotion had ended. The Shadow was walking back toward the cookshack, with the pan tucked underneath its arm, and Greasy was climbing down off the shovel. The men were all gathered around the shovel, making a lot of noise, and I figured that it would take a long, long time for Greasy to live down what had happened. Although, I realized, he had it coming to him.

I went back into Mack's tent and found the others there. All three of them were standing beside the table, looking down at what lay there upon the surface.

The bag had disappeared and had left behind a little pile of trinkets. Looking at the pile, I could see that they were miniatures of frying pans and kettles and all the other utensils that Greasy worked with. And there, half protruding out of the pile, was a little statuette of Greasy.

I reached out a hand and picked up the statuette. There was no mistaking it – it was Greasy to a T. It was made of some sort of stone, as if it might have been a carving, and was delicate beyond all belief. Squinting closely, I could even see the lines on Greasy's face.

"The bag just went away," said Knight. "It was lying here when we dashed out, and when we came back, it was gone and all this junk was lying on the table."

"I don't understand," Carr said.

And he was right. None of us did.

"I don't like it," Mack said slowly.

I didn't like it, either. It raised too many questions in my head and some of them were resolving into some miserable suspicions.

"They're making models of our stuff," said Knight. "Even down to the cups and spoons."

"I wouldn't mind that so much," Carr said. "It's the model of Greasy that gives me the jitters."

"Now let's sit down," Mack told us, "and not go off on any tangents. This is exactly the sort of thing we could have expected."

"What do you mean?" I prompted.

"What do we do when we find an alien culture? We do just what the Shadows are doing. Different way, but the same objective. We try to find out all we can about this alien culture. And don't you ever forget that, to the Shadows, we're not only an alien culture, but an *invading* alien culture. So if they had any sense at all, they'd make it their business to find out as much about us as they could in the shortest time."

That made sense, of course. But this making of models seemed to be carrying it beyond what was necessary.

And if they had made models of Greasy's cups and spoons, of the dishwasher and the coffee pot, then they had other models, too. They had models of the earthmovers and the shovels and the dozers and all the rest of it And if they had a model of Greasy, they had models of Mack and Thorne and Carr and all the rest of the crew, including me.

Just how faithful would those models be? How much deeper would they go than mere external appearances?

I tried to stop thinking of it, for I was doing little more than scaring myself stiff.

But I couldn't stop. I went right on thinking.

They had been gumming up equipment so that the mechanics had to rip the machines all apart to get them going once again. There seemed no reason in the world why the Shadows should be doing that, except to find out what the innards of those machines were like. I wondered if the models of the equipment might not be faithful not only so far as the outward appearance might go, but faithful as well on the most intricate construction of the entire machine.

And if that was true, was that faithfulness also carried out in the Greasy statuette? Did it have a heart and lungs, blood vessels and brain and nerve? Might it not also have the very essence of

Greasy's character, the kind of animal he was, what his thoughts and ethics might be?

I don't know if, at that very moment, the others were thinking the same thing, but the looks on their faces argued that they might have been.

Mack put out a finger and stirred the contents of the pile, scattering the miniatures all about the tabletop.

Then his hand darted out and picked up something and his face went red with anger.

Knight asked: "What is it, Mack?"

"A peeper!" said Mack, his words rasping in his throat. "There's a model of a peeper!"

All of us sat and stared and I could feel the cold sweat breaking out on me.

"If Greasy has a peeper," Mack said woodenly, "I'll break his scrawny neck."

"Take it easy, Mack," said Carr.

"You know what a peeper is?"

"Sure, I know what a peeper is."

"You ever see what a peeper does to a man who used one?"

"No, I never did."

"I have." Mack threw the peeper model back on the table and turned and went out of the tent. The rest of us followed him.

Greasy was coming down the street, with some of the men following along behind, kidding him about the Shadow treeing him.

Mack put his hands on his hips and waited.

Greasy got almost to us.

"Greasy!" said Mack.

"Yes, Mack."

"You hiding out a peeper?"

Greasy blinked, but he never hesitated. "No, sir," he said, lying like a trooper. "I wouldn't rightly know one if somebody should point it out to me. I've heard of them, of course."

"I'll make a bargain with you," said Mack. "If you have one, just hand it over to me and I'll bust it up and fine you a full month's wages and that's the last that we'll say about it. But if you lie to me and we find you have one hidden out, I'll can you off the job."

I held my breath. I didn't like what was going on and I thought what a lousy break it was that something like this should happen just when I had swiped the peeper. Although I was fairly sure that no one had seen me sneak into the cookshack – at least I didn't think they had.

Greasy was stubborn. He shook his head. "I haven't got one, Mack."

Mack's face got hard. "All right. We'll go down and see."

He headed for the cookshack and Knight and Carr went along with him, but I headed for my tent.

It would be just like Mack, when he didn't find the peeper in the cookshack, to search the entire camp. If I wanted to stay out of trouble, I knew, I'd better be zipping out of camp and take the peeper with me.

Benny was squatted outside the tent, waiting for me. He helped me get the roller out and then I took the specimen bag with the peeper in it and stuffed it in the roller's carrying bag.

I got on the roller and Benny jumped on the carrier behind me and sat there showing off, balancing himself – like a kid riding a bicycle with no hands.

"You hang on," I told him sharply. "If you fall off this time, I won't stop to pick you up."

I am sure he didn't hear me, but however that may be, he put his arms around my waist and we were off in a cloud of dust.

Until you've ridden on a roller, you haven't really lived. It's like a roller coaster running on the level. But it is fairly safe and it gets you there. It's just two big rubber doughnuts with an engine and a seat and it could climb a barn if you gave it half a chance. It's too rambunctious for civilized driving, but it is just the ticket for an alien planet.

We set off across the plain toward the distant foothills. It was a fine day, but for that matter, every day was fine on Stella IV. It was an ideal planet, Earth-like, with good weather nearly all the time, crammed with natural resources, free of vicious animal life or deadly virus – a planet that virtually pleaded for someone to come and live on it.

And in time there'd be people here. Once the administration center was erected, the neat rows of houses had been built, once the shopping center had been installed, the dams built, the power plant completed – then there would be people. And in the years to come, sector by sector, project community by community, the human race would spread across the planet's face. But it would spread in an orderly progression.

Here there would be no ornery misfits slamming out on their own, willy-nilly, into the frontier land of wild dream and sudden death; no speculators, no strike-it-rich, no go-for-broke. Here there would be no frontier, but a systematic taking over. And here, for once, a planet would be treated right.

But there was more to it than that, I told myself.

If Man was to keep going into space, he would have to accept the responsibility of making proper use of the natural resources that he found there. Just because there might be a lot of them was no excuse for wasting them. We were no longer children and we couldn't gut every world as we had gutted Earth.

By the time an intelligence advances to a point where it can conquer space, it must have grown up. And now it was time for the human race to prove that it was adult. We couldn't go ravaging out into the Galaxy like a horde of greedy children.

Here on this planet, it seemed to me, was one of the many proving grounds on which the race of Man must stand and show its worth.

Yet if we were to get the job done, if we were to prove anything at all, there was another problem that first must be met and solved. If it was the Shadows that were causing all our trouble, then somehow we must put a stop to it. And not merely put a stop to it, but understand the Shadows and their motives. For how can anybody fight a thing, I asked myself, that he doesn't understand?

And to understand the Shadows, we'd agreed back in the tent, we had to know what kind of critters they might be. And before we could find that out, we had to grab off one for examination. And that first grab had to be perfect, for if we tried and failed, if we put them on their guard, there'd be no second chance.

But the peeper, I told myself, might give us at least one free try. If I tried the peeper and it didn't work, no one would be the wiser. It would be a failure that would go unnoticed.

Benny and I crossed the plain on the roller and headed into the foothills. I made for a place that I called the Orchard, not because it was a formal orchard, but because there were a lot of fruit-bearing trees in the area. As soon as I got around to it, I was planning to run tests to see if any of the fruit might be fit for human food.

We reached the Orchard and I parked the roller and looked around. I saw immediately that something had happened. When I had been there just a week or so before, the trees had been loaded with fruit and it seemed to be nearly ripe, but now it all was gone.

I peered underneath the trees to see if the fruit had fallen off and it hadn't. It looked for all the world as if someone had come in and picked it.

I wondered if the Shadows had done the picking, but even as I thought it, I knew it couldn't be. The Shadows didn't eat

I didn't get the peeper out right away, but sat down beneath a tree and sort of caught my breath and did a little thinking.

From where I sat, I could see the camp and I wondered what Mack had done when he hadn't found the peeper. I could imagine he'd be in a towering rage. And I could imagine Greasy, considerably relieved, but wondering just the same what had happened to the peeper and perhaps rubbing it into Mack a little how he had been wrong.

I got the feeling that maybe it would be just as well if I stayed away a while. At least until mid-afternoon. By that time, perhaps, Mack would have cooled off a little.

And I thought about the Shadows.

Lousy savages, Thorne had said. Yet they were far from savages. They were perfect gentlemen (or ladies, God knows which they were, if either) and your genuine savage is no gentleman on a number of very fundamental points. The Shadows were clean in body, healthy and well mannered. They had a certain cultural poise. They were, more than anything else, like a group of civilized campers, but unencumbered by the usual camp equipment.

They were giving us a going over – there could be no doubt of that. They were learning all they could of us and why did they want to know? What use could they make of pots and pans and earthmovers and all the other things?

Or were they merely taking our measure before they clobbered us?

And there were all the other questions, too.

Where did they hang out?

How did they disappear, and when they disappeared, where did they go?

How did they eat and breathe?

How did they communicate?

Come right down to it, I admitted to myself, the Shadows undoubtedly knew a great deal more about us than we knew about them. Because when you tried to chalk up what we knew about them, it came out to almost exactly nothing.

I sat under the tree for a while longer, with the thoughts spinning in my head and not adding up. Then I got to my feet and went over to the roller and got out the peeper.

It was the first time I'd ever had one in my hands and I was interested and slightly apprehensive. For a peeper was nothing one should monkey with.

It was a simple thing to look at – like a lopsided pair of binoculars, with a lot of selector knobs on each side and on the top of it.

You looked into it and you twisted the knobs until you had what you wanted and then there was a picture. You stepped into the picture and you lived the life you found there – the sort of life you picked by the setting of the knobs. And there were many lives to pick from, for there were millions of combinations that could be set up on the knobs and the factors ranged from the lightest kind of frippery to the most abysmal horror.

The peeper was outlawed, naturally – it was worse than alcoholism, worse than dope, the most insidious vice that had ever hit mankind. It threw psychic hooks deep into the soul and tugged forevermore. When a man acquired the habit, and it was easy to acquire, there was no getting over it. He'd spend the rest of his life trying to sort out his life from all the fantasied ones, getting further and further from reality all the while, till nothing was real any more.

I squatted down beside the roller and tried to make some sense out of the knobs. There were thirty-nine of them, each numbered from one to thirty-nine, and I wondered what the numbering meant.

Benny came over and hunkered down beside me, with one shoulder touching mine, and watched what I was doing.

I pondered over the numbering, but pondering did no good. There was only one way to find out what I was looking for. So I set all the knobs back to zero on the graduated scales, then twisted No. 1 up a notch or two.

I knew that was not the way to work a peeper. In actual operation, one would set a number of the knobs at different settings, mixing in the factors in different proportions to make up the kind of life that one might want to sample. But I wasn't after a life. What I wanted to find out was what factor each of the knobs controlled.

So I set No. 1 up a notch or two and lifted the peeper and fitted it to my face and I was back again in the meadow of my boyhood – a meadow that was green as no meadow ever was before, with a sky as blue as old-time watered silk and with a brook and butterflies.

And more than that – a meadow that lay in a day that would never end, a place that knew no time, and a sunlight that was the bright glow of boyish happiness.

I knew exactly how the grass would feel beneath bare feet and I could remember how the sunlight would bounce off the wind-ripples of the brook. It was the hardest thing I ever did in my entire life, but I snatched the peeper from my eyes.

I squatted there, with the peeper cradled in my lap. My hands were unsteady, longing to lift the peeper so I could look once again at that scene out of a long-lost boyhood, but I made myself not do it.

No. 1 was not the knob I wanted, so I turned it back to zero and, since No. 1 was about as far away as one could imagine from what I was looking for, I turned knob 39 up a notch or two.

I lifted the peeper halfway to my face and then I turned plain scared. I put it down again until I could get a good grip on my courage. Then I lifted it once more and stuck my face straight into a horror that reached out and tried to drag me in.

I can't describe it. Even now, I cannot recall one isolated fragment of what I really saw. Rather than seeing, it was pure impression and raw emotion – a sort of surrealistic representation of all that is loathsome and repellent, and yet somehow retaining a hypnotic fascination that forbade retreat.

Shaken, I snatched the peeper from my face and sat frozen. For a moment, my mind was an utter blank, with stray wisps of horror streaming through it.

Then the wisps gradually cleared away and I was squatting once again on the hillside with the Shadow hunkered down beside me, his shoulder touching mine.

It was a terrible thing, I thought, an act no human could bring himself to do, even to a Shadow. Just turned up a notch or two, it was terrifying; turned on full power, it would twist one's brain.

Benny reached out a hand to take the peeper from me. I jerked it away from him. But he kept on pawing for it and that gave me time to think.

This, I told myself, was exactly the way I had wanted it to be. All that was different was that Benny, by his nosiness, was making it easy for me to do the very thing I'd planned.

I thought of all that depended on our getting us a Shadow to examine. And I thought about my job and how it would bust my heart if the inspector should come out and fire us and send in another crew. There just weren't planets lying around every day in the week to be engineered. I might never get another chance.

So I put out my thumb and shoved knob 39 to its final notch and let Benny have the peeper.

And even as I gave it to him, I wondered if it would really work or if I'd just had a pipe-dream. It might not work, I thought, for it was a human mechanism, designed for human use, keyed to the human nervous system and response.

Then I knew that I was wrong, that the peeper did not operate by virtue of its machinery alone, but by the reaction of the brain and the body of its user – that it was no more than a trigger mechanism to set loose the greatness and the beauty and the horror that lay within the user's brain. And horror, while it might take a different shape and form, appear in a different guise, was horror for a Shadow as well as for a human.

Benny lifted the peeper to that great single eye of his and thrust his head forward to fit into the viewer. Then I saw his body jerk and stiffen and I caught him as he toppled and eased him to the ground.

I stood there above him and felt the triumph and the pride – and perhaps a little pity, too – that it should be necessary to do a thing like this to a guy like Benny. To play a trick like this on my Shadow who had sat, just moments ago, with his shoulder touching mine.

I knelt down and turned him over. He didn't seem so heavy and

I was glad of that, because I'd have to get him on the roller and then make a dash for camp, going as fast as I could gun the roller, because there was no telling how long Benny would stay knocked out.

I picked up the peeper and stuck it back into the roller's bag, then hunted for some rope or wire to tie Benny on so he would not fall off.

I don't know if I heard a noise or not. I'm half inclined to think that there wasn't any noise – that it was some sort of built-in alarm system that made me turn around.

Benny was sagging in upon himself and I had a moment of wild panic, thinking that he might be dead, that the shock of the horror that leaped out of the peeper at him had been too much for him to stand.

And I remembered what Mack had said: "Never kill a thing until you have figured out just how efficiently it may up and kill you back."

If Benny was dead, then we might have all hell exploding in our laps.

If he was dead, though, he sure was acting funny. He was sinking in and splitting at a lot of different places, and he turning to what looked like dust, but wasn't dust, and there wasn't any Benny. There was just the harness with the bag and the jewel and then there wasn't any bag, but a handful of trinkets lying on the ground where the bag had been.

And there was something else.

There still was Benny's eye. The eye was a part of a cone that been in Benny's head.

I recalled how the survey party had seen other cones like that. But had not been able to get close to them.

I was too scared to move. I stood and looked and there were a lot of goose pimples rising on my hide.

For Benny was no alien. Benny was no more than the proxy of some other alien that we had never seen and could not even guess at.

All sorts of conjectures went tumbling through my brain, but they were no more than panic-pictures, and they flipped off and on so fast, I couldn't settle on any one of them.

But one thing was clear as day – the cleverness of this alien for which the Shadows were the front.

Too clever to confront us with anything that was more remotely human in its shape – a thing for which we could feel pity or contempt or perhaps exasperation, but something that would never rouse a fear within us. A pitiful little figure that was a caricature of our shape and one that so stupid that it couldn't even talk. And one that was sufficiently alien to keep us puzzled and stump us on so many basic points that we would, at last, give up in sheer bewilderment any attempts that we might make to get it puzzled out.

I threw a quick glance over my shoulder and kept my shoulders hunched, and if anything had moved, I'd have run like a frightened rabbit. But nothing moved. Nothing even rustled. There was nothing to be afraid of except the thoughts within my head.

But I felt a frantic urge to get out of there and I went down on my hands and knees and began to gather what was left of Benny.

I scooped up the pile of trinkets and the jewel and dumped them in the bag along with the peeper. Then I went back and picked up the cone, with the one eye looking at me, but I could see that the eye was dead. The cone was slippery and it didn't feel like metal, but it was heavy and hard to get a good grip on and I had quite a time with it. But I finally got it in the bag and started out for camp.

I went like a bat winging out of hell. Fear was roosting on one shoulder and I kept that roller wheeling.

I swung into camp and headed for Mack's tent, but before I got there, I found what looked like the entire project crew working at the craziest sort of contraption one would ever hope to see. It was a mass of gears and cams and wheels and chains and whatnot, and it sprawled over what, back home, would have been a good-sized lot, and there was no reason I could figure for build-ing anything like that.

I saw Thorne standing off to one side and superintending the work, yelling first at this one and then at someone else, and I could see that he was enjoying himself. Thorne was that kind of bossy jerk.

I stopped the roller beside him and balanced it with one leg.

"What's going on?" I asked him.

"We're giving them something to get doped out," he said. "We're going to drive them crazy."

"Them? You mean the Shadows?"

"They want information, don't they?" Thorne demanded. "They've been underfoot day and night, always in the way, so now we give them something to keep them occupied."

"But what does it do?"

Thorne spat derisively. "Nothing. That's the beauty of it."

"Well," I said, "I suppose you know what you're doing. Does Mack know what's going on?"

"Mack and Carr and Knight are the big brains that thought it up," said Thorne. "I'm just carrying out orders."

I went on to Mack's tent and parked the roller there and I knew that Mack was inside, for I heard a lot of arguing.

I took the carrier bag and marched inside the tent and pushed my way up to the table and, up-ending the sack, emptied the whole thing on the tabletop.

And I plumb forgot about the peeper being in there with all the other stuff.

There was nothing I could do about it. The peeper lay naked on the table and there was a terrible silence and I could see that in another second Mack would blow his jets.

He sucked in his breath to roar, but I beat him to it.

"Shut up, Mack!" I snapped. "I don't want to hear a word from you!"

I must have caught him by surprise, for he let his breath out slowly, looking at me funny while he did it, and Carr and Knight were just slightly frozen in position. The tent was deathly quiet.

"That was Benny," I said, motioning at the tabletop. "That is all that's left of him. A look in the peeper did it."

Carr came a bit unfrozen. "But the peeper! We looked everywhere –"

"I knew Greasy had it and I stole it when I got a hunch. Remember, we were talking about how to catch a Shadow –"

"I'm going to bring charges against you!" howled Mack. "I'm going to make an example out of you! I'm going to –"

"You're going to shut up," I said at him. "You're going to stay quiet and listen or I'll heave you out of here tin cup over appetite."

"Please!" begged Knight. "Please, gentlemen, let's act civilized."

And that was a hot one – him calling us gentlemen.

"It seems to me," said Carr, "that the matter of the peeper is somewhat immaterial if Bob has turned it to some useful purpose."

"Let's all sit down," Knight urged, "and maybe count to ten. Then Bob can tell us what is on his mind."

It was a good suggestion. We all sat down and I told them what had happened. They sat there listening, looking at all that junk on the table and especially at the cone, for it was lying on its side at one end of the table, where it had rolled, and it was looking at us with that dead and fishy eye.

"Those Shadows," I finished up, "aren't alive at all. They're just some sort of spy rig that something else is sending out. All we need to do is lure the Shadows off, one by one, and let them look into the peeper with knob 39 set full and –"

"It's no permanent solution," said Knight. "Fast as we destroyed them, there'd be other ones sent out."

I shook my head. "I don't think so. No matter how good that alien race may be, they can't control those Shadows just by mental contact. My bet is that there are machines involved, and when we destroy a Shadow, it would be my hunch that we knock out a machine. And if we knock out enough of them, we'll give those other people so much headache that they may come out in the open and we can dicker with them."

"I'm afraid you're wrong," Knight answered. "This other race keeps hidden, I'd say, for some compelling reason. Maybe they have developed an underground civilization and never venture on the surface because it's a hostile environment to them. But maybe they keep track of what is doing on the surface by means of these cones of theirs. And when we showed up, they rigged the cones to look like something slightly human, something they felt sure we would accept, and sent them out to get a good close look."

Mack put up his hands and rubbed them back and forth across his head. "I don't like this hiding business. I like things out in the open where I can take a swipe at them and they can take a swipe at me. I'd have liked it a whole lot better if the Shadows had really been the aliens."

"I don't go for your underground race," Carr said to Knight. "It doesn't seem to me you could produce such a civilization if you lived underground. You'd be shut away from all the phenomena of nature. You wouldn't –"

"All right," snapped Knight, "what's *your* idea?"

"They might have matter transmission – in fact, we know they do – whether by machine or mind, and that would mean that they'd never have to travel on the surface of the planet, but could transfer from place to place in the matter of a second. But they still would need to know what was going on, so they'd have their eyes and ears like a TV radar system –"

"You jokers are just talking round in circles," objected Mack. "You don't know what the score is."

"I suppose you do," Knight retorted.

"No, I don't," said Mack. "But I'm honest enough to say straight out I don't."

"I think Carr and Knight are too involved," I said. "These aliens might be hiding only until they find out what we're like

– whether they can trust us or if it would be better to run us off the planet."

"Well," said Knight, "no matter how you figure it, you've got to admit that they probably know practically all there is to know about us – our technology and our purpose and what kind of animals we are and they probably have picked up our language."

"They know too much," said Mack. "I'm getting scared."

There was a scrabbling at the flap and Thorne stuck in his head.

"Say, Mack," he said, "I got a good idea. How about setting up some guns in that contraption out there? When the Shadows crowd around –"

"No guns," Knight said firmly. "No rockets. No electrical traps. You do just what we told you. Produce all the useless motion you can. Get it as involved and as flashy as possible. But let it go at that."

Thorne withdrew sulkily.

Knight explained to me: "We don't expect it to last too long, but it may keep them occupied for a week or so while we get some work done. When it begins to wear off, we'll fix up something else."

It was all right, I suppose, but it didn't sound too hot to me. At the best, it bought a little time and nothing more. It bought a little time, that is, if we could fool the Shadows. Somehow, I wasn't sure that we could fool them much. Ten to one, they'd spot the contraption as a phony the minute it was set in motion.

Mack got up and walked around the table. He lifted the cone and tucked it beneath one arm.

"I'll take this down to the shop," he said. "Maybe the boys can find out what it is."

"I can tell you now," said Carr. "It's what the aliens use to control the Shadows. Remember the cones the survey people saw? This is one of them. My guess is that it's some kind of a signal device that can transmit data back to base, wherever that might be."

"No matter," Mack said. "We'll cut into it and see what we can find."

"And the peeper?" I asked.

"I'll take care of that."

I reached out a hand and picked it up. "No, you won't. You're just the kind of bigot who would take it out and smash it."

"It's illegal," Mack declared.

Carr sided with me. "Not any more. It's a tool now – a weapon that we can use."

I handed it to Carr. "You take care of it. Put it in a good safe place. We may need it again before all this is over."

I gathered the junk that had been in Benny's bag and picked up the jewel and dropped it into a pocket of my coat.

Mack went out with the cone underneath his arm. The rest of us drifted outside the tent and stood there, just a little footloose now that the excitement was all over.

"He'll have Greasy's hide," worried Knight.

"I'll talk to him," Carr said. "I'll make him see that Greasy may have done us a service by sneaking the thing out here."

"I suppose," I said, "I should tell Greasy what happened to the peeper."

Knight shook his head. "Let him sweat a while. It will do him good."

Back in my tent, I tried to do some paper work, but I couldn't get my mind to settle down on it. I guess I was excited and I'm afraid that I missed Benny and I was tangled up with wondering just what the situation was, so far as the Shadows were concerned.

We had named them well, all right, for they were little more than shadows – meant to shadow us. But even knowing they were just camouflaged spy rigs, I still found it hard not to think of them as something that was alive.

They were no more than cones, of course, and the cones probably were no more than observation units for those hidden people who hung out somewhere on the planet. For thousands of years, perhaps, the cones had been watching while this race stayed in hiding somewhere. But maybe more than watching. Maybe the cones were harvesters and planters – perhaps hunters and trappers – bringing back the plunder of the wilds to their hidden masters. More than likely, it had been the cones that had picked all the Orchard fruit.

And if there was a culture here, if another race had primal rights upon the planet, then what did that do to the claims that Earth might make? Did it mean we might be forced to relinquish this planet, after all – one of the few Earthlike planets found in years of exploration?

I sat at my desk and thought about the planning and the work and the money that had gone into this project, which, even so, was no more than a driblet compared to what eventually would be spent to make this into another Earth.

Even on this project center, we'd made no more than an initial start. In a few more weeks, the ships would begin bringing in the steel mill and that in itself was a tremendous task – to bring it in, assemble it, mine the ore to get it going and finally to put it into operation. But simpler and easier, infinitely so, than freighting out from Earth all the steel that would be needed to build this project alone.

We couldn't let it go down the drain. After all the years, after all the planning and the work, in face of Earth's great need for more living space, we could not give up Stella IV. And yet we could not deny primal rights. If these beings, when they finally showed themselves, would say that they didn't want us here, then there would be no choice. We would simply have to clear out.

But before they threw us out, of course, they would steal us blind. Much of what we had would undoubtedly be of little value to them, but there would be some of it that they could use. No race can fail to enrich itself and its culture by contact with another. And the contact that these aliens had established was a completely one-sided bargain – the exchange flowed only in their direction.

They were, I told myself, just a bunch of cosmic sharpers.

I took the junk that had been in Benny's bag out of my pocket and spread it on the desk and began to sort it out. There was the sector model and the roller and the desk and my little row of books and the pocket chess set and all the other stuff that belonged to me.

There was all the stuff but me.

Greasy's Shadow had carried a statuette of Greasy, but I found none of me and I was a little sore at Benny. He could have gone to the extra effort to have made a statuette of me.

I rolled the things around on the desk top with a finger and wondered once again just how deeply they went. Might they not be patterns rather than just models? Perhaps, I told myself, letting my imagination run away with me, perhaps each of these little models carried in some sort of code a complete analysis and description of whatever the article might be. A human, making a survey or an analysis, would write a sheaf of notes, would capture the subject matter in a page or two of symbols. Maybe these little models were the equivalent of a human notebook, the aliens' way of writing.

And I wondered how they wrote, how they made the models, but there wasn't any answer.

I gave up trying to work and went out of the tent and climbed up the little rise to where Thorne and the men were building their flytrap for the Shadows.

They had put a lot of work and ingenuity into it and it made no sense at all – which, after all, was exactly what it was meant to do.

If we could get the Shadows busy enough trying to figure out what this new contraption was, maybe they'd leave us alone long enough to get some work done.

Thorne and his crew had gotten half a dozen replacement motors out of the shop and had installed those to be used as power. Apparently they had used almost all the spare equipment parts they could find, for there were shafts and gears and cams and all sorts of other things all linked together in a mindless pattern. And here and there they had set up what looked like control boards, except, of course, that they controlled absolutely nothing, but were jammed with flashers and all sorts of other gimmicks until they looked like Christmas trees.

I stood around and watched until Greasy rang the dinner bell, then ran a foot race with all the others to get to the tables.

There was a lot of loud talk and joking, but no one wasted too much time eating. They bolted their food and hurried back to the flytrap.

Just before sunset, they set it going and it was the screwiest mass of meaningless motion that anyone had ever seen. Shafts were spinning madly and a million gears, it seemed, were meshing, and cams were wobbling with their smooth, irregular strokes, and pistons were going up and down and up and down.

It was all polished bright and it worked slicker than a whistle and it was producing nothing except motion, but it had a lot of fascination – even for a human. I found myself standing rooted in one spot, marveling at the smoothness and precision and the remorseless non-purpose of the weird contraption.

And all the time the fake control boards were sparkling and flashing with the lamps popping on and off, in little jagged runs and series, and you got dizzy watching them, trying to make some pattern out of them.

The Shadows had been standing around and gaping ever since work had started on the trap, but now they crowded closer and stood in a tight and solemn ring around the thing and they never moved.

I turned around and Mack was just behind me. He was rubbing his hands in satisfaction and his face was all lit up with smiles.

"Pretty slick," he said.

I agreed with him, but I had some doubts that I could not quite express.

"We'll string up some lights," said Mack, "so they can see it day and night and then we'll have them pegged for good."

"You think they'll stay with it?" I asked. "They won't catch on?"

"Not a chance."

I went down to my tent and poured myself a good stiff drink, then sat down in a chair in front of the tent.

Some of the men were stringing cable and others were rigging up some batteries of lights and down in the cookshack I could hear Greasy singing, but the song was sad. I felt sorry for Greasy.

Mack might be right, I admitted to myself. We might have built a trap that would cook the Shadows' goose. If nothing else, the sheer fascination of all that motion might keep them stuck there. It had a hypnotic effect even for a human and one could never gauge what effect it might have on an alien mind. Despite the evident technology of the aliens, it was entirely possible that their machine technology might have developed along some divergent line, so that the spinning wheel and the plunging piston and the smooth fluid gleam of metal was new to them.

I tried to imagine a machine technology that would require no motion, but such a thing was entirely inconceivable to me. And for that very reason, I thought, the idea of all this motion might be just as inconceivable to an alien intellect.

The stars came out while I sat there and no one wandered over to gab and that was fine. I was just as satisfied to be left alone.

After a time, I went into the tent, had another drink and decided to go to bed.

I took off my coat and slung it on the desk. When it hit, there was a thump, and as soon as I heard that thump, I knew what it was. I had dropped Benny's jewel into the pocket of the coat and had then forgotten it.

I fished into the pocket and got out the jewel, fearing all the while that I had broken it. And there was something wrong with it — it had somehow come apart. The jewel face had come loose from the rest of it and I saw that the jewel was no more than a cover for a box-shaped receptacle.

I put it on the desk and swung the jewel face open and there, inside the receptacle, I found myself.

The statuette was nestled inside a weird piece of mechanism and it was as fine a piece of work as Greasy's statuette.

It gave me a flush of pride and satisfaction. Benny, after all, had not forgotten me!

I sat for a long time looking at the statuette, trying to puzzle out the mechanism. I had a good look at the jewel and I finally figured out what it was all about.

The jewel was no jewel at all; it was a camera. Except that instead of taking two-dimensional pictures, it worked in three dimensions. And that, of course, was how the Shadows made the models. Or maybe they were patterns rather than just models.

I finished undressing and got into bed and lay on the cot, staring at the canvas, and the pieces all began to fall together and it was beautiful. Beautiful, that is, for the aliens. It made us look like a bunch of saps.

The cones had gone out and watched the survey party and had not let it get close to them, but they had been ready for us when we came. They'd disguised the cones to look like something that we wouldn't be afraid of, something perhaps that we could even laugh at it. And that was the safest kind of disguise that anyone could assume – something that the victim might think was mildly funny. For no one gets too upset about what a clown might do.

But the Shadows had been loaded and they'd let us have it and apparently, by the time we woke up, they had us pegged and labeled.

And what would they do now? Still stay behind their log, still keep watching us, and suck us dry of everything that we had to offer?

And when they were ready, when they'd gotten all they wanted or all they felt that they could get, they'd come out and finish us.

I was somewhat scared and angry and felt considerably like a fool and it was frustrating just to think about.

Mack might kid himself that he had solved the problem with his flytrap out there, but there was still a job to do. Somehow

or other, we had to track down these hiding aliens and break up
their little game.

Somewhere along the way, I went to sleep, and suddenly
someone was shaking me and yelling for me to get out.

I came half upright and saw that it was Carr who had been
shaking me. He was practically gibbering. He kept pointing outside and babbling something about a funny cloud and I couldn't
get much more out of him.

So I shucked into my trousers and my shoes and went out
with him and headed for the hilltop at a run. Dawn was just
breaking and the Shadows still were clustered around the flytrap
and a crowd of men had gathered just beyond the flytrap and
were looking toward the east.

We pushed our way through the crowd up to the front and
there was the cloud that Carr had been jabbering about, but it was
a good deal closer now and was sailing across the plains, slowly
and majestically, and flying above it was a little silver sphere that
flashed and glittered in the first rays of the sun.

The cloud looked, more than anything, like a mass of junk. I
could see what looked like a derrick sticking out of it and here and
there what seemed to be a wheel. I tried to figure out what it might
be, but I couldn't, and all the time it was moving closer to us.

Mack was at my left and I spoke to him, but he didn't answer
me. He was just like Benny – he couldn't answer me. He looked
hypnotized.

The closer that cloud came, the more fantastic it was and the
more unbelievable. For there was no question now that it was a
mass of machinery, just like the equipment we had. There were
tractors and earthmovers and shovels and dozers and all the other
stuff, and in between these bigger pieces was all sorts of little stuff.

In another five minutes, it was hovering almost over us and
then slowly it began to lower. While we watched, it came down
to the ground, gently, almost without a bump, even though there
were a couple or three acres of it. Besides the big equipment,

there were tents and cups and spoons and tables and chairs and benches and a case or two of whisky and some surveying equipment – there was, it seemed to me, almost exactly all the items there were in the camp.

When it had all sat down, the little silver sphere came down, too, and floated slowly toward us. It stopped a little way away from us and Mack walked out toward it and I followed Mack. Out of the corner of my eye, I saw that Carr and Knight were walking forward, too.

We stopped four or five feet from it and now we saw that the sphere was some sort of protective suit. Inside it sat a pale little humanoid. Not human, but at least with two legs and arms and a single head. He had antennae sprouting from his forehead and his ears were long and pointed and he had no hair at all.

He let the sphere set down on the ground and we got a little closer and squatted down so we would be on a level with him.

He jerked a thumb backward over his shoulder, pointing at the mass of equipment he'd brought.

"Is pay." he announced in a shrill, high, piping voice.

We didn't answer right away. We did some gulping first.

"Is pay for what?" Knight finally managed to ask him.

"For fun," the creature said.

"I don't understand," said Mack.

"We make one of everything. We not know what you want, so we make one of all. Unfortunate, two lots are missing. Accident, perhaps."

"The models," I said to the others. "That's what he's talking about. The models were patterns and the models from Greasy's Shadow and from Benny –"

"Not all," the creature said. "The rest be right along."

"Now wait a minute," said Carr. "Let us get this straight. You are paying us. Paying us for what? Exactly what did we do for you?"

Mack blurted out: "How did you make this stuff?"

"One question at a time," I pleaded.

"Machines can make," the creature said. "Knowing how, machines can make anything. Very good machines."

"But why?" asked Carr again. "Why did you make it for us?"

"For fun," the creature explained patiently. "For laugh. For watch. Is a big word I cannot –"

"Entertainment?" I offered.

"That is right," the creature said. "Entertainment is the word. We have lot of time for entertainment. We stay home, watch our entertainment screen. We get tired of it. We seek for something new. You something new. Give us much interesting. We try to pay you for it."

"Good Lord!" exclaimed Knight. "I begin to get it now. We were a big news event and so they sent out all those cones to cover us. Mack, did you saw into that cone last night?"

"We did," said Mack. "As near as we could figure, it was a TV sender. Not like ours, of course – there would be differences. But we figured it for a data-sending rig,"

I turned back to the alien in his shiny sphere. "Listen carefully," I said. "Let's get down to business. You are willing to keep on paying if we provide you entertainment?"

"Gladly," said the creature. "You keep us entertained, we give you what you want."

"Instead of one of everything, you will make us many of one thing?"

"You show it to us," the creature said. "You let us know how many."

"Steel?" asked Mack. "You can make us steel?"

"No recognize this steel. Show us. How made, how big, how shaped. We make."

"If we keep you entertained?"

"That right." the creature said.

"Deal?" I asked.

"Deal," the creature said.

"From now on? No stopping?"

"As long as you keep us happy."

"That may take some doing," Mack told me.

"No, it won't," I said.

"You're crazy!" Mack yelped. "They'll never let us have them!"

"Yes, they will," I answered. "Earth will do anything to cinch this planet. And don't you see, with this sort of swap, we'll beat the cost. All Earth has to do is send out one sample of everything we need. One sample will do the trick. One I-beam and they'll make a million of them. It's the best deal Earth has ever made."

"We do our part," the creature assured us happily. "Long as you do yours."

"I'll get that order right off now," I said to Mack. "I'll write it up and have Jack send it out."

I stood up and headed back toward camp.

"Rest of it," the creature said, motioning over his shoulder.

I swung around and looked.

There was another mass of stuff coming in, keeping fairly low. And this time it was men – a solid press of men.

"Hey!" cried Mack. "You can't do that! That just isn't right!"

I didn't need to look. I knew exactly what had happened. The aliens had duplicated not only our equipment, but the men as well. In that crowd of men were the duplicates of every one of us – everyone, that is, except myself and Greasy.

Horrified as I might have been, outraged as any human would be, I couldn't help but think of some of the situations that might arise. Imagine two Macks insisting on bossing the operation! Picture two Thornes trying to get along together!

I didn't hang around. I left Mack and the rest of them to explain why men should not be duplicated. In my tent, I sat down and wrote an imperative, high-priority, *must-deliver* order for five hundred peepers.

SO BRIGHT THE VISION

This story was probably completed early in 1955 under the title "Writ by Hand" before finally being sold to Leo Margulies at Fantastic Universe Science Fiction, *to whom Cliff had been selling pieces the top-ranked markets rejected. Any critical mention that "So Bright the Vision" has received since being published in August 1956 has largely been due to comment on its vision of the writerly craft in a computerized future. And while such comment is both accurate and deserved, it completely overlooks the story's criticisms of both the literary establishment in general and the science fiction establishment in particular: The machine, Cliff argued, was being allowed to set the norm for literature, which had the effect of setting up a pattern that would be deadly to good fiction.*

For all the seriousness of that subject, this story is just kind of fun, showing what can be done by an author willing to break out of the prevailing SF pattern of the fifties. And I remain – as I said in my comment in an earlier volume of these collections, on the story "Ogre" – utterly tickled by Cliff's use of that story's "life blanket" idea in the context of this story.

—dww

I

The showroom was in the decorous part of town, where Kemp Hart seldom found himself. It was a long way from his usual haunts and he was surprised to find that he had walked so far. In fact, he would not have walked at all if his credit had been good at the Bright Star bar where his crowd hung out.

As soon as he realized where he was he knew he should turn around and walk rapidly away, for he was out of place in this district of swank publishers, gold-plated warrens and famous eateries. But the showroom held him. It would not let him go. He stood in front of it in all his down-at-heels unkemptness, one hand thrust in a pocket, fugitively rubbing between thumb and finger the two small coins that still remained to him.

Behind the glass the machines were shining-wonderful, the sort of merchandise that belonged on this svelte and perfumed street. One machine in the corner of the showroom was bigger and shinier than the others and had about it a rare glint of competence. It had a massive keyboard for the feeding in of data and it had a hundred slots or so for the working tapes and films. It had a mood control calibrated more sensitively than any he had ever seen and in all probability a lot of other features that were not immediately apparent.

With a machine such as that, Hart told himself, a man could become famous almost automatically and virtually overnight. He could write anything he wished and he would write it well and the doors of the most snooty of the publishers would stand open to him.

But much as he might wish to, there was no use of going in to see it. There was nothing to be gained by even thinking about it. It was just something he could stand and look at from beyond the showroom's glass.

And yet, he told himself, he had a perfect right to go in and look it over. There was not a thing to stop him. Nothing, at least, beyond the sneer upon the salesman's face at the sight of him – the silent, polite, well-disciplined contempt when he turned and slunk away.

He looked furtively up and down the street and the street was empty. The hour was far too early for this particular street to have come to life, and it occurred to him that if he just walked in and asked to see the machine, it would be all right. Perhaps he could explain he did not wish to buy it, but just to look at it. Maybe if he did that they wouldn't sneer at him. Certainly no one could object. There must be a lot of people, even rich and famous people, who only came to look.

He edged along the showroom, studying the machines and heading for the door, telling himself that he would not go in, that it was foolish to go in, but secretly knowing that he would.

He reached the door and opened it and stepped inside. The salesman appeared almost as if by magic.

"The yarner in the corner," Hart said. "I wonder if I might –"

"Most certainly," said the salesman. "If you'll just come along with me."

In the corner of the showroom, the salesman draped his arm across the machine affectionately.

"It is our newest model," he said. "We call it the Classic, because it has been designed and engineered with but one thought in mind – the production of the classic. It is, we think, a vast improvement over our Best Seller Model, which, after all, is intended to turn out no better than best sellers – even though on occasion it has turned out certain minor classics. To be quite honest with you, sir, I would suspect that in almost every one of those instances, it had been souped up a bit. I am told some people are very clever that way."

Hart shook his head. "Not me. I'm all thumbs when it comes to tinkering."

"In that case," said the salesman, "the thing for you to do is buy the best yarner that you can. Used intelligently, there's virtually no limit to its versatility. And in this particular model the quality factor is much higher than in any of the others. Although naturally, to get the best results you must be selective in your character films and your narrative problem tapes. But that needn't worry you. We have a large stock of tapes and films and some new mood and atmosphere fixers that are quite unique. They come fairly high, of course, but —"

"By the way, just what is the price of this model?"

"It's only twenty-five thousand," the salesman told him, brightly. "Don't you wonder, sir, how it can be offered at so ridiculous a figure? The engineering that went into it is remarkable. We worked on it for ten full years before we were satisfied. And during those ten years the specifications were junked and redrawn time and time again to keep pace with our developmental research."

He slapped the shiny machine with a jubilant hand.

"I can guarantee you, sir, that nowhere can you get a product superior to this. It has everything. Millions of probability factors have been built into it, assuring you of sure-fire originality. No danger of stumbling into the stereotype, which is not true at all with so many of the cheaper models. The narrative bank alone is capable of turning out an almost infinite number of situations on any particular theme and the character developer has thousands of points of reference instead of the hundred or so you find in inferior models. The semantics section is highly selective and sensitive and you must not overlook —"

"It's a good machine," interposed Hart. "But it costs a bit too much. Now, if you had something else . . ."

"Most certainly, sir. We have many other models."

"Would you take a machine in trade?"

"Gladly. What kind of machine do you have, sir?"

"An Auto-Author Ninety-six."

The salesman froze just slightly. He shook his head, half sadly, half in bewilderment. "Well, now, I don't know if we could allow you much for that. It's a fairly old type of machine. Almost obsolete."

"But you could give me something?"

"I think so. Not a great deal, though."

"And time payment?"

"Yes, certainly. We could work something out. If you would give me your name."

Hart told him what it was.

The salesman jotted it down and said, "Excuse me a moment, sir."

Hart stood for a moment, looking after him. Then, like a sneak thief in the night, he moved softly to the front door and walked swiftly down the street.

There was no use in staying. No use at all of waiting for the salesman to come back and shake his hand and say, "We're very sorry, sir."

We're very sorry, sir, because we've looked up your credit rating and it's absolutely worthless. We checked your sales record and found you sold just one short story in the last six months.

It had been a mistake to go for a walk at all, Hart told himself, not without bitterness.

II

Downtown, in a section of the city far removed from the glamorous showroom, Hart climbed six flights of stairs because the elevator was out of whack again.

Behind the door that said *Irving Publications*, the preoccupied receptionist stopped filing her nails long enough to make a motion with her thumb toward the inner office.

"Go on in and see him," she said.

Ben Irving sat behind a heaped-up desk cluttered with manuscripts, proofs and layout sheets. His sleeves were rolled up to his elbows and he wore an eyeshade. He always wore the eyeshade and that was one of the minor mysteries of the place, for at no time during the day was there light enough in his dingy office to blind a self-respecting bat.

He looked up and blinked at Hart.

"Glad to see you, Kemp," he said. "Sit down. What's on your mind today?"

Hart took a chair. "I was wondering. About that last story that I sent you –"

"Haven't got around to it yet," said Irving. He waved his hand at the mess upon his desk by way of explanation.

"Mary!" he shouted.

The receptionist stuck her head inside the door.

"Get Hart's manuscript," he said, "and let Millie have a look at it."

Irving leaned back in his chair. "This won't take long," he said. "Millie's a fast reader."

"I'll wait," said Hart.

"I've got something for you," Irving told him. "We're starting a new magazine, aimed at the tribes out in the Algol system. They're a primitive sort of people, but they can read, Lord love them. We had the devil's own time finding someone who could do the translations for us and it'll cost more than we like to pay to have the type set up. They got the damnedest alphabet you ever saw. We finally found a printer who had some in his fonts."

"What kind of stuff?" Hart asked.

"Simple humanoid," Irving replied. "Blood and thunder and a lot of spectacle. Life is tough and hard out there, so we have to give them something with plenty of color in it that's easy to read. Nothing fancy, mind you."

"Sounds all right."

"Good basic hack," said Irving. "See how it goes out there and if it goes all right we'll make translations for some of the primitive groups out in the Capella region. Minor changes, maybe, but none too serious."

He squinted meditatively at Hart.

"Not too much pay. But if it goes over we'll want a lot of it."

"I'll see what I can do," said Hart. "Any taboos? Anything to duck?"

"No religion at all," the editor told him. "They've got it, of course, but it's so complicated that you'd better steer clear of it entirely. No mushy stuff. Love don't rate with them. They buy their women and don't fool around with love. Treasure and greed would be good. Any standard reference work will give you a line on that. Fantastic weapons – the more gruesome the better. Bloodshed, lots of it. Hatred, that's their dish. Hatred and vengeance and hell-for-leather living. And you simply got to keep it moving."

"I'll see what I can do."

"That's the second time you've said that."

"I'm not doing so good, Ben. Once I could have told you yes. Once I could have hauled it over by the ton."

"Lost the touch?"

"Not the touch. The machine. My yarner is haywire. I might just as well try to write my stories by hand."

Irving shuddered at the thought.

"Fix it up," he said. "Tinker with it."

"I'm no good at that. Anyhow, it's too old. Almost obsolete."

"Well, do the best you can. I'd like to go on buying from you."

The girl came in. Without looking at Hart she laid the manuscript down upon the desk. From where he sat, Hart could see the single word the machine had stamped upon its face: REJECTED.

"Emphatic," said the girl. "Millie almost stripped a gear."

Irving pitched the manuscript to Hart.

"Sorry, Kemp. Better luck next time."

Hart rose, holding the manuscript in his hand. "I'll try this other thing," he said.

He started for the door.

"Just a minute," Irving said, his voice sympathetic.

Hart turned back.

Irving brought out his billfold, stripped out two tens and held them out.

"No," said Hart, staring at the bills longingly.

"It's a loan," said the editor. "Damn it, man, you can take a loan. You'll be bringing me some stuff."

"Thanks, Ben. I'll remember this."

He stuffed the bills into his pocket and made a swift retreat.

Bitter dust burned in his throat and there was a hard, cold lump in the center of his belly.

Got something for you, Ben had said. *Good basic hack.*

Good basic hack.

So that was what he'd sunk to!

Angela Maret was the only patron in the Bright Star bar when Hart finally arrived there, with money in his pocket and a man-sized hankering for a glass of beer. Angela was drinking a weird sort of pink concoction that looked positively poisonous. She had her glasses on and her hair skinned back and was quite obviously on a literary binge. It was a shame, Hart thought. She could be attractive, but preferred not to be.

The instant Hart joined her Blake, the bartender, came over to the table and just stood there, with his fists firmly planted on his hips.

"Glass of beer," Hart told him.

"No more cuff," Blake said, with an accusing stare.

"Who said anything about cuff? I'll pay for it."

Blake scowled. "Since you're loaded, how about paying on the bill?"

"I haven't got that kind of money. Do I get the beer or don't I?"

Watching Blake waddle back to the bar, Hart was glad he had had the foresight to stop and buy a pack of cigarettes to break one of the tens. Flash a ten in this joint and Blake would be on it in a second and have it chalked against his bill.

"Staked?" Angela asked sweetly.

"An advance," Hart told her, lying like a gentleman. "Irving has some stuff for me to do. He'll need a lot of it. It doesn't pay too well, of course."

Blake came with the beer and plunked it down on the table and waited pointedly for Hart to do the expected thing.

Hart paid him and he waddled off.

"Have you heard about Jasper?" Angela asked.

Hart shook his head. "Nothing recent," he said. "Did he finish his book?"

Angela's face lit up. "He's going on vacation. Can you imagine that? *Him* going on vacation!"

"I don't see why not," Hart protested. "Jasper has been selling. He's the only one of us who manages to stay loaded week after week."

"But that's not it, Kemp. Wait until I tell you – it simply is a scream. Jasper thinks he can write better if he goes off on vacation."

"Well, why not? Just last year Don went to one of those summer camps. That Bread Loaf thing, as they call it."

"All they do there," she said, "is brush up on mechanics. It's a sort of refresher course on the gadgetry of yarners. How to soup up the old heap so it'll turn out fresher stuff."

"I still don't see why Jasper can't take a vacation if he can afford it."

"You're so dense," said Angela. "Don't you get the point at all?"

"I get the point all right. Jasper thinks there's still a human factor in our writing. He's not entirely satisfied to get his facts out of a standard reference work or encyclopedia. He's not content to let the yarner define an emotion he has never felt or the color of a sunset he has never seen. He was nuts enough to hint at that and you and the rest of them have been riding him. No wonder the guy is eccentric. No wonder he keeps his door locked all the time."

"That locked door," Angela said cattily, "is symbolic of the kind of man he is."

"I'd lock my door," Hart told her. "I'd be eccentric too – if I could turn it out like Jasper. I'd walk on my hands. I'd wear a sarong. I'd even paint my face bright blue."

"You sound like you believe the same as Jasper does."

He shook his head. "No, I don't think the way he does. I know better. But if he wants to think that way let him go ahead and think it."

"You do," she crowed at him. "I can see it in your face. You think it's possible to be independently creative."

"No, I don't. I know it's the machines that do the creating – not us. We're nothing but attic tinkers. We're literary mechanics. And I suppose that's the way it should be. There is, naturally, the yearning for the past. That's been evident in every age. The 'good old days' complex. Back in those days a work of fiction was writ by hand and human agony."

"The agony's still with us, Kemp."

He said: "Jasper's a mechanic. That's what's wrong with me. I can't even repair that junk-heap of mine and you should see the way Jasper has his clunk souped up."

"You could hire someone to repair it. There are firms that do excellent work."

"I never have the money."

He finished his beer.

"What's that stuff you're drinking?" he asked. "Want another one?"

She pushed her glass away. "I don't like that mess," she said. "I'll have a beer with you, if you don't mind."

Hart signaled to Blake for two beers.

"What are you doing now, Angela?" he asked. "Still working on the book?"

"Working up some films," she said.

"That's what I'll have to do this afternoon. I need a central character for this Irving stuff. Big and tough and boisterous – but not too uncouth. I'll look along the riverfront."

"They come high now, Kemp," she said. "Even those crummy aliens are getting wise to us. Even the ones from *way out*. I paid twenty for one just the other day and he wasn't too hot, either."

"It's cheaper than buying made-up films."

"Yes, I agree with you there. But it's a lot more work."

Blake brought the beers and Hart counted out the change into his waiting palm.

"Get some of this new film," Angela advised. "It's got the old stuff beat forty different ways. The delineation is sharper and you catch more of the marginal factors. You get a more rounded picture of the character. You pick up all the nuances of the subject, so to speak. It makes your people more believable. I've been using it."

"It comes high, I suppose," he said.

"Yes, it's a bit expensive," she admitted.

"I've got a few spools of the old stuff. I'll have to get along with that."

"I've an extra fifty you can have."

He shook his head. "Thanks, Angela. I'll cadge drinks and bum meals and hit up for a cigarette, but I'm not taking a fifty you'll need yourself. There's none of us so solvent we can lend someone else a fifty."

"Well, I would have done so gladly. If you should change your mind –"

"Want another beer?" Hart asked, cutting her short.

"I have to get to work."

"So have I," said Hart.

III

Hart climbed the stairs to the seventh floor, then went down the corridor and knocked on Jasper Hansen's door.

"Just a minute," said a voice from within the room.

He waited for three minutes. Finally a key grated in the lock and the door was opened wide.

"Sorry I took so long," apologized Jasper. "I was setting up some data and I couldn't quit. Had to finish it."

Hart nodded. Jasper's explanation was understandable. It was difficult to quit in the middle of setting up some data that had taken hours to assemble.

The room was small and littered. In one corner stood the yarner, a shining thing, but not as shiny as the one he'd seen that morning in the uptown showroom. A typewriter stood on a littered desk, half covered by the litter. A long shelf sagged with the weight of dog-eared reference works. Bright-jacketed books were piled helter-skelter in a corner. A cat slept on an unmade bed. A bottle of liquor stood on a cupboard beside a loaf of bread. Dirty dishes were piled high in the sink.

"Heard you're going on vacation, Jasper," Hart said.

Jasper gave him a wary look. "Yes, I thought I might."

"I was wondering, Jasper, if you'd do something for me."

"Just name it."

"When you're gone, could I use your yarner?"

"Well, now, I don't know, Kemp. You see –"

"Mine is busted and I haven't the cash to fix it. But I've got a line on something. If you'd let me use yours, I could turn out enough in a week or two to cover the repair bill."

"Well, now," said Jasper, "you know I'd do anything for you. Anything at all. But that yarner – I just can't let you use it. I got it jiggered up. There isn't a circuit in it that has remained the way it was originally. There isn't a soul but myself who could operate it. If someone else tried to operate it they might burn it out or kill themselves or something."

"You could show me, couldn't you?" Hart asked, almost pleadingly.

"It's far too complicated. I've tinkered with it for years," said Jasper.

Hart managed a feeble grin. "I'm sorry, I thought –"

Jasper draped an arm around his shoulder. "Anything else. Just ask me anything."

"Thanks," said Hart, turning to go.

"Drink?"

"No, thanks," said Hart, and walked out of the door.

He climbed two more flights to the topmost floor and went into his room. His door was never locked. There was nothing in it for anyone to steal. And for that matter, he wondered, what did Jasper have that anyone might want?

He sat down in a rickety chair and stared at his yarner. It was old and battered and ornery, and he hated it.

It was worthless, absolutely worthless, and yet he knew he would have to work with it. It was all he had. He'd slave and reason with it and kick it and swear at it and he'd spend sleepless nights with it. And gurgling and clucking with overweaning gratitude, it would turn out endless reams of mediocrity that no one would buy.

He got up, and walked to the window. Far below lay the river and at the wharfs a dozen ships were moored, disgorging rolls of paper to feed the hungry presses that thundered day and night. Across the river a spaceship was rising from the spaceport, with the faint blue flicker of the ion stream wisping from the tubes. He watched it until it was out of sight.

There were other ships, with their noses pointed at the sky, waiting for the signal – the punched button, the flipped switch, the flicker of a piece of navigation tape – that would send them bounding homeward. First out into the blackness and then into that other place of weird other-worldness that annihilated time and space, setting at defiance the theoretic limit of the speed of light. Ships from many stars, all come to Earth for one thing only, for the one commodity that Earthmen had to sell.

He pulled his eyes from the fascination of the spaceport and looked across the sprawling city, the tumbled, canted, box-like rectangles of the district where he lived, while far to the north shone the faery towers and the massive greatness of the famous and the wise.

A fantastic world, he thought. A fantastic world to live in. Not the kind of world that H. G. Wells and Stapledon had dreamed. With them it had been far wandering and galactic empire, a glory and a greatness that Earth had somehow missed when the doors to space had finally been opened. Not the thunder of the rocket, but the thunder of the press. Not the great and lofty purpose, but the faint, quiet, persistent voice spinning out a yarn. Not the far sweep of great new planets, but the attic room and the driving fear that the machine would fail you, that the tapes had been used too often, that the data was all wrong.

He went to the desk and pulled all three of the drawers. He found the camera in the bottom one beneath a pile of junk. He hunted for and found the film in the middle drawer, wrapped in aluminum foil.

Rough and tough, he thought, and it shouldn't be too hard to find a man like that in one of the dives along the riverfront, where the space crews on planet leave squandered their pay checks.

The first dive he entered was oppressive with the stink of a group of spidery creatures from Spica and he didn't stay. He grimaced distastefully and got out as fast as he could. The second was repellently patronized by a few cat-like denizens of Dahib and they were not what he was looking for.

But in the third he hit the jackpot, a dozen burly humanoids from Caph – great brawling creatures with a flair for extravagance in dress, a swashbuckling attitude and a prodigious appetite for lusty living.

They were grouped about a large round table out in the center of the room and they were whooping it up. They were pounding the table with their tankards and chivvying the scuttling proprietor about and breaking into songs that they repeatedly interrupted with loud talk and argument.

Hart slipped into an unoccupied booth and watched the Caphians celebrate. One of them, bigger and louder and rowdier than the rest, wore red trousers, and a bright green shirt. Looped necklaces of platinum and outlandish alien gems encircled his throat and glittered on his chest, and his hair had not been trimmed for months. He wore a beard that was faintly satanic and, startlingly enough, his ears were slightly pointed. He looked like an ugly customer to get into a fracas with, and so, thought Hart, he's just the boy I want.

The proprietor finally lumbered over to the booth.

"Beer," said Hart. "A big glass."

"Buster," said the man, "no one drinks beer here."

"Well, then, what have you got?"

"I got *bocca* and *igno* and *hzbut* and *greno* and –"

"*Bocca*," said Hart. He knew what *bocca* was and he didn't recognize any of the others. Lord knows what some of them might do to the human constitution. *Bocca*, at least, one could survive.

The man went away and in a little while came back with a mug of *bocca*. It was faintly greenish and it sizzled just a little. What was worse, it tasted like a very dilute solution of sulphuric acid.

Hart squeezed himself back into the corner of the booth and opened his camera case. He set the camera on the table, no farther forward than was necessary to catch Green Shirt in the lens. Sighting through the finder, he got the Caphian in focus, and then quickly pressed the button that set the instrument in motion.

Once that was done, he settled down to drinking *bocca*.

He sat there, gagging down the *bocca* and manipulating the camera. Fifteen minutes was all he needed. At the end of fifteen minutes Green Shirt would be on film. Probably not as good as if he had been using the new-fangled spools that Angela was using, but at least he'd have him.

The camera ground on, recording the Caphian's physical characteristics, his personal mannerisms, his habits of speech, his thought processes (if any), his way of life, his background, his theoretic reaction in the face of any circumstance.

Not three-dimensional, thought Hart, not too concise, nor too distinctive, not digging deep into the character and analyzing him – but good enough for the kind of tripe he'd have to write for Irving.

Take this joker and surround him with a few other ruffians chosen haphazardly from the file. Use one of the films from the Deep Dark Villain reel, throw in an ingenious treasure situation and a glob of violence, dream up some God-awful background, and he'd have it. He'd have it, that is, if the yarner worked . . .

Ten minutes gone. Just five more to go. In five more minutes he'd stop the camera, put it back into its case, slip the case into his pocket and get out of the place as fast as he could. Without causing undue notice, of course.

It had been simple, he thought – much simpler than he could possibly have imagined.

They're getting on to us, Angela had said. *Even these crummy aliens.*

Only three more minutes to go.

A hand came down from nowhere, and picked up the camera. Hart swiveled around. The proprietor stood directly behind him, with the camera under his arm.

Good Lord, thought Hart, *I was watching the Caphians so closely I forgot about this guy!*

The proprietor roared at him: "So! You sneak in here under false pretenses to get your film! Are you trying to give my place a bad name?"

Swiftly Hart flung himself out of the booth, one frantic eye on the door. There was just a chance that he might make it. But the proprietor stuck out an expert foot and tripped him. Hart landed on his shoulders and somersaulted. He skidded across the floor, smashed into a table and rolled half under it.

The Caphians had come to their feet and were looking at him. He could see that they were hoping he'd get his head bashed in.

The proprietor hurled the camera with great violence to the

floor. It came apart with an ugly, splintering sound. The film rolled free and snaked across the floor. The lens wobbled crazily. A spring came unloose from somewhere and went *zing*. It stood out at an angle, quivering.

Hart gathered his feet beneath him, and leaped out from the table. The Caphians started moving in on him – not rushing him, not threatening him in any way. They just kept walking toward him and spreading out so that he couldn't make a dash for the door.

He backed away, step by careful step, and the Caphians still continued their steady advance.

Suddenly he leaped straight toward them in a direct assault on the center of the line. He yelled and lowered his head and caught Green Shirt squarely in the belly. He felt the Caphian stagger and lurch to one side, and for a split second he thought that he had broken free.

But a hairy, muscular hand reached out and grabbed him and flung him to the floor. Someone kicked him. Someone stepped on his fingers. Someone else picked him up and threw him – straight through the open door into the street outside.

He landed on his back and skidded, with the breath completely knocked out of him. He came to rest with a jolt against the curbing opposite the place from which he had been heaved.

The Caphians, the full dozen of them, were grouped around the doorway, aroar with booming laughter. They slapped their thighs, and pounded one another on the back. They doubled over, shrieking. They shouted pleasantries and insults at him. Half of the jests he did not understand, but the ones that registered were enough to make his blood run cold.

He got up cautiously, and tested himself, He was considerably bruised and battered and his clothes were torn. But seemingly he had escaped any broken bones. He tried a few steps, limping. He tried to run and was surprised to find that he could.

Behind him the Caphians were still laughing. But there was no telling at what moment they might cease to think that his predicament was funny and start after him in earnest – for blood.

He raced down the street and ducked into an alley that led to a tangled square. He crossed the square into another street without pausing for breath and went running on. Finally he became satisfied that he was safe and sat down on a doorstep in an alley to regain his breath and carefully review the situation.

The situation, he realized, was bad. He not only had failed to get the character he needed. He had lost the camera, suffered a severe humiliation and barely escaped with his life.

There wasn't a thing that he could do about it. Actually, he told himself, he had been extremely lucky. For he didn't have a legal leg to stand on. He'd been entirely in the wrong. To film a character without the permission of the character's original was against the law.

It wasn't that he was a lawbreaker, he thought. It wasn't as if he'd deliberately set out to break the law. He'd been forced into it. Anyone who might have consented to serve as a character would have demanded money – more money than he was in a position to shell out.

But he did desperately need a character! He simply had to have one, or face utter defeat.

He saw that the sun had set, and that twilight was drifting in. The day, he thought, had been utterly wasted, and he had only himself to blame.

A passing police officer stopped and looked into the alley.

"You," he said to Hart. "What are you sitting there for?"

"Resting," Hart told him.

"All right. You're rested. Now get a move on."

Hart got a move on.

IV

He was nearing home when he heard the crying in the areaway between an apartment house and a bindery. It was a funny sort of crying, a not-quite-human crying – perhaps not so much a crying as a sound of grief and loneliness.

He halted abruptly and stared around him. The crying had cut off, but soon it began again. It was a low and empty crying, a hopeless crying, a crying to one's self.

For a moment he stood undecided, then started to go on. But he had not gone three paces before he turned back. He stepped into the areaway and at the second step his foot touched something lying on the ground.

He squatted and looked at the form that lay there, crying to itself. It was a bundle – that described it best – a huddled, limp, sad bundle that moaned heartbrokenly.

He put a hand beneath it and lifted it and was surprised at how little weight it had. Holding it firmly with one hand, he searched with the other for his lighter. He flicked the lighter and the flame was feeble, but he saw enough to make his stomach flop. It was an old blanket with a face that once had started out to be humanoid and then, for some reason, had been forced to change its mind. And that was all there was – a blanket and a face.

He thumbed the lighter down and crouched in the dark, his breath rasping in his throat. The creature was not only an alien. It was, even by alien standards, almost incredible. And how had an alien strayed so far from the spaceport? Aliens seldom wandered. They never had the time to wander, for the ships came in, freighted up with fiction, and almost immediately took off again. The crews stayed close to the rocket berths, seldom venturing farther than the dives along the riverfront.

He rose, holding the creature bundled across his chest as one would hold a child – it was not as heavy as a child – and feeling the infant-like warmth of it against his body and a strange companionship. He stood in the areaway while his mind went groping back in an effort to unmask the faint recognition he had felt. Somewhere, somehow, it seemed he once had heard or read of an alien such as this. But surely that was ridiculous, for aliens did not come, even the most fantastic of them, as a living blanket with the semblance of a face.

He stepped out into the street and looked down to examine the face again. But a portion of the creature's blanket-body had draped itself across its features and he could see only a waving blur.

Within two blocks he reached the Bright Star bar, went around the corner to the side door and started up the stairs. Footsteps were descending and he squeezed himself against the railing to let the other person past.

"Kemp," said Angela Maret. "Kemp, what have you there?"

"I found it in the street," Hart told her.

He shifted his arm a little and the blanket-body slipped and she saw the face. She moved back against the railing, her hand going to her mouth to choke off a scream.

"Kemp! How awful!"

"I think that it is sick. It —"

"What are you going to do?"

"I don't know," Hart said. "It was crying to itself. It was enough to break your heart. I couldn't leave it there."

"I'll get Doc Julliard."

Hart shook his head. "That wouldn't do any good. Doc doesn't know any alien medicine. Besides, he's probably drunk."

"No one knows any alien medicine," Angela reminded him. "Maybe we could get one of the specialists uptown." Her face clouded. "Doc is resourceful, though. He has to be, down here. Maybe he could tell us —"

"All right," Hart said. "See if you can rout out Doc."

In his room he laid the alien on the bed. It was no longer whimpering. Its eyes were closed and it seemed to be asleep, although he could not be sure.

He sat on the edge of the bed and studied it and the more he looked at it the less sense it seemed to make. Now he could see how thin the blanket body was, how light and fragile. It amazed him that a thing so fragile could live at all, that it could contain in so inadequate a body the necessary physiological machinery to keep itself alive.

He wondered if it might be hungry and if so what kind of food it required. If it were really ill how could he hope to take care of it when he didn't know the first basic thing about it?

Maybe Doc – But, no, Doc would know no more than he did. Doc was just like the rest of them, living hand to mouth, cadging drinks whenever he could get them, and practicing medicine without adequate equipment and with a knowledge that had stopped dead in its tracks forty years before.

He heard footsteps coming up the stairs – light steps and trudging heavy ones. It had to be Angela with Doc. She had found him quickly and that probably meant he was sober enough to act and think with a reasonable degree of coordination.

Doc came into the room, followed by Angela. He put down his bag and looked at the creature on the bed.

"What have we here?" he asked and probably it was the first time in his entire career that the smug doctorish phrase made sense.

"Kemp found it in the street," said Angela quickly. "It's stopped crying now."

"Is this a joke?" Doc asked, half wrathfully. "If it is, young man, I consider it in the worst possible taste."

Hart shook his head. "It's no joke. I thought that you might know –"

"Well, I don't," said Doc, with aggressive bitterness.

He let go of the blanket edge and it quickly flopped back upon the bed.

He paced up and down the room for a turn or two. Then he whirled angrily on Angela and Hart.

"I suppose you think that I should do something," he said. "I should at least go through the motions. I should act like a doctor. I'm sure that is what you're thinking. I should take its pulse and its temperature and look at its tongue and listen to its heart. Well, suppose you tell me how I do these things. Where do I find the pulse? If I could find it, what is its normal rate? And if I could figure out some way to take its temperature, what is the normal temperature for a monstrosity such as this? And if you would be so kind, would you tell me how – short of dissection – I could hope to locate the heart?"

He picked up his bag and started for the door.

"Anyone else, Doc?" Hart pleaded, in a conciliatory tone. "Anyone who'd know?"

"I doubt it," Doc snapped.

"You mean there's *no one* who can do a thing? Is that what you're trying to say?"

"Look, son. Human doctors treat human beings, period. Why should we be expected to do more? How often are we called upon to treat an alien? We're not *expected* to treat aliens. Oh, possibly, once in a while some specialist or researcher may dabble in alien medicine. But that is the correct name for it – just plain dabbling. It takes years of a man's life to learn barely enough to qualify as a human doctor. How many lifetimes do you think we should devote to curing aliens?"

"All right, Doc. All right."

"And how can you even be sure there's something wrong with it?"

"Why, it was crying and I quite naturally thought –"

"It might have been lonesome or frightened or grieving. It might have been lost."

Doc turned to the door again.

"Thanks, Doc," Hart said.

"Not at all." The old man hesitated at the door. "You don't happen to have a dollar, do you? Somehow, I ran a little short."

"Here," said Hart, giving him a bill.

"I'll return it tomorrow," Doc promised.

He went clumping down the stairs.

Angela frowned. "You shouldn't have done that, Kemp. Now he'll get drunk and you'll be responsible."

"Not on a dollar," Hart said confidently.

"That's all you know about it. The kind of stuff Doc drinks –"

"Let him get drunk then. He deserves a little fun."

"But –" Angela motioned to the thing upon the bed.

"You heard what Doc said. He can't do anything. No one can do anything. When it wakes up – *if* it wakes up – it may be able to tell us what is wrong with it. But I'm not counting on that."

He walked over to the bed and stared down at the creature. It was repulsive and abhorrent and not in the least humanoid. But there was about it a pitiful loneliness and an incongruity that made a catch come to his throat.

"Maybe I should have left it in the areaway," he said. "I started to walk on. But when it began to cry again I went back to it. Maybe I did wrong bothering with it at all. I haven't helped it any. If I'd left it there it might have turned out better. Some other aliens may be looking for it by now."

"You did right," said Angela. "Don't start in fighting with windmills."

She crossed the room and sat down in a chair. He went over to the window and stared somberly out across the city.

"What happened to you?" she asked.

"Nothing."

"But your clothes. Just look at your clothes."

"I got thrown out of a dive. I tried to take some film."

"Without paying for it."

"I didn't have the money."

"I offered you a fifty."

"I know you did. But I couldn't take it. Don't you understand, Angela? *I simply couldn't take it.*"

She said softly, "You're bad off, Kemp."

He swung around, outraged. She hadn't needed to say that. She had no right to say it. She –

He caught himself up before the words came tumbling out.

She had the right. She'd offered him a fifty – but that had been only a part of it. She had the right to say it because she knew that she could say it. No one else in all the world could have felt the way she did about him.

"I can't write," he said. "Angela, no matter how I try, I can't make it come out right. The machine is haywire and the tapes are threadbare and most of them are patched."

"What have you had to eat today?"

"I had the beers with you and I had some *bocca*."

"That isn't eating. You wash your face and change into some different clothes and we'll go downstairs and get you some food."

"I have eating money."

"I know you have. You told me about the advance from Irving."

"It wasn't an advance."

"I know it wasn't, Kemp."

"What about the alien?"

"It'll be all right – at least long enough for you to get a bite to eat. You can't help it by standing here. You don't know how to help it."

"I guess you're right."

"Of course I am. Now get going and wash your dirty face. And don't forget your ears."

V

Jasper Hansen was alone in the Bright Star bar. They went over to his table and sat down. Jasper was finishing a dish of sauerkraut and pig's knuckles and was drinking wine with it, which seemed a bit blasphemous.

"Where's everyone else?" asked Angela.

"There's a party down the street," said Jasper. "Someone sold a book."

"Someone that we know?"

"Hell, no," Jasper said. "Just someone sold a book. You don't have to know a guy to go to his party when he sells a book."

"I didn't hear anything about it."

"Neither did the rest of the bunch. Someone looked in at the door and hollered about the party and everyone took off. Everyone but me. I can't monkey with no party. I've got work to do."

"Free food?" asked Angela.

"Yeah. Don't it beat you, though. Here we are, honorable and respected craftsmen, and every one of us will break a leg to grab himself a sandwich and a drink."

"Times are tough," said Hart.

"Not with me," said Jasper. "I keep working all the time."

"But work doesn't solve the main problem."

Jasper regarded him thoughtfully, tugging at his chin.

"What else is there?" he demanded. "Inspiration? Dedication? Genius? Go ahead and name it. We are mechanics, man. We got machines and tapes. We went into top production two hundred years ago. We mechanized so we could go into top production, so that people could turn out books and stories even if they had no talent at all. We got a job to do. We got to turn out tons of drivel for the whole damn galaxy. We got to keep them drooling over what is going to happen next to sloe-eyed Annie, queen of the far-flung spaceways. And we got to shoot up the lad with her and patch him up and shoot him up and patch him up and . . ."

He reached for an evening paper, opened it to a certain page and thumped his fist upon it.

"Did you see this?" he asked. "The Classic, they call it. Guaranteed to turn out nothing but a classic."

Hart snatched the paper from him and there it was, the wondrous yarner he had seen that morning, confronting him in all its glory from the center of a full-page ad.

"Pretty soon," said Jasper, "all you'll need to write is have a lot of money. You can go out and buy a machine like that and say turn out a story and press a button or flip a switch or maybe simply kick it and it'll cough out a story complete to the final exclamation point.

"It used to be that you could buy an old beat-up machine for, say, a hundred dollars and you could turn out any quantity of stuff – not good, but salable. Today you got to have a high-priced machine and an expensive camera and a lot of special tape and film. Someday," he said, with a sudden flare of anger, "the human race will outwit itself. Someday it will mechanize to the point where there won't be room for humans, but only for machines."

"You do all right," said Angela.

"That's because I keep dinging my machine up all the time. It don't give me no rest. That place of mine is half study and half machine shop and I know as much about electronics as I do about narration."

Blake came shuffling over.

"What'll it be?" he growled.

"I've eaten," Angela told him. "All I want is a glass of beer."

He turned to Hart. "How about you" he demanded.

"Give me some of that stuff Jasper has – without the wine."

"No cuff," said Blake.

"Damn it, who said anything about cuff? Do you expect me to pay you before you bring it?"

"No," said Blake. "But immediately I bring it."

He turned and shuffled off.

"Some day," said Jasper, "there has to be a limit to it. There must be a limit to it and we must be reaching it. You can only mechanize so far. You can assign only so many human activities and duties to intelligent machines. Who, two hundred years ago, would have said that the writing of fiction could have been reduced to a matter of mechanics?"

"Who, two hundred years ago," said Hart, "could have guessed that Earth could gear itself to a literary culture? But that is precisely what we have today. Sure, there are factories that build the machines we need and lumbermen who cut the trees for pulp and farmers who grow the food, and all the other trades and skills which are necessary to keep a culture operative. But by and large the Earth today is principally devoted to the production of a solid stream of fiction for the alien trade."

"It all goes back to one peculiar trait," said Jasper. "A most unlikely trait to work – as it does – to our great advantage. We just happen to be the galaxy's only liars. In a mass of stars where truth is accepted as a universal constant, we are the one exception."

"You make it sound so horrible," protested Angela.

"I suppose I do, but that's the way it is. We could have become great traders and skinned all and sundry until they got wise to us. We could have turned our talent for the untruth into many different channels and maybe even avoided getting our heads bashed in. But instead we drifted into the one safe course. Our lying became an easy virtue. Now we can lie to our hearts' content and they lap it up. No one, nowhere, except right here on Earth, ever even tried to spin a yarn for simple entertainment, or to point a moral or for any other reason. They never attempted it because it would have been a lie, and we are the only liars in the universe of stars."

Blake brought the beer for Angela and the pig knuckles for Hart. Hart paid him out of hand.

"I've still got a quarter left," he said. "Have you any pie?"

"Apple."

"Here," said Hart, "I'll pay you in advance."

"First," went on Jasper, "it was told by mouth. Then it was writ by hand and now it's fabricated by machine. But surely that's not the end of it. There must be something else. There must be another way, a better way. There must be another step."

"I would settle for anything," said Hart. "Any way at all. I'd even write by hand if I thought I could go on selling."

"You can't!" Angela told him, sharply. "Why, it's positively indecent to even joke about it. You can say it as a joke just among the three of us, but if I ever hear you –"

Hart waved his hand. "Let it go. I'm sorry that I said it."

"Of course," said Jasper, "it's a great testimonial to the cleverness of Man, to the adaptability and resourcefulness of the human race. It is a somewhat ludicrous application of big business methods to what had always been considered a personal profession. But it works. Some day, I have no doubt, we may see the writing business run on production lines, with fiction factories running double shifts."

"No," Angela said. "No, you're wrong there, Jasper. Even with the mechanization, it's still the loneliest business on Earth."

"It is," agreed Jasper. "But I don't regret the loneliness part. Maybe I should, but I don't."

"It's a lousy way to make a living," said Angela, with a strange half-bitterness in her voice. "What are we contributing?"

"You are making people happy – if you can call some of our readers people. You are supplying entertainment."

"And the noble ideas?"

"There are even a few of those."

"It's more than that," said Hart. "More than entertainment, more than great ideas. It's the most innocent and the deadliest propaganda in all of human history. The old writers, before the first space flight, glorified far wandering and galactic conquest and I think that they were justified. But they missed the most important development completely. They couldn't possibly fore-see the way we would do it – with books, not battleships. We're softening up the galaxy with a constant stream of human thought. Our words are reaching farther than our spaceships ever could."

"That's the point I want to make," Jasper said, triumphantly. "You hit the point exactly. But if we are to tell the galaxy a story it must be a *human* story. If we sell them a bill of goods it must be a *human* bill of goods. And how can we keep it human if we relegate its telling to machines?"

"But they're human machines," objected Angela.

"A machine can't be purely human. Basically a machine is uni-versal. It could be Caphian as well as human, or Aldebaran or Draconian or any other race. And that's not all. We let the machine set the norm. The one virtue of mechanics is that it sets a pattern. And a pattern is deadly in literary matters. It never changes. It keeps on using the same old limp plots in many different guises.

"Maybe at the moment it makes no difference to the races who are reading us, for as yet they have not developed anything approaching a critical faculty. But it should make some difference to us. It should make some difference in the light of a certain pride of workmanship we are supposed to have. And that is the trouble with machines. They are destroying the pride in us. Once writing was an art. But it is an art no longer. It's machine-produced, like a factory chair. A good chair, certainly. Good enough to sit on, but not a thing of beauty or of craftsmanship or –"

The door crashed open and feet pounded on the floor.

Just inside the door stood Green Shirt and behind him, grinning fiendishly, his band of Caphians.

Green Shirt advanced upon them happily, with his arms flung wide in greeting. He stopped beside Hart's chair and clapped a massive hand upon his shoulder.

"You recall me, don't you?" he asked in slow and careful English.

"Sure," Hart said, gulping. "Sure, I remember you. This is Miss Maret and over there is Mr. Hansen."

Green Shirt said, with precise bookishness, "So happy, I assure you."

"Have a seat," said Jasper.

"Glad to," said Green Shirt, hauling out a chair. His necklaces jingled musically as he sat down.

One of the other Caphians said something to him in a rapid-fire alien tongue. Green Shirt answered curtly and waved toward the door. The others marched outside.

"He is worried," Green Shirt said. "We will slow – how do you say it – we will slow the ship. They cannot leave without us. But I tell him not to worry. The captain will be glad we slow the ship when he see what we bring back."

He leaned forward and tapped Hart upon the knee. "I look for you," he said. "I look high and wide."

"Who is this joker?" Jasper asked.

"Joker?" asked Green Shirt, frowning.

"A term of great respect," Hart hastily assured him.

"So," said Green Shirt. "You all write the stories?"

"Yes. All three of us."

"But *you* write them best."

"I wouldn't say that exactly. You see –"

"You write the wild and woolly stories? The bang-bangs?"

"Yeah. I guess I'm guilty."

Green Shirt looked apologetic. "Had I known, we would not from the tavern have thrown you out. It was just big fun. We did not know you write the stories. When we find out who you are we try to catch you. But you run and hide."

"Just what is going on here, anyhow?" Angela demanded.

Green Shirt whooped for Blake.

"Set them up," he shouted. "These are my friends. Set up the best you have."

"The best I have," Blake said icily, "is Irish whiskey and that costs a buck a shot."

"I got the cash," said Green Shirt. "You get this name I cannot say, and you will get your cash."

He said to Hart, "I have a surprise for you, my friend. We love the writers of the bang-bangs. We read them *always*. We get much stimulation."

Jasper guffawed.

Green Shirt swung about in amazement, his bushy brows contracting.

"He's just happy," Hart explained, quickly. "He likes Irish whiskey."

"Fine," said Green Shirt, beaming. "You drink all you wish. I will give the cash. It is – how do you say – on me."

Blake brought the drinks and Green Shirt paid him.

"Bring the container," he said.

"The container?"

"He means the bottle."

"That'll be twenty dollars," said Blake.

"So," said Green Shirt, paying him.

They drank the whiskey and Green Shirt said to Hart, "My surprise is that you come with us."

"You mean in the ship?"

"We have never had a real live writer on our planet. You will have a good time. You will stay and write for us."

"Well," said Hart, "I'm not sure –"

"You try to take the picture. The tavern man explain it all to us. He say it is against the law. He say if I complain it will come big trouble."

"You can't do it, Kemp," protested Angela. "Don't let this big hyena bluff you. We'll pay your fine."

"We not complain," said Green Shirt, gently. "We just with you mop up the condemned place."

Blake brought the bottle and thumped it down in the center of the table. Green Shirt picked it up and filled their glasses to the brim.

"Drink up," he said and set a fine example.

He drank and Green Shirt filled his glass again. Hart picked up his glass and twirled it in his fingers.

There had to be a way out of this mess, he told himself. It was absurd that this thundering barbarian from one of the farther suns should be able to walk into a bar and tell a man to come along with him.

However, there was no percentage in stirring up a fight – not with ten or eleven Caphians waiting just outside.

"I explain it to you," said Green Shirt. "I try hard to explain it well so that you will – so that you will –"

"Understand," supplied Jasper Hansen.

"I thank you, Hansen man. So you will understand. We get

the stories only shortly ago. Many of the other races got them long ago, but with us it is new and most wonderful. It takes us – how would you say – out of ourselves. We get many things from other stars, useful things, things to hold in the hand, things to see and use. But from you we get the going of far places, the doing of great deeds, the thinking of great things."

He filled the glasses all around again.

"You understand?" Green Shirt asked.

They nodded.

"And now we go."

Hart rose slowly to his feet.

"Kemp, you can't!" screamed Angela.

"You shut the mouth," said Green Shirt.

Hart marched through the door and out into the street. The other Caphians oozed out of dark alleyways and surrounded him.

"Off we go," said Green Shirt, happily. "It gives big time on Caph."

Halfway to the river, Hart stopped in the middle of the street.

"I can't do it," he said.

"Can't do what?" asked Green Shirt, prodding him along.

"I let you think," said Hart, "that I was the man you wanted. I did it because I'd like to see your planet. But it isn't fair. I'm not the man you want."

"You write the bang-bangs, do you not? You think up the wild and woolies?"

"Certainly. But not really good ones. Mine aren't the kind where you hang on every word. There's another man who can do it better."

"This man we want," said Green Shirt. "Can you tell us where to find him?"

"That's easy. The other man at the table with us. The one who was so happy when you ordered whiskey."

"You mean the Hansen man?"

"He is the one, exactly."

"He write the bang-bangs good?"

"Much better than I do. He's a genius at it."

Green Shirt was overcome with gratitude. He hugged Hart to him in an extravagant expression of good will.

"You fair," he said. "You fine. It was nice of you to tell us."

A window banged up in a house across the street and a man stuck his head out.

"If you guys don't break it up," he bellowed, "I'll call the cops."

"We shatter the peace," sighed Green Shirt. "It is a queer law you have."

The window banged down again.

Green Shirt put a friendly hand upon Hart's shoulder. "We love the wild and woolies," he said gravely. "We want the very best. We thank you. We find this Hansen man."

He turned around and loped back up the street, followed by his ruffians.

Hart stood on the corner and watched them go. He drew a deep breath and let it slowly out.

It had been easy, he told himself, once you got the angle. And it had been Jasper, actually, who had given him the angle. *Truth is regarded as a universal constant*, Jasper had said. *We are the only liars.*

It had turned out tough on Jasper – a downright dirty trick. But the guy wanted to go on vacation, didn't he? And here was the prospect of a travel jaunt which would be really worthwhile. He'd refused the use of his machine and he had guffawed insultingly when Green Shirt had asked about the wild and woolies. If ever a guy had it coming to him, Jasper Hansen was that guy.

And above and beyond all that, he always kept his door locked – which showed a contemptible suspicion of his fellow writers.

Hart swung about and walked rapidly away in an opposite direction. Eventually he'd go back home, he told himself. But not right now.

Later on he'd go, when the dust had settled slightly.

VI

It was dawn when Hart climbed the stairs to the seventh floor and went down the corridor to Jasper Hansen's door. The door was locked as usual. But he took out of his pocket a thin piece of spring steel he'd picked up in a junkyard and did some judicious prying. In the matter of seconds, the lock clicked back and the door swung open.

The yarner squatted in its corner, a bright and lovely sight.

Jiggered up, Jasper had affirmed. If someone else ever tried to use it, it would very likely burn out or kill him. But that had been just talk, just cover-up for his pig-headed selfishness.

Two weeks, Hart told himself. If he used his head he should be able to operate it without suspicion for at least two weeks. It would be easy. All he'd have to say was that Jasper had told him that he could borrow it any time he wished. And if he was any judge of character, Jasper would not be returning soon.

But even so, two weeks would be all the time he'd need. In two weeks, working day and night, he could turn out enough copy to buy himself a new machine.

He walked across the room to the yarner and pulled out the chair that stood in front of it. Calmly he sat down, reached out a hand and patted the instrument panel. It was a good machine. It turned out a lot of stuff – good stuff. Jasper had been selling steadily.

Good old yarner, Hart said.

He dropped his finger to the switch and flipped it over. Nothing happened. Startled, he flipped it back, flipped it on again. Still nothing happened.

He got up hastily to check the power connection. There was no power connection! For a shocked moment, he stood rooted to the floor.

Jiggered up, Jasper had said. Jiggered up so ingeniously that it could dispense with power?

It just wasn't possible. It was unthinkable. With fumbling fingers, he lifted the side panel, and peered inside.

The machine's innards were a mess. Half of the tubes were gone. Others were burned out, and the wiring had been ripped loose in places. The whole relay section was covered with dust. Some of the metal, he saw, was rusty. The entire machine was just a pile of junk.

He replaced the panel with suddenly shaking fingers, reeled back blindly and collided with a table. He clutched at it and held on tight to still the shaking of his hands, to steady the mad roaring in his head.

Jasper's machine wasn't jiggered up. It wasn't even in operating condition.

No wonder Jasper had kept his door locked. He lived in mortal fear that someone would find out that he wrote by hand!

And now, despite the dirty trick he'd played on a worthy friend, Hart was no better off than he had been before. He was faced with the same old problems, with no prospect of overcoming them. He still had his own beaten-up machine and nothing more. Maybe it would have been better if he had gone to Caph.

He walked to the door, paused there for an instant, and looked back. On the littered desk he could see Jasper's typewriter, carefully half-buried by the litter, and giving the exact impression that it was never used.

Still, Jasper sold. Jasper sold almost every word he wrote. He sold – hunched over his desk with a pencil in his hand or hammering out the words on a muted typewriter. He sold without using the yarner at all, but keeping it all bright and polished, an empty, useless thing. He sold by using it as a shield against the banter and the disgust of all those others who talked so glibly and relied so much upon the metal and the magic of the ponderous contraption.

First it was told by mouth, Jasper had said that very evening. *Then it was writ by hand. Now it's fabricated by machine.*

And what's next, he'd asked – as if he had never doubted that there would be something next.

What next? thought Hart. Was this the end and all of Man – the moving gear, the clever glass and metal, the adroit electronics?

For the sake of Man's own dignity – his very sanity – there *had* to be a next. Mechanics, by their very nature, were a dead end. You could only get so clever. You could only go so far.

Jasper knew that. Jasper had found out. He had discarded the mechanistic aid and gone back to hand again.

Give a work of craftsmanship some economic value and Man would find a way to turn it out in quantity. Once furniture had been constructed lovingly by artisans who produced works of art that would last with pride through many generations. Then the machine had come and Man had turned out furniture that was purely functional, furniture that had little lasting value and no pride at all.

And writing had followed the same pattern. It had pride no longer. It had ceased to be an art, and become a commodity.

But what was a man to do? What *could* he do? Lock his door like Jasper and work through lonely hours with the bitter taste of nonconformity sharp within his mind, tormenting him night and day?

Hart walked out of the room with a look of torment in his eyes. He waited for a second to hear the lock click home. Then he went down the hall and slowly climbed the stairs.

VII

The alien – the blanket and the face – was still lying on the bed. But now its eyes were open and it stared at him when he came in and closed the door behind him.

He stopped just inside the door and the cold mediocrity of the room – all of its meanness and its poverty – rose up to clog his nostrils. He was hungry, sick at heart and lonely, and the yarner in the corner seemed to mock at him.

Through the open window he could hear the rumble of a spaceship taking off across the river and the hooting of a tug as it warped a ship into a wharf.

He stumbled to the bed.

"Move over, you," he said to the wide-eyed alien, and tumbled down beside it. He turned his back to it and drew his knees up against his chest and lay huddled there.

He was right back where he'd started just the other morning. He still had no tape to do the job that Irving wanted. He still had a busted-up haywire machine. He was without a camera and he wondered where he could borrow one – although there would be no sense of borrowing one if he didn't have the money to pay a character. He'd tried once to take a film by stealth and he wouldn't try again. It wasn't worth the risk of going to prison for three or four years.

We love the wild and woolies, Green Shirt had said. *From them we get the going of far places.*

And while with Green Shirt it would be the bang-bangs and the wild and woolies, with some other race it would be a different type of fiction – race after race finding in this strange product of Earth a new world of enchantment. The far places of the mind, perhaps – or the far places of emotion. The basic differences were not too important.

Angela had said it was a lousy way to make a living. But she had only been letting off steam. All writers at times said approximately the same thing. In every age men and women of every known profession at some time must have said that theirs was a lousy way to make a living. At the moment they might have meant it, but at other times they knew that it was not lousy because it was important.

And writing was important, too – tremendously important. Not so much because it meant the "going of far places," but because it sowed the seed of Earth – the seed of Earth's thinking and of Earth's logic – among the myriad stars.

They are out there waiting, Hart thought, for the stories that he would never write.

He would try, of course, despite all obstacles. He might even do as Jasper had done, scribbling madly with a sense of shame, feeling anachronistic and inadequate, dreading the day when someone would ferret out his secret, perhaps by deducing from a certain eccentricity of style that it was not machine-written.

For Jasper was wrong, of course. The trouble was not with the yarners nor with the principle of mechanistic writing. It was with Jasper himself – a deep psychopathic quirk that made a rebel of him. But even so he had remained a fearful and a hidden rebel who locked his door, and kept his yarner polished, and carefully covered his typewriter with the litter on his desk so no one would suspect that he ever used it.

Hart felt warmer now and he seemed to be no longer hungry and suddenly he thought of one of those far places that Green Shirt had talked about. It was a grove of trees and a brook ran through the grove. There was a sense of peace and calm and a touch of majesty and foreverness about it. He heard birdsong and smelled the sharp, spice-like scent of water running in its mossy banks. He walked among the trees and the Gothic shape of them made the place seem like a church. As he walked he formed words within his mind – words put together so feelingly and so rightly and so carefully that no one who read them could mistake what he had to say. They would know not only the sight of the grove itself, but the sound and the smell of it and the foreverness that filled it to overflowing.

But even in his exaltation he sensed a threat within the Gothic shape and the feeling of foreverness. Some lurking intuition told him that the grove was a place to get away from. He tried for a moment to remember how he had gotten there, but there was no memory. It was as if he had become familiar with the grove only a second or two before and yet he knew that he had been walking beneath the sun-dappled foliage for what must have been hours or days.

He felt a tingling on his throat and raised a hand to brush it off and his hand touched something small and warm that brought him upright out of bed.

His hand tightened on the creature's neck. He was about to rip it from his chest when suddenly he recalled, full-blown, the odd circumstance he had tried to remember just the night before.

His grip relaxed and he let his hand drop to his side. He stood beside the bed, in the warm familiarity of the room, and felt the comfort of the blanket-creature upon his back and shoulders and around his throat.

He wasn't hungry and he wasn't tired and the sickness that he'd felt had somehow disappeared. He wasn't even worried and that was most unusual, for he was customarily worried.

Twelve hours before he had stood in the areaway with the blanket creature in his arms and had sought to pry out of a suddenly stubborn mind an explanation for the strange sense of recognition he'd experienced – the feeling that somewhere he had read or heard of the crying thing he'd found. Now, with it clasped around his back and clinging to his throat, he knew.

He strode across the room, with the blanket creature clinging to him, and took a book down from a narrow, six foot shelf. It was an old and tattered book, worn smooth by many hands, and it almost slipped from his clasp as he turned it over to read the title on the spine:

Fragments from Lost Writings.

He reversed the volume and began to leaf through its pages. He knew now where to find what he was looking for. He remembered exactly where he had read about the thing upon his back.

He found the pages quickly enough – a few salvaged para-

graphs from some story, written long ago and lost, He skipped
the first two pages, and came suddenly upon the paragraphs he
wanted:

*Ambitious vegetables, the life blankets waited, probably only
obscurely aware of what they were waiting for. But when the humans
came the long, long wait was over. The life blankets made a deal with
men. And in the last analysis they turned out to be the greatest aid to
galactic exploration that had ever been discovered.*

And there it was, thought Hart – the old, smug, pat assurance
that it would be the humans who would go into the galaxy to
explore it and make contact with its denizens and carry to every
planet they visited the virtues of the Earth.

*With a life blanket draped like a bobtailed cloak around his
shoulders, a man had no need to worry about being fed, for the life
blanket had the strange ability to gather energy and convert it into
food for the body of its host.*

*It became, in fact, almost a second body – a watchful, fussy,
quasiparental body that watched over the body of its host, keeping
metabolism in balance despite alien conditions, rooting out infec-
tions, playing the role of mother, cook and family doctor combined.*

*But in return the blanket became, in a sense, the double of its
host. Shedding its humdrum vegetable existence, it became vicari-
ously a man, sharing all of its host's emotions and intelligence, living
the kind of life it never could have lived if left to itself.*

*And not content with this fair trade, the blankets threw in a
bonus, a sort of dividend of gratitude. They were storytellers and
imaginers. They could imagine anything – literally anything at all.
They spent long hours spinning out tall yarns for the amusement of
their hosts, serving as a shield against boredom and loneliness . . .*

There was more of it, but Hart did not need to read on. He
turned back to the beginning of the fragment and he read: Author
Unknown. Circa 1956.

Six hundred years ago! Six hundred years--and how could any
man in 1956 have known?

The answer was he couldn't.

There was no way he could have known. He'd simply *dreamed* it up. And hit the truth dead center! Some early writer of science fiction had had an inspired vision!

There was something coming through the grove and it was a thing of utter beauty. It was not humanoid and it was not a monster. It was something no man had ever seen before. And yet despite the beauty of it, there was a deadly danger in it and something one must flee from.

He turned around to flee and found himself in the center of the room.

"All right," he said to the blanket. "Let's cut it out for now. We can go back later."

We can go back later and we can make a story of it and we can go many other places and make stories of them, too. I won't need a yarner to write those kind of stories, for I can recapture the excitement and splendor of it, and link it all together better than a yarner could. I'll have been there and lived it, and that's a setup you can't beat.

And there it was! The answer to the question that Jasper had asked, sitting at the table in the Bright Star bar.

What next?

And this was next: a symbiosis between Man and an alien thing, imagined centuries ago by a man whose very name was lost.

It was almost, Hart thought, as if God had placed His hand against his back and propelled him gently onward, for it was utterly fantastic that he should have found the answer crying in an areaway between an apartment house and a bindery.

But that did not matter now. The important thing was that he'd found it and brought it home – not quite knowing why at the time and wondering later why he had even bothered with it.

The important thing was that *now* was the big pay-off.

He heard footsteps coming up the stairs and turning down the hall. Alarmed by their rapid approach he reached up hastily and snatched the blanket from his shoulders. Frantically he looked about for a place to hide the creature. Of course! His desk. He jerked open the bottom drawer and stuffed the blanket into it, ignoring a slight resistance. He was kicking the drawer shut when Angela came into the room.

He could see at once that she was burned up.

"That was a lousy trick," she said. "You got Jasper into a lot of trouble."

Hart stared at her in consternation. "Trouble? You mean he didn't go to Caph?"

"He's down in the basement hiding out. Blake told me he was there. I went down and talked to him."

"He got away from them?" Hart appeared badly shaken.

"Yes. He told them they didn't want a man at all. He told them what they wanted was a machine and he told them about that glittering wonder – that Classic model – in the shop uptown."

"And so they went and stole it."

"No. If they had it would have been all right. But they bungled it. They smashed the glass to get at it, and that set off an alarm. Every cop in town came tearing after them."

"But Jasper was all –"

"They took Jasper with them to show them where it was."

Some of the color had returned to Hart's face. "And now Jasper's hiding from the law."

"That's the really bad part of it. He doesn't know whether he is or not. He's not sure the cops even saw him. What he's afraid of is that they might pick up one of those Caphians and sweat the story out of him. And if they do, Kemp Hart, you have a lot to answer for."

"Me? Why, I didn't do a thing –"

"Except tell them that Jasper was the man they wanted. How did you ever make them believe a line like that?"

"Easy. Remember what Jasper said. Everyone else tells the truth. We're the only ones who lie. Until they get wise to us, they'll believe every word we say. Because, you see, no one else tells anything but the truth and so –"

"Oh, shut up!" Angela said impatiently.

She looked around the room. "Where's that blanket thing?" she asked.

"It must have left. Maybe it ran away. When I came home it wasn't here."

"Haven't you any idea what it was?"

Hart shook his head. "Maybe it's just as well it's gone," he said. "It gave me a queasy feeling."

"You and Doc! That's another thing. This neighborhood's gone crazy. Doc is stretched out dead drunk under a tree in the park and there's an alien watching him. It won't let anyone come near him. It's as if it were guarding him, or had adopted him or something."

"Maybe it's one of Doc's pink elephants come to actual life. You know, dream a thing too often and –"

"It's no elephant and it isn't pink. It's got webbed feet that are too big for it and long, spindly legs. It's something like a spider, and its skin is warts. It has a triangular head with six horns. It fairly makes you crawl just to look at it."

Hart shuddered. Ordinary aliens could be all right, but a thing like that –

"Wonder what it wants of Doc."

"Nobody seems to know. It won't talk."

"Maybe it can't talk."

"You know all aliens talk. At least enough of our language to make themselves understood. Otherwise they wouldn't come here."

"It sounds reasonable," said Hart. "Maybe it's acquiring a second-hand jag just sitting there beside Doc."

"Sometimes," said Angela, "your sense of humor is positively disgusting."

"Like writing books by hand."

"Yes," she said. "Like writing books by hand. You know as well as I do that people just don't talk about writing anything by hand. It's like – well, it's like eating with your fingers or belching in public or going without clothes."

"All right," he said, "all right. I'll never mention it again."

VIII

After she had left, Hart sat down and gave some serious thought to his situation.

In many ways he'd be a lot like Jasper, but he wouldn't mind if he could write as well as Jasper.

He'd have to start locking his door. He wondered where his key was. He never used it and now he'd have to look through his desk the first chance he got, to see if he couldn't locate it. If he couldn't find it, he'd have to have a new key made, because he couldn't have people walking in on him unexpectedly and catching him wearing the blanket or writing stuff by hand.

Maybe, he thought, it might be a good idea to move. It would be hard at times to explain why all at once he had started to lock his door. But he hated the thought of moving. Bad as it was, he'd gotten used to this place and it seemed like home.

Maybe, after he started selling, he should talk with Angela and see how she felt about moving in with him. Angela was a good kid, but you couldn't ask a girl to move in with you when you were always wondering where the next meal was coming from. But now, even if he didn't sell, he'd never have to worry where his next meal was coming from. He wondered briefly if the blanket could be shared as a food provider by two persons and he wondered how in the world he'd ever manage to explain it all to Angela.

And how had that fellow back in 1956 ever thought of such a

thing? How many of the other wild ideas concocted out of tortuous mental efforts and empty whiskey bottles might be true as well?

A dream? An idea? A glimmer of the future? It did not matter which, for a man had thought of it and it had come true. How many of the other things that Man had thought of in the past and would think of in the future would also become the truth?

The idea scared him.

That "going of far places." The reaching out of the imagination. The influence of the written word, the thought and power behind it. It was deadlier than a battleship, he'd said. How everlastingly right he had been.

He got up and walked across the room and stood in front of the yarner. It leered at him. He stuck out his tongue at it.

"That for you," he said.

Behind him he heard a rustle and hastily whirled about.

The blanket had somehow managed to ooze out of the desk drawer and it was heading for the door, reared upon the nether folds of its flimsy body. It was slithering along in a jerky fashion like a wounded seal.

"Hey, you!" yelled Hart and made a grab at it. But he was too late. A being – there was no other word for it – stood in the doorway and the blanket reached it and slithered swiftly up its body and plastered itself upon its back.

The thing in the doorway hissed at Hart: "I lose it. You are so kind to keep it. I am very grateful."

Hart stood transfixed.

The creature was a sight. Just like the one which Angela had seen guarding Doc, only possibly a little uglier. It had webbed feet that were three times too big for it, so that it seemed to be wearing snowshoes, and it had a tail that curved ungracefully halfway up its back. It had a melon-shaped head with a triangular face, and six horns and there were rotating eyes on the top of each and every horn.

The monstrosity dipped into a pouch that seemed to be part of its body, and took out a roll of bills.

"So small reward," it piped and tossed the bills to Hart.

Hart put out a hand and caught them absent-mindedly.

"We go now," said the being. "We think kind thoughts of you."

It had started to turn around, but at Hart's bellow of protest it swiveled back.

"Yes, good sir?"

"This – blanket – this thing I found. What about it?"

"We make it."

"But it's alive and –"

The thing grinned a murderous grin. "You so clever people. You think it up. Many times ago."

"That story!"

"Quite so. We read of it. We make it. Very good idea."

"You can't mean you actually –"

"We biologist. What you call them – biologic engineers."

It turned about and started down the hall.

Hart howled after it. "Just a minute! Hold up there! Just a min –"

But it was going fast and it didn't stop. Hart thundered after it. When he reached the head of the stairs and glanced down it was out of sight. But he raced after it, taking the stairs three at a time in defiance of all the laws of safety.

He didn't catch it. In the street outside he pulled to a halt and looked in all directions but there was no sign of it. It had completely disappeared.

He reached into his pocket and felt the roll of bills he had caught on the fly. He pulled the roll out and it was bigger than he remembered it. He snapped off the rubber band, and examined a few of the bills separately. The denomination on the top bill, in galactic credits, was so big it staggered him. He riffled through the entire sheaf of bills and all the denominations seemed to be the same.

He gasped at the thought of it, and riffled through them once again. He had been right the first time – all the denominations *were* the same. He did a bit of rapid calculation and it was strictly unbelievable. In credits, too – and a credit was convertible, roughly, into five Earth dollars.

He had seen credits before, but never actually held one in his hand. They were the currency of galactic trade and were widely used in interstellar banking circles, but seldom drifted down into general circulation. He held them in his hand and took a good look at them and they sure were beautiful.

The being must have immeasurably prized that blanket, he thought – to give him such a fabulous sum simply for taking care of it. Although, when you came to think of it, it wasn't necessarily so. Standards of wealth differed greatly from one planet to another and the fortune he held in his hands might have been little more than pocket money to the blanket's owner.

He was surprised to find that he wasn't too thrilled or happy, as he should have been. All he seemed to be able to think about was that he'd lost the blanket.

He thrust the bills into his pocket and walked across the street to the little park. Doc was awake and sitting on a bench underneath a tree. Hart sat down beside him.

"How you feeling, Doc?" he asked.

"I'm feeling all right, son," the old man replied.

"Did you see an alien, like a spider wearing snowshoes?"

"There was one of them here just a while ago. It was here when I woke up. It wanted to know about that thing you'd found."

"And you told it."

"Sure. Why not? It said it was hunting for it. I figured you'd be glad to get it off your hands."

The two of them sat silently for a while.

Then Hart asked, "Doc, what would you do if you had about a billion bucks?"

"Me," said Doc, without the slightest hesitation, "I'd drink myself to death. Yes, sir, I'd drink myself to death real fancy, not on any of this rotgut they sell in this end of town."

And that was the way it went, thought Hart. Doc would drink himself to death. Angela would go in for arty salons and the latest styles. Jasper more than likely would buy a place out in the mountains where he could be away from people.

And me, thought Hart, what will I do with a billion bucks – take or give a million?

Yesterday, last night, up until a couple of hours ago, he would have traded in his soul on the Classic yarner.

But now it seemed all sour and off-beat.

For there was a better way – the way of symbiosis, the teaming up of Man and an alien biologic concept.

He remembered the grove with its Gothic trees and its sense of foreverness and even yet, in the brightness of the sun, he shivered at the thought of the thing of beauty that had appeared among the trees.

That was, he told himself, a surely better way to write – to know the thing yourself and write it, to live the yarn and write it.

But he had lost the blanket and he didn't know where to find another. He didn't even know, if he found the place they came from, what he'd have to do to capture it.

An alien biologic concept, and yet not entirely alien, for it had first been thought of by an unknown man six centuries before. A man who had written as Jasper wrote even in this day, hunched above a table, scribbling out the words he put together in his brain. No yarner there – no tapes, no films, none of the other gadgets. But even so that unknown man had reached across the mists of time and space to touch another unknown mind and the life blanket had come alive as surely as if Man himself had made it.

And was that the true greatness of the human race – that they could imagine something and in time it would be so?

And if that were the greatness, could Man afford to delegate it to the turning shaft, the spinning wheel, the clever tubes, the innards of machines?

"You wouldn't happen," asked Doc, "to have a dollar on you?"

"No," said Hart, "I haven't got a dollar."

"You're just like the rest of us," said Doc. "You dream about the billions and you haven't got a dime."

Jasper was a rebel and it wasn't worth it. All the rebels ever got were the bloody noses and the broken heads.

"I sure could use a buck," said Doc.

It wasn't worth it to Jasper Hansen and it wasn't worth it to the others who must also lock their doors and polish up their never-used machines, so that when someone happened to drop in they'd see them standing there.

And it isn't worth it to me, Kemp Hart told himself. Not when by continuing to conform he could become famous almost automatically and virtually overnight.

He put his hand into his pocket and felt the roll of bills and knew that in just a little while he'd go uptown and buy that wonderful machine. There was plenty in the roll to buy it. With what there was in that roll he could buy a shipload of them.

"Yes, sir," said Doc, harking back to his answer to the billion dollar question. "It would be a pleasant death. A pleasant death, indeed."

IX

A gang of workmen were replacing the broken window when Hart arrived at the uptown showroom, but he scarcely more than glanced at them and walked straight inside.

The same salesman seemed to materialize from thin air.

But he wasn't happy. His expression was stern and a little pained.

"You've come back, no doubt," he said, "to place an order for the Classic."

"That is right," said Hart and pulled the roll out of his pocket.

The salesman was well-trained. He stood wall-eyed for just a second, then recovered his composure with a speed which must have set a record.

"That's fine," he said. "I knew you'd be back. I was telling some of the other men this morning that you would be coming in."

I just bet you were, thought Hart.

"I suppose," he said, "that if I paid you cash you would consider throwing in a rather generous supply of tapes and films and some of the other stuff I need."

"Certainly, sir. I'll do the best I can for you."

Hart peeled off twenty-five thousand and put the rest back in his pocket.

"Won't you have a seat," the salesman urged. "I'll be right back. I'll arrange delivery and fix up the guarantee . . ."

"Take your time," Hart told him, enjoying every minute of it.

He sat down in a chair and did a little planning.

First he'd have to move to better quarters and as soon as he had moved he'd have a dinner for the crowd and he'd rub Jasper's nose in it. He'd certainly do it – if Jasper wasn't tucked away in jail. He chuckled to himself, thinking of Jasper cringing in the basement of the Bright Star bar.

And this very afternoon he'd go over to Irving's office and pay him back the twenty and explain how it was he couldn't find the time to write the stuff he wanted.

Not that he wouldn't have liked to help Irving out. But it would be sacrilege to write the kind of junk that Irving wanted on a machine as talented as the Classic.

He heard footsteps coming hurriedly across the floor behind him and he stood up and turned around, smiling at the salesman.

But the salesman wasn't smiling. He was close to apoplexy.

"You!" said the salesman, choking just a little in his attempt to remain a gentleman. "That money! We've had enough from you, young man."

"The money," said Hart. "Why, it's galactic credits. It –"

"It's play money," stormed the salesman. "Money for the kids. Play money from the Draconian federation. It says so, right on the face of it. In those big characters."

He handed Hart the money.

"Get out of here!" the salesman shouted.

"But," Hart pleaded, "are you sure? It can't be! You must be mistaken –"

"Our teller says it is. He has to be an expert on all sorts of money and he *says it is!*"

"But you took it. You couldn't tell the difference."

"I can't read Draconian. But the teller can."

"That damn alien!" shouted Hart in sudden fury. "Just let me get my hands on him!"

The salesman softened just a little.

"You can't trust those aliens, sir. They are a sneaky lot."

"Get out of my way," Hart shouted. "I've got to find that alien!"

The man at the Alien bureau wasn't very helpful.

"We have no record," he told Hart, "of the kind of creature you describe. You wouldn't have a photo of it, would you?"

"No," said Hart. "I haven't got a photo."

The man started piling up the catalogs he had been looking through.

"Of course," he said, "the fact we have no record of him doesn't mean a thing. Admittedly, we can't keep track of all the various people. There are so many of them and new ones all the time. Perhaps you might inquire at the spaceport. Someone might have seen your alien."

"I've already done that. Nothing. Nothing at all. He must have come in and possibly have gone back, but no one can remember him. Or maybe they won't tell."

"The aliens hang together," said the man. "They don't tell you nothing."

He went on stacking up the books. It was near to quitting time and he was anxious to be off.

The man said, jokingly, "You might go out in space and try to hunt him up."

"I might do just that," said Hart and left, slamming the door behind him.

Joke: You might go out in space and find him. You might go out and track him across ten thousand lightyears and among a million stars. And when you found him you might say I want to have a blanket and he'd laugh right in your face.

But by the time you'd tracked him across ten thousand lightyears and among a million stars you'd no longer need a blanket, for you would have lived your stories and you would have seen your characters and you would have absorbed ten thousand backgrounds and a million atmospheres.

And you'd need no yarner and no tapes and films, for the words would be pulsing at your fingertips and pounding in your brain, shrieking to get out.

Joke: Toss a backwoods yokel a fistful of play money for something worth a million. The fool wouldn't know the difference until he tried to spend it. Be a big shot cheap and then go off in a corner by yourself and die laughing at how superior you are.

And who had it been that said humans were the only liars?

Joke: Wear a blanket around your shoulders and send your ships to Earth for the drivel that they write there – never knowing, never guessing that you have upon your back the very thing that's needed to break Earth's monopoly on fiction.

And that, said Hart, is a joke on you.

If I ever find you, I'll cram it down your throat.

X

Angela came up the stairs bearing an offering of peace. She set the kettle on the table. "Some soup," she said. "I'm good at making soup."

"Thanks, Angela," he said. "I forgot to eat today."

"Why the knapsack, Kemp? Going on a hike?"

"No, going on vacation."

"But you didn't tell me."

"I just now made up my mind to go. A little while ago."

"I'm sorry I was so angry at you. It turned out all right. Green Shirt and his gang made their getaway."

"So Jasper can come out."

"He's already out. He's plenty sore at you."

"That's all right with me. I'm no pal of his."

She sat down in a chair and watched him pack.

"Where are you going, Kemp?"

"I'm hunting for an alien."

"Here in the city? Kemp, you'll never find him."

"Not in the city. I'll have to ask around."

"But there aren't any aliens –"

"That's right."

"You're a crazy fool," she cried. "You can't do it, Kemp. I won't let you. How will you live? What will you do?"

"I'll write."

"Write? You can't write! Not without a yarner."

"I'll write by hand. Indecent as it may be, I'll write by hand because I'll know the things I write about. It'll be in my blood and at my fingertips. I'll have the smell of it and the color of it and the taste of it!"

She leaped from the chair and beat at his chest with tiny fists.

"It's filthy! It's uncivilized! It's –"

"That's the way they wrote before. All the millions of stories, all the great ideas, all the phrases that you love to quote. And that is the way it should have stayed. This is a dead-end street we're on."

"You'll come back," she said. "You'll find that you are wrong and you'll come back."

He shook his head at her. "Not until I find my alien."

"It isn't any alien you are after. It is something else. I can see it in you."

She whirled around and raced out the door and down the stairs.

He went back to his packing and when he had finished, he sat down and ate the soup. Angela, he thought, was right. She was good at making soup.

And she was right in another thing as well. It was no alien he was seeking.

For he didn't need an alien. And he didn't need a blanket and he didn't need a yarner.

He took the kettle to the sink and washed it beneath the tap and dried it carefully. Then he set it in the center of the table where Angela, when she came, would be sure to see it.

Then he took up the knapsack and started slowly down the stairs.

He had reached the street when he heard the cry behind him. It was Angela and she was running after him. He stopped and waited for her.

"I'm going with you, Kemp."

"You don't know what you're saying. It'll be rough and hard. Strange lands and alien people. And we haven't any money."

"Yes, we have. We have that fifty. The one I tried to loan you. It's all I have and it won't go far, I know. But we have it."

"You're looking for no alien."

"Yes, I am. I'm looking for an alien, too. All of us, I think, are looking for your alien."

He reached out an arm and swept her roughly to him, held her close against him.

"Thank you, Angela," he said.

Hand in hand they headed for the spaceport, looking for a ship that would take them to the stars.

CLIFFORD D. SIMAK, during his fifty-five year career, produced some of the most iconic science fiction stories ever written. Born in 1904 on a farm in southwestern Wisconsin, Simak got a job at a small-town newspaper in 1929 and eventually became news editor of the *Minneapolis Star-Tribune,* writing fiction in his spare time.

Simak was best known for the book *City,* a reaction to the horrors of World War II, and for his novel *Way Station.* In 1953 *City* was awarded the International Fantasy Award, and in following years, Simak won three Hugo Awards and a Nebula Award. In 1977 he became the third Grand Master of the Science Fiction and Fantasy Writers of America, and before his death in 1988, he was named one of three inaugural winners of the Horror Writers Association's Bram Stoker Award for Lifetime Achievement.

DAVID W. WIXON was a close friend of Clifford D. Simak's. As Simak's health declined, Wixon, already familiar with science fiction publishing, began more and more to handle such things as his friend's business correspondence and contract matters. Named literary executor of the estate after Simak's death, Wixon began a long-term project to secure the rights to all of Simak's stories and find a way to make them available to readers who, given the fifty-five-year span of Simak's writing career, might never have gotten the chance to enjoy all of his short fiction. Along the way, Wixon also read the author's surviving journals and rejected manuscripts, which made him uniquely able to provide Simak's readers with interesting and thought-provoking commentary that sheds new light on the work and thought of a great writer.

THE COMPLETE SHORT FICTION
OF CLIFFORD D. SIMAK

FROM OPEN ROAD MEDIA

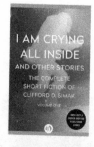

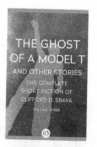

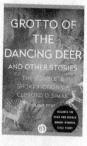
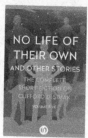

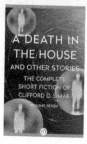
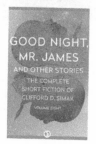

OPEN ROAD

INTEGRATED MEDIA

OPEN ROAD

INTEGRATED MEDIA

Find a full list of our authors and
titles at www.openroadmedia.com

FOLLOW US
@OpenRoadMedia